BEWITCHED BY THE BLUESTOCKING

The Perks of Being an Heiress
Book One

By Jillian Eaton

ARE YOU SIGNED UP FOR
DRAGONBLADE'S BLOG?

You'll get the latest news and information on exclusive giveaways, exclusive excerpts, coming releases, sales, free books, cover reveals and more.

Check out our complete list of authors, too!

No spam, no junk. That's a promise!

Sign Up Here

www.dragonbladepublishing.com

Dearest Reader;

Thank you for your support of a small press. At Dragonblade Publishing, we strive to bring you the highest quality Historical Romance from the some of the best authors in the business. Without your support, there is no 'us', so we sincerely hope you adore these stories and find some new favorite authors along the way.

Happy Reading!

CEO, Dragonblade Publishing

CHAPTER ONE

London, England
August 19, 1870
The Office & Private Residence of Mr. Thomas Kincaid, Private Investigator

MANY PEOPLE—AND things—had shown up on Kincaid's doorstep seeking help during his three years as a private investigator. Wives wanting to know if their husbands were having an affair behind their backs. Husbands wanting to know if their wives were having an affair behind *their* backs (fidelity, it seemed, was not exceedingly common these days).

Occasionally, someone would come searching for a missing relative, and this past winter he'd solved the mystery of a missing cow. His first bovine case, as it so happened. Then there was the time he'd arrived home to discover two tiny kittens on his doorstep; both of whom now happily resided in the flat above his office.

But in all those years, he'd never—not once—opened his door to find a blue-eyed American heiress with hair the color of fire and a plump mouth that immediately brought to mind all sorts of wicked, carnal thoughts. Until one rainy morning in the middle of August, when he proceeded to do precisely that. Truth be told, Kincaid would have preferred more kittens.

"Can I help you?" he asked warily, his dark brows gathering above thin wire spectacles. A light mist fell from the gloomy London sky, coating the lenses of his glasses and causing him to squint at the woman perched on his doorstep.

She wasn't wearing a cloak, leaving her slender arms exposed to the rain. Kincaid had a primal urge to throw his jacket over her trembling shoulders and draw her into the warmth of his chest, but he'd learned long ago to be leery of beautiful women. And this one, with her thick, auburn lashes and high cheekbones and soft, soft lips, was absolutely stunning.

"I hope so." Her husky voice—smoke and velvet wrapped together—hit him like a punch to the gut. "Are you Mr. Thomas Kincaid?"

He gave a curt nod. "Kincaid is fine. Might I inquire as to who is asking?"

"Joanna Thorncroft." Without waiting for an

invitation, she slipped past him, the side of her breast leaving a burning path along his forearm as she marched into the foyer and turned around. "Well?" she said impatiently. "Are you going to take my case or not?"

Kincaid blinked at her, then slowly closed the door. It was clear from the hard inflections of her words—and her sheer audacity—that his unexpected visitor was an American. Heralding from somewhere in Massachusetts, if he had to guess. Coupled with a keen sense of observation, he also had an excellent ear for dialects. It was what made him good at his job. Something *else* that made him good at his job was knowing when to recognize trouble. And it had just walked through his door dressed in rain and smelling of violets.

"I am afraid I am not taking any new clients at this time, Miss Thorncroft." The world around him blurred as he took off his glasses and wiped them dry on the cuff of his sleeve. He'd worn spectacles since he was a young boy at the orphanage, and had been teased mercilessly for it. Those cruel taunts were what had prompted him to become a peeler as soon as he came of age.

Named for their founder, Robert Peel, the peelers were Britain's first—and only—organized police force. Kincaid had worn his blue coat with pride, and quickly climbed the ranks from constable to sergeant. Five years in, he was named an inspector and given his own division.

With nearly twenty-four men under his command, he'd earned a reputation as a demanding, but fair leader. From sunup to sundown, and often late into the night, his career had consumed him.

It was gritty, exhausting, and dangerous work. Work that often exposed the darkest, vilest underbelly of human existence. But it had given him purpose. It had given him the opportunity to stand up against the bullies and the bruisers. It had allowed him to protect the vulnerable and save the innocent. To rescue the boy he'd been. The boy no one had ever stood up for. The boy no one had ever cared about.

The boy no one had ever loved.

Some might have taken all of that pain and anguish and drank themselves to death with it. Kincaid had used it to fuel his grueling ambition to make London a better place. A safer place. A place where babies weren't abandoned by their parents and children weren't beaten by those charged to keep them safe.

He hadn't always succeeded, and sometimes those bitter failures weighed heavier on his soul than the triumphs. But he had made a difference. He'd been *making* a difference.

Then he met *her*.

Lady Lavinia Townsend.

The conniving bitch who had cost him everything.

His position. His career. His good name. She'd taken it all from him because she could, and laughed gleefully while she'd done it.

But she'd also taught him a valuable lesson.

Because of Lavinia, he knew what happened when the lines between his professional life and his personal life blurred. Because of Lavinia, he knew never to trust another woman with his heart. Because of Lavinia, he knew he couldn't help Miss Thorncroft.

He wanted to. A single glimpse into those luminous blue eyes and he was tempted to move heaven and earth to give her whatever she asked of him.

But he couldn't.

He *wouldn't*.

Kincaid had learned in the hardest possible of ways to avoid temptation. And Joanna Thorncroft had temptation written across every inch of her damp, delectable little body.

Sliding his spectacles back into place, he cleared his throat. "There are several investigators I could recommend. Good men, all, and—"

"I don't want them." Joanna stepped closer to him, her leather boots leaving small, muddy footprints on the wooden floor. Her tantalizing perfume lingered in the air between them, causing his nostrils to flare. "I want *you*."

Steeling himself against the urge to reach out

and trace the sharp curve of her cheekbone, then bury his fingers in her hair, Kincaid shoved his hands behind his back and disguised his desire behind a clipped, businesslike tone. "As I said, Miss Thorncroft, I am not accepting new clients at this time."

Her eyes flashed with annoyance. "Then you'll have to make an exception, Kincaid, because I have come a very long way, I am very tired, and I am not leaving here unless you agree to help me."

He'd missed the stubbornness in her chin before, but he saw it now. Along with a tiny freckle in the middle of her collarbone.

He wondered what it tasted like.

He wondered what *she* tasted like.

Scowling, Kincaid squeezed the back of his neck where the corded muscles were as hard as granite.

They weren't the only part of his anatomy that had gone hard.

"Miss Thorncroft, I *must* insist—"

"Kincaid," she interrupted smoothly, "I can see that you are reluctant to hear me out. I can understand. I am a stranger, after all. And an American at that." A wry smile twisted those plump lips. "However, I am sure that after I've had the opportunity to tell you why I came here, you will agree that my case is of the utmost importance. Do you have an office?"

"Yes, it's through there." He nodded at a door across the foyer that was partially ajar.

Originally, the room had been a parlor, but now housed an old desk cluttered with papers, shelves cluttered with books, and chairs cluttered with cats. There was also a bed shoved into the corner and his jaw clenched taut when his mind conjured a vivid image of Joanna sprawled across the mattress while he peeled off her wet clothes...with his teeth.

He ran a hand across his mouth.

This would not do.

This would not do at all.

But before he could put his foot down and demand Joanna get the hell out, she flitted past him and into his office, leaving him staring after her in stunned, stormy silence.

"Oh, you have a cat!" she exclaimed, pointing to the top of a bookshelf where a sleek, black feline lounged on its side.

"*Two*," he managed in a strangled voice. "I have two cats. That's James. Jane is most likely upstairs."

"I've always wanted a cat, but my sister seems to be allergic to them. Well?" Joanna's head canted. "Won't you come in, Kincaid? Do have a seat. You're looking rather...flushed. Are you feeling all right?"

The irony of being invited into his *own bloody office* was not lost on Kincaid as he stalked through the doorway, sat down at his desk, and selected a pen from the jumbled pile of writing utensils jammed inside the top drawer.

It was clear Joanna was not leaving until he listened to what she had to say. It was even clearer he was dangerously close to yanking her into his arms and kissing her senseless. Since he obviously couldn't do the latter, he would grit his teeth and do the former. Then he'd escort her out, tear up his notes, and go on with his day as if she'd never walked through his door.

"I am fine," he said curtly as he flipped to a fresh page in the leather-bound journal where he kept track of all his various cases. Not that there were very many to keep track of at the moment. Business always slowed when the *ton* flocked en masse to their estates in the countryside. As it stood, his only other case regarded another missing cow. The poor things must have had a dreadful sense of direction. Ordinarily, he'd be reluctant to take on work involving farm animals, something which never would have been asked of him as an inspector, but beggars couldn't be choosers.

He hadn't earned much as a peeler. Certainly not enough to compensate him for all of the long hours, nor the life-threatening danger he'd found himself in more often than not. But part of his salary had included an allowance for rent, and clothes, and food. It hadn't been much, yet he had gotten by. And there'd been a certain security in knowing that at the end of every week he would have money to bring to the bank.

As a private detective, he earned more quid outright, but it came in sporadic bursts that were dependent on the number of cases he took on. In the beginning, not a single person had dared darken the door of a disgraced policeman. By sheer will and persistence, he'd managed to secure a handful of clients, who had then discreetly spread his name to their friends. Now that he was nearing the end of his third year as a detective, he was turning a respectable profit. But he still had bills to pay, and a house in need of repairs, and cats to feed.

Traitorous little buggers that they were.

Abandoning his perch on top of the bookshelf, James leapt onto Joanna's lap as soon as she sat down. Purring loudly, he kneaded her thigh before turning in two circles and curling into a ball. If Kincaid didn't know any better, he would have sworn the damned cat smirked at him before James yawned, exposing a mouthful of pointy white canines, and closed his eyes.

"He's absolutely charming," said Joanna, stroking his back. "And *soft*."

Kincaid had endured low points in his life. A beating at the orphanage that had left him black and blue for weeks. The betrayal of the woman he loved. But never—not once—had he sunk so low as to be jealous of a cat.

Before now.

Forcing his gaze away from James (*you and I will discuss this later*, he told the feline silently) he jabbed his pen into an open inkwell and held it poised in midair. "Why don't you enlighten me as to why you are here, Miss Thorncroft?"

"I'd be delighted." Her hand paused in the middle of James' back. "But first, I believe I should be upfront about something. I do not—as it currently stands—possess the necessary monetary funds to pay for your services, Kincaid."

In Kincaid's experience, most women—hell, most men—would have stuttered and hemmed and blushed their way through such an admission. Money, particularly the *lack* of money, was never an easy subject to address. Which was why his standard policy was to demand a generous down payment on services to be rendered upfront. But Miss Joanna Thorncroft, with her clear blue eyes the color of an autumn sky, did not so much as blink. Nor did she blush, much to his disappointment.

He'd always been attracted to a blushing woman.

"I am sorry to hear that, Miss Thorncroft." A lie, of course. Except that it wasn't. Not entirely. Because there was a part of him that *did* want to take her on a client. The same part of him that wanted to kiss her. The same part of him that had imagined her on his bed. The same part of him that was fascinated by that damned freckle on her collarbone. Which, as far as he was concerned, was simply more evidence that he should not, under any circumstance, agree to help Joanna. "I can recommend—"

"Yes," she cut him off, waving her arm in the air, "you mentioned that. But the fact remains I want you to be my investigator. And it is you I intend to have, by whatever means necessary."

Was she *trying* to heat his blood, Kincaid wondered?

If so, it was working.

Any hotter and he'd burst into flames.

"That may be. But if you cannot afford my services, I am afraid we will not be able to proceed." Closing his journal with a loud, purposeful *snap*, he slid it away from him across the desk. "Thank you for coming in, Miss Thorncroft. Please let me show you to the door."

He stood up.

Joanna did not.

"I believe I was very clear, Kincaid." She arched a russet brow. "I temporarily lack the *monetary* funds to hire you, but that does not mean I am incapable of paying by other means."

Kincaid sat down so hard his chair slid back and hit the wall. "What—what are you implying, Miss Thorncroft?" he croaked as his mind immediately conjured a flurry of scenarios, each one more wicked than the last.

Joanna against the wall, sighing his name as he kissed her neck.

Joanna naked on her knees, eyes heavy-lidded with desire as she beckoned him towards her with a crook of her finger.

Joanna leaning back against his desk, her skirts lifted above her waist as she ran a hand down the flat plane of her belly and pressed her fingers between her thighs—

Stop it, he ordered himself fiercely.

What the devil had come over him?

Kincaid wasn't a monk. Far from it. But in the four years since Lavinia had shredded his heart with all the maliciousness of a feral she-wolf and reduced his career to a smoking pile of ash, he had selected his partners with the utmost discretion. Seeking blind pleasure over emotional attachment, he'd always been exceedingly careful to choose women far outside of his professional circle.

His last mistress, a widow several years his senior, hadn't even lived in London. He had visited her when time allowed, and when they'd mutually decided to end their affair last month, there were no hard feelings. There'd been no feelings at all. Which was exactly what Kincaid preferred.

And how he knew, he *knew*, he couldn't

allow himself to become tangled up with a feisty red-haired American. Because the ripe, tangy passion Joanna invoked within him was the same he'd felt with Lavinia.

And everyone this side of the Thames knew how *that* had ended.

He had been stupid enough to fall in love once and it had nearly ruined him. He wasn't going to make the same mistake again. He wasn't even going to allow himself to be *tempted* to make the same mistake again. Which meant, as deliciously enticing as trading sexual favors for investigative work appeared on the surface, he needed to decline Joanna's offer.

"Miss Thorncroft, while I appreciate—greatly—your proposition, I'm afraid I must turn it down."

She frowned at him and tucked a damp tendril of hair behind her ear. Her dress, a simple green gown with black buttons down the middle and a matching sash at the waist, was nearly dry with the exception of her breasts. Full and voluptuous, Joanna's bosom must have caught the rain as she walked, and Kincaid's tongue stuck to the roof of his mouth when he noted the hard peaks of her nipples straining against the light cotton fabric.

"But I haven't even told you what it is yet," she said.

"What?" Tearing his gaze away from her

bodice—no small feat—Kincaid forced himself to focus solely on Joanna's countenance. That hardly helped matters, as every inch of her face was just as stunningly beautiful as the rest of her.

Thick, arching brows a few shades darker than all that wild, red hair. Pale ivory skin saved from coldness by a charming spattering of freckles across the bridge of her nose. A full mouth that was slightly top heavy, and an elegant jawline leading to that delightfully stubborn chin.

"My offer. I haven't told you what it is yet," she repeated.

Kincaid gripped either side of his desk and bore down with such strength he wouldn't have been surprised to see the wood crack in half. "That won't be necessary, Miss Thorncroft. I've a vivid enough imagination."

Her freckles bunched as her nose wrinkled. "What are you imagining?"

Was the woman *trying* to kill him?

"Miss Thorncroft." Taking a deep breath, he chose his words with the utmost care. "Please do not misunderstand. I would *very* much enjoy engaging in an—an intimate relationship. However, given the—"

"What are you talking about?" she interrupted.

His brows drew together. "What are *you* talking about?"

"Secretarial work." She looked oddly at him.

"Obviously."

"Secretarial work," he repeated in a strangled voice.

"Yes." Joanna scratched James under his whiskery chin, then took a pointed glance around the room. "It is clear you would benefit from some organization. Your office is, if I may be so blunt, an absolute disaster. As it happens, my organizational skills are second to none. In addition, given my lackluster welcome, I believe you would benefit greatly from a secretary."

"Do you?" Kincaid didn't know whether he felt relieved...or disappointed.

"Indeed. Someone to greet your potential clients as they come in. Take their coats, serve them tea, make sure they are comfortable." She leaned forward, further exposing her breasts to his carnal stare, and Kincaid liked to believe it was a mark of his good character that he didn't whimper. "Surely we can work something out. My services in exchange for yours."

Once again dragging his gaze from Joanna's curvaceous frame, he grimaced fiercely at a painting hanging crookedly on the wall. It had been a gift from a wealthy dowager countess after he'd discovered who had been siphoning money off of her estate. A greedy nephew, as it happened, with no regard for his elderly aunt's welfare. The countess had been so pleased with Kincaid's detective work, she'd doubled his fee and given him an oversized canvas depicting her three beloved cocker spaniels as a reward. He'd tried hanging the painting in his bedroom, but James and Jane wouldn't hear of it, and thus the artwork had been relegated to the office.

The frame was in need of a good dusting, he noted. As did everything else.

Joanna was right. The room *was* a disaster. But then, he was an investigator, not a bloody maid, and he had neither the time nor the inclination to keep things neat and tidy. That being said, he was the first to admit his office could surely benefit from a bit more...orderliness. And a secretary to take notes, keep his files straight, and greet clients with the warmth and tactfulness he admittedly lacked, certainly wouldn't hurt anything either. In fact, it might even get him some of the meeker clients his gruff demeanor tended to frighten away.

Yes, now that he thought about, he didn't know why he hadn't hired someone sooner.

But he'd be damned if that someone was going to be Miss Joanna Thorncroft.

"No," he said flatly as he picked up a pile of papers and shuffled them into place.

"*No?*" Joanna said in the incredulous tone of someone unacquainted with the word. "I don't understand."

"Have you ever been a secretary before?"

"Not exactly, but—"

"Have you ever worked for a detective?"

"Well, no, but—"

"Are you acquainted with British law?"

"How does that—"

"I am sorry, but you do not have the proper qualifications." He met her gaze, registered the angry indignation swirling in the depths of those vivid blue eyes, and glanced promptly away. "As you can see, I am a very busy man. If you would, please put down my cat and see yourself out."

She stomped her foot. "I will not!"

"All right, you can keep the cat," he said graciously.

"I don't want the cat. No offense intended," she said when James lifted his head and gave a grumpy *meow*. "What I want—and need—is a private investigator. You've come highly recommended, Kincaid. I should think you would view that as a compliment. And while I realize exchanging my services for yours is a tad...*unconventional*, shall we say, I truly believe such a bargain will be immensely beneficial to us both." She smiled hopefully. "Why don't we shake on it and see how things go? Surely you can commit to a trial period of a week. A fitting compromise, don't you agree?"

Kincaid didn't like what that smile did to him.

Or maybe he liked it *too* much.

Either way, the answer was still...

"No, Miss Thorncroft. I *don't* agree."

Her smile disappeared. Her eyes narrowed. Her chin lifted. "Is this because I am a woman? Is that why you don't believe I meet your lofty qualifications? Perhaps I've never been employed as a secretary before, but I can assure you I am as intelligent and well-read as any man. I'm also more than capable of handling any tasks you put before me."

Kincaid didn't doubt that Joanna could topple mountains if she put her mind to it. For such a little slip of a thing, her courage and persistence was formidable. But he'd drawn his line, and he wouldn't cross it. No matter how sweet the enticement was on the other side.

He had been down this road to hell before. He had the scars to prove it.

And he had no desire to travel it again.

"Miss Thorncroft, my inability to take you on as a secretary—or a client—has nothing to do with your intelligence, or your work ethic." Having shuffled and straightened every piece of paper on his desk, he laid his hands flat and pushed his weight into them. "This is a personal decision."

"Personal?" Her head tilted in confusion. "But you don't know me well enough to dislike me yet. It usually takes a few days. Or so I've been told." She bit her lip and gave a small, apologetic shrug. "It seems I can be ra-ther...obstinate."

"Really?" Kincaid said dryly. "I hadn't noticed."

A huff of breath whistled between her lips. "Kincaid, I must implore you to reconsider. My sister and I have traveled a very long way—"

"You've a sister?" he interrupted.

Wonderful.

As if one gorgeous, stubborn American running amok in London wasn't bad enough, there was a pair of them. And no, he wasn't going to allow himself to imagine them naked. Together. Doing things.

Naughty things.

No, he wasn't going to imagine that at all.

Absolutely not.

"Yes," Joanna replied. "Well, two sisters actually, but—"

Bloody hell.

"—Claire stayed at home."

Thank God for small favors.

"Miss Thorncroft." Gritting his teeth, he latched on to his self-control with all the desperate strength of a drowning sailor clinging onto the side of a sinking ship. "I do not know how many different ways I can say the same thing. I cannot, under any circumstances, hire you on. It's completely out of the question."

"I...I see." Giving James a final scratch behind the ears, Joanna gently set him aside and stood up. Walking towards Kincaid, she extended her hand across the desk. "Very well, Kincaid. I respect your decision, in as much as I disagree with it. Thank you for taking the time to meet with me."

"You're welcome." Relief flowed through Kincaid as he took her small, delicate hand in his considerably larger one. He began to shake it. And then he saw her stubborn chin wobble.

Such a tiny movement, really.

Hardly perceptible.

Easy to ignore.

Except he couldn't ignore it. Nor could he ignore the sudden clench in his gut. His fingers tightened around hers, unconsciously drawing her closer.

"Miss Thorncroft…"

"Yes?" she whispered.

Kincaid closed his eyes.

Don't do it.

Don't do it.

Don't do it.

"A week-long trial, did you say?" With great reluctance, he opened his eyes.

"Yes!" Her entire countenance lit up, as bright as the sun. "Just seven days. If I haven't found what I'm looking for, or either of us decides our arrangement is no longer sustainable, then I'll get another detective and you'll never have to see me again. I swear."

Never see her again?

Kincaid's stomach tightened again. Although this time, it was for an entirely different reason. Quickly releasing Joanna's hand, he sat back in his chair and motioned for her to do the same.

He knew he was going to hate himself for this later.

He knew he was making a terrible mistake.

But he also knew it was the right thing to do.

Picking up a pen, he reopened his journal. "Why don't we begin by you telling me what it is you're doing here, and what, precisely, you're searching for?"

"I thought you'd never ask." Resuming her seat, Joanna beckoned James into her lap. With a happy *meow* the traitorous feline accepted the invitation and began to purr as she stroked his tail. "You see, it all began with a ring…"

CHAPTER TWO

Somerville, Massachusetts
Three Months Ago

"MISS JOANNA THORNCROFT." Taking a deep breath, Charles Gaines dropped down to one knee in the middle of the park and pulled a small, velvet box from the inside pocket of his gray frock coat. "Will you do me the great honor of being my wife?"

He flipped the box open with his thumb to reveal a very large, very shiny diamond ring. Or perhaps it only appeared so large because the box was so small.

Joanna squinted.

No, she decided.

It was definitely large. Ostentatious, even. Then again, Charles *was* wearing silk trousers.

Pink ones, at that.

Or maybe they were peach.

She'd been trying to avoid looking at them.

"Charles," she began.

"Yes?" he said eagerly.

"No."

His smile slipped a notch. "No?"

"No," she confirmed with a sigh. "Please get up. I wouldn't want you to ruin your pants."

"Quite right." He leapt to his feet as if the ground had suddenly caught fire and used a handkerchief to delicately brush a few loose pieces of grass off his knee. "Mother would have my head if these became stained. They're from—"

"Paris, yes. You told me last week. They're...unique," Joanna said generously.

Charles brightened. "Do you think so?"

"I do."

"But you're still refusing my proposal?"

"I am."

"But..." A troubled frown replaced his smile. "I was certain you'd say yes."

Joanna wondered if he knew that was what every suitor had said before him. Except for Mr. Browning, who had turned bright red from the tips of his ears to the tip of his nose and run away without saying a single word.

Of all her proposals, his was her favorite.

"I'm sorry, Charles. I truly am. It's a beautiful ring, and I am certain it will make a special woman *very* happy someday. But that woman is not going to be me."

"Why not?" he demanded.

Joanna pursed her lips. Why did men think so little of a woman's mind that they believed a few words could change it? Or that women always owed an explanation for their decision? When a man said no, he was *never* questioned. And he never had to explain himself.

It was horribly unfair.

More than that, it was annoying.

And Joanna Thorncroft did not have patience for things that annoyed her. Especially when they were wearing pink/peach trousers.

"Charles—"

"I would be a good husband to you." Drawing back his shoulders, Charles made himself as tall as he possibly could, but even by stretching into every inch of his five foot, seven inch frame, the top of his head still barely reached Joanna's nose. "I have a good job."

"Your *father* has a good job," she corrected mildly.

"I will be receiving an excellent inheritance."

"From your father."

"I have a large house with ample cropland."

"Charles, you still live with your parents!"

"And?" he asked, his brows knitting together.

"And…and I do not love you. I'm sorry," she said. "I realize that must be difficult to hear."

But Charles didn't look hurt. He looked confused. "What does love have to do with anything?"

Her eyes narrowed. "Charles, why do you want to marry me?"

"Because—because I do." Snapping the ring box closed, he shoved it back into his pocket and glanced away from her as the corners of his mouth pinched in a boyish pout. "Mother told me you would do this."

"What exactly have I done?"

"You broke my heart."

Oh, for heaven's sake.

"Charles," Joanna said firmly, placing her hands on his shoulders so he was forced to meet her gaze, "I did *not* break your heart, you are *not* in love with me, and you do *not* want to marry me. You fancy me because I'm something you cannot have, but what you've failed to realize is that you don't really want me. You don't even know me."

"I do," he protested. "I know all about you."

A light summer breeze tickled the satin ribbons underneath Joanna's chin. With a grimace, she untied them, then whisked off her bonnet and tucked it under her arm.

"Do you know I despise hats?" she asked. "Cannot stand them. They itch, and they obscure my vision, and I wish I didn't have to wear one every time I stepped outside."

JILLIAN EATON

Charles frowned. "But that wouldn't be proper.

"I *also* despise being proper. There are too many rules to follow." Her bonnet fluttered to the ground as she flung her hands out to the side. "Women can do this, but not that. We are supposed to be intelligent, but only concerning topics such as fashion, and household management, and what wine pairs best with what dish. We are supposed to be pretty, but not in a manner that would cause distraction. We are supposed to be perfect, but not so perfect that the men of our acquaintance feel undermined or challenged." She dragged in a mouthful of air and Charles, who had remained silent during her impassioned speech, took a large step in retreat.

"You're right, Miss Thorncroft." He tugged at the collar of his jacket. "I—I do not believe we will suit."

Joanna watched with some bemusement as Charles pivoted and walked briskly way...in the *opposite* direction of his carriage. He'd realize his error soon enough. Just like he had realized they weren't a good fit for marriage.

Thank goodness.

Picking up her bonnet, she gave it a quick shake before carelessly plopping it back on her head and striking out towards home. She knew Charles was what every young, unwedded girl from Somerville to Salem would consider a fine catch. He was pleasing to the eye, had all his teeth, and was as rich as a king. Or rather, his father was. How unfortunate, then, that Charles wasn't looking for a wife.

No, what Charles—and all of Joanna's previous suitors—desired was a pretty vase they could put up on a shelf. Something to admire from afar, and occasionally take down to show off to friends before they returned it to the top of the bookcase.

Well, she was no vase.

And she had absolutely no intention of spending the rest of her life accruing dust on some shelf. Even if the shelf was in a lovely mansion and her family could have desperately used the money such an affluent match would bring.

Something her sister, Evelyn (Evie to family and close friends), brought up as soon as Joanna walked through the door of their small, creaky house on the outskirts of the village square.

"He proposed, didn't he?" Evie said after she'd taken one glance at Joanna's face. "And you said no. *Again.*" Her mouth curling, Evie crossed her arms and scowled at Joanna from across the foyer. Which also doubled as a parlor. And a music room. And, when they had a guest, a bedroom as well.

Not so very long ago, Joanna and her sisters had lived in a grand brick manor in the center of town. There had been plenty of bedrooms to spare, as well as parlors with fifteen foot ceilings, and drawing rooms with beautiful, white wainscoting, and a sun-filled studio for Claire, the youngest, to do her art. Their home had been *so* large that their father, a physician of much acclaim, was able to see his patients in the formal study and their grandmother, who had helped raise the girls since their mother died when Claire was only a baby, had her very own wing.

They'd had tutors, and carriages, and an entire closet devoted to Evie's extensive shoe collection. Money was of no consequence and, while they remained humble at heart, the Thorncrofts were considered to be one of Somerville's most affluent families.

Then came the War of the Great Rebellion.

Four years of devastation that tore the country apart from the inside out. Family fighting against family. Brother again brother. Citizen against citizen. Dr. Jacob Thorncroft had been reluctant to leave his daughters, but his services were needed on the front lines, and he'd never refused to help those in needs.

For nearly eight months, their only correspondence with him had been through letters. He hadn't made it home for Joanna's sixteenth birthday, or Evie's leading role as Juliet in the fall play at Chesterbrook Academy for Young Ladies, or Christmas.

But he'd always sent his letters, and his love, and there was never a doubt in Joanna's mind that one day he would return to them.

And then one day he had.

In a pine box.

With his name scrawled at the bottom in pencil.

Once the initial shock had passed and the grief had changed from a knife being dragged through the flesh into a dull throbbing, Joanna and her sisters were dealt another blow. Without their father's income, they could not afford to sustain the lifestyle they'd grown accustomed to.

At first, under the guidance of their grandmother, they made do by selling off the paintings and the furniture. Then the carriages and the horses. Finally, on a day stained by tears and helpless regret, they said goodbye to their beloved childhood manor and used the money garnered by the sale to purchase a two-bedroom cottage a mile out of the village.

It had been a difficult transition, made even harder by all the other changes that soon followed. Evie had to leave Chesterbrook mid-year as the tuition was prohibitively expense, Claire was never given the opportunity to attend, and Joanna halted all plans to go on a grand tour of France with her dearest friend, Louisa, a trip they'd been planning since they were practically in pinafores.

Their forced sacrifices allowed them to survive and, in the six years that followed, they learned to make do with simple things. But none of the sisters, with perhaps the exception of Claire, who was nearly too young to remember, forgot what it was like to have everything. Which was why, when Joanna and Evie came of marriageable age, they set their sights on making a fortuitous match that would help lift them out of poverty.

Or, at least Evie did.

"I *knew* you'd refuse Charles. I just knew it." As different from Joanna in appearance as she was in demeanor, Evie had lustrous black hair she brushed exactly one hundred times each morning, a flawless, ivory countenance with nary a blemish or freckle to be seen, and blue eyes that held a hint of violet. She was also shorter, only five feet two inches to Joanna's five foot nine, but what she lacked in height she more than made up for in temperament.

Born only eighteen months apart, the two sisters had begun quarreling in infancy and they'd never stopped. Or so that was how it often felt.

One issue that had been particularly contentious as of late was Joanna's adamant refusal to take any of her many marriage proposals. Evie saw nothing wrong with marrying a man because of what he could provide, regardless if those provisions included love or not. And Joanna didn't care what her future husband could provide so long as he loved her unconditionally.

Their differences in opinion, Joanna had long ago concluded, came from the very different ways they had healed after their father's death. Whereas the unexpected passing of the sibling's only remaining parent had made Joanna all the more determined to follow her heart, it had left Evie with a lingering sense of bitterness and longing. The middle Thorncroft sister wanted what she'd had to give up, and she was willing to do whatever it took to get it all back.

The beautiful house in the middle of town. A gleaming carriage that turned heads as it passed down the street. Hats and gowns and rooms filled with shoes. Material belongings that meant little to Joanna, and everything to Evie.

There was nothing wrong with either position, except that they were *so* very opposite there seemed to be no way a compromise could be reached. Added to that, their grandmother had tacitly refused to give her blessing for Evie to marry until Joanna found a husband first, and thus the sisters found themselves at each other's throats more often than not.

"I did not *want* to refuse Charles." Tossing her bonnet onto an empty table, Joanna reached to the nape of her neck and pulled out the pins holding her heavy coiffure in place. Giving a blissful sigh when her hair tumbled freely down her back, she surrendered herself to the nearest chair and kicked her feet up on a worn leather ottoman. Tiny dust plumes flew into the air, illuminated by rays of late morning sunlight trickling in through the curtainless windows.

"Then why did you?" Evie demanded.

"Because he didn't give me any choice in the matter." Joanna started to close her eyes, then opened them with a grimace when it became obvious by the tension simmering in the air that Evie had no intention of letting the matter drop. "I did not love him. He did not love me. What else is there to say? Of *course,* I declined his proposal. It would have been a disservice to both of us had I accepted."

"What in the world does love have to do with anything?" Evie asked, unknowingly repeating what Charles had said nearly verbatim. "Charles Gaines is the wealthiest bachelor in all of Somerville. You would want for nothing as his wife. *We* would want for nothing. Surely you don't have to be in love in order to see that."

"You're right, I don't have to be love. But I do *want* to be in love." When Joanna heard the patter of feet on the stairs, she sat up straight and greeted her youngest sister with a warm, affectionate smile. "There you are. I was wondering if you'd returned from the market yet."

"Half an hour ago." As fair as Evie was dark, Claire's light blonde curls framed a delicate face with high arching brows, soft cheekbones, and a mouth shaped like a cupid's bow. She had a sensitive nature, and a sweet heart, and was adored by all who knew her. "I was able to get more flour and eggs, but butter has gone up to nearly fifteen cents a pound."

"Fifteen cents?" said Joanna incredulously. "That's absurd! Mr. Hemphill acts as if his cows are churning out gold."

The corners of Claire's lips twitched. "For their sake, I'm glad they are not. That sounds as if it would be very uncomfortable. How was your stroll with Mr. Gaines?" Nudging Joanna's feet aside, Claire sat on the edge of the ottoman. "Did he—"

"Ask her to marry him?" Evie interrupted with a glare at Joanna. "Yes, as a matter of fact, he did. I'll give you three guesses as to what our dear sister said, but you're only going to need one."

Clair sighed. "Oh, Jo, not *again*. I was under the impression you liked Charles."

"I *did* like him. Although his choice in pants was admittedly questionable."

"How did he take the news?"

Leave it to Claire to worry about the man her sister had spurned.

"As well as can be expected, I suppose." Joanna gave a small shrug. "He'll be fine, I'm sure. There's a line of women from here to Boston waiting to marry him."

"Yes, but you were at the *head* of the line."

Like a cat with its hackles raised, Evie began to pace back and forth across the room, her skirts swishing angrily between her ankles. "You *know* Mr. Bridgeton has asked to court me. Not only is his father a senator, but he's considering a run for the governorship at the end of next year! I could be a governor's daughter-in-law. Think of all the high society I'd be able to entertain! Why, we'd probably even get to go to Washington and meet President Grant. But if I cannot accept Mr. Bridgeton's proposal because *you* keep refusing yours, then there's no point to it, is there?"

"How do you know Mr. Bridgeton *would* propose?" Joanna asked.

"Jo," Claire chided gently. "That's not very nice."

"But it's true. Who's to say whether he and Evie would get on or not? After all, that's the entire point of a courtship, isn't it? To decide if the person bringing you flowers and reciting poetry under the full moon is someone you want to spend the rest of your life with." Joanna brushed an auburn curl behind her ear. "For what it is worth, I've always found Mr. Bridgeton a tad dull."

Evie stopped short. "Mr. Bridgeton is not *dull*. He is refined."

"I believe if you look in Roget's Thesaurus you'll find that refined is another word for dull."

"Oh, dear," Claire murmured with a distressed glance between her sisters. "Can't we just—"

"Why must you be *such* a brat?" Evie hissed.

Joanna's eyes narrowed. She didn't *like* to fight with her sister. But she couldn't very well let an insult pass without returning it in kind. What sort of precedent would that set? Evie was already unbearable under the best of circumstances. Allowing her to get away with her abominable behavior would only make it worse.

"If anyone is being a brat here," she said, jabbing her finger at Evie, "it's *you*. I've every right to accept—or refuse—any marriage proposal given to me."

"Not when your refusal has dire implications for the entire family!"

"What would you have me do?" she exclaimed. "Marry someone I don't love?"

Evie set her jaw. "Do you love the roof over our heads? Do you love the food on our table? Do you love the clothes on our backs? Because if you don't marry soon, and marry well, not being able to afford a pound of butter is going to be the *least* of our concerns."

Joanna flicked a glance at Claire's face, which had drained of all color, and then scowled at Evie, who at least had the good sense to appear somewhat contrite.

The elder sisters took no prisoners when they attacked each other, but it was never their intention to upset the baby of the family. Never mind that Claire had turned eighteen just last week. To Joanna and Evie, she would always be a little girl clutching her doll as she struggled to keep up with them on their various escapades.

By silent agreement, Joanna, Evie, and their grandmother had vowed to hide the worst of their financial woes from Claire. It was a burden they didn't want her to carry. Not when her life was already so different from what Joanna and Evie's had been at her age.

When Joanna was eighteen, the war hadn't even started. There were rumblings. Whispers. News of a rebellion growing in the south. But Somerville had remained untouched, even well after the first battle that burned Charleston to the ground, and their lives had remained largely unchanged.

It wasn't until their father gave them each a piece of chocolate and bid them farewell with a kiss upon their heads that the full weight of the war began to sink in. The enormity of what could be gained if the Union won. And what might be lost if it didn't.

Even then, even when Joanna watched the dust kick up from the hooves of her father's horse as he rode away until her eyes stung, she never imagined that would be the last time she'd ever see him. Certainly Claire, all gangly limbs and earnest questions, hadn't known what would happen. And when it did, when the absolute worst occurred, Joanna and Evie tried the best they could to shield their sister from the grief, and the loss, and the devastation only a parent's death could bring.

They'd protected her ever since.

Joanna knew that Claire was not oblivious. Her little sister understood they weren't as wealthy as they'd once been. Heavens, a blind person could see that. Still, Joanna had taken great pains to shield Claire from the extent of their sacrifice. But a stain could only be covered by a rug for so long, and they'd sold off the last of the floor coverings months ago to pay for food.

"Don't listen to Evie," Joanna advised, giving Claire a nudge with her foot. "She's always prone to dramatics. We've still plenty left from selling the house. We'll be fine. It will *all* be fine." But even to her own ears, her words sounded hollow. A collection of empty promises she had no way of keeping unless she did the one thing she couldn't bring herself to do: marry for money instead of love.

If only Evie had been born first! *She* certainly had no such compunctions in regards to marrying a man for his wealth and social stature. But for reasons that had always baffled Joanna, their grandmother was insistent that her granddaughters marry in the order they'd entered the world. Which meant Joanna either needed to seriously reconsider Charles' offer, or find another way to save the family from financial ruin.

Given Charles' proclivity for silk pants, she had her hopes pinned on the latter.

"We cannot continue on with our heads buried in the sand." Evie put her hands on her hips. "You know as well as I, and maybe it's time Claire knew as well, that we've not enough to see us comfortably through the winter. What little we had was spent on new slate shingles for the roof last fall and rebuilding the summer kitchen after *you* burned it to the ground."

"That wasn't my fault," Joanna snapped. Even though it had happened last year, the topic of the summer kitchen—and its subsequent burning—was still a tender subject.

Joanna had been cooking (always a dangerous feat) when she found herself distracted by a fawn in the meadow across the way. She'd taken care to move the pot she was using off the fire before she flitted out to watch the young deer but, apparently, she hadn't moved it far enough, and when the pot boiled over, the resulting heat from the steam caused a pile of straw to catch fire. The summer kitchen had gone up in flames despite Joanna's best efforts to save it, and all she'd gotten for her trouble was a white puckered scar on the inside of her forearm from a floating ash.

It wasn't often she made mistakes. At least,

not of that magnitude. She would've liked to have forgotten the entire thing ever happened, but Evie had an uncanny knack for bringing it up at the absolute worst possible times.

Like right now.

"You left the pot on, didn't you?"

"Yes, but—"

"Then you burned it down," Evie said with unmistakable smugness.

If Joanna had that pot handy, she would have thrown it at Evie's head. Unfortunately, she had to settle for her shoe. Evie ducked, and the ankle boot bounced harmlessly off the wall just as their grandmother entered the room carrying a basket of carrots she'd picked from the garden behind the house.

"My dears," Ruth Thorncroft scolded, her thin gray brows gathering in disapproval over a hawkish nose. "It is not yet noon. Can we save the shoe throwing for after lunch?"

Joanna sank low in her chair. "Evie started it."

"And I am finishing it." Although small and slight in appearance, their grandmother had a will that was as strong as iron. A good thing, as she'd needed that will to see her through the death of her husband, the loss of her only child, and raising her three granddaughters as her own.

The matriarch of the Thorncroft family, Ruth was both stern and loving, strict and compassionate. When the sisters lost their mother to scarlet fever, she'd stepped in without hesitation, and had been caring for them ever since. She'd nursed their hurts, taught them their letters, and modeled the proper way to execute a curtsy. Joanna quite simply did not know how they would have gotten through the past few years without her unwavering support or wisdom, and her face heated beneath the scolding weight of Ruth's stare.

"I didn't *actually* hit her," she muttered beneath her breath.

"Not for lack of trying, I'm sure." Ruth clucked her tongue. "Pick up your boot, darling. We may live in a house the size of a pincushion, but the last I checked it wasn't a barn."

Obeying her grandmother's request without argument, Joanna removed her remaining ankle boot before grabbing the one she'd thrown and adding them to the line of shoes beside the door. For a second, her attention lingered on the assortment of footwear, all of it scuffed and worn and patched.

Not too long ago, the leather would have had a shiny new finish and the buttons would have been covered in silk instead of cheap pewter. Another reminder, however slight, of what had once been before the war.

When the back of her throat tightened, Joanna made herself to turn around. The death of her father was not something she liked to dwell on. For while the general heartache had lessened over time, the razor sharp grief still remained, like a needle lost in the folds of a skirt.

There would be hours, days, even months where she did not miss him at all. Or, when she thought of him, it was only of their happy times together. Then out of nowhere, she would feel the stab of that pesky needle, and all the pain came rushing back.

Placing her hand at the base of her neck, she willed the cool tips of her fingers to soften the shards of glass within as she forced herself to slowly inhale through her nostrils and breathe out through her mouth.

Joanna had always experienced her emotions more keenly than those around her. Or at least, that was how it often seemed. Most likely, because she was incapable of disguising how she felt. If she was sad, she cried. If she was happy, she laughed. If she was angry, she threw shoes. Nobody ever had to guess what Joanna was feeling, because, for better or for worse, it was always right there on her face.

At the moment, the same could be said for Evie.

"I can only assume from the murderous look Evelyn is giving you from across the room— careful, dear, you don't want your mouth to fix like that—you've left another broken heart in your wake?" Ruth asked Joanna as she set the basket of carrots aside and wiped her hands clean on the apron she wore over a faded green and white gingham dress.

"Charles' heart was far from broken." Tucking her grief aside, Joanna gave a snort. "I believe he was more upset about almost getting a grass stain on his pants."

Ruth sat down in her favorite chair, a wooden rocker that had belonged to *her* grandmother, and drew a blanket across her lap. "As long as you were kind in your refusal, I see no reason to make a fuss." She gave a pointed glance at Evie, who pursed her lips and looked away. "When you find the man you are meant to be with, he won't let you go as easily as that."

Joanna tucked a loose piece of hair behind her ear. "Evie thinks I should have accepted his proposal."

"Is that so?" Ruth murmured. "It's such a lovely morning. Claire, do you mind opening a window? I do so enjoy when you can smell the sea in the air."

While not considered a coastal town, Somerville was only a stone's throw from the ocean, and on a clear day, Joanna could taste the sharp, tangy salt water on her tongue and hear the piercing cry of gulls circling the massive sailing ships docked at Boston Harbor.

"I think Joanna should have at least *considered*

Charles' offer," Evie put in. Retreating to the staircase, she sat on the third step and scowled at Joanna, who scowled right back. "Especially considering our current circumstances."

"And what circumstances are those?" Ruth asked mildly.

"It's all right." Having finally managed to wrench the window open, Claire turned around. "I...I know. About everything. You needn't hide it from me anymore as if I were still a child."

"No one is hiding anything from you," Joanna protested even as guilt tickled her conscience, for that was *precisely* what they'd been doing. "We just didn't want you to worry."

"Then you should have given me more money for market," Claire said, her lips twisting in a wry smile, "and I would have been able to afford the butter."

"How much was the butter?" Ruth queried.

"Fifteen cents a pound."

"That much! Mr. Hemphill certainly thinks highly of his cows, doesn't he?" Their grandmother shook her head. "At that rate, we'd do better to buy a cow and churn the butter ourselves."

"Which is *exactly* why Joanna could have said yes to Charles." Evie's voluminous skirt, complete with a large silk bustle, rustled loudly as she stood up.

Unlike Joanna and Claire, who had taken to

wearing simpler garments now that they no longer entertained at the house (even with just the four of them the parlor/foyer/guest bedroom was noticeably crowded), Evie still insisted on dressing her very best every single day.

Appearance, she insisted, made all the difference between genteel poverty and actual poverty. Never mind that they hardly had two nickels to rub together. If someone saw Evie walking down the street with her hair perfectly pinned beneath a velvet half-bonnet and enough ruffles on her gown to suffocate an elephant, they'd naturally assume she heralded from a wealthy family. Which, of course, was exactly what she wanted them to think.

For her part, Joanna had never much cared for the opinions of others, regardless of whether they were friends or foes. The intricate and ever-changing rules of fashion had always eluded her. She'd much rather spend her time *doing* than dressing.

Yet another reason why she and Evie rarely saw eye to eye.

"How many times do I have to say I did not love him?" Joanna wondered aloud. "I'm beginning to sound like a parrot."

Evie crossed her arms. "You act as if love is the most important thing in the world. As if it is something that will pay for itself. But it isn't, and it *won't*. Women have been making strategic marriages to advance themselves both economically and socially for centuries. It is not a foreign concept."

"And I suppose if one of these women jumped off a bridge, you'd do that as well?" Joanna bit out as she struggled to rein in her temper. She'd had just about *enough* of Evie's nonsense, and she was tired of listening to it.

"Might we all try to get along?" Claire asked timidly. "I'm sure if we—"

"Don't be ridiculous," Evie scoffed, glaring at Joanna. "I'd ruin my dress."

"Your dress. Your *dress*." Joanna threw her hands in the air. "Because that's all you care about, hairstyles and dresses and pretty things."

"What's wrong with pretty things?"

"They're useless!"

"I really think—" Claire began.

"Are you saying *I'm* useless?" Evie's eyes flashed a dangerous shade of blue. "Just because we like different things doesn't mean what *I* like is any less valuable or unimportant. That's your problem, you know."

Anger boiled in Joanna's blood, hot and thick. No one could rile her up quite like Evie. She almost wished they were children again, so that she might resort to yanking on Evie's braids. But the last time she'd tried to pull Evie's hair in the heat of an argument, Ruth had snapped a ruler across Joanna's knuckles and told her in no uncertain terms that she was too old for such antics and, as a young lady, if she wanted to attack or defend herself she would have to learn how to do it with words.

The issue with words was that they required both thought and discipline. Joanna, on the other hand, had always preferred to act first and consider the potential consequences of those actions later.

"What, *exactly*, is my problem?" She advanced on Evie until they were nose to nose. Well, almost nose to nose. Joanna was several inches taller than both her sisters. Taller than almost every woman in the village, truth be told. "My string bean" her father had called her with great affection, and while other women might have felt self-conscious about their height being so different from their peers, Joanna had never given it a second thought.

"You think you're always right just because you're the eldest." A storm cloud had gathered between Evie's brows and lightning shot between them, leaving a groove in the middle of her flawlessly plucked arches. "And because you think you're always right, you also believe things are just going to magically work out. But they're *not*, and your foolish optimism has blinded you to the stark reality of our situation."

"I'd rather have my optimism than your cynicism!" Joanna retorted.

"Would you rather starve than marry?"

"If it meant marrying someone I didn't love, then maybe I would!"

"That's absurd."

"Perhaps, but no more absurd than trading my freedom for a fancy house high on a hill." She gave a willful toss of her head. "I will *not* marry for any reason other than love. You cannot convince me otherwise."

"And you call *me* dramatic?" Evie said. "What freedoms would you be giving up by marrying Charles Gaines? The freedom to live in this tiny little shack while everyone mocks us in the village? The freedom to not be able to afford butter or new clothes or wood for the winter? The freedom to not send Claire to finishing school?"

"I'd be giving up the freedom to be myself! Charles and all the other suitors preceding him would see me suffocated in beautiful gowns and tea parties and luncheons. They'd parade me about as if I were some fine show horse before they gave me a carrot and put me away while they went to smoke cigars and give themselves pats on the back for how well-behaved their wives are."

Evie looked genuinely puzzled. "And what's wrong with that?"

"It's not for me. If I could find a wealthy man who had all the traits I desired, and who loved me for who I am now instead of who he wants to mold me into, then I would marry him in a second!" Joanna cried passionately. "But if such a man exists, he isn't here in Somerville. Trust me." Her mouth flattened. "I've searched."

"Well you'd best keep searching, because we've no other way to keep the creditors at bay."

"I—I could find someone to marry," Claire interceded hesitantly.

"No," Joanna and Evie said in unison.

Claire frowned. "But the butcher's son, Eric, has been slipping two extra slices of bacon into our order." Her face was overcome by a rosy blush. "I think...I think he might be sweet on me."

Joanna shook her head. "Free bacon does not a marriage make."

"But—"

"Joanna will be the first to marry," Ruth announced, finally breaking her silence as she set her blanket aside and stood up from the rocking chair. "I've few rules in this house, but that is one which you *all* will abide by. Furthermore, I'm weary of all this squabbling. You two,"—she pointed at Joanna and Evie—"have worn my nerves to the bone with your constant bickering. If your father could see you now, he'd be *most* disappointed in how you are treating each other."

Shame burned the back of Joanna's neck.

There was not a crueler thing that Ruth

could have said.

But she was right.

If Father could see them now, he *would* be disappointed.

He'd always been so proud of how his daughters had gotten along. Oh, they'd had their occasional disagreements. Three girls under a single roof, how could they not? But they'd never fought like this. And never over things of such a personal nature.

The uncertainty of the war, the death of their father, and the loss of their home and the life they knew had combined to create the perfect storm of emotions that neither Joanna nor Evie knew how to navigate. The sad truth, Joanna assumed, was that they'd grown so accustomed to pointing out each other's differences that they'd forgotten how to celebrate their similarities.

On a hard swallow, she met Evie's gaze.

Her sister's eyes were wide, wider than normal, and there was a suspicious glint in them even though Evie refused to let herself cry (she was convinced that tears caused wrinkles).

"I never liked the way Charles always used his salad fork for the main course," Evie said with a sniff. "You couldn't possibly marry someone who did not use their silverware in the correct order. What would people say?"

It wasn't a perfect apology. It wasn't even really an apology at all. But the intent was there, and that was all that mattered.

"Not to mention his choice in fashion," Joanna said.

Evie blinked. "Are you referring to his salmon trousers?"

"Are they salmon? I thought they were pink."

"Salmon," Evie confirmed. "And imported straight from Paris."

"You don't say."

"Have we managed to reach a compromise?" Ruth asked with a cool, measured stare at her oldest granddaughters.

Joanna glanced at Evie, who gave a small, nearly imperceptible nod.

"Yes," she said, "I believe we have."

"Good," said Ruth matter-of-factly. "I realize all of you girls are concerned, and you've every right to be. The truth of the matter is that our situation *is* precarious. But *no one* is going to marry someone they do not want to. Nor will they be pressured into doing so by any member of this family. Is that understood?"

"Then what would you have us do?" Claire asked softly.

Ruth hesitated. She seemed to be battling back and forth with something, before she squared her shoulders and lifted her chin. "You can sell the ring."

All three sisters gave an audible gasp and looked at each other.

After a moment of stunned silence, Joanna was the first to speak.

"You mean...Mother's ring?" she said disbelievingly.

Ruth lifted an eyebrow. "Is there another priceless ruby ring I am unaware of in your possession?"

"No," said Evie. "It's just that..."

"It's *Mother's* ring," Claire finished.

Found in a box in the attic seven weeks after their father passed when they were packing up their belongings, the ring in question was an enormous heart-shaped ruby with glittering diamonds on either side. They knew it had belonged to their mother because her name had been inscribed on the inside of the gold band.

Anne, my love ~ JW

The identity of "JW", where the ring had come from, and why it had been hidden all these years...well, that remained a mystery.

When Joanna had first discovered the ring, tucked away with a lock of their mother's hair (red, just like her own), she and her sisters had discussed selling it. But still reeling from the loss of their father, they hadn't been able to part with something that had belonged to their mother.

Even if it was something they knew nothing about.

Late at night, with nothing else to fill her mind, Joanna had closed her eyes and wondered…but she'd never allowed, nor wanted, her mind to travel down a road where her mother had been given a piece of jewelry worth a large fortune from a man whose initials did not match her husband's.

Thus the ring's very existence had been largely—and purposefully—ignored.

Until now.

"The ring is worth an immense amount. I've never seen a stone of its equal in all my years." Ruth walked to the window. "You would need to take it to a jeweler in Boston. I have one I can recommend. No merchant here in Somerville would be able to give you even half its value. But if you went into the city, and held out for a higher price, the money earned would be more than enough to see us comfortably through the next few years."

An unpleasant feeling pooled in Joanna's belly. Not quite guilt, not quite excitement, but an uncomfortable combination of the two that tasted sour on the back of her tongue. Like the time she'd bitten into a blackberry that wasn't yet ripe.

"I'm not sure…" she said with a glance at Evie, who appeared equally uneasy.

Ruth peered at them over her shoulder. Her gaze was sharp, and uncharacteristically calculating. "Evie, you could purchase that beautiful silk shawl you've swooned over every time we've gone into the village. Joanna, you could go on that trip with your friend. And Claire, you could start up your singing lessons again." Her gaze softened as she looked at her youngest granddaughter. "You've a rare talent, my dear, and I should like to see you pursue it."

The praise brought a blush to Claire's cheeks. "Thank you, Grandmother."

"I suppose…" Joanna hesitated. Here, at last, was the opportunity she'd been hoping for. The chance to fill their pockets and alleviate their financial burdens without having to marry a man like Charles. Still, it didn't seem right. To sell something that had never belonged to them. To sell something their mother had taken such pains to keep secret. But then, what other choice did they have? "I suppose it wouldn't hurt to take the ring to Boston and see how much it is actually worth. After that, we can decide whether we'd like to sell it or not."

"I agree," said Evie.

"But it's the last thing we have of hers," Claire protested. "Except for her lock of hair, and the painting."

Joanna's gaze automatically went to the brick fireplace on the other side of the room. There, propped on top of the old wooden mantel, was the only painting they had of their mother. The commissioned artwork had been a wedding gift. It depicted Anne and Jacob Thorncroft on the day of their marriage. Their mother, stunning in white with her auburn hair hidden beneath a veil, was looking directly at the artist while their father, handsome in a black suit, gazed adoringly at his bride. Both of them were glowing with happiness, the love and devotion they felt towards each other all but radiating off the canvas.

Since she was a little girl, Joanna couldn't remember a day that had gone by where she hadn't paused whatever she was doing to admire the painting. She'd memorized every brush stroke, from the slight curve of her mother's mouth to the sparkle in her father's eyes. It was a beautiful piece of artwork. But more than that, it was a glimpse into the past. A glimpse at a mother she could hardly remember. A glimpse at what awaited Joanna if she could find her own true love.

"Mother would never want us to marry someone we didn't love." Of this, Joanna was absolutely certain. "For that reason, I believe *she* would approve of us selling the ring."

Claire bit her lip. "How could you possibly know that?"

Joanna gestured at the painting. "Because I can see how much Mother loved Father. And the last thing she'd want is for us to commit ourselves to a husband out of obligation or necessity. That's not to say we *will* part with the ring. But if we did, I don't think she would look poorly upon us for it."

"You're right," said Evie.

Joanna nearly fell over. "I'm sorry, what?"

Evie rolled her eyes. "You needn't look shocked."

"I *am* shocked." She pressed the back of her hand to Evie's temple. "How are you feeling? Any hot or cold flashes? How many fingers am I holding up?"

"Very amusing," Evie said before she swatted Joanna's arm away.

"Then you'll go to Boston?" Ruth asked.

Joanna and Evie nodded.

After a long pause, Claire did the same.

For once, all three Thorncroft sisters were in agreement.

If only they knew how much that unity was going to change all of their lives...forever.

CHAPTER THREE

L IKE MOST OF the country, Boston was
undergoing a massive restoration. There was
a new university, a new children's hospital, and
even a new association dedicated solely to the
women's suffrage movement.

Everywhere Joanna looked, there were horses pulling carts piled high with bricks and oxen
dragging enormous wooden beams. Well-dressed
women sauntered by on the arms of equally well-
dressed men, while young boys darted through
the streets hawking newspapers and young girls
sold roses. A governess steered her charges past a
new building that was only halfway assembled as
a crew of burly men worked on demolishing the
one next to it. There was a memorial dedicated to
Massachusetts Fifty-fourth Regiment being
constructed in the middle of Boston Common,
and an entire housing development being built on

Black Bay, a portion of land that had once been part of the river before it was filled in.

Composed of an eclectic mixture of Americans, many of whom had recently fled the devastated south, Irish immigrants, and French Canadians, the city was a loud, disorganized jumble of different people seeking a new life in a revitalized city.

And Joanna loved every bit of it.

"Do you see that?" she exclaimed, pointing her finger at a chimney sweep casually walking across the top of a steeply pitched roof. "And that! And *that*!"

"It's deafening," Claire winced, clapping her hands over her ears.

"And dirty," Evie complained, lifting her skirts out of the mud.

"It's *exciting*," Joanna corrected. Pulling a crinkled piece of paper out of her purse, she squinted at her own messy handwriting. Their grandmother had given them directions to a very old and very highly regarded jeweler on the corner of Bridge Street and…

"Is that a J or a T?" she asked, shoving the paper underneath Evie's nose.

"I don't know," Evie said, pushing Joanna's arm away with a grimace. "*You're* the one who wrote it."

"We need to find Truman Avenue." Stopping in the middle of the busy sidewalk, Claire flattened a hand against her temple and stood up on her toes in an effort to see above the crowded swarm of pedestrians. "I see it!" she said, her face brightening with relief. Unlike Joanna, who loved the business of the city, and Evie, who was in awe of the fashion, Claire much preferred the quietness of Somerville. She'd been visibly overwhelmed ever since they'd arrived, and was eager to have the ring appraised as fast as possible and return home. "Right over there, beside the bakery, just like Grandmother said."

"Then over there we shall go," Joanna announced, barely contained excitement adding an extra bounce to her step as she linked arms with her sisters and half-walked, half-dragged them past the bakery and into a small, narrow shop with a gold sign above the door that read *Bernard's Fine Estate Jewelry and Antiquities.*

In the two days since they'd decided to have the ring appraised and possibly sold, Joanna had felt light as a feather. Finally, *finally,* there was a potential solution to her dilemma of marrying to save her family instead of marrying to fulfill her heart's desire. Because if she had to—if she *really* had to—she would accept Charles' proposal. Or the one that had come before it. Or the one that had come before that. Somerville had plenty of men from wealthy families, with no exceedingly remarkable traits to distinguish them from each other. Oh, John Yardley preferred fishing to hunting and Henry Wellsboro had never met a deer he didn't want to kill, but in their bones and their blood they were all cut from the same cloth.

Except for Charles, who preferred silk.

If she said yes to any of them, she'd be saying yes to all of them. It wouldn't matter which suitor she chose. But with the ring and the money it brought, she wouldn't have to. With the ring, she could pursue her dream of traveling the world without being weighed down by the guilt of letting her family down. With the ring, she could fall in love with whomever she wanted. With the ring, she could choose someone because of *who* they were instead of how *wealthy* they were. With the ring, she could be free.

A plush green carpet muffled her footsteps as she followed her sisters into the jewelry shop and allowed the door to swing closed behind her. At once, she was assailed by the overwhelming scent of a heavy floral perfume. The kind their grandmother kept on her dressing table but never used.

At first glance, there was no one about. As Joanna's eyesight adjusted to the dimly lit interior, she noticed a long, glass case that ran the entire length of the back wall. Inside the case was jewelry of all sorts, from necklaces to earrings to an enormous sapphire brooch that immediately captured Evie's attention.

"Oh," she sighed, pressing her face to the

glass, "it's *gorgeous*."

"You've an excellent eye, Miss. That particular piece belonged to the Duchess of Knoxleigh," said a short, middle-aged man as he stepped out from behind a velvet curtain on the other side of the case. Wearing a pleasant smile and an old-fashioned waistcoat with a gold pocket watch tucked in the front pocket, he inclined his head in greeting. "Mr. Bernard at your service, young ladies. How can I help you today?"

As the eldest, Joanna was accustomed to taking the lead. "We've come to have a ring appraised. It belonged to our mother." Opening her purse where she'd carefully secured the ring inside a leather pouch, she placed it in the middle of her palm and held out her arm. Evie and Claire crowded on either side of her, and all three sisters held their breath as Mr. Bernard leaned forward to examine the ring.

"Exquisite," he murmured. "Positively exquisite." His head lifted sharply. "How did you say the ring came to be in your possession?"

"It was our mother's," Joanna repeated. "I found it in the attic a number of years after she had passed."

"I am sorry for your loss," said Mr. Bernard without taking his eyes off the ring. "You'd like to know its worth? Are you interested in selling it?"

"We haven't decided," Claire said with an anxious glance at Joanna, who took her sister's hand and gave it a reassuring squeeze.

She knew Claire still harbored some reservations about parting with the ring. She also knew why. While Joanna and Evie still retained some memories of their mother, however obscure and fleeting they may have been, Claire had none. The ring was an attachment to the woman who had given birth to her. The woman she was incapable of remembering. The woman she'd always yearned to know.

If Claire did not want to sell the ring after they learned its monetary value, then they wouldn't sell it. It was as simple as that. In the Thorncroft family, sisters came first. No matter how much they bickered on small matters, they always presented a united front on the things that were most important.

While selling the ring was the easiest and simplest solution to all of their problems, if one of them didn't want to do it, then none of them would do it.

They'd find another way.

They always did.

"We'd like to have it appraised first," Joanna said matter-of-factly. "Then discuss possibly putting it on consignment. Our Grandmother, Ruth Thorncroft, told us you sold several pieces of jewelry for her."

"Mrs. Thorncroft. Yes. I remember her very well. Very well, indeed. Lovely woman. Drove a hard bargain, I will admit." Mr. Bernard rocked onto his heels and tucked his hands into the pockets of his waistcoat. "Her granddaughters, did you say?"

"I am Joanna, this is Evie, and Claire." Joanna's eyes narrowed as she studied the jeweler. She didn't know why, exactly, but she didn't like the way his gaze kept darting to the ring. Or how his tongue ran across his bottom lip every time he stared at it. "Can you tell us anything about the ring?"

"I'd have to examine it, naturally. May I?" Opening a drawer, Mr. Bernard removed a square piece of black velvet and laid it flat across the top of the glass case.

After a moment's hesitation, Joanna placed the ring in the middle of the velvet and then watched, nibbling on her bottom lip, as the jeweler slipped on a pair of heavyset spectacles with what appeared to be miniature magnifying glasses attached to the ends.

"What are those?" Claire asked, nodding at the unusual spectacles.

"These," said Mr. Bernard as he grasped the ring with a pair of tweezers and held it up to his right eye which appeared comically large, "are called a jeweler's loupe. Think of them as a telescope, except they're used to look at gemstones instead of planets and stars. Interesting." He turned the ring from side to side. "Quite interesting."

"What is?" Evie said breathlessly.

Carefully returning the ring to the velvet, Mr. Bernard pushed his jeweler's loupe to the top of his head. "Your mother's ring was undoubtedly custom made and in pristine condition for its age."

"Its age?" Joanna's brow creased. "How old is it, precisely?"

"Given the type of setting, my best guess would be the mid-18th century."

The sisters exchanged a startled glance, and Joanna knew they were all thinking the same thing. How in the world had their mother come to be in possession of a ring that was nearly one hundred and twenty years old?

"The ruby itself is likely to be much older than that," Mr. Bernard continued. "It's a marquise cut, four carats, framed in twelve half-carat diamonds. Absolutely top grade. What's *interesting* is that the designer of such a magnificent piece of work would usually leave a signature mark. Not unlike an artist signing his painting. What makes this ring very unique, aside from its size and clarity, is that there is no such signature mark. It is, for all intents and purposes, anonymous."

"And that's rare?" said Evie.

"Exceedingly so."

"Then you don't know who made the ring?"

asked Claire.

"No, I am afraid not," Mr. Bernard said quickly.

Too quickly to Joanna's way of thinking.

As the fine hairs on her nape stood straight on end, she snatched up the ring and closed it protectively in her fist. She still couldn't pinpoint the source of her uneasiness, but she'd learned to trust her gut a long time ago. And right now, it was telling her something wasn't right.

"What is it worth?" she asked.

"I…" Removing a linen handkerchief from his pocket, Mr. Bernard ran it across his temple. "I would need more time to do a thorough exam. Standard procedure, you understand. It should only take a day or two, three at the most."

"What sort of exam?" she asked suspiciously.

"Tests," he mumbled vaguely. "Standard procedure, as I said."

"What *sort* of tests?"

Again Mr. Bernard swiped his handkerchief along his forehead, which was now beginning to gleam with sweat beneath the soft glow of the light hanging above their heads. "The—the usual sort. Nothing out of the ordinary."

"Jo, just give him the ring," said Evie, her voice tinged with exasperation. "It's not as if Mr. Bernard is trying to *steal* it from us. He's a highly respected jeweler! Aren't you, Mr. Bernard?"

"H—highly respected," Mr. Bernard stuttered.

"There, you see?" Then she frowned. "Mr. Bernard, are you well? You're turning rather red."

"Very red," Claire agreed.

The jeweler tugged at his necktie. "I...I...oh, to hell with it. Just give me the ring!"

Evie shrieked when Mr. Bernard lunged across the counter at Joanna. "Bad jeweler!" she cried, striking at him with the parasol she always carried with her regardless of fair weather or foul. "Bad jeweler!"

As her sister bludgeoned the jeweler over the head, Joanna leapt nimbly out of reach of his waving arms. Her heel caught on a fold in the carpet, and she nearly fell. Catching her balance, she tightened her grip on the ring until the point of the ruby cut into the palm of her hand, but she hardly registered the pain over the sound of her heartbeat roaring in her ears.

"We're leaving," she announced. "Claire, Evie, let's go."

"Wait!" Mr. Bernard cried after them as they hurried out the door.

But the sisters didn't stop. Not before they'd raced around the corner and slipped into an alley carved between two towering brick buildings. Spying a mountain of crates, Joanna ducked behind them and motioned for her siblings to do the same.

Claire immediately followed suit.

But Evie stopped short.

"It's *dirty*," she complained. "Isn't there someplace else we can go? A nice pastry shop, perhaps?"

Joanna gaped at her sister. "Mr. Bernard just tried to physically assault us in order to steal our most valuable possession, and you want to eat *pastries*? Get down here before he sees you!"

"I didn't say I wanted to eat pastries," Evie grumbled as she crouched gingerly beside Claire. "I'd just prefer a place to hide that wasn't infested with rats."

"There are rats?" Claire squeaked in alarm.

"No," Joanna said firmly. "There aren't any rats."

At least, she hoped not.

Still, a rat or two would be vastly preferable to a crazed jeweler.

"I knew something was wrong with him." She shook her head. "As soon as he saw the ring, his entire demeanor changed. Almost as if…"

"He recognized it," Claire whispered. She raised wide, fearful, blue eyes to Joanna. "I found his behavior peculiar as well. But how could he have seen Mother's ring before? It was in that attic for years and years."

"I'm not sure. But he seemed to know an awful lot about it." Uncurling her fingers, Joanna studied the ring with a renewed sense of interest…and wariness. What secrets were embedded within the ruby? Why had their mother kept it hidden for their entire lives? And why had Mr. Bernard tried to steal it from them?

For once, Joanna didn't have any answers.

It wasn't a good feeling.

As the oldest, she was accustomed to fixing things. To solving problems. To righting wrongs. But there was no easy solution to be found in any of this.

Only more questions.

Carefully slipping the ring back into its leather carrying pouch, she put the pouch in her purse and slipped her wrist through the leather handles.

"What do we do now?" Claire asked, unknowingly echoing Joanna's exact thoughts.

"I'm not sure. Take it to another jeweler, I suppose. Someone who doesn't know anything about us, or our family, or the ring." Slowly standing, she peeked around the corner of a crate. When she didn't see anything out of the ordinary, she waved her arm to indicate the path was clear.

"Finally." With a huff, Evie used her parasol to push herself to her feet and then gave a gasp of outrage when dust rose in a billowing cloud of red from her skirts as she spun around in a circle. "*Look* at this! I told you we should have gone to a pastry shop. Do you know how hard it is to get stains out of bombazine?"

"God bless you," Claire said politely.

Joanna rolled her eyes. "We've more to

worry about than a little dirt on our dresses."

"Easy for you to say," Evie scowled. "You never care *what* you look like."

"It's served me well this far." Not wanting to go back the way they'd come in case Mr. Bernard was still after them, Joanna crossed the street and turned left. Thankfully, Boston was a large, sprawling metropolis, and the chances of crossing paths with a single person out of thousands was incredibly slim. "There should be another jeweler near the commons. If not, we can double back to our carriage and return home."

For the journey into the city they'd borrowed a square gig from a friend in the village, which Claire had driven. While timid with people, she'd always had an affinity for animals, and had handled the three-hour trip with remarkable ease, particularly given the condition of some of the roads.

"I hope we can find someone reputable to appraise the ring," Claire said fretfully as the sisters pressed up against the side of a store to make room for two men carrying a large crate between them. "I shouldn't like to come here again."

"We could always spend the night," Evie suggested, her gaze lingering on the display of colorful shawls hanging in the window. "Start fresh in the morning."

"How are we to afford lodging?" Joanna

asked.

Tearing her gaze away from the window, Evie kicked at a pebble with her shoe. "I *despise* being poor."

"It is not ideal," Claire agreed. "Still, we have each other, don't we?"

"Of course. *And* we still have the ring," Joanna pointed out. "Which means our plan remains the same as it did before. We just need to find another jeweler."

"Preferably one I don't have to beat over the head with a parasol," said Evie.

Joanna grinned. "Excellent work, by the by. Mr. Bernard quite literally did not know what hit him."

"Thank you," said Evie, appearing pleased by the praise.

They rounded a busy corner. Joanna began to search the signs hanging above the various stores, looking for one that could provide them the service they required. "I'm certain Mr. Bernard was nothing more than a stroke of bad luck. I know we can find—*oompf!*"

She was nearly knocked off her feet when a boy, a tuft of black hair sticking out from beneath an oversized hat, slammed into Claire, who in turn crashed into Evie, who bumped hard into Joanna.

Clutching each other for balance, the sisters whipped around just in time to watch the boy's retreating back as he dashed off in the direction of the harbor, fearlessly winding and weaving his way through the heavy traffic.

"I never," Evie sniffed as she patted her hair.

"He was in a very big hurry." A bit wobbly on her feet, Claire leaned against the lamppost. "I wonder where he is—"

"The ring." As a pit opened up in her belly, Joanna yanked her purse off her arm and began to feverishly sift through its contents.

There wasn't much.

An ivory comb.

A small mirror.

A pencil.

Noticeably missing?

A leather pouch with their mother's 120-year-old ring.

"It was right here!" Her heart pounding, she whirled in a circle and jabbed a finger at the harbor where billowing white sails snapped in the wind and, somewhere, a pickpocket was making off with their inheritance. "That little thief stole the ring!"

"*No*," Evie gasped.

Claire paled. "What do we do?"

"We go after him. Follow me!" Filled with determination, Joanna took off like a thorough-bred who had just heard the toll of a race bell. Her height gave her a stride advantage over both her sisters and, within seconds, she had outdistanced them considerably. Dimly, she could hear Evie calling at her to wait, to stop, but she was not about to allow someone to escape with their fortune…and their future.

She knocked into a man with a dark beard. He yelled angrily at her and waved his fist. She shouted an apology over her shoulder, but didn't slow down. The street narrowed, then widened as it approached the harbor. Large factories puffing black smoke out of tall, brick chimneys gave way to long docks and even longer ships. Joanna ducked under the arm of a sailor carrying an enormous coil of rope, then nearly collided with another as he rolled a barrel along the pier.

"Watch where ye're going," he snarled in a heavy cockney accent.

"I'm sorry. I didn't mean…" Panting, Joanna leaned forward and braced her hands on her knees. She'd lost her hat somewhere along the way, and her hair spilled over her shoulders in a wave of red. "Did you see a boy come through here? Lean as a whip. Black hair. Large hat." Dragging in a lungful of air, she managed to stand upright despite the vicious cramp piercing her left side. "He stole something very valuable from me and my sisters."

"Prob'y down on the docks by now, gettin' in a boat. The *Queen Mary* sails for London in a minute or so. They've already pulled the anchor." The sailor jerked his head at the largest ship in the harbor, a schooner with three masts and too many sails to count. Men swarmed the top deck shouting orders to each other while seagulls squawked loudly overhead. As the last ropes were yanked from the water, the grand ship began to inch away from the pier.

Slanting a hand against her temple to block out the sun, Joanna's gaze flew across the wooden gangplanks for a sign of the thief. There were just so many *people*. Crewmen, merchants, passengers. Finding the little rapscallion would be like finding a needle in a haystack.

Then, by some small miracle, she noticed a slim figure scaling the side of the *Queen Mary*.

"There! He's right there!" she yelled. "We need to stop him. Can you help me?"

The sailor followed the direction of frantic pointing and snorted. "Aye. Good luck with that, luv. The Mary's good as gone." Then his gaze dropped to her breasts, and his lips peeled back in a leer. "If ye need someone to console ye…"

Why was it, in times of great desperation, men's thoughts always seemed to center on one thing?

With a pinched expression of disgust, Joanna shoved past the sailor. She reached the docks just as the schooner's sails were released. They caught the wind with a deafening *snap* and she was forced to watch as the *Queen Mary*, bound for England, surged towards open waters.

"No," she whispered, pressing her hand to her mouth. "No, no, *no*."

Joanna was not accustomed to failing, and the weight of this defeat nearly sent her to her knees. Because it was more than a lost ring. It was a lost hope. It was a lost dream. It was a lost future.

How could this have happened?

How could she have *let* it happen?

Turning around, Joanna staggered up the gangplank on legs that were numb from exhaustion and disappointment. When Evie and Claire found her, she was sitting on a bench, staring blindly out at the harbor.

"It's gone," she said before they could speak a word. "The ring is gone."

CHAPTER FOUR

R UTH WAS WAITING up for them in the parlor.
Flickering candlelight illuminated the sisters'
bleak faces, alerting their grandmother at once
that something was amiss. Alarmed, she rose
from her rocking chair as they filed stiffly past
her.

"What happened?" she demanded.

"Someone stole the ring," Evie said flatly. It
was the first time she'd spoken since they'd left
Boston, and her quiet fury rolled across the room
like a wave. Slipping out of her shoes, she gave
them an angry kick across the room. "It's on a
ship heading to London. We'll never get it back."

"I'm going to make us all some tea," Claire
murmured, flitting away to the kitchen.

"Joanna?" Ruth asked, turning to her eldest
granddaughter with knitted brows.

Exhaustion seeped into Joanna's bones like

lead. Sinking down onto the sofa, she dragged a blanket over her lap and in dull, halting tones, told their grandmother everything that had happened, beginning with taking the ring to Mr. Bernard and ending with watching it sail away on the *Queen Mary*. When she'd finished, she could only shake her head in bewilderment. "I just don't understand. Of all the people in Boston, why would a thief choose *me*? How did he know I even *had* the ring? And why take it to *England*, of all places? It doesn't make any sense."

"I am going to bed," Evie announced. "This was a horrific day, and I should like very much for it to end."

"I'll join you," Claire said as she returned with the tea. Setting it on a table, she kissed Ruth on the cheek, glanced sadly at Joanna, and then followed Evie up the staircase.

Joanna dropped her head into her hands.

"They blame me," she said, her voice muffled. "And they're right. It's my fault the ring was stolen. I should have protected it better. I should have had us go straight home. Then none of this would have happened." Biting hard on the inside of her cheek to quell the tears that threatened to spill off her lashes, she lifted her chin and gazed helplessly at her grandmother. "What are we supposed to do?"

"First of all, you are going to stop blaming yourself. Because what happened is *not* your fault.

75

It's mine." Ruth helped herself to a cup of tea before she sat back down in her rocking chair.

"What do you mean?" Joanna blinked in confusion. "Grandmother, you weren't even there."

A faint smile softened the stern brackets on either side of Ruth's mouth as she turned her gaze to the painting of Joanna's parents on the mantel. "Jacob was always handsome, even as a young boy. And he so did love your mother." Her smile slowly faded as her gaze darkened. "There are things you are not aware of, Joanna. Family secrets I've kept from you and your sisters at the request of your father. Secrets that are tied to that damned ring." She took a long sip of tea. "I selfishly thought that if the ring was sold then its troubled past would go with it. Clearly, I was mistaken."

Uneasiness prickled along the nape of Joanna's neck like tiny, little needles. In all her life, she'd never known her grandmother to hide anything. Ruth was honest to a fault, and blunt along with it. But clearly there was *something* she'd been hiding. Something that had begun unraveling the moment her grandmother suggested they sell the ring.

"What secrets?" she asked.

Ruth stared at the portrait for a long time. When she finally looked away, there was a glint of sadness in her eyes Joanna had never seen.

"Painful ones. I am going to tell you the truth, my dearest, and leave it to you to decide if you wish to tell your sisters."

Now, Joanna was more bewildered than ever. Yes, she and Evie could go at each other like cats and dogs, but when the dust settled, there was no one she trusted more. Except for Claire, of course. They were a bonded trio, their sisterhood forged by love and loss. There was nothing she would keep from her siblings, and nothing they would keep from her.

Surely, their grandmother knew that.

"Go on," she said, even as part of her was tempted to plaster her hands over her ears and not listen to a word. She had no inkling as to what her grandmother was going to say, but she did know one thing: it wasn't going to be good.

Secrets never were.

"I suppose I should start at the beginning." Ruth paused. "But before I do that, I should like you to remember that you were truly the apple of your father's eye. He adored you beyond measure, my dear. Nothing I say is going to change that."

Joanna remained silent, dread and curiosity rising within her in equal measure.

"Your parents were childhood sweethearts. I honestly believe that from the first moment they met, they were in love. After your father graduated medical college in New York, their plan was to marry and settle here, in Somerville. He already had the house in town picked out, and your mother was all but decorating the nursery. But then…then things changed."

"What things?" Joanna said warily as a rippling unease made its way down her spine. She knew her parents had fallen in love when they were very young. And she knew they'd married soon after her father became a doctor. Shortly thereafter, they had her, and then Evie, and then Claire. She'd heard the story a hundred times. Mayhap even a thousand. Yet in all its various retellings, there had never been a "but then".

"While your father was in his last year of medical school, your mother traveled to London."

Stunned, Joanna could only stare blankly at her grandmother. "She—she did?"

"Indeed." Ruth clasped her hands together in the middle of her lap. Her fingers were clenched. Her knuckles white. "Her mother, *your* other grandmother who passed right before you were born, was born and raised there."

"Her name was…" Joanna hesitated as she searched her memory. "Mabel. Mabel…Ellin?"

"Ellinwood. Your grandmother's maiden name was Ellinwood. Mabel was the daughter of a viscount, and it seems her family was quite disappointed when she chose to marry an American and move to Boston. When your mother came of age, Mabel decided she wanted her to have a traditional coming out in High British Society. An attempt, I would assume, to reconcile with her family."

Joanna's head was spinning. She'd known—vaguely—that her Grandmother Mabel was from England, but she'd never given it much consideration. Her mother's side of the family had always been a bit obscure. Especially given she and her sisters had never had the opportunity to meet any of them.

"Neither of your parents wanted Anne to travel overseas," Ruth continued. "But Mabel was adamant, and gave little choice in the matter. Jacob wrote to her nearly every day and, at first, she wrote him back, but gradually the letters slowed, and then stopped." Once again, Ruth looked to the painting. She stared at it for several seconds. Then she sighed, straightened her spine, and met Joanna's wide gaze. "When your mother returned, some nine months later, she was carrying a child."

Had Joanna been drinking something, she would have spat it out, so great was her shock. She threw the blanket over her legs aside, but paused shy of leaping to her feet. "What are you saying? Mother was—Mother was *pregnant* when she returned from London? But...Father wasn't there."

"No," Ruth said quietly. "He wasn't."

"I don't understand. I—we—have a brother or a sister? A half-brother or sister we've never known about? *That's* the secret?" As a wave of relief cooled the fires of Joanna's disbelief, she slumped in her seat. All things considered, a hidden sibling wasn't such a terrible thing. And if the indiscretion had occurred before her parents were married, well, then, it wasn't even really an affair. Certainly it was not *preferable*. But neither was it wrong. Except…

"Why?" she asked. "Why would Father have kept this a secret? Why would he have kept our sibling from us? Were they taken back to England to be raised with the Ellinwoods?"

"Not exactly." Ruth's eyes glistened. "The baby, a girl, was kept here."

"Then why have we never met her?"

"Because, my dear, that baby is *you*."

"No." Joanna's denial was swift and immediate. "No, that's not right. That's not true." Auburn curls whipped across her face as she shook her head wildly from side to side. "I was born after Mother and Father were married."

"Yes, you were." Pushing out of the rocking chair, Ruth walked to Joanna and sat down beside her. She gently took her granddaughter's trembling hand. "When your mother came home and shared that she was expecting, your father married her the very next day. It was a lovely ceremony. Sweet, and simple, and full of love.

After it was over, your parents never spoke of Anne's indiscretion ever again. You were, for all intents and purposes, their firstborn child, Joanna. And they made the decision to raise you as such."

There was a ball of ice in the middle of the Joanna's chest, growing larger and larger with every inhalation. Her breath hitched. Tears swarmed, stinging the corners of her eyes like the jabs of angry hornets. Her skin felt alternately hot and then freezing cold. Her teeth began to chatter. "But I wasn't...I'm not...I'm not my father's daughter. I'm not *your* granddaughter."

Ruth slapped her.

The sound was like a gunshot.

Joanna's head whipped to the side. She gave a sharp gasp and gently cupped the side of her face where the throbbing outline of Ruth's hand was burning to the touch.

"You—you *hit* me," she accused.

"And I'll do it again," Ruth said evenly, "if you ever dare speak such nonsense. I *am* your grandmother. You *are* my granddaughter. Maybe not by blood. But in every other way that matters, we *are* a family, Joanna. You, and I, and your sisters. And we will continue to be a family. This changes nothing."

Except it did.

It changed *everything*.

If there was one thing Joanna had always been certain of, if there was one thing she had always believed in, it was where she came from. Those ties, those *roots*, made her who she was. She had red hair and blue eyes because of her mother. She had an inherent stubbornness because of her father. She had an iron will because of her grandmother.

Or at least, that was what she'd always assumed.

But how could she inherit a trait from someone she was not related to?

How could she be part of a family when her very existence was a secret?

How could her father and grandmother have *lied* to her all these years?

Her heart felt as if it had been cleaved in two.

One piece from before she knew the truth.

One piece from after.

And they were both bleeding.

"Who is he?" Unable to sit beside Ruth any longer, Joanna sprang to her feet. At the moment, she didn't know what was worse. Learning she wasn't who she thought she was...or the knowledge that the truth had been withheld from her for all these years. "My...that is to say, the man who my mother..."

"The man who sired you?" Ruth said gently.

"Yes." Her hands curled into fists. *"Him."*

"I don't know. I don't," Ruth repeated when Joanna's eyes flashed. "Your mother never shared his name with anyone. Not even your father.

After your parents were married, they never spoke of your mother's time in England ever again. It was as if it never happened."

"But it *did*." Because she wanted to throw something, Joanna pinned her hands behind her back and started to pace. "It did happen, or else I wouldn't be here."

"I understand you're upset—" Ruth began.

"Upset?" Joanna interrupted. "*Upset?* I'm upset when Evie beats me in a game of checkers! I'm upset when it rains on a day I'd planned to go walking. This is more than being upset, Grandmother. This is...this is...I don't know." She stopped short. Threw her arms wide. "I haven't a word for it."

Or maybe she had too many words.

Distress.

Anger.

Confusion.

Betrayal.

Her mother, her father, her grandmother...they had all conspired to keep this from her. Together, they'd buried the truth of who she was. And that pain cut the deepest.

Joanna had been hurt when her father died. She *still* hurt to this day. But this was different. This was...this was dishonesty, and duplicity, and she found it difficult to meet Ruth's gaze.

"Why now? Why tell me all this now, and not before? Or not at all?" She looked at the painting. But even that, too, felt like a lie. Her parents, their beaming smiles disguising the fact that her mother was already carrying a child. A child that was *not* her husband's.

"Your parents asked for my silence shortly after you were born." And if the slight tick of a muscle in her jaw was any indication, Ruth had not been overly pleased to give it. "I went along, because it was their choice to make. Over time…over time, it became an easy thing to forget. You are the mirror image of your mother. Sometimes, I catch a glimpse of you out of the corners of my eyes and have to remind myself that you're not her. And ever since you were a born, you had your father wrapped around your adorable little finger. My son loved all of his daughters. But you, my dear…he always had a special bond with you." Ruth smiled fondly. "To watch the two of you, peas in a pod, talking about books you'd read and the grand adventures you were going to take together. It was a special thing to behold."

Which was exactly why Joanna felt flayed to the very bone. Because she did have a special bond with her father. And now to learn he wasn't her real father…to learn that he'd *lied* to her all these years…

It was incomprehensible.

"That all being said," her grandmother went on, "I knew the day you unearthed that ring in the attic we would have this conversation. I hoped that if it could be removed from our keeping, once and for all, the past might finally rest, and your mother's secret along with it. But now that the ring has been stolen...I am afraid I had no choice but to go against your parents' wishes and tell you the truth." She closed her eyes. "I can only hope they forgive me."

"But what does the ring have to do—wait." Joanna's mind flashed to the inscription carved into the band of the ring. An inscription she'd never understood...until this second.

Anne, my love ~ JW.

"It was from *him*, wasn't it?" she demanded.

"Yes." Ruth gave a clipped nod. "The only remaining clue to the identity of the man with whom your mother had her...liaison."

Something in her grandmother's tone gave Joanna pause. "You don't think...you don't think *he* stole it, do you?" She couldn't bring herself to call him her father. Even "sire" sounded wrong, as if she were describing some breeding stallion. She wished she had a name. Instead, all she had were two initials. J and W. Letters that were meaningless without context.

"Or he had it stolen."

"Are you saying, all these years, he has just been waiting for the ring to resurface?" Joanna gave a short, incredulous shake of her head. "That would be impossible."

A humorless smile laid claim to Ruth's lips. "I should think nothing about this situation should be considered impossible. I'd remind you that as we speak, your mother's ring is on a ship bound for London. That's an awfully large coincidence, don't you agree? Added to that, I've known Mr. Bernard for nearly three decades. His behavior towards you girls was *highly* out of character. I have to wonder if you would have met a similar outcome at every other jeweler in Boston." She hesitated. "I told you I do not know the identity of your real father, and I don't. But I've long suspected, from little things your mother accidentally shared here and there, that he was a person of great wealth and power. And people of great wealth and power are capable of extraordinary things. Particularly when they wish to acquire something not in their possession."

Joanna sat back down. It was either that, or slowly fall into a crumpled heap upon the floor. Her mind was still spinning a hundred miles an hour, but her body felt as if she'd just swam ten laps around Boston Harbor.

Her limbs were heavy.

Her mouth was dry.

And her heart…her heart *ached*.

"What am I supposed to do with all of this?" She drew her legs to her chest and wrapped her arms around her knees, just as she'd done when she was a child and it was storming outside. Curling into a ball had soothed her fears and uneasiness. But there was no comfort to be found now. "What am I—what am I supposed to think?"

"I've told you everything I know, Joanna. I probably should have told you sooner, and for that...for that, I am sorry." Ruth glanced down at the floor. She was not a woman who apologized easily, or often. "But it is up to *you* to decide what you'd like to do going forward. You're the eldest. The leader. The one your sisters look to in times of trouble. This does not change that."

Joanna bit down hard on the inside of her cheek. "But without the ring, we've nothing."

Ruth lifted her head. "Then go get it."

JOANNA HARDLY SLEPT at all that night. How could she, with all that she'd learned? Secrets piled upon secrets, with still more questions than answers.

When dawn crept across the sky in a spill of pink and orange, she was the first to wake. Or so she thought, before Evie tiptoed across the bedroom they shared and climbed into bed with her.

"I heard everything," Evie said without preamble, her voice hushed so as not to awake Claire who still slept, blissfully unaware of all that had been unveiled.

"But of course you did." Joanna jabbed her elbow into her sister's side. "You're a renowned eavesdropper, and a gossip besides."

Evie winced, then gave Joanna a jab right back. "I am neither, thank you very much. And it's not *my* fault you and Grandmother were speaking loud enough to wake the dead."

Joanna wished she *could* wake dead. For then, she'd be able to ask her mother why she'd had an illicit affair with an Englishman whose initials were JW. And she could ask her father why he'd agreed to cover it all up and raise another man's daughter as his own.

Had he thought of her differently than Evie and Claire? That was what she *really* wanted to know. Had he looked at her and seen the man his wife had betrayed him with? Or had she always been his, right from the very beginning?

She liked to think it was the latter.

She *hoped* it was.

But how could she ever be certain?

How could she ever be certain about anything, ever again?

Sitting up, she pulled a pillow against her stomach and hugged it tight. "Did you know?"

Looking offended that Joanna would even ask, Evie gave an adamant shake of her head that sent her long hair, black as a raven's wing, spilling across her shoulders. "No. I had absolutely no idea. I...I am sorry, Jo."

"As am I." Joanna clasped the pillow even harder, fingers digging into the soft feathers in a desperate need to cling to something tangible. "Grandmother believes I should go after the ring."

"She wants you to go all the way to *England*?" Evie's eyes widened. "I must have missed that part."

"Eavesdropping isn't perfect, I suppose."

"I told you I wasn't eavesdropping."

"Then what would you call sitting at the top of the stairs and listening in on a private conversation?"

Evie pursed her lips. "Being observant."

"What are you two discussing?" Her voice groggy with sleep, Claire sat up in bed and peered drowsily at them. "And why are you up so early?"

For an instant, Joanna considered hiding the truth from her little sister. But now that she knew what it felt like to have secrets withheld from *her*, she couldn't do the same thing to Claire. Claire may have been the youngest, but she was also compassionate, and intelligent, and wise beyond her years. If they were going to get through this, they'd need to do it together or not at all.

Taking a breath, she began from the beginning, repeating everything Ruth had told her and Evie had overheard. Their mother's affair in

England, the quick wedding upon her return, the decision to raise Joanna as if she were Jacob's daughter, and, finally, the significance of the ring.

Claire listened intently and did not interrupt with the exception of a soft gasp here and there, which Joanna could hardly blame her for. Even to Joanna's own ears, the story sounded...well, it sounded made up. Like the plot of some gothic romance whereupon the heroine discovers she is the hidden by-blow of a mysterious English lord who then goes to great extremes to steal the only item that could link him to his illegitimate child.

But it wasn't made up.

It was real.

And *she* was the hidden by-blow.

"That's...that's incredible," Claire said once Joanna had finished. Sliding off her mattress, she hurried barefoot across the small bedroom and squeezed into bed between her two sisters. "I cannot believe Grandmother didn't tell us— didn't tell *you*—sooner. Or Father, for that matter."

Out of habit, Joanna began to comb the tangles from Claire's golden locks with her fingers. "I can only assume they were trying to protect me."

She'd come to that realization in the middle of the night, while sleep danced elusively in a cloud of black and the stars flashed like diamonds in the sky. It made it better, just a little bit better, to acknowledge that her parents and her grandmother had acted out of love. But they'd still deceived her. They'd still lied to her.

And it still hurt.

"I cannot dwell on it, though." She began to twist Claire's hair together to form a long braid down the center of her back. "Not when I have a ring to find."

Claire blinked in astonishment. "But...you can't mean to *really* go to England."

"Why not?"

"Because...because it's England. It's an entire ocean away!"

"Exactly." Right now, an entire ocean away sounded perfect to Joanna. "We *need* that ring. It belonged to our mother, and now it belongs to us, and someone stole it. They stole it, and if I don't get it back, who will?"

"We couldn't afford to hire a hackney to take us to Boston," Evie pointed out. "How are we to come up with passage across the pond, let alone room and board once we're there?"

"*We?*" Joanna repeated, lifting a brow. "I never said anyone would accompany me."

"As if I'd let you go alone," Evie scoffed. "Do you know what they have in England that they haven't here?"

"Crumpets?" Claire ventured.

"*Dukes.*" Evie's blue eyes gleamed. "They've dukes. Dozens of them, so I hear. Practically dangling out of trees just waiting for a beautiful woman of impeccable manners and fashion to cross their paths."

Claire frowned. "I don't know if that's how it works."

"Have you ever *met* a duke?" asked Evie.

"Have *you*?" Joanna countered.

"No, which is exactly why I'm coming with you." Climbing off the bed, Evie opened the closet and began to yank out dresses. "What do you think the weather is like there this time of year? I've been told it rains a lot."

"Haven't you heard? The tree dukes hold out parasols." Despite the seriousness of the situation and the heaviness in her heart, Joanna couldn't help but snicker. "You needn't worry about the rain at all."

Holding up her prettiest gown, an elaborate concoction of bows and bustle and green silk, Evie whirled around. "That *isn't* funny."

"Maybe not, but I've just had an idea on how we can afford to travel to London," said Joanna as her gaze lingered on Evie's ball gown.

Following the direction of her sister's stare, Evie immediately bristled. "No. Absolutely not. I won't sell it. I refuse."

"Dukes," Joanna reminded her.

"And crumpets," Claire put in brightly.

Evie wrapped her arms protectively around her gown. "But if I sell my best dress, what duke will bother to look at me?"

"I guess you'll have to win him over with your charm and wit. I wish there was another way," said Joanna, and she genuinely meant it. "But that dress is the only thing of value we've left in the entire house. Once we get the ring back, you'll have enough money to buy *ten* green frilly dresses."

"It's not green," Evie sniffed. "It's chartreuse. And how, exactly, are you planning to find Mother's ring in the first place? The thief isn't going to be waiting for us with a sign saying, here I am."

"We'll hire a private investigator. The ring is very unique. With the inscription, it's one of a kind." Joanna finished plaiting Claire's hair and looked around for a piece of ribbon to hold it in place. "Whoever JW is, he went to great pains to steal the ring. I'm sure a trail was left. All we need to is go to England, pick up the trail, find the ring, and steal it back."

"Oh, is that all?" Evie said dryly.

"It does seem rather daunting," Claire admitted.

"And when do I meet a duke?"

Joanna closed her eyes. "I don't know. I don't have *all* the answers." Her eyes snapped open. "I don't even know what questions to ask to *get* the answers. But I do know that without Mother's ring, and the money we'll make by selling it, we will be huddling together for warmth come winter. It is our best—and *only*—option."

Evie sobered. "If Grandmother's theory about who had the ring stolen is correct, then finding the ring will mean finding your…that is to say, your…er…"

"Birth father?" Joanna had come up with the term last night as she'd restlessly tossed beneath her sheets. She needed to call him *something*, and it seemed as good as anything else. "I understand that. I think…" She plucked at a loose thread on the corner of the pillowcase. "I think that is why Grandmother wants me to go to England more than anything else. To search out that side of me. To find out who, and where, half of me comes from."

"You come from here," Claire said with shocking fierceness. "You come from *us*." Her newly fashioned braid whipped through the air as she leapt off the bed and spun in a half-circle. "Going to another country and finding out who your—who your *birth father* is isn't going to change that. You're *our* sister. You're Mother and Father's eldest daughter. You were born right here, in Somerville. *That's* who you are. *That's* where you came from."

Evie whistled under her breath. "Look at you, little duck," she said, referring to a nickname they'd given Claire when she was a toddler and waddled when she walked. "I've not seen you this riled up since Georgie Pin pinched your arm at the village fair when you were six. Do you remember how red her face turned, Jo?"

"I remember."

Claire flushed. "I don't understand what came over me. Joanna, you're the one who should be upset, not me. I just...I just know I haven't the courage to travel across an ocean. I could hardly make it to Boston! And I know I'll worry about you every second that you're gone." She gazed beseechingly at Joanna. "Please promise that you...that you won't forget me."

"*Forget* you?" Aghast at the very idea, Joanna jumped to her feet and flung her arms around Claire in a hug that left them both breathless. Clasping her sister by the shoulders, she rocked back on her heels and said sternly, "Don't be ridiculous. If Evie and I go to England, it will be *because* of you. And even though you won't be there in person, you'll still be with us every step of the way."

Evie gave a long, loud sigh. "You mean when. *When* we go to England. I'm so sorry," she murmured, and it took Joanna a moment to realize she was talking to her gown. "I will never forget you."

Had she not known how very much Evie's dresses meant to her, Joanna might have been tempted to laugh. As it stood, she needed all of her facial muscles not to smile. "Are you certain?"

she asked. "I don't want to force you to do something you don't want to do."

"I'm certain," Evie said firmly. "It's only fabric, after all. And this…this is family."

A burst of unexpected excitement flared within Joanna's chest. Four days ago, she'd been turning down yet another lackluster engagement proposal. Now, she was on the brink of setting sail on a grand adventure that had the potential to change her past, her present…and her future.

"I'm going to England." She whispered the words, then shouted them. "I'm going to England!"

"*We're* going to England," Evie corrected. "Where I will marry a duke, become a duchess, and live happily-ever-after in a grand palace with swans."

"What color swans?" Claire wondered.

"Two of each color." Evie tapped her chin. "And a herd of peacocks for good measure. Or is it a peck? A peck of peacocks."

"A pride, I believe," said Claire.

"A *pride* of peacocks?" Evie shook her head. "That doesn't sound right."

Joanna held up her hand. "Mother's ring first, dukes and birds second."

"But what if I meet a duke before we—oh, all right," Evie grumbled when Joanna stared at her. "But I cannot be expected to wait *forever*. A woman has to have her priorities straight."

"As soon as we find the ring, you can hunt tree dukes and pick out your peck of peacocks to your heart's desire."

"I really think it's a pride," Claire said hesitantly.

Joanna pinched the bridge of her nose. "Peck or pride, it doesn't matter. We are going to England. And we are *going* to get our ring back."

CHAPTER FIVE

London, England
August 19, 1870
Mrs. Privet's Boarding House for Young, Unaccompanied Women

"HE AGREED TO help!" Joanna shouted triumphantly as she let herself into the small, dimly lit bedroom she and Evie were renting for $3 a week. The cost of rent included a single candle, and the proprietor of the boarding house, a stern, heavyset woman by the name of Mrs. Privet, had made it clear that no more candles would be forthcoming if they squandered the one they'd been given.

"Who did?" Evie asked from the bed, her voice muffled from the blanket over her head. It was better, she claimed, to look at nothing than to see the hideous green and yellow wall hangings that covered every inch of their room.

Including the ceiling.

Joanna had to admit their accommodations weren't *exactly* what she had imagined when they'd embarked on their grand adventure across the pond. She'd pictured an old English manor with ivy crawling up the side and servants in lace caps and tea being served every hour on the hour. Unfortunately, while she'd seen such houses from afar (usually tucked behind tall, iron gates), it appeared the majority of London was a crowded sprawl of townhouses and narrow alleys and busy streets.

Or at least, the part of London they could afford.

Evie's dress hadn't fetched nearly as much as Joanna had hoped it would, leaving them with limited options. But while Mrs. Privet's taste in décor may have been questionable, at least they had a roof over their heads.

Sort of.

"How long has this puddle been here?" Grabbing a pitcher from the wash stand, Joanna shoved it in the corner of the room where a pool of water, courtesy of the steady drizzle falling on the roof, had started to collect. Exasperated, she turned to the bed and the sister-sized lump huddled in the middle of it. "Evie, I know you do not feel well, but you must get up at *some* point."

"Easy for you to say," Evie mumbled from underneath the blanket. "You didn't spend eight weeks throwing up into a tin pail."

"Maybe not," Joanna retorted, "but I *did* spend eight weeks holding your hair and chucking the contents of said tin pail out a porthole the size of a dinner plate. I'm sorry the trip wasn't pleasant,"—to put it mildly—"but we're here now, and I just had a splendid visit with Kincaid, who has agreed to help us!"

Considering the bad luck that had followed them ever since the ring was stolen in Boston, Joanna was still surprised that she'd been able to coax Kincaid into taking their case. Particularly since she'd had no money to pay him. He hadn't exactly seemed pleased, but an agreement was an agreement, and she intended to hold him to his end of the bargain.

By force, if necessary.

Evie peeked out from beneath the blanket. "Who is Kincaid?"

"The private investigator Mrs. Benedict told us about, remember?" On their first night at the boarding house, Joanna had made quick work of asking their fellow tenants if they could recommend someone to help find the ring. Mrs. Benedict, a quiet widow, had suggested Mr. Thomas Kincaid.

Apparently, she had hired him two years ago to track down her sister after she'd eloped with a footman, and she'd employed his services again just this past winter to find a missing necklace.

"There's no one better," she'd told Joanna. "He's also a gentleman through and through, so you needn't worry about him trying to...well, *you know*."

Truth be told, now having met Kincaid, Joanna didn't think she'd mind a little *"you know"*.

From the moment she had walked into his house, she had felt an instant connection. A recognition of sorts, even though they'd never met and he was *nothing* like what she had been expecting.

For some reason (she blamed her risqué dime novels), she thought a private investigator would have an eyepatch and a mouth curled in a menacing sneer and a pistol sitting on the edge of his desk. But Kincaid, with his angular face and tousled, brown hair and somber, amber gaze, had none of those things.

Instead of an eyepatch, he had thin, wire frame spectacles. Instead of a menacing sneer, he wore a politely detached smile. And instead of a pistol, he had a very friendly cat named James.

She'd liked James.

She'd also liked Kincaid.

Her feelings for the cat she understood.

Her feelings for the private investigator she...did not.

"I might recall you mentioning him." Throwing back the covers, Evie opened her mouth in a jaw-cracking yawn and sat up. "That's good he can help us, I suppose. But how can we afford him? We can barely afford to stay off the streets. Although, I'm beginning to wonder if a nice alley wouldn't be preferable to *this*." She gestured to the room with a broad sweep of her arm. "The pillows are so hard my neck is beginning to ache, and I swear I saw a mouse run across the floor this morning. A mouse!"

"For the last time, this isn't meant to be a vacation." Trying—and failing—not to roll her eyes, Joanna picked up one of the pillows in question and gave it a good hard whack to even out the lumps before tossing it back on the bed. "There, all better. As for being able to afford Kincaid, he and I agreed to a trade. My services for his."

Evie gasped. "Joanna! You cannot *possibly* mean to—to sell yourself to this man!"

"What? No! That isn't what I…no." Unable to stop the blush that flooded her cheeks with heat, she quickly went to the dressing table and began to mindlessly line up all of Evie's little beauty tinctures and potions into two straight rows. "He is in need of a secretary. Someone to greet potential clients as they arrive, organize his office, and keep his schedule in order. As the oldest of three siblings, I believed myself suited to the task."

"Naturally," Evie said with an unmistakable bite of sarcasm.

Holding a small bottle of rose water intended to soften the complexion, Joanna spun towards her sibling with narrowed eyes. "What is *that* supposed to mean?"

"It means that just because you're the eldest doesn't mean you're the only one who can accomplish things."

"I never claimed I was!"

"But you act like you are," Evie countered. "I'm only eighteen months younger than you, yet you constantly still treat me as if I were a child."

"Maybe I wouldn't *treat* you like a child if you didn't *act* like a child. Lying in bed all day, complaining about pillows and mice! That's something a child would do."

Evie's brows snapped together. "You know that I've been ill!"

"Which was why I took it upon myself to find us a private investigator."

"I could have found one."

"Hiding under the blankets? I highly doubt that. Ouch!" she cried when a pillow struck her on the shoulder.

Goodness.

They *were* rather hard.

"I do not even know why you are upset." Picking up the pillow, she tossed it back at her sister who managed to catch it right before it hit her on the side of the head.

"I am upset," Evie said between gritted teeth, "because you always take it upon yourself to do things without consulting me. We came here together. We should make decisions *together*. You are not our mother, as much as you'd like to pretend you are!"

This time when the pillow came sailing towards her, Joanna managed to snatch it out of the air.

"I've never pretended anything of the sort!" As Joanna's chest heaved with indignation, it occurred to her, somewhat belatedly, that perhaps Evie was right. Joanna did—very rarely— treat her sisters as if she were their superior instead of their equal. That included making decisions (like hiring Kincaid without giving Evie the opportunity to meet him) on their behalf. But she *was* older, if only by eighteen months. Surely that made her somewhat wiser, even if Evie didn't think so.

"Why can't we just get on?" she asked in frustration as she let the pillow drop. "We've traveled across an ocean, and we're *still* fighting."

"We can't get on because we're so different. We always have been." Rising, Evie went to the wash basin and dipped a cloth into the lukewarm water. "You've never cared what others think about you, and I…"

"Care too much," Joanna supplied when Evie trailed away.

"Yes," said Evie, catching Joanna off guard with her honest admission. "I am well aware I've always put too much weight in other people's opinions of me."

"Then why don't you stop?"

Evie met her gaze in the mirror's silvery reflection. "Why don't *you* start?"

"Point taken," Joanna murmured. "I suppose we are who we are."

"I suppose so."

"That doesn't mean there isn't room for change. For improvement. I hate these little squabbles. I don't *want* to fight with you," Joanna said earnestly as she crossed to her bed and sat down on the edge of it. With an ominous creak and a groan, it sagged beneath her weight until she was nearly sitting on the floor. "In the moment, it feels like the right thing to do. But after…"

"You feel horrible?"

Joanna nodded.

"I do as well."

"Then why do we do it?"

"As I said, we're different." After washing her face and neck, Evie laid the cloth on the edge of the basin and turned around. "If we weren't sisters, I honestly don't believe we'd be friends."

It was painful, but true.

Evie adored clothes, and attending parties, and flirting with handsome men. Joanna liked reading, and going on walks through the countryside, and visiting new places regardless of how fashionable they were.

They had absolutely nothing in common.

But they *were* sisters.

Well, half-sisters.

"I know exactly what you're thinking," Evie said when a grimace flitted across Joanna's countenance. "I want you to stop. Us having different fathers by blood doesn't change *anything*. I hope you realize that."

"I do. Up here." Joanna tapped the side of her skull. Then she pressed a closed fist to the middle of her chest where a weight had been consistently growing ever since she'd learned the truth. "But in my heart...it's going to be difficult to reconcile. What this changes and what it doesn't."

Throughout all the hard times—the war, their father's death, selling the house, being so poor they couldn't afford butter at fifteen cents a pound—she'd clung to the certainty of who she was and where she'd come from. It had been an unconscious source of strength. Something she hadn't even realized she was drawing on when a problem or struggle presented itself. But it had seen her through nevertheless.

Asking herself what her father would do had seen her through. Channeling his strength and his wisdom had seen her through. But now…now that she knew her father *wasn't* her father, how was she expected to see anything?

She felt like a ship adrift in a stormy sea, and the lighthouse beckoning it towards safer shores had just gone out. She felt lost, and angry, and *betrayed*.

Betrayed by a father who was never hers.

Betrayed by a mother she could hardly remember.

Betrayed by a grandmother who had kept it all a secret.

The Thorncrofts may have lost all of their material belongings, but they'd always been rich in family, and Joanna had taken pride in that. She was proud of the strong bond that connected them. Proud of the way they'd always protected each other. Proud of the way they'd held their chins up through good times and bad.

But how could she be proud of a family built on a lie?

"Not to worry," said Evie as she pivoted back to the mirror and picked up the vial of rose water. "I found you bossy and irritating in Somerville, and I still find you bossy and irritating in London. *That* isn't going to change anytime soon."

A reluctant smile teased the corners of Joanna's mouth.

"Brat," she said with great affection.

"So, tell me more about this private investigator you've hired." Pouring a small amount of rose water into her left hand, Evie rubbed her palms together and began to massage the sweet-smelling tonic onto her face. "Mr. Kensington?"

"Kincaid," Joanna corrected. "As I said, he came highly recommended by Mrs. Benedict. I thought him to be very competent and nice. He was also quite handsome." Joanna frowned. She didn't know why she'd just said that. Kincaid's physical appearance had no bearing on his ability to conduct a thorough investigation. She wanted to take the words back, but it was too late. Mentioning a handsome man in front of Evie was like waving a red flag in front of a bull.

The damage had already been done.

"He is?" Having finished applying the rose water, Evie moved on to a glass jar filled with white cream.

Joanna had no idea what the cream contained. Knowing how seriously her sister took her beauty regiment, it was probably the sacrificial blood of a newborn lamb.

Or maybe it was just honey and glycerin.

"What does this Kincaid look like?" Evie asked as she smeared the lotion onto her forehead.

"Er…" Joanna thought back to the morning and her first impression of Kincaid. Wet from the rain, she'd been chastising herself for not bringing an umbrella when the door opened…and the most striking man in all of her life had appeared.

The sheer *size* of him was what she'd noticed most. As a woman of taller than average height, Joanna was accustomed to either looking men straight in the eyes or looking down on them. But for Kincaid, she'd had to look *up*. Up into a serious gaze the color of coffee with a bit of cream lightly stirred in.

His brows had been thick and forbidding above the thin wire rim of his spectacles. His mouth had been twisted into a grimace before she'd even had the chance to introduce herself. And his jaw, that hard, clean-shaven jaw, with its lines and angles, had been *sternly* disapproving.

A jaw like that could make a girl swoon if she wasn't careful.

Which Joanna rarely was.

"Well?" Evie prompted. "I'm waiting."

"He has brown hair."

Evie rolled her eyes. "How descriptive. You should be an artist. Is he tall? Muscular? Both?"

"I don't know. Unlike you, I am not here to find a *husband*, Evelyn." Scowling, Joanna stood up and crossed her arms. "He looked like a private investigator. He stood about this high"— she waved her hand vaguely in the air four inches above her own head—"and physically fit with broad shoulders."

And strong thighs.

And a very taut backside.

Her cheeks heated.

Evie gasped with delight.

"Jo, you're *blushing!*" she crowed.

"I am not," Joanna protested even as she slapped her hands over her cheeks and turned her back on her sister. "It's just...warm in here."

"Stifling, but that's not why you're blushing. You *like* Kincaid, don't you?" Evie came up behind Joanna and gave her arm a playful pinch. "No wonder you wanted to be his secretary. Was this your ploy all along? Come to England and fall in love with a dashing detective?"

Joanna slapped her sister's arm away. "Don't be absurd. Kincaid is going to help us retrieve Mother's ring and identify my birth father. That's all. Our relationship is strictly professional."

But if that was true...why had she tingled when he'd touched her? Just a glancing sweep of his fingertips across the small of her back as she'd preceded him into his office, but still...

She had never *tingled* before.

Certainly not for Charles, or any of the beaus that had preceded him. Yet she'd tingled for Thomas Kincaid. All the way from her nose to her toes...and everywhere in between.

"You will not speak of this conversation to anyone." Because she knew exactly how her sister operated, she wagged her finger warningly at Evie's lotion-covered countenance. "That specifically includes Kincaid."

"Why would you presume I would tell Kincaid anything?" Evie said, all wide-eyed innocence brimming with thinly veiled mischief. "I do not even know the man."

"Because you love nothing more than to play match maker. But there's no match to be made here. We did *not* come to London to fall in love."

"I did," said Evie unabashedly. "With a duke. A blindingly gorgeous, adorably charming, obscenely wealthy duke. He'll fall in love with me at first sight. We will take carriage rides around the park and attend the theater and send the *ton* into an absolute tizzy. You'll see."

Joanna had no doubt that she would. Once Evie set her mind to something, she was a force to be reckoned with. Her sister's duke—whoever he may be—did not stand a chance. But while Evie was dreaming of romance, Joanna had no such notions.

"I am to report to his office first thing tomorrow morning," she said, striving for nonchalance. "You may come, if you'd like."

"And interrupt your alone time?" A sly smile curled Evie's mouth. "I wouldn't dare."

"It isn't *alone* time."

"Oh?" She batted her lashes. "Is someone else going to be there?"

"For your information, yes. There is."

"Who might that be?"

"James and Jane."

"Are they investigators as well?"

"Not exactly," Joanna hedged.

"Servants?"

"They're cats, if you *must* know."

"Cats!" Evie chortled, her slender body shaking with giggles as she fell back onto the bed. Bouncing lightly, she sat up on her elbows and grinned. "*Cats!* Joanna, you do make me laugh."

"So glad to be of service," Joanna said sourly. "I was going to walk up to Bond Street since the rain has stopped. If you're finished taking amusement at my expense, would you care to join me?"

Evie's gaze sharpened like a fox who had just smelled a rabbit. "Isn't Bond Street where all the best shops are?"

"According to Mrs. Privet. We cannot afford anything, but—"

"I'll be ready in a moment!" Moving with surprising speed given how sick she'd been all morning, Evie rolled off the mattress and disappeared behind a changing screen tucked away in the corner of the room.

With a long sigh, Joanna sat down to wait. When Evie and clothes were involved, there was no such thing as "in a moment". While she had only brought a single traveling trunk, neatly packed with three dresses, a shawl, and an extra pair of shoes, Evie's wardrobe had taken two sailors to haul it onboard the ship.

After a small eternity, Evie emerged from the screen in a sunny yellow gown with a full skirt, cinched waist, and elbow-length sleeves trimmed with ivory lace.

"Can you help with the buttons?" she asked, scooping her dark hair out of the way as she presented her back to Joanna.

Tucking her tongue between her teeth, Joanna made quick work of the long line of black glass buttons that ran from Evie's neck all the way to the base of her spine. When she'd finished, she waited several more minutes for Evie to pick out *just* the right hat and then they were off, passing Mrs. Benedict on the way down the narrow, creaky staircase.

"Aren't you two lovely!" exclaimed the young widow. "Off to explore a bit of the city, I take it?"

"Bond Street," Joanna confirmed with a nod.

"Do you know if there will be any dukes there?" Evie said anxiously.

Mrs. Benedict blinked. "There's always the possibility, I suppose."

"You're welcome to come with us," Joanna invited.

"That's nice of you to ask, but I am having my sister over for tea. Another time, perhaps." Mrs. Benedict started past them, then stopped and glanced over her shoulder. "Were you able to speak with Kincaid?"

"I did, just this morning." As her heart gave a sudden and unexpected *thump*, Joanna bit back a smile. "He is going to take our case. Thank you again for recommending him."

"My pleasure. If anyone can help you, it's Mr. Kincaid. Such a kind fellow."

Joanna did not know if she would describe Kincaid as *kind*. Polite, perhaps, in that he hadn't tossed her out on her ear when she'd revealed she had no money with which to pay him. But there'd been an edge beneath that disheveled, bookish veneer. A sense of danger. A lingering hint of the man he was before he took up as a private investigator helping widows find their missing sisters and old ladies retrieve their misplaced jewelry.

"Joanna is going to be his secretary," Evie put in.

Mrs. Benedict's brows rose ever-so-slightly. "That's wonderful. Kincaid has been a bachelor for as long as I've known him. His home and office would benefit greatly from a woman's touch."

"I'm not going to *touch* him," Joanna began, only to stop short at Mrs. Benedict's resulting expression. "That's—that's not what you meant."

"Enjoy town," said Mrs. Benedict. Then she dashed up the stairs.

"I must say, I don't know if I've ever seen you in such a state," Evie said as the two sisters continued on outside. The rain from the earlier in the day had finally cleared and the clouds were beginning to lift, exposing a sky painted in various shades of clear, crisp blue. "Blushing. Fumbling your words. It's really not like you, Jo. If I did not know any better, I'd believe you *were* quite taken with Kincaid."

"Evie?" Joanna said sweetly.

"Yes?"

"Shut up."

CHAPTER SIX

A LL THINGS CONSIDERED, Kincaid had a better chance of finding a virgin in a brothel than the stolen ring of an American. Make that the stolen ring of an American's deceased *mother*. Who may or may not have received said ring from a British lord with the initials JW.

Twenty-two years ago.

It would be like searching for the proverbial needle in a haystack. And ever since he'd received eighteen stiches across the back of his skull following a scuffle with a bloke who very much did *not* want to be dragged in front of the magistrate, Kincaid had a particular aversion to needles.

The fact of the matter was that he never should have agreed to take the case. He *certainly* never should have allowed himself to become bewitched by guileless, blue eyes and a siren's smile. But he had, and he was, and there was no going back on it now. He'd given his word. He would honor it. Then he'd put Joanna Thorncroft on the first ship setting sail for Boston and never think of her again.

"Don't look at me like that," he muttered to James when the cat slanted him a cool, unblinking stare from his lofty perch atop the bookshelf. "Fat lot of help *you* were this morning. If you'd acted like the devil I know you to be instead of preening about like a besotted idiot, we wouldn't be in this bloody predicament. Was a tiny, little bite too much to ask?"

James yawned.

"Regardless, I am *not* going to make the same mistake again," Kincaid said fervently. Standing up from behind his desk, he crossed to the window. His townhouse was only four blocks from the river. On a clear day, if he stood in the attic and squinted just right, he could make out the towering mast of a massive sailing vessel as it edged its way towards London Bridge.

As a police officer, he'd spent more time at the harbor than anywhere else in the city. It was a crowded, rat-infested den of crime that stank to the high heavens of fish and rot. He couldn't begin to count the number of bloated bodies he'd hauled out of the water. He'd loathed that part of the job the most. The senseless loss. The stomach-twisting violence. The mindless destruction of life and limb.

Kincaid had never imagined how mindlessly *cruel* people could be to each other before he became a peeler. Maybe that was why, three years into the madness and the muck, he'd found himself drawn to Lady Lavinia.

Lady Lavinia, with her enchanting laugh and sweet aura of innocence. She'd been a beacon of hope in the dismal abyss of endless depravity. A chance to breathe clean, fresh air after suffocating in the stench of moral decay.

If only he'd known how unscrupulous she *really* was. Instead, he had been blind to her spider's web until it was too late. Until the harder he struggled, the more entangled he became. And when it was finally over, when the smoke had cleared and the damage had been done, he had vowed to himself he would never again risk his heart for a client.

Or a client's wife.

Kincaid jumped, startled out of his thoughts when James nudged his leg.

"What do *you* want?" he asked sourly, still annoyed by the cat's betrayal. If a man didn't have the loyalty of his own pet, what did he have? An ungrateful mouth to feed, that's what. "I know you liked Miss Thorncroft. I did, too."

It was true, he realized with a sinking sensation in the pit of his stomach. He *had* liked Joanna. As far as first impressions went, the fearless, red-haired American had made an indelible one. Why else would he still be in his office going over their conversation hours after she'd left? Perhaps because even though she was gone, her scent still remained.

Violets. Joanna had smelled of rain and violets. Not the sort that grew in pretty, potted plants in shop windows, but the sort that sprawled across the Highlands in a wild tangle of purple petals and glossy, green leaves.

At his feet, James gave a plaintive *meow*.

"I told you not to look at me like that," Kincaid said gruffly, even as he scooped the cat up and gave him a scratch behind his ear. "This isn't going to be like it was. I've gone down that road once, and have no intention of traveling that way again. Not that you'd know anything about it. You weren't even born yet, you scrawny bastard."

His ill-fated affair with Lavinia had ended well before some arse dropped two kittens on his doorstep. While most would have given the scrawny, flea-infested little buggers away (if not drowned them outright), Kincaid had always had a soft spot in his heart for the weak and the vulnerable. Besides, he'd desperately needed the company. And while James in particular had tested his patience over the years, he didn't regret taking them in and giving them a home.

Today being the exception.

Both man and cat turned their attention to the door when a firm knock sounded on the other side of it. A quick glimpse at the longcase clock in the corner and Kincaid mumbled a curse. He'd allowed himself to become so distracted by Joanna that he had forgotten he was expecting a visitor.

"Come in," he called out, his deep baritone carrying easily across the office. A second's pause, and then the door swung inward to reveal a well-dressed gentleman with black hair just long enough to touch the collar of his jacket, intelligent, gray eyes, and the large, bulky build of a boxer.

Despite his size, Sterling Nottingham, Duke of Hanover, moved lightly on his feet as he walked into the office. A grin lit up his face when he saw Kincaid and the two men were quick to embrace, their hands slapping loudly on each other's backs before they pulled apart.

"Kincaid. As I live and breathe. How long has it been?"

"Too long." Kincaid had met Sterling—as he preferred to be called by his closest acquaintances—when he'd still been just a constable. The duke's sister had been kidnapped by highwaymen and was being held for ransom. Sterling had immediately paid what they were asking, but when his sister wasn't delivered as promised, he turned to Scotland Yard (as it was better known now) for help. Thankfully, the story had a happy ending, with Kincaid and Sterling striking up a friendship despite their differences in class and fortune.

They'd maintained contact over the years, occasionally exchanging a letter or meeting for a drink whenever their paths happened to cross. Sterling had even stuck by him when the rest of London turned their backs on him. But in all that time, Sterling had never reached out in a professional capacity, which was why Kincaid had been so surprised to receive a note from the duke requesting a private meeting.

"Have a seat," he said, pointing at the same chair Joanna had sat in just a few hours ago. Leaning back against his desk, he thumbed through his journal to an empty page. "I hope this has nothing to do with Sarah again."

"No, no." Sterling shook his head as he settled his large body into the chair and stretched his legs out in front of him. His black leather Hessians were splattered with mud, indicating he'd walked rather than taken a carriage as would be expected of a duke. But then, Sterling had never fully come to terms with his title or the tragic event that led to him inheriting it.

The younger of two sons, he should have been the spare. But when his brother was killed in an illegal duel, Sterling became Duke of Hanover. Most would have secretly celebrated such an accession.

Sterling had been devastated.

One night, when he was long into his cups, he'd confessed to Kincaid that the title felt like a bloody yoke around his neck. He'd never wanted to be burdened by all the responsibilities that came with such a lofty rank. But more than that, the title was a constant reminder that his brother should have been the duke. After all, Sterling was the one who had goaded him into the duel...never dreaming in his worst nightmares that Sebastian would actually go through with it. He carried the weight of that loss to this day, but was always quick to hide it behind an engaging grin or a quick jest.

Were Kincaid not so attuned to the nuanced expressions of those around him, he might have thought as others did: that the Duke of Hanover was nothing more than a renowned rake, womanizer, and ne'er-do-well. But he knew a thing or two about facades, which was how he was able to see so clearly past Sterling's.

Sterling may have been a rake, and a womanizer, and all right, yes, a ne'er-do-well. But he was also a good man, and a good friend, and Kincaid would do whatever he could to help him.

"Sarah is fine," Sterling continued. "Better than fine, actually. She is engaged to be married."

"Please be sure to pass on my congratulations."

"I will." The duke hesitated, then shook his head, a bemused smile twisting his lips. "I suppose there's no way around it. I've come to you today because I have an...*unusual* problem I'd like your help in solving."

Intrigued, Kincaid reached for his pen. "What kind of unusual problem?"

Sterling grimaced. "I've been accused of murdering my mistress."

"I'm sorry," Kincaid said politely. "You've what?"

"I didn't do it." His grimace deepening into a scowl, Sterling surged to his feet. "Do you have anything to drink that doesn't have cat hair in it?"

"I wouldn't think that you did. And there's a bottle of brandy in that cabinet there. Might as well pour two glasses." Ordinarily, Kincaid would never share alcohol with a client, but there was nothing *ordinary* about a duke being accused of murder.

Filling a glass to the brim and placing it on the edge of Kincaid's desk, Sterling reserved the bottle for himself. He did not return to his seat, but rather went to the window, his gray gaze unreadable as he stared out through the glass at the dull, dreary sky beyond. "I didn't do it," he repeated before he tilted the brandy to his lips and indulged in a long, liberal swallow that had Kincaid's brows rising. "Admittedly, Eloise and I had a tempestuous relationship at times, but I would never cause her physical harm."

Kincaid pressed the tip of his pen to parchment. "Eloise is…"

"*Was* my mistress," Sterling said darkly.

"Can you describe her?" Part of being a good detective was knowing when to calm a client down and when to incite them. Given the rigidity of Sterling's broad shoulders, it was clear what the duke required. And there was no better way to cut through tension than with talking.

"Eloise was gorgeous, of course." His tone wry, Sterling glanced back at Kincaid. "I'd never take up with anyone *plain*."

No, he wouldn't. Because that might mean he would be forced to see past the superficiality of his lover's physical appearance, and Kincaid knew that Sterling would rather eat rocks for the rest of his life than become engaged in a personal relationship. Which was also why he knew, deep in his gut, that the Duke of Hanover really *was* innocent. Not because they were friends, but because Sterling simply didn't care enough about any other human being to bother with murdering them.

Any genuine emotion Sterling had once possessed had disappeared when his brother was killed. What remained was a caricature of whom the *ton* wanted him to be: a devilish duke with a penchant for fast horses and beautiful women.

Nothing more, nothing less.

"Could you be more specific?" Kincaid asked, tapping his pen against the side of his jaw.

"Silky black hair, straight as a pin. Big blue eyes. The nicest tits I've ever seen."

"Black hair, blue eyes, large breasts," Kincaid muttered as he took notes. "Any distinguishing characteristics? A scar, or a birth mark..."

"A freckle, here." Sterling pointed to the middle of his collarbone. "She also had a slight accent. Her mother was a French courtesan, her father a British diplomat. She was brought to England when she was a girl, and raised in the country by governesses. When she was seventeen, she came to London and quickly made a name for herself on the stage. I'll never forget her performance in Shakespeare's *Cleopatra*."

"She sounds like she was a very talented young woman."

"She was," the duke said wistfully. "The things she could do with her thighs—"

"I'm sure were extraordinary," Kincaid interrupted. "Why are *you* being accused of her murder?"

Sterling's expression shuttered. "Because the night she was killed, I was the last person to see her alive. And we argued. Screamed at each other, more like."

Kincaid's pen stilled. "That's not good."

"Well, not when you say it like *that*."

"What were you arguing about?"

"Nothing important. I got caught up at the tables, and was nearly two hours late coming to see her. Had I been there when I was supposed to be, I doubt we'd have fought at all. Or maybe we would have." Sterling gave a shrug. "It was our way of communicating. Foreplay, if you will."

"And after you were done fighting, you…"

"Fucked," the duke said bluntly. "Then I left."

"Did anyone see you leaving?"

"It was late. The servants had all gone to bed."

Kincaid closed his journal and leaned back in his chair. "I'll have to interview your driver. The staff. Your mates at the club. Anyone and everyone who can corroborate the events of that night as you'd told them to me."

"Then you'll take my case?"

"I will."

"And you believe we've a fair chance of proving my innocence?"

Kincaid hesitated. "I do."

For the first time since he'd entered the office, Sterling's mouth, always more prone to smirks than sneers, stretched in a grin. "I hope so. Lord knows I'm far too handsome to hang."

AFTER A LONG night of rain, the morning dawned bright and clear with nary a cloud in sight. Her waning spirits bolstered by the weather—and the knowledge that she was soon to be in Kincaid's company again—Joanna carefully avoided a line of puddles on her way to her new place of employment.

Tucked between two larger homes, the detective's townhouse maintained a gruff sense of charm, not unlike its owner. White paint was beginning to peel off the brick exterior, but the flower boxes in the windows were blooming with color and the large slabs of slate leading up to the blue front door had been freshly swept of debris. While the chimney was a tad crooked and could have used some repair, the balcony jutting out from the second floor looked like a lovely place to sit on a warm summer's evening and watch the sun set over the Thames.

Letting herself through a metal gate that squeaked on its hinges, Joanna walked briskly—she had never perfected the art of small, ladylike steps—up to the front door and lifted the gold door knocker in the shape of a lion's head. Three successive whacks and, from somewhere within the house, she heard Kincaid beckon her inside.

Taking off her frock coat and bonnet, (*"It's London, you absolutely* have *to wear a hat,"* Evie had chided when Joanna had tried to sneak out without one) she laid them neatly over her arm, then turned her focus to the foyer. It was the first room a client would see when they walked through the door. It should have radiated warmth and invitation. But despite Kincaid's office being an eclectic hodgepodge of disorder, the rest of his house—and the foyer in particular—was cold and barren.

There were no paintings on the white walls. No rugs on the oak floors. No benches to sit on. No magazines or books to read. What was a person supposed to occupy themselves with while they waited for their appointment? Stare at the cracks in the ceiling?

"This won't do," she murmured as she opened a door to her left and peered into a larger room that was just as empty save a rectangular table and a single chair. "This won't do at all."

Returning to the foyer, she opened another door and discovered the kitchen which led into a small parlor. The parlor, at least, had a sofa and footstool in front of the fireplace. But both were covered in a thin layer of dust, indicating they hadn't been used in quite some time, which led her to assume Kincaid lived exclusively upstairs.

She wondered what his bedchamber was like. A hapless mess like his office? Or was it as sterile and unwelcoming as the foyer? Did he neatly make his bed every day, or leave the sheets in a rumpled pile that smelled of him?

Sandalwood and citrus, she recalled, her cheeks

pinkening with another damnable blush as she unwittingly envisioned Kincaid's long, lanky body sprawled from one end of the mattress to the other, his scowl lost to slumber as his chest rose and fell with each heavy breath.

His scent was sandalwood and citrus.

And she had absolutely *no* business imagining him in bed.

After waiting for the redness in her cheeks to subside (any more blushing and she'd turn into Claire), and then waiting some more for Kincaid to come out of his office, Joanna made up her mind to go in. She knew the rules of polite society dictate she wait for an invitation, but she had a feeling she would be waiting for a very long while. And Joanna waited for no one, least of all a man.

Even ones that made her tingle.

Rapping her knuckles against the door to give fair warning of her impending entrance, she let herself into Kincaid's office without bothering to wait for a reply and found him sitting behind his desk, his brow furrowed as he studied something he'd written in the leather journal she'd seen him carrying yesterday.

"Miss Thorncroft." Visibly startled by her appearance, he rose halfway out of his chair, amber eyes widening behind his spectacles. "I was…I was coming to let you in."

"Alas, here I am. Regrettably, patience is not

a virtue of mine." She flashed him a smile as a peculiar fluttering filled her belly. If she didn't know any better, she'd think she had swallowed a butterfly and the poor thing was flying around inside of her trying to find a way out. *Make that twenty butterflies*, she thought silently when Kincaid raked his fingers through his unruly hair and a brown curl tumbled across his brow.

"Maybe not," he said, "but it seems punctuality is. I wasn't expecting you this early."

"You told me to return in the morning," she pointed out, folding her hands behind her back after she'd hung her coat and bonnet on the hall tree shoved into the corner.

"Yes, but I didn't…" He glanced at the window, where the sun had barely crept above the horizon and the sky was still turning from orange to blue. "Never mind. I suppose it's a good thing I am an early riser as well, or you might have walked in on me only half-dressed. Wait." His tone turned slightly panicked while Joanna tried—and failed—not to picture Kincaid without his shirt on. "That's not what I meant to say. I…*do* have a seat, Miss Thorncroft. Would you care for some, uh…coffee?"

Her nose wrinkling at the sight of the cold, brown sludge sitting in a clear pot, Joanna gave a firm shake of her head. Sweeping her skirts to the side, she sank gracefully into the same chair she'd occupied the day prior. "This is *exactly* why you need a secretary, Kincaid."

"I will admit, the idea never occurred to me," Kincaid revealed as he sat down at his desk. "But we did have one at Scotland Yard." His gaze swept across Joanna and the corners of his mouth tightened imperceptibly. "A quiet, elderly widow who made the best sugar biscuits I've ever tasted."

It was clear by the flicker of disapproval in his eyes that Kincaid would have preferred a secretary who fit those qualifications. A doddering old grandmother type who patted him on the head and said things like, *"There's a good lad"* and *"Have another treat, my boy, you're much too thin"*.

Instead, he had...well, he had *her*. A brash American who was rarely quiet, often spoke before she thought, and couldn't bake a sugar cookie to save her life.

If only he knew how lucky he was.

"How long were you a policeman before you became a detective?" Joanna asked.

A shadow darkened Kincaid's countenance. "Long enough to decide I'd rather work for myself. Miss Thorncroft, let's begin by reviewing your—"

"What drew you to such a job?" she interrupted. Having never met a detective—crime wasn't exactly rampant in quiet, sleepy Somerville—she was naturally curious as to why

Kincaid had chosen such a dangerous, demanding line of work…and what had made him leave it to become a private investigator.

"Because I wanted to help people," he said curtly. "Do you have a picture of—"

"Why did you leave the police force?"

Brandy-colored eyes burned into hers. "Miss Thorncroft, I have agreed to take on your case in exchange for your secretarial skills, as unproven as they are. If you wish to begin our agreement by asking prying questions which I've no obligation to answer, then I'd just as soon show you the door."

Well, then.

She'd certainly been put in her place, hadn't she?

How unfortunate (for Kincaid) that she had no intention of staying there. Still, it wouldn't do to be sacked on her first day. Especially when she found her employer so *very* intriguing.

She liked his spectacles, which gave him an air of propriety. And she liked his scowl, which did not. She also liked the way she had felt when he touched her yesterday. That little sizzling *shock* of awareness that had made her breath catch and left her thinking about him long after they'd said goodbye. It made her wonder what it would feel like if he touched her deliberately…and if those proper spectacles would fog with passion when they kissed.

Joanna blinked.

She couldn't remember the last time she'd lusted over a man. Charles and his pink pants hadn't exactly invoked dreams of desire. On the two occasions she *had* granted him permission to kiss her (ever polite, Charles had always made sure to ask before he attacked her lips with all the fervor of a small Pomeranian yapping at the heels of its master), she'd immediately regretted her decision. But she had an inkling that if Kincaid kissed her, the last thing she'd feel was regret.

"I apologize for my questions," she said, offering her most contrite smile. "Normally, it is my sister, Evelyn, who is the nosy one. But I must admit I find you utterly fascinating, Kincaid. I hope that is not too forward a thing to say. As we get to know each other, I believe you'll find I have the bad habit of almost always speaking what's on my mind."

His scowl deepened. "I can assure you there is nothing fascinating about me, Miss Thorncroft."

Oh, Joanna doubted that.

She doubted that very much.

If ever there was a person who was hiding something, it was Kincaid. She'd already told him all of her scandalous secrets. By the time they were through, she was determined to learn his.

One way or another.

"Should we get on with my case?" she asked

brightly.

With clear relief, Kincaid nodded. "Indeed. Your case." He picked up a pen, and briefly consulted his journal. "I've already requested the passenger manifest for the *Queen Mary* and should have a copy by the end of the day."

Joanna sat up. "That's brilliant!"

"However—"

"Never a good word," she mumbled.

"—I doubt very much if the pickpocket we're searching for will show up on it. He was most likely a stowaway, or used a different name. Which means we know the ring arrived in London when the *Queen Mary* made port but, after that, we've no way to trace it."

"What about the inscription?" she asked. "And the initials. JW."

"Yes." Kincaid tapped the pen against his chin. "I've given that a great deal of consideration. I do believe your grandmother's theory is correct. This was no random robbery. That boy, whoever he is, was dispatched specifically to steal *your* ring and bring it here. If I were to question every jeweler in Boston and the surrounding area, I should think we'd discover they were paid, and paid handsomely, to send the ring to England should it ever come to be in their possession."

She slumped in her chair. "Then by the very act of having the ring appraised, we allowed it to be stolen."

Kincaid put down his and pen and frowned at her. "This not your fault, Miss Thorncroft. You, and your sisters, are the victims here. Per the inscription on the ring, you are also its rightful owners. Clearly, it was intended as a gift to your mother. It's also clear that the person who gave your mother that ring, or someone closely associated with them, has gone to great lengths to get it back. My assumption is that they do not wish for your mother's...*relationship*...with whomever gave her the ring to come to light."

"You can call it an affair. It's all right." Ignoring the pang in her chest, Joanna gave her best attempt at a lighthearted shrug. "That's what it was, after all. I suppose I should be grateful the affair happened, for had it not, I would never have been born."

"Yes, well." Kincaid cleared his throat. "I can assure you I will do my best to find your ring, Miss Thorncroft. As well as the identity of your..."

"Birth father," she supplied.

"Indeed." He stood up behind his desk and brought his pen and journal to her. "Would you be able to draw a picture of the ring? You've described it in detail, but a visual is always best."

Yes, Joanna thought as she suddenly found herself eye-level with Kincaid's nether regions. A visual *was* always best.

Goodness.

Who knew a man could be so well...*endowed*...in that area?

Maybe it was because she'd never paid much attention, having never had loins thrust in front of her. But it seemed Kincaid's height wasn't the only thing about him that was larger than average.

Slowly, her gaze traveled up the length of his torso, lingering on the V of flesh that was exposed by his partially unbuttoned shirt until she finally reached his face.

Their eyes met.

With a delicate cough, Joanna's gaze flicked down, then up again.

"Miss Thorncroft, what is the—*oh*." As he suddenly realized the close proximity of his groin to her countenance, Kincaid's body went as stiff as a board.

His *entire* body, she noted with some interest.

"Here," he said, all but throwing the journal and pen into her lap. "Draw the ring to the best of your ability and I'll return shortly."

Before she could ask him where he was going, he had quit the room.

"Hmmm," Joanna murmured to James, who had watched the entire exchange from his lofty perch atop the bookcase. "How do you like that?"

CHAPTER SEVEN

IN THE FOYER, Kincaid closed his eyes and let his skull fall back against the plaster wall with an audible *thud*.

Bloody hell.

He'd hoped his flare of attraction towards Joanna had been a one-time anomaly. A result of him being caught unawares by a damp, delectable beauty forcing her way into his office. Surely, he'd told himself, when he saw her again there would no sexual friction between them. She was his client, *and* his employee, and he could—he *would*—conduct himself in a manner that conveyed his utmost professionalism.

"Kincaid? I'm all done."

As Joanna's melodious voice floated through the door, his bollocks tightened.

Done?

No, they hadn't even gotten started.

And he already needed an ice bath.

"I'm coming," he called back, then winced.

Bad choice of words, that.

Not to mention they did piss all to help with his growing arousal.

Shoving his hands through his hair, he forced himself to count to ten. Twice. When he'd finished and his trousers *still* fit a bit more snugly than he was comfortable with, he cursed under his breath and went upstairs to fetch a long overcoat. Holding it closed, he re-entered his office, marched straight to his desk, and sat down.

"Cold?" Joanna asked with a glance at his coat.

"Let's just see the drawing." Normally, Kincaid wasn't so abrasive. Under the right circumstances, he could almost be as charming as Sterling (no easy feat). But these were far from the right circumstances, and given how tenuous his grip was on his self-control, he wanted to conclude this meeting with all haste and get Joanna the hell out of his house.

"Here." Leaning forward in her chair, she slid the journal across his desk. "My sister, Claire, would have done a much better job. She's the artistic one in the family. But this should give you a fair idea of what the ring looks like."

Kincaid picked up the journal. His brows drew together. Joanna was right. She wasn't an artist. But her rudimentary sketch gave him a clear picture of what he was searching for.

Sort of.

"Is the ring on a large boat, or…"

Joanna's eyes narrowed. "That is my mother's hand."

"Ah." Kincaid tilted his head and squinted. "Yes, I see it now."

"Give me that." Snatching the journal back, she pressed the tip of the pen between her lips— dear God in heaven—before adding a few lines to the drawing, then a few a more. She held the journal back out. "There. That should be better."

"Thank you," Kincaid croaked as he took the journal.

"The ruby is a vibrant red." She tucked the pen behind her ear. "Mr. Bernard, the jeweler, said it was a marquise cut, and quite old."

"An heirloom, no doubt. In the peerage, it's common for certain pieces of jewelry to be handed down through the generations. If it was given to your mother without the family's knowledge or permission, that might also explain why they went to such lengths to have it returned to them."

A tiny notch appeared in the middle of her brows. "But you said the ring rightfully belongs to me and my sisters."

"Morally, it does."

"*Morally*?"

"British law is…complicated. Particularly

when it involves the aristocracy." Kincaid shifted his weight in his chair as, at long last, the blood in his groin began to recede. Nothing like a healthy law discussion to quell a man's arousal. "I should forewarn you that even if we manage to find who took the ring, they may be under no legal obligation to return it."

Anger swirled in the depths of Joanna's gaze. "That's not right. They stole the ring. They *have* to give it back."

"Hopefully, they will."

"And if they don't?" she demanded.

"We'll cross that bridge when we come to it. As I said, I will have the opportunity to examine the *Queen Mary's* manifest this afternoon. If I find anything of interest, I'll be sure to let you know." He closed his journal. Cleared his throat. "It looks to be a clear, sunny day. You and your sister should do some sightseeing."

Joanna stood when he did. "Are you dismissing me, Kincaid?"

Damned right he was.

The sooner his office didn't smell of violets, the better. Maybe then, he'd actually be able to focus on her case instead of stealing glances at her breasts like some lovesick young pup.

"I can recommend Hyde Park," he said as he opened the door. "There are several miles of walking trails. There's also Trafalgar Square where you'll find the National Gallery. I believe they're currently showcasing an exhibition featuring new European artists. There's one in particular I like, although I doubt you've ever heard of him. Claude Monet?"

"No, I am afraid not."

"If you enjoy watching plays, the Gaiety Theater shouldn't be too far from your boarding house. The acting troupe that's currently touring there is quite entertaining."

Joanna tilted her head. "Do you enjoy the theater, Kincaid?"

"Occasionally." Back when he was a peeler, Kincaid had worked, gone to bed, woken up, and returned to work. There'd simply been no time to take a stroll through the park, or admire paintings at the National Gallery, or see a play. After he was let go (as kind a way to put it as any), he'd drank himself into oblivion. When he'd finally surfaced from the self-inflicted haze of cheap gin, he had found himself with nothing to do.

Needing *something* to fill the long, empty evenings that gnawed at him like a dog on a bone, he'd followed Sterling's suggestion and attended the theater. Better to spend his money on that, he'd supposed, than a bottle of gin. To his surprise, he'd actually enjoyed himself, and had seen several plays since.

"They're debuting an operetta tonight, I believe." A combination of humor and vocal talent, operettas were shown exclusively at the Gaiety Theater as they weren't considered prestigious enough for The Globe or Charring Cross, both of which appealed to a more exclusive set of people than Kincaid preferred to run with. "You should go see it, Miss Thorncroft. Take in a bit of the local talent during your stay."

Her blue eyes brightened. "What a nice invitation, Kincaid. I would love to accompany you."

"What?" he said blankly. "No, I didn't...that is to say, I wasn't..."

"I'll be ready at half-past seven." With that, she picked up her bonnet and coat and sailed past him before he could sputter another word.

"ARE YOU SURE you don't want to come with me?" Joanna asked for the fifth time. "I am certain Kincaid could get another ticket."

"And spoil your evening alone?" Evie teased. "I wouldn't dare dream of it. Besides, Mrs. Benedict is going to teach me how to play whist and then we're going for a stroll around Cremorne Gardens. She says it's *the* place to be if I want to meet a duke."

"Because of all the trees?" Joanna asked innocently, then promptly ducked when Evie threw a pillow at her head.

"You *know* I was speaking metaphorically." Carefully adjusting a shiny, black curl she'd laid just so over her shoulder, Evie put her hands on her hips and turned her head to the side. "How do I look?"

"Beautiful, as always. That color is stunning on you."

"It's not *too* yellow, is it?" Evie fretted, glancing down at her voluminous skirt.

"If there's a duke to be had, he'll be eating out of your palm in no time at all," Joanna said with the utmost confidence.

Evie smiled. "Thank you. I must say, you don't look *nearly* as dowdy as you usually do."

"What a wonderful compliment," Joanna said dryly. For her night out with Kincaid, she'd chosen a gown in emerald green silk with a square neckline, pointed waist, and a modest bustle that paled in comparison to the small mountain that currently resided on Evie's rear end. She'd tamed her thick mass of red curls into a braid, and then twisted the braid into a bun on top of her head. A pair of simple pearl earrings and matching necklace completed the outfit.

"Come to think of it," said Evie said thoughtfully, "I don't know if you've ever been this dressed up. Are you wearing a corset?"

"Maybe," Joanna said defensively. "What does it matter?"

"You *never* wear a corset."

"Because they're barbaric monstrosities created to suppress women."

"And yet you're wearing one."

"The dress required it."

"Ah, of course." Evie's smile grew. "The *dress* required it."

Joanna began to cross her arms, but was forced to drop them back to her sides when the edges of her corset dug into her ribs. They really *were* devilish contraptions. "What does that mean?"

"It means I was right. You *are* sweet on Kincaid."

"I'm nothing of the kind," she scoffed. "This is merely a—a business meeting between associates. Men have them all the time."

"You aren't a man," said Evie. "And I've never heard of a meeting being conducted in the middle of a play."

"It's an operetta."

"Whatever it is, I'm certain Kincaid did not invite you to discuss *business*."

"I don't know if he invited me so much as I invited *him*." And for as long as she lived, Joanna would never forget the way the blood had drained from Kincaid's face, as if she'd proposed they fling themselves off London Bridge instead of attend a play. Truth be told, she didn't know whether to be insulted or amused by the obvious horror he'd experienced upon realizing she had tricked him into a night at the theater.

A bit of both, she decided as she picked up her beaded handbag and slipped it around her wrist.

Which was why she had decided to wear the corset.

"All right," she confessed. "Maybe I *do* find Kincaid somewhat...attractive."

"I knew it!" Evie said triumphantly.

"But finding the ring is still my highest priority." As she spoke, Joanna honestly didn't know whether she was trying to convince Evie...or herself. "Any feelings I may or may not be developing for Kincaid must remain secondary."

"Well I, for one, think it is romantic."

Joanna gazed dubiously at her sister. "This from the person who doesn't believe in love?"

"I never said I didn't believe *in* love. I just don't believe in marrying *for* love unless it is financially beneficial." Consulting her warlike assortment of beauty products and potions, Evie opened a tin of beeswax and used her fingertip to apply a light sheen to her lips. "The more I think about it, the more I think *you're* the one who doesn't believe in love. All these suitors you've had, and not a single one has ever made your heart flutter?"

"No," Joanna said without hesitation.

"And what about Kincaid? Does *he* make

your heart flutter?"

A blush warmed her cheeks. "He...he makes me tingle."

Evie nodded approvingly. "Tingling is good."

"Yes, but as I said, my highest priority is—"

"Finding the ring." A dusting of rouge on her cheeks, and Evie stepped back to admire her reflection in the dressing mirror. "That's another thing I've noticed about you, Jo. For all your impassioned speeches about unconditional love, you've always managed to come up with a litany of excuses to cut your suitors off before they even have the chance to prove themselves. Do you want to know what I think about *that*?"

"Not really," Joanna said grumpily, "but I have the feeling you're going to tell me anyways."

"I think you don't *want* to fall in love." Apparently satisfied with her appearance, Evie turned and regarded her sister with an arched brow. "Because your *real* highest priority has always been me and Claire. You've raised us every bit as much as Grandmother has, and if you fell in love and got married, you'd have to leave us, and *that's* why you've found a reason to dismiss every man who has ever attempted to court you."

"That's—that's preposterous," Joanna said, even as the truth of Evie's words resonated somewhere deep inside of her like the low tolling of a church bell whose rippling sound could be heard from miles away. "I want to marry. And I will. When I meet the right man."

"Is that man Kincaid?"

"No. Maybe. Most likely not." If her corset had allowed it, she would have released a loud huff of breath. Instead she had to make do with a slow whistling hiss between her teeth. And a glare. "We did *not* come here to find husbands."

"Speak for yourself," Evie sniffed. "I'm going to meet mine tonight."

CHAPTER EIGHT

"**I**S SOMETHING THE matter, Miss Thorn-croft?"

Joanna peeked at Kincaid out of the corners of her eyes. It was the third time he'd asked her that question since they'd stepped into the long line of people waiting to enter the Gaiety Theater, and she still didn't have an answer for him.

She couldn't say nothing was wrong, for that would be a lie.

But neither could she say what was *really* bothering her. How could she possibly explain that she was afraid Evie was right? That she really *didn't* want to fall in love. Not with Charles. Not with Kincaid.

Not with anyone.

"My sister and I had a disagreement. That's all." The line shuffled forward a few steps, with

Joanna and Kincaid moving along with it. She slanted him another glance.

Positively dashing in a black tailcoat and royal blue ascot, the detective had slicked his hair back but forgotten to shave his jaw, leaving a shadow of dark scruff that gave him a rakish appearance she found secretly appealing.

If she *was* going to fall in love, surely it would be with someone like Kincaid. Evie could keep her wealthy dukes and Claire her sweet, well-meaning butchers. Joanna would much rather have a man who knew what it was to live on the edge of danger. Who had seen and done things others couldn't even imagine. Who was sharp and prickly around the edges, but still kind enough to help a complete stranger track down her mother's stolen ring.

"Do you have any siblings, Kincaid?" she asked him.

"No," he said in a clipped tone that invoked more questions than it did answers.

"I couldn't imagine being an only child. My sisters and I argue more than we probably should, but when we get on we're as close as three peas in a pod. I cannot remember the last time we've ever been separated." She frowned. "Come to think of it, I don't believe we ever have. At least not by an entire ocean."

"How is your sister liking London?"

"Oh, Evie loves it. I invited her to accompany

us tonight, but she's already made fast friends with another one of the tenants at the boarding house and they're going to a place called..." Joanna paused as she tried to remember the name. "Cremorne Gardens."

Kincaid stopped short. "The *pleasure* garden?"

"I don't know." Her frown returned. "What is a pleasure garden?"

For some reason, the detective's countenance reddened. "If you're unaware of what the purpose of a pleasure garden is, Miss Thorncroft, I'm hardly the one to educate you."

"I see. Then I suppose I'll just have to ask a stranger. Excuse me!" she called out to the couple standing in front of them. "Yes, hello. Do you know what a—"

"All right," Kincaid growled. "I'll tell you."

"Thank you," she told the couple sweetly, "but it seems my companion has suddenly recalled the answer to my question."

Kincaid looked at her with suspicion. "You did that on purpose."

"Yes," she said unabashedly. "But it worked, didn't it? Now, what is a pleasure garden? It sounds very...wicked."

"It's certainly not a suitable place for a young, unmarried woman, if that's what you're asking. To be perfectly blunt, a pleasure garden is a place where lasciviousness and carnality are openly encouraged."

"But my sister is going there to meet a duke!" Joanna exclaimed.

"A scoundrel, more like. Any peer wary of ruining their reputation does well to avoid Cremorne Gardens, dukes included."

"If Evie ruins her reputation, then she ruins any chances of marrying a British nobleman. We have to warn her!"

"What are you doing?" Kincaid said warily when she grabbed his arm and pulled him out of the queue. "You cannot be serious. The theater is one thing, but I'll be damned if I take you to a pleasure garden. There are lines, Miss Thorncroft, that exist between an employer and employee, and I won't cross them." His mouth tightened. "I refuse."

"Should I go there by myself, then?" she challenged with a toss of her head.

He muttered a curse. "I'll get us a hackney."

THEY WENT TO the boarding house first. Joanna hoped she might be able to head off Evie before her sister and Mrs. Benedict left, but she was too late. The house was quiet, and Evie was gone.

"How far is it to Cremorne Gardens?" she anxiously asked Kincaid as she climbed back up into the hackney and squeezed in beside him.

The detective had tried to hail a larger carriage, but they'd all been taken. The creaky little hansom cab with its patched roof and dusty velvet seat that smelled vaguely of cigar smoke was the only one that had stopped when Kincaid stepped out in the busy street with his arm raised and with no other options, they'd been forced to take it.

Joanna didn't mind, but it was clear by Kincaid's stony expression and the stiffness of his body that he would have vastly preferred roomier accommodations.

"A half-hour, give or take," he replied without looking at her.

"That long?" she said in dismay.

"The gardens are all the way in Chelsea by the end of the King's Road. If the traffic doesn't thin out soon, it may take even longer. Rest assured, however, we'll get there."

Yes, they'd get there.

But would it be in time to prevent Evie from being ruined?

Joanna knew her sister could take care of herself. But she also knew this wasn't Somerville. The Thorncroft women had gone from the pond to the ocean, and they weren't accustomed to how deep the water was...or the size of the sharks circling beneath their feet.

Evie may have had her heart set on a duke, but what did she know of the *ton* or the litany of unspoken rules that governed their actions? As an American with no dowry (at least, not before they recovered the ring), she was already at a severe disadvantage. If she found her reputation in tatters, there was no nobleman in all of England who would have her.

At least, not for marriage.

Pulling her handbag off her wrist, Joanna set it on her knees, fingers digging into the worn leather as their carriage bounced over a large rut. "Have you ever been there? To the pleasure gardens, I mean." If she was going to be trapped beside Kincaid for the next thirty minutes (give or take), she couldn't sit in deafening quiet, her mind constantly veering towards the worst possible outcome.

"On occasion, I was required to patrol the grounds," he said evasively. The wind ruffled his hair, whisking it away from his temple and giving her a clear, unfettered view of his profile.

All sharp angles and lines, she noted, with only the rounded edge of his spectacles to soften a countenance that otherwise could have been carved from granite.

"Have you ever gone when it *wasn't* required of you?" she asked.

A muscle leapt in his jaw. "That is a very personal question, Miss Thorncroft."

"We're practically sitting on each other's laps in a carriage bound for a place that you have described as lascivious and carnal," she pointed out. "How much more personal could we possibly get?"

Finally, he glanced at her.

And the blaze of heat in his amber eyes took her breath away.

"Oh, I can think of several ways," he said in a husky tone she'd never heard him use.

Close, she thought with a vague stirring of alarm as he shifted his weight and his thigh brushed against her knee. They were too close. Or maybe they weren't close enough. Either way, she had the sudden and distinct impression that she would have been much wiser to maintain her silence.

As her pulse skittered like an autumn leaf blown across the ground and her palms grew slick with sweat inside her plain suede gloves, Joanna was startled to realize that she was nervous. No one—man or woman—had ever made her *nervous*.

It was a strange feeling, and she didn't like it.

But she *did* like Kincaid.

What a vexing dilemma to find herself in.

"If you wish to kiss me," she said breathlessly, "you have my permission."

His gaze dropped to her mouth, where it lingered for the span of three heartbeats. A small eternity in the timespan of desire. Something flashed in his eyes—regret?—before he lifted his head and scowled at her. "You forget your place, Miss Thorncroft. You are my secretary. You are also my client. Any relationship of a physical nature would only serve to complicate things."

He was right, of course.

She *knew* he was right.

Unfortunately, that did nothing to quell her disappointment. Or the nagging suspicion that even though Kincaid seemed to distance himself from everyone, he loathed *her* in particular.

Had she done something to offend him? Maybe she'd been too presumptuous when she had all but forced him to take her to the theater. Kincaid did not seem like the sort of man who enjoyed being told what to do. Despite that, he had still been at the boarding house to collect her at precisely half-past seven. Now, they were on their way to rescue Evie from an ill-mannered rogue at London's premiere pleasure garden. If *that* wasn't complicated, she didn't know what was.

On a sigh, Joanna turned her attention to the passing scenery as Kincaid returned to staring straight ahead. Like two ships passing in the night, they did not acknowledge each other until the cab slowed, then turned down a dirt lane that brought them to an enormous, black, wrought iron gate with a coat of arms above and a towering stone wall on either side.

From within the expansive gardens came the

unmistakable sounds of music and laughter. Old-fashioned torchlight revealed a large brick pathway that branched off into smaller walking trails guarded by shrubbery. Most of the light and noise seemed concentrated in the middle of the park, where Joanna could just make out a large pavilion through the trees.

The air smelled of honeysuckle and sinful decadence.

After paying the driver, Kincaid exited the carriage and then offered his arm to Joanna. Placing her small hand in his larger one, she joined him on the ground in a graceful swirl of skirts. Her eyes widened when the gate swung inward, beckoning them into the gardens like a lover coaxing his mistress into bed.

"Stay close to me," Kincaid warned, his grip tightening as they slipped beneath the coat of arms and into a world unlike anything Joanna had ever witnessed.

Amidst the sin and the starlight, there were couples everywhere.

Strolling arm in arm down the paths. Standing in clusters in the shadows. Sprawled across wooden benches.

Some were talking. Some were kissing. And some were…

"Are they, er…*fornicating*?" Joanna hissed, staring in scandalized fascination at a partially naked man and woman lounging against a tree.

The man's trousers were bunched at his knees as he lazily moved his hips back and forth. As Joanna watched, the woman lifted her lips from her partner's neck and winked.

"Come on," Kincaid growled, dragging her past. "We're here to find your sister, not partake in an orgy."

"Are you sure that was an orgy?" Her brow creased as she slowed her step. "I was always under the impression it required at least four participants."

"Miss Thorncroft…" he said between clenched teeth.

"All right, all right. I was just trying to *clarify*." Increasing her stride length to match his, she stayed close to his side as they drew nearer to the center of the gardens where the lights were brighter and the music was almost loud enough to drown out the gasps and moans coming from the bushes.

Dozens of people waltzed across a raised wooden platform while servants moved amidst them carrying large silver trays filled with golden champagne. There were even more guests crowded onto the large pavilion behind the dance floor, their glazed expression and lopsided grins indicating they'd already partaken in quite a few glasses of the bubbly spirits.

Joanna considered grabbing one herself, but Kincaid must have sensed that was her intention for he abruptly turned her away from a passing servant and steered her towards an empty bench partially hidden behind a cluster of lilacs.

"Sit," he ordered. "Stay."

"Should I bark as well?" she asked, annoyed with his handling of her. "Or lift my paw?"

He dragged a hand through his hair. "Just remain here until I return. I can cover more ground if I'm not worrying about you wandering off."

Her irritation grew. "I can take care of myself, Kincaid. I am not a wayward child."

"No, you're something far worse," he said grimly. "You're an American. Promise me you'll stay on this bench, Miss Thorncroft, and wait for my return. It's the safest place you could be while I search for your sister."

"But you don't even know what Evie looks like!"

He snorted. "If she's anything like you, she'll be the one causing the most trouble."

"Arrogant bastard," Joanna mumbled under her breath as Kincaid walked swiftly away.

For all of ten seconds, she obeyed his request to remain on the bench. But Thorncroft women were not renowned for their ability to follow rules, and after a furtive glance around to ensure her domineering detective had truly gone, she jumped up and scurried off down the nearest path.

Winding through a thicket of rosebushes, the walkway, illuminated only by moonlight, soon branched into two separate parts. Joanna stopped and studied each way in equal measure, until she ultimately decided to head towards the left.

She quickened her pace when she heard raised voices ahead. Without warning, the path she'd chosen twisted around an ancient oak and ended abruptly at a small alcove surrounded by marble statues...of nude warriors.

"Goodness," she breathed, her eyes growing to the size of dinner plates as she took in the detailed anatomy of an archer with his bow drawn. He had one leg extended while the other stretched behind him, revealing a muscular backside and extraordinarily large...er...phallus.

"They are Greek Gods," drawled a masculine voice from directly behind her.

On a gasp, Joanna whirled around. "You—you shouldn't sneak up on people like that," she said as she found herself face to face with a young, blonde-haired gentleman with brown eyes that were crinkled with amusement at the corners and a slightly sardonic tilt to his mouth.

"How else am I to get close to beautiful women?" he asked, canting his head to the side while his gaze traveled leisurely across her body as if she were standing there for his own personal enjoyment.

Flushing beneath his intimate—not to mention rude—perusal, Joanna hugged her arms around herself to ward off a sudden chill of warning that trickled down her spine like a bead of condensation sliding down the outside of a glass. "You could introduce yourself," she suggested. "And not lurk in the shadows."

"Was I lurking?" he said. "I hadn't any idea. My apologies, sweet. Colin Farnsworth, Duke of Telford. At your pleasure."

This was a duke?

This was what Evie had crossed an ocean to marry?

How utterly disappointing.

Oh, he was pleasant enough to look at. Joanna would give him that. But his obvious sense of self-importance, combined with his lewd staring, left an unpleasant taste in her mouth. A taste that only grew more bitter when he reached out with all the quickness of a snake, grabbed her arm, and jerked her against him.

"Don't be impolite, sweet." His breath reeked of strong spirits as it wafted past her nose. "I told you who I am. Who are you?" He slid a hand around her waist, fingers digging painfully into her hip. "Besides a goddess sent from the heavens above to tempt this poor mortal's soul."

Joanna craned away from him. "Does that bit work?"

"Usually." There was a flicker of annoyance in his dark eyes, and then he shrugged. "But it doesn't matter. I don't *really* need to know your name. Even if you did tell me, I'd probably forget it tomorrow. What do you have under this bustle, sweet?"

"Let me *go!*" Joanna snapped, outraged when his hand slipped around her waist to squeeze her bottom. She brought her arms up between them and tried to push herself free, but the duke's grip only tightened, like a serpent coiling around its prey.

"Now, now," he said, leering at her. "No need to play hard to get. We both know why you came to the gardens."

"I *came* here to find my sister!" Bringing her leg back, she kicked it forward with all the strength she could muster and hit him squarely in the middle of his shin.

With a howl, he released her, but before she could escape back down the path he grabbed her wrist and spun her towards him. She struggled to free herself, but it was to no avail. The duke was physically stronger and, within seconds, he had her pinned against the base of the archer statue with his knee thrust between her thighs and her arms stretched high above her head.

"That," he bit out, "wasn't very nice."

"Neither is accosting a female when it's clear she finds you repulsive!" Joanna spat, her chest heaving with indignation...and a tiny, but rapidly growing, sliver of fear.

There were at least four other people milling about the statue garden, but it was clear none of them had any plans to come to her aid.

She should have stayed on the bench.

"You're feisty, sweet." A drunken grin stumbled across the duke's mouth as he reached between them to rub himself suggestively. "I like that."

"You're disgusting," she hissed, pinching her eyes shut and turning her head to the side when he tried to place a sloppy kiss on her lips. "Release me this instant!"

"Or what?" he sneered.

"Or I'll break your fucking face." Moving through the darkness like a shadow, Kincaid materialized behind the Duke of Telford and wrapped his forearm around the duke's throat. "I believe Miss Thorncroft asked you to release her."

"The hell I will," the duke retorted. "Do you have any idea who I am? Sod off and find yourself another fine piece. This wench is—*ahhh*," he gurgled when Kincaid applied pressure to the duke's windpipe, effectively silencing him.

"You're going to apologize to Miss Thorncroft," the detective said calmly. "Then you are going to get the hell out of her sight, or I'm going to snap your neck like a bloody twig. Do you understand?"

The duke wheezed something unintelligible.

"What was that?" Kincaid asked, loosening his grip a fraction of an inch.

"I—I'm sorry," he gasped. "T—truly."

"Is that sufficient, Miss Thorncroft?" Although Kincaid's tone was pleasant, even polite, his eyes burned black fury as he met her gaze.

Joanna sucked in a startled breath.

Gone was the quiet, mild-mannered private investigator who rescued cats and left mugs of coffee scattered around his office (seven, at last count). In his place stood a man who was every bit as much a warrior as the statues that surrounded him. He was fierce, and frightening, and there wasn't a doubt in Joanna's mind that he wouldn't hesitate to make good on his threat to kill the Duke of Telford in cold blood.

All for the sin of touching her.

"Yes," she said quickly. "Yes, it's sufficient. You can let him go."

Please let him go, she thought, for even though the duke had treated her abominably, she didn't want his death on her conscience.

To her great relief, Kincaid honored his word and released the duke.

After nearly collapsing to his knees, the nobleman righted himself, but he was either too pompous or too stupid to heed Kincaid's warning.

"You're going to pay for this!" he said shrilly. "I'll see you thrown in Newgate! Then I'm going to take your little whore and—"

Whatever the duke's nefarious intentions were, he never had the chance to speak them aloud for with a sickening *crunch* of bone striking bone, Kincaid slammed a fist into the middle of the duke's nose and he sank to the ground like a stone.

"That's one way to shut him up, I suppose." Lifting her skirts, Joanna stepped neatly over the Duke of Telford's body. "Shall we?" she asked Kincaid.

"I told you to remain on the bench," he growled as they left the statue garden.

"I'm not very good at following directions," she admitted.

"Obviously." Drawing her to the side of the path, he lightly grasped her elbows as his dark gaze, more amber than obsidian as his anger slowly receded, raked across her with a blush-inducing intensity. "Are you injured, Miss Thorncroft? Did he hurt you in any way? If you need to see a doctor—"

"I'm fine. Truly," she insisted when he still appeared dubious. "The only thing injured was my pride, but I'm confident it shall recover in due time." She bit her lip. "That—that was a duke. Granted, I'm not all that familiar with British titles yet, but I know that's an important one. Won't you suffer repercussions for assaulting him?"

The detective's eyes flashed. "He put his hands on you. He should consider himself lucky I didn't kill him."

And now Kincaid had *his* hands on her, but she didn't mind.

She didn't mind at all.

The Duke of Telford had repulsed her from the very first word he'd spoken. Even before his mouth turned cruel and his grip turned demanding, she hadn't trusted him. Her instincts had warned her something was wrong. The very same instincts that told her Thomas Kincaid was right. That he *felt* right. That standing here, with him, with moonlight in her hair and a mad fluttering in her heart, was where she was meant to be.

Her lashes skimmed across her cheekbones, disguising her uncertainty...and her hope. She might have crossed the Atlantic to find a ring, but that did not mean it was the only thing of value worth discovering. In Somerville, love had eluded her more times than she cared to acknowledge. And despite Evie's theory, she refused—*refused*—to believe it was because she didn't want to fall in love.

Maybe her heart had just been waiting for the right person.

Never knowing that right person was on the other side of the ocean.

"Are you certain you are all right, Miss

Thorncroft?"

Joanna blinked, then raised her gaze. "Yes. I...I am appreciative of the lengths which you employed to ensure my safety, Kincaid. I realize that was not part of our original agreement."

She'd meant to compliment him but, for some reason, her words only seemed to cause him annoyance. Then again, he was always in such a perpetual state of irritation it was difficult to gauge whether he was scowling because of something she'd said or he was scowling because he was breathing.

"There's a carriage waiting for us," he said curtly.

"Wait," she called out, hurrying to catch up to him when he started to walk away. "What about Evie?"

"She's not here."

Bunching her skirts in her fists, Joanna broke into a light jog. "She's not here?" she repeated, panting slightly as she struggled to keep pace with the detective's considerably longer stride. "What do you mean?

Kincaid halted with such abruptness that she plowed into the back of him. They both fell forward, and would have continued falling had he not twisted around and wrapped his arms around her.

"I mean," he snarled, his face an inch from her own as he hauled her upright, "that she left as soon as she saw what kind of place this is. Because, unlike her sister, she is *sensible*."

"I'm sensible," Joanna protested.

"You are many things, Miss Thorncroft. Sensible is not one of them." With that, he released her and stalked through the gate, leaving her to follow after or be left behind.

After a quick glance over her shoulder, she followed him to a different carriage than the shoddy cab they'd arrived in. This one was large, and sleek, and its glossy black surface reflected her pale, tired countenance back at her as she climbed inside and sat across from Kincaid.

He acknowledged her presence with a low grunt, the only sound he made for the entirety of the ride. She could *tell* he was angry at her but, after everything she'd been through over the past hour, she did not have the energy, or the will, to pry the reason out of him.

When they finally reached the boarding house, it was nearly half-past midnight, and she was relieved to see the soft glow of candlelight coming from the room she and Evie were sharing.

"Thank you," she told Kincaid while she waited for the driver to come round and open the door. "For…for everything. The theater, and coming with me to find my sister, and giving the Duke of Telford what he deserved."

"It was nothing."

"It was hardly *nothing*." She waited for him to say something else. To say *anything* else. When he remained cloaked in stubborn silence, she gave a small sigh. "Goodnight, Kincaid. I shall see you at your office in the morning."

"Miss Thorncroft," he said after she'd departed the carriage.

"Yes?" She turned towards him expectantly, only to be greeted by a swath of shadows. Just the lower half of his jaw was visible, and it was so rigidly held it was a wonder he could move it enough to form words.

"If I were to ever kiss you, I would not need to ask permission." With that, the door slammed shut and the carriage rolled away...leaving Joanna to wonder if she wasn't alone in waiting for love.

CHAPTER NINE

T HE ICE HOUSE was colder than a witch's tit. Kincaid's teeth chattered lightly together as he waited at the mouth of the well for the iceman to return. Somewhere down in that deep, dark chasm there was over four long tons of ice, cut into rough blocks and stacked as high as seven men. Kincaid only needed a pound of it to wrap around the hand he'd plowed into the Duke of Telford's ugly arse face.

An impulsive bit of violence, that.

The likes of which he hadn't employed since his days as a peeler.

He had more self-restraint now. More control. Or at least, that's what he liked to believe. But when he'd stepped into that statue garden and witnessed Telford grabbing Joanna, the last thing he'd felt was in control.

The duke was lucky he wasn't dead, or

JILLIAN EATON

worse.

"Those are some ugly knuckles you've got there," the iceman, a skinny fellow with a head as bald as an ivory cue ball, remarked as he climbed out of the well and handed Kincaid a slab of ice wrapped in a dirty, brown cloth.

"You should see the other bastard." Fishing a shilling out of his pocket, Kincaid paid for the ice and immediately applied it to his throbbing hand before he headed towards home.

He'd been so enraged, he had forgotten to untuck his thumb when he punched, and was paying a fine price for such an amateur mistake. His entire arm throbbed like the dickens, and he wouldn't have been surprised if one, if not more, fingers were broken.

Still, the pain was a small price to pay for the satisfaction of watching Telford crumple to the ground...and the knowledge that *he'd* put him there.

The sheer *rage* that had flowed over him...it was like nothing he'd experienced. And nothing he hoped to experience again. For the duke wasn't the only recipient of his anger. He had *told* Joanna to stay put, hadn't he? Remain on the bench, he'd said. Wait for him to return, he'd said.

Yet what had she done at the first opportunity?

Run off to a garden filled with naked statues

of men.

Naked, *well-endowed* statues of men.

And a foxed duke who should have known better than to go chasing after his woman.

Everything inside of Kincaid stilled.

Including his heart.

Bloody hell.

His woman?

Joanna Thorncroft wasn't his.

She was…she was a menace to society, that's what she was. And he just happened to have gotten himself sucked into the storm of chaos that seemed to follow her wherever she went. That didn't mean he thought of her as *his*. That would be…that would be ludicrous.

Almost as ludicrous as taking a gorgeous American he hardly knew to a damned *pleasure garden* to search for her sister who he didn't know at all.

"I need a drink," he snapped at James and Jane as he let himself to his house and went straight to the liquor cabinet in his office. The two cats trailed after him, their petulant meows a reminder that they hadn't yet received their dinner. Dumping what remained of the rapidly melting ice in a bucket, he glared at the felines. "Go catch a mouse. That's what you're here for, and there's plenty of them scurrying about in the attic."

Jane, the shyer of the two, darted away.

James merely sat on his haunches at his master's feet, opened his mouth, and yowled.

"All right, all right." Cringing at the horrendous sound, Kincaid rummaged around in a cabinet with his good hand and managed to procure half a loaf of bread and hunk of hard cheese. There was no telling how long they'd been in there, but James didn't seem to mind. Tearing off a piece of bread for himself, Kincaid poured a glass of whiskey and nursed it by the window.

Clouds obscured the sky, blocking out the stars and the moon and turning London as black as pitch save for the intermittent glow of cast iron lamp posts. Somewhere out in all that inky darkness were the peelers, combing the streets and the alleys and the docks. Four years ago, he would have been out there with them. Risking life and limb to protect a city that didn't give a damn about him. Now, he was in his house with his cats, trying not to let his mind be led astray by a titian-haired beauty with eyes as blue as the ocean and the most temptingly kissable mouth he'd ever seen.

It was a miracle, really.

That he hadn't kissed her yet.

God, did he want to.

Truthfully, he didn't know if he'd ever wanted anything more.

And that terrified him more than when he'd

found himself on the wrong end of a pistol after he was sent to break up a brawl at a riverside pub.

Grimacing, Kincaid sipped his whiskey, then took a bite of the bread before promptly spitting it back out. Hell, but it was stale. Like chewing on an old rubber shoe. Chasing the taste out of his mouth with more whiskey, he happened to glance down and saw James looking up, his yellow eyes slanted in annoyance.

"It's not my fault," Kincaid said defensively. "When I bought the bread it was fine. Try the cheese."

Lowering his head, James gave the cheese a dainty sniff, then abruptly recoiled and batted at it with his paw.

Kincaid glared at the picky feline. "Don't bloody well start with me. You're a *cat*. Not the King of England. Who cares if it's a little off color? If I can eat it, so can you." Scooping the cheese off the floor—he'd gotten his food from worse places—he tried it. Then promptly spat that out, too, as James watched smugly.

"Go catch a mouse," Kincaid repeated. Picking up his whiskey, he returned to staring out the window. The clouds had shifted, allowing a shimmer of moonlight to peek through. Instantly, he was reminded of the streaks of silvery moonlight in Joanna's hair as she'd walked into Cremorne Gardens. If he hadn't known better, he would have sworn she was a goddess of old.

Aphrodite, perhaps.

Or Athena, the goddess of war and wisdom.

Athena, he decided as he sipped his drink.

Most definitely.

While the wisdom of Joanna's decision to sail across the Atlantic in search of a ring and a father she'd never met was debatable, her courage was not. It was clear she'd go to great lengths to protect her sisters. She already had. And if that wasn't the sign of a true warrior, what was?

If Kincaid wasn't determined to dislike her, he'd having nothing but admiration for her.

And lust.

Quite a bit of lust.

Along with…other feelings.

Feelings he didn't want to feel, which was where the dislike came in.

Never mind that there was absolutely nothing he'd disliked about Joanna tonight. The notable exception being her refusal to follow even the simplest of commands. But even that, in and of itself, was a source of grudging appreciation. She was as headstrong a woman as he'd ever encountered, and he couldn't fault her for it. Not when it was what had first drawn him to her.

"Will you *stop* looking at me like that?" he snapped when he turned round to find James was staring at him with a smirk.

Or so it seemed.

Were cats capable of smirking?

Kincaid did not have any idea. But if there was ever a feline who *could* pull off such a human expression, it was James.

"I'll get you fresh fish at the market tomorrow. Does that meet your fancy, m'lord," he said with a mocking bow, "or should I pull it out of the river with my teeth?"

James' smirk only grew.

"You're a bastard, you know that, right?" Tipping his glass, Kincaid finished the rest of the whiskey, considered pouring himself another, then put the bottle back on the shelf with some regret. It was already late, and the morning was going to come early, and if he was going to continue to dislike Miss Joanna Thorncroft, he needed his wits about him.

Scooping James up in his arms—he could hardly leave the cat downstairs all alone now, could he?—Kincaid clomped off to bed.

JOANNA WAS BORED.

No, that didn't do it justice.

She was bored of *being* bored.

And it was all Kincaid's fault.

Since she'd arrived in his office some three hours ago, he had hardly taken the time to acknowledge her aside from dumping a large bin of paper on her lap and asking her to organize it by date while he conducted interviews with potential clients.

She realized he was busy. By her estimation, more than seven people had walked through the door this morning. A man in search of his missing horse, a woman in search of her missing necklace, and (the most interesting case by far, in Joanna's opinion) a baroness who wanted to open an investigation into the sudden and unexpected death of her husband.

Sir Edgar Chamberlain, it seemed, had recently engaged in an affair with an actress—or *that harlot*, as Lady Chamberlain had referred to her—and upon his demise, the actress' theater group had inherited a considerable percentage of Sir Edgar's fortune. If Lady Chamberlain could prove Sir Edgar had been killed by the actress, the bulk of his estate would revert back to his wife.

It was a fascinating mystery, and one Joanna would have very much liked to assist on…if she wasn't being completely ignored.

The *least* Kincaid could do was spare a bit of attention. Especially since his parting words from the night before had kept her up tossing and turning until Evie had thrown a pillow at her head and demanded that she either fall asleep or go find another room.

If I were to ever kiss you, I would not need to ask permission.

How could he say that to her, and then pretend the next day as if she didn't exist? How could he knock a duke flat on his backside for the crime of simply *touching* her, and then greet her the next morning as if they were perfect strangers?

"I am glad to see you are well, Miss Thorncroft. Here are twenty thousand pages of busywork I need you to do. Please proceed with all haste, and disregard the occasional glare in your direction as I am suffering from gastrointestinal upset."

Or something to that effect.

Waiting for the last client to leave (a husband who wanted his mistress followed as he suspected she was guilty of taking up with another lover, never mind that he was guilty of doing exactly what he was accusing his mistress of), Joanna dumped the pile of meaningless receipts off her lap and stood up, stretching her arms high above her head to work the stiffness from her muscles.

Honestly, did Kincaid *really* need to know what he'd paid for a slab of beef two years ago? Half of the papers would make excellent kindling, and the other half would fare perfectly fine in the bottom of a bin somewhere.

The floorboards creaked as she crossed the room and poured herself a cup of coffee. She'd made the dark brew herself, and was pleased to note it was neither cold nor strong enough to knock a grown man off his feet. After grinding the beans she had added a spoonful of burned sugar for sweetness, a trick her grandmother had taught her. The result was a coffee that was actually palatable, unlike the black swamp water Kincaid had tried to serve her.

Stirring in some thick, white cream, she blew across the top of the ceramic mug, took a sip, and then proceeded to walk straight up to his desk.

"It was the wife," she announced in no uncertain terms. Placing her coffee on a book so as not to stain the wood finish, she crossed her arms and stared directly at Kincaid's bent head. He was jotting down notes in that journal of his, and made no indication that he heard her. "Lady Chamberlain killed her husband."

Kincaid's pen paused for a split second. "It was not the wife."

Joanna pursed her lips. "I think it was."

He resumed writing. Then on a loud, exasperated sigh, he dropped his pen. "Why do you think it's the wife?"

"Because it's *always* the wife." She uncrossed her arms and reached for her coffee. "If Lady Chamberlain didn't do it herself, she hired the person who did. You said he was poisoned?"

"That is the working theory, yes. Oleander, perhaps, as his last twelve hours on earth were reportedly not very...pleasant." Kincaid removed his spectacles and pinched the bridge of his nose. "The coroner should be able to confirm when the exam is complete."

Joanna nodded. "Most definitely the wife. If I was going to murder my husband, that's how I would do it."

Kincaid's brows snapped together. "Why the devil would you murder your husband?"

"The usual reasons, I suppose," she said with a shrug.

"The usual—*Miss Thorncroft*," he said in a strangled voice.

She blinked at him. "Yes?"

"You *do* realize you've just admitted to plotting murder."

"Don't be silly," she said with a wave of her hand. "I'm not even married yet."

An odd flicker of emotion passed across Kincaid's countenance. He leaned forward onto his desk and clasped his hands together. "Still, I would caution you to consider the potential impact of your words before you speak them. *And* to be careful about making accusations you've no evidence with which to confirm."

There was a lock of rich mahogany dangling just above his right eye. Joanna's fingers itched to comb it back from his face, but she had a feeling he wouldn't appreciate the gesture.

Too bad.

There were some people who desperately needed affection, and Kincaid was one of them. He was all sharp lines and defensive angles, but with the right touch—*her* touch—some of those peaks could be softened.

If I were to ever kiss you, I would not need to ask permission.

"I shall take your advice under consideration." She sipped her coffee. "As long as you take mine and investigate Lady Chamberlain. A woman scorned is a powerful entity."

"Do you speak from experience, Miss Thorncroft?" Kincaid asked, his serious gaze intent on her face and every nuanced expression that inadvertently flitted across it.

It was an experience in and of itself, she found, to be gazed upon with such ferocity. As a tall woman with bright red hair, Joanna was accustomed to men staring *at* her. But they never stared *into* her.

Except for Thomas Kincaid.

He looked at her…well, he looked at her as if he wanted to know everything about her. As if he wanted to devour every thought inside of her mind. As if he wanted to peel away her layers until he reached her soul.

What would he find, if he went that far?

What would he discover in her secret heart of heats?

Did she want him to know?

Did *she* even know?

Three months ago, she would have said yes. Unequivocally. She knew exactly who she was. She knew just what she wanted. But now…now with old secrets exposed, and a future that was ripe with uncertainty, and a growing attraction to a British detective who didn't seem to like her very much, let alone return her interest, she wasn't so certain.

About anything.

It was a very uncomfortable position to be in.

Especially for someone accustomed to being in control.

Disguising her discomfort behind a wry smile, she used her thumb to wipe away a spot of dust on the edge of his desk. "I imagine one would have to be in love in order to be scorned, and I'm afraid I have never been blessed with that particular pleasure."

"Good," he said, rather abruptly.

Now *her* eyebrows rose. "Good?"

"I...that's not what I meant to say." With a grimace, Kincaid raked a hand through his hair and shoved his spectacles into place then promptly removed them, polished the lenses on his sleeve, and then put them back on.

Crookedly.

Joanna lifted her mug to disguise her growing smile. This was the first time she had ever seen the detective visibly flustered, and she found it very...appealing. Maybe—just maybe—he wasn't as unaffected by her as he'd like her to believe. Maybe—just maybe—he really *did* like her.

"What did you mean to say, then?" she asked,

placing her coffee down on the desk with a hard *click* that made him flinch. Her head canted. "Are you glad I've never been in love, Kincaid?"

"Yes. No. I...that is to say...bollocks." Flipping his journal to a clean page, he picked up his pen and wrote with such speed the words seemed to blur. "Here," he said, ripping the paper free. "There are supplies I need from a bookshop on the corner. Paper, envelopes, more ink. I've an account with the shopkeeper, you need only give him my name."

"You want me to go *now*?" she asked.

"Do you've a more pressing matter to attend to, Miss Thorncroft?"

"No, it's just that I thought we might discuss the Chamberlain case in more detail." *And find out why you seem relieved that I've never fallen in love,* she added silently.

"Your position does not entail solving cases." He stood up, walked around his desk, and held out the list.

She took it. Their fingers brushed. Heat flared between them, like the strike of a match against flint. With a startled gasp, she looked swiftly up at his face, searching for a sign that Kincaid had felt what she had. But to her overwhelming disappointment, his gaze was shuttered and his emotions were concealed.

A wall of stone would have been able to tell her more about what it was feeling, and she felt a surge of frustration at Kincaid's refusal to reveal even the tiniest hint of desire.

"The bookstore is easy to find," he said in a clipped tone. "Turn left, walk to the end of the street where the large oak tree is, then turn right. It will be on the corner. The white building with blue shutters. The proprietor, Mr. Bingley, is very helpful. He should have everything you need."

As she folded the list and tucked it inside her reticule, it occurred to Joanna, somewhat belatedly, that if Kincaid hadn't experienced a jolt of sensation when their hands had collided, then he'd have nothing to hide. Maybe the very fact that his entire countenance was as empty as his foyer was actually an indication that he had *felt* something.

He was just better at disguising it than she was.

Joanna frowned. Thomas Kincaid presented a problem she'd never faced before. In the past, her suitors had never needed any encouragement. As soon as she had refused one, another had lined up, eager to try for her hand. Truth be told, she had never quite understood her own appeal. But she had also never questioned it, and— eventually—she'd come to take the attention for granted. Which meant she had never developed a key ingredient to any successful courtship: the ability to flirt.

Now here she was, actually *wanting* a man's

attention for once in her life, and Kincaid could not have been more dismissive.

It was all very infuriating.

And confusing.

And *very* inconvenient.

But then…when had she ever let a little inconvenience stop her? She'd sailed across an ocean in search of a stolen ring, for goodness' sake. Surely winning the affection of a bookishly handsome (albeit emotionally aloof) private investigator couldn't be *that* difficult. After all, she was, if nothing else, a problem solver.

And this was just another problem.

"Miss Thorncroft," Kincaid said warily. "What are you *doing*?"

"Testing a theory." Never taking her eyes away from his, she slowly traced a path from his elbow to the blue and purple veins on the inside of his wrist. He wore only a linen shirt with the sleeves rolled partially up, exposing his forearms to her inquisitive fingertips. "I've a very scientific mind, Kincaid. And I have always enjoyed…experiments."

He expelled a ragged breath when she lightly circled her thumb around the throb of his pulse. His pupils dilated, amber eyes darkening to aged cognac. The muscles in his arm tightened, and when he spoke it was not with the tone of a man unaffected by pleasure, but one trying not to drown in it.

184

"This—this is not proper, Miss Thorncroft," he rasped.

A smile teased her lips. "You forget I am an American, Kincaid. We've never been overly fond of British propriety." She lifted his hand and lowered her lashes to conceal the glint of sensual mischief in her gaze as she pressed her lips to the heel of his palm.

A growl tore itself loose from the depths of his throat, and her heart thrummed wildly in response.

She'd never made a man *growl* before.

It was all quite wolfish...and wicked. She was tempted to do more. To *demand* more. But having gotten an irrefutable answer to her question of whether Kincaid felt something for her or not (it was clear that he did), perhaps it was time for a tactful retreat.

"I should go see about that list," she murmured, turning away.

His stare burned a hole in the small of her back as she sauntered out of the room, her uncharacteristically lascivious gait empowered by the passion running hot and heavy through her veins. She closed the door then sagged against it, wondering what she'd started...and how it would end.

CHAPTER TEN

WHEN JOANNA RETURNED from her errand an hour later, Kincaid was gone and his office was empty.

She'd intended to be quicker, but there had been too many books to look at. She could have easily spent half a day browsing through the shelves, particularly since the majority of the novels were by authors unfamiliar to her, but she hadn't wanted to give Kincaid an excuse to fire her off. Despite their undeniable physical attraction, it was obvious her presence unsettled him, and she wouldn't be surprised if he used the tiniest excuse to end their agreement and let her go.

Leaving the items he'd requested in a neat pile beside his desk, she considered poking around, but how would she explain herself if Kincaid suddenly showed up and she was elbow deep in a drawer searching for his inner-most secrets?

Better to curb her curiosity and return to-morrow. At least, that *was* the plan until she saw James on top of the bookshelf. Naturally, she couldn't leave without coaxing him down for a nuzzle. That would just be rude. And when he leapt off the shelf and accidentally knocked over a stack of papers, she couldn't *not* pick them up. And when she saw how woefully disorganized Kincaid's books were, she couldn't *help* but sort them in alphabetical order by title. And when she finished categorizing the books, she couldn't very well leave before she'd cleaned up the rest of the shelves, could she?

"Miss Thorncroft, what the *hell* are you doing up there?"

Joanna froze halfway up the bookshelf. She'd been trying to reach the top, and with no ladder to be found, she had decided to simply climb, arranging things as she went. But it seemed she had lost track of time...and if the sharp bite of annoyance in Kincaid's tone was any indication, he was *not* pleased she was still in his office.

"My job?" she said innocently, swiveling her head. Unfortunately, she'd allowed herself to become distracted by Kincaid's return and the slight movement caused her to lose her balance. The flat soles of her ankle boots slid off the shelf. Her fingers started to slip. With a shriek, she fell backwards…and landed right in Kincaid's arms.

He had moved across the room with light-ning quickness to scoop her out of the air. Cradling her against his chest, he glared down at her, his eyes nearly black with fury.

"You little fool," he snarled, his face inches from her own. "You could have broken your neck! What were you thinking?"

Joanna's heart pounded like a drum inside her chest. "I was only trying to—"

"You will *not* put yourself in peril again!" His grip tightened. "Do you understand me?"

In the blink of an eye, he'd once again trans-formed into the dangerous, deadly rogue she'd first glimpsed in the pleasure gardens. A rogue who wouldn't hesitate to slay the dragon with his bare hands and then rescue the damsel in distress.

Except Joanna was no damsel.

She was the dragon.

And it was time Kincaid tasted some of her fire.

Before she could consider the potentially serious repercussions of her actions, she grabbed a fistful of his shirt to hold herself upright, and dragged his mouth onto hers.

For a moment, he was frozen.

For a moment, everything was still.

Then his arms banded around her, and his lips parted, and the world stopped spinning as everything in it blurred, then came into sharp, stunning focus.

With a possessive snarl that was more animal than man, Kincaid shoved her back against the very same shelf he'd just saved her from. Her skirts bunched as he hitched her legs up over his hips, and she locked her ankles together as he deepened the kiss with a demanding thrust of his tongue.

Books toppled all around them. One grazed Joanna's shoulder. She barely felt it. She barely felt anything except for a wild *pulsing* inside of her that had grown so loud it drowned out the sound of her own heartbeat roaring in her ears.

Heat licked across her body like a flame, burning away everything in its path.

Inhibitions.

Logic.

Self-restraint.

They were all reduced to smoking piles of ash when she arched against Kincaid, clinging to his broad back as her hard nipples scraped against his chest and a damp ache gathered between her thighs.

This was what she'd been missing. *This* was what she'd been craving. *This* was the proof she'd been searching for that passion, real, bone-melting passion, truly existed. Kissing Kincaid, being kissed *by* Kincaid, was like opening her eyes for the first time and seeing a midnight sky filled with shooting stars after a lifetime of empty darkness.

Her nails dug into sinewy muscle as he drew her bottom lip between his teeth. She gasped, the muscles in her belly tightening as he nipped, and then suckled, and then nipped again. Bristle scraped against the edge of her jaw when he lowered his head and skimmed his mouth down her neck, leaving a fiery trail of kisses in his wake. Her head fell back, exposing the slender line of her collarbone and lifting her breasts.

He cupped a heavy globe in the palm of his hand, his thumb strumming across her nipple over the thin fabric of her muslin bodice. A strangled *mewl* spilled from the depths of her throat and her fingers swept across his shoulders to tangle in his hair, sinking into all of that delicious, glossy mahogany as he continued to fondle her.

She would have had their embrace go on forever if she could. But shooting stars only lasted for a moment, and after a final, lingering brush of his lips across hers, Kincaid gently set her down on her feet.

"I…" He cupped the back of his neck, his expression was adorably rueful. Like a boy who had gotten caught with his hand in a jar of sweets. "I apologize, Miss Thorncroft. I do not…I do not know what came over me."

"Mindless lust?" she suggested dazedly.

Goodness.

Joanna had been kissed before. Charles had even touched her left breast, although he'd immediately apologized and turned so red she had feared he was going to suffer an apoplexy. Because of her previous experience, she'd considered herself—if not an expert—at least somewhat well versed in the art of seduction.

What a fool she was!

Her previous encounters had done *nothing* to prepare her for this. Nothing could have. It would be like describing all the colors in the rainbow to a blind person, or the ocean to someone who had never seen a drop of water. Impossible to describe, the fiery desire she'd discovered in Kincaid's arms could only be felt. And once felt, never forgotten.

Nearly a minute since he had ended it and her body was *still* humming with tiny little aftershocks of pleasure. Her nipples were still aroused. The soft, secret place between her thighs still ached. And all this, from a single kiss.

It was mindboggling.

"Lust is one way to describe it," Kincaid agreed. "Still, it is no excuse for the way in which I behaved. I should not have allowed myself to lose control, and I humbly ask that you accept my apology."

Joanna resisted the urge to roll her eyes. He was certainly acting very prim and proper for a man who'd just had his tongue between her lips and his hands all over her breasts. She found she liked the juxtaposition between the rogue who had ravished her and the detective who was—

"Are you *blushing*?" she asked in amazement.

"Absolutely not," he scoffed. "It's just...warm in here."

It *was* warm, she'd give him that.

But the steam in the room had nothing to do with the temperature.

"*I* kissed *you*," she reminded him as she tucked a loose tendril behind her ear. Kincaid had inadvertently loosened several pins during their embrace, and the heavy mass was all but undone. A shake of her head, and it would come tumbling down in a thick spill of auburn curls. "If any blame is to be assigned, I fully accept all of it." She smiled engagingly. "I can apologize to *you*, if you'd like. I've never initiated a kiss. You're my first."

"Don't tell me that," he muttered, his expression pained as he yanked a hand through his hair.

"Tell you what?" she asked. "That you're the first man I've—"

"This is *not* a conversation we are having," he interrupted.

Her brows gathered. "Why not?"

"Because this,"—he gestured between them—"will not happen again."

"Won't it?"

"No," he said emphatically.

She sighed. "That's a pity, as I've already put it on your schedule." Lifting her arm, she mimed writing in the air with a pen. "*Ravish Miss Thorncroft at five o'clock.*"

Kincaid's mouth twitched.

Joanna stared, stunned at what she was seeing.

Was that—was that an actual *smile?*

A trick of the light, she decided when he scowled and stalked across the room to pour himself a glass of water from the pitcher on the windowsill. After quenching his thirst, he turned to face her. A storm cloud on the brink of releasing a torrent of rain and booming thunder would have appeared less ominous.

"*Miss* Thorncroft—"

"*Mr.* Kincaid," she quipped.

"This is not a joke."

"I never said it was." Kneeling, she began to gather the books they'd knocked down during their moment of passion. As good a way as any to describe what had occurred between them, she supposed. And no matter what Kincaid claimed to the contrary, it *was* going to happen again.

Sooner rather than later, if she had anything to say about it.

"Why don't you like me?" Clutching a dictionary to her chest, she sat on her haunches amidst a pool of skirts. "I understand I can be somewhat vexing at times—"

"*Somewhat* vexing?" he said incredulously.

"But we've never argued or spoken unkindly to each other. Why, then, do I find myself the constant recipient of so much…" She searched for the right word. "Antagonism?"

"Miss Thorncroft, all we *do* is argue," he said, leaning back against his desk.

"That's not true," she protested.

He lifted a brow. "We're *literally* arguing right now."

"You're trying to change the subject."

"No, I am trying to avoid the conversation altogether."

She rested her chin on the spine of the dictionary. "Why?"

"Because it's not one we should be having."

"*Why?*"

A muscle ticked in his jaw. "Because you are my employee, *and* my client, and our relationship is already complicated enough. I do not dislike you, Miss Thorncroft. Neither do I like you. I…I feel nothing towards you. As it should be." He crossed his arms. "Which is why these discussions of an intimate nature serve absolutely no purpose."

Joanna slowly rose to her feet as a spark of anger ignited within her belly. Despite their short acquaintance, she'd already come to several conclusions in regards to Kincaid's character. She knew he was cold. Occasionally even callous. But he was also compassionate. Dedicated Protective.

One thing she'd never suspected him of being?

A liar.

"Here." Marching up to him, she more or less threw the dictionary at his chest.

He caught it with a grunt. "What the devil is this for?"

"So you can look up the definition of the word hypocrite!" She whirled around, prepared to dash out in a huff of righteous indignation—if she were on stage, surely it would be an exit worthy of a standing ovation—but Kincaid spoiled her theatrical debut when he grabbed her around the waist and spun her towards him.

Their bodies collided.

Their eyes flashed.

First with warning…

…and then in recognition of the inevitable.

"Damn you," Kincaid growled as he pushed his fingers into her hair and tilted her head back. Free of its coiffure, her wild mane tumbled over his hands in a waterfall of red silk. He cursed again while her breath quickened in anticipation. "I don't want this."

"Hypocrite," she whispered.

He kissed her.

No, Joanna registered with a small stirring of alarm as he nipped her bottom lip with his teeth and then soothed the bite with his tongue.

Kincaid wasn't kissing her. He was *possessing* her. With a fierce, nearly carnal hunger that left her gasping for air when he wrenched free of her lips, cleared his desk of papers with a violent sweep of his arm, and sat her in the middle of it.

She clung to his neck as he stepped between her legs, anchored his arms on either side of her trembling body, and proceeded to devour her mouth like a man starved. He took her lips as though they belonged to him, as though *she* belonged to him and, for once in her life, Joanna was more than happy to relinquish control.

Her head rolled limply to the side when he kissed her neck. He suckled at the deliciously sensitive juncture between her throat and collarbone, and she gasped when he went even lower, tugging her bodice down with one hand while the other cupped the underside of her breast…and raised its dusky center to his mouth.

Lust. Passion. Arousal.

Joanna had not understood their true meaning before this. Before she found herself sprawled on a man's desk, her thighs wantonly splayed apart and her pupils dilated with desire, while a man teased her nipple through her cotton undergarments.

With his tongue.

She whimpered when Kincaid moved to her other breast; a tiny, mewling sound that only seemed to inflame his ardor. He kissed his way down her ribcage, peeling her gown off as he went. It bunched at her wrists and her waist, and his snarl of frustration made her smile.

"How do you get this bloody thing off?" he demanded, tugging at her corset.

Joanna shook her head regretfully. "I wish I knew."

He took off his spectacles and tossed them carelessly on the desk. They skidded across and dropped to the floor, but he didn't even seem to notice. He was too intent of ridding her of anything that separated his lips from her flesh, and she jumped when he grabbed her corset by its seams and quite simply ripped it apart.

The boning had left faint red lines in a vertical row around her torso. Anger darkened Kincaid's countenance when he saw the marks the corset had left. She quivered when he traced them first with his fingertips and then with his mouth, following a line all the way down to the jut of her hipbone.

"Never wear one of those again," he said, glaring at the torn corset which now laid in a sad crumple at her feet. "Such beauty doesn't deserve to be contained."

"All right." Resisting the primitive urge to cover herself, she lifted her chin instead, bravely exposing every inch of her naked bosom to Kincaid's gaze as he turned his head. "I won't."

The detective swallowed.

Audibly.

"Beauty," he repeated, his voice little more than a rasp.

Joanna closed her eyes and arched her spine away from the desk when he cupped her breasts, his thumbs circling round her nipples until they were hard and aching and all but begging to be licked.

Kincaid obliged, leisurely suckling one swollen peak and then the other. Soon, her entire body was as taut as a bowstring and she feared she might explode. There was a...a *tension* rising within her. Unlike anything she'd ever encountered before. The tension only increased when his hand slipped beneath her skirts and found the inside of her leg.

Her drawers were loosely fitted, allowing more than enough room for his fingers to glide up to the juncture of her thighs. He paused just shy of touching the curls that nestled there and met her gaze. His amber eyes gleamed with a wolfish intensity, and she understood the question he was asking before he could form the sentence.

"Yes," she whimpered, shamelessly rubbing herself against the hand beneath her dress when he rolled her nipple between his thumb and finger. "Oh, *yes*."

He kissed her.

Stroking her above the waist and below, he

kissed her.

Slowly at first, so slowly she nearly stomped her foot in frustration, and then the tempo increased as his tongue stole boldly between her lips and his finger stroked the small nub buried between her slick folds from which all of that delicious tension was radiating.

Faster, and faster, and faster he pleasured her. She writhed on the desk, her hips instinctively rising to meet his hand as she returned his kiss with a desperate enthusiasm.

Almost, she wanted to beg. *Almost*.

She didn't understand what she was reaching towards, only that Kincaid was bringing her closer and closer to it with every wicked flick of his wrist. Her nails streaked up and over his shoulders, unconsciously urging him on as she rode his hand with all the wild abandon of some dockside hussy.

Then, a final stroke.

The peak.

A guttural noise rose from the depths of Kincaid's throat as she clamped her thighs around his hand and cried out. Her head fell back, her arms went limp. If it was possible, she could have sworn her heart stopped as well. At the very least, it stuttered.

And why wouldn't it? She'd just touched lightning. Had been touched *by* lightning. Surely that was the only comparable explanation of what had occurred. Of what Kincaid had done to her. Of what he'd done *for* her. He had taken passion, wrapped it in a pretty box, added a bow, and given it to her. A gift she hadn't expected, but one which she was exceedingly pleased to have received.

Much more practical than flowers and sweet candies.

Her eyes were still squeezed shut. She opened them to see Kincaid was still hovering above her. His gaze was unreadable, his nostrils flared. A thin sheen of perspiration gleamed high on his brow and his hair was in disarray. Reaching out, she tucked a piece behind his ear. For an instant, he leaned into her embrace. For an instant, she held the weight of his heart in the palm of her hand. Then he stiffened, and pulled back.

"Miss Thorncroft—"

"I am sitting on your desk half-naked with my skirts above my knees," she interrupted. "Surely we can dispel with the formalities."

Other women in her position may have felt self-conscious. Embarrassed. Perhaps even a little ashamed. But Joanna did not find any shame in what she'd done with Kincaid. Quite the opposite, in fact.

She felt liberated.

She felt empowered.

She also felt a slight chill.

"Would you mind?" she asked, turning her back towards Kincaid so that he could assist in helping her redress. There was no saving the corset, but after a few tugs and adjusting a button here and there, she managed without it. Her hair was another matter. Tangled beyond repair, the best she could manage was shoving it behind her shoulders.

"I'll make certain to wear my hat when I leave." Her lips, swollen from his kisses, twitched at the corners. "Wouldn't want the neighbors gossiping if they saw the state of my coiffure."

His mouth flattened. "Miss Thorncroft—"

"Joanna," she said. "Call me Joanna."

Something flickered in the depths of his amber gaze. "That would be unprofessional."

She snorted. She couldn't help it. "If using my Christian name is unprofessional, what would you call...well..."—she pointed at the desk—"*that*?"

"A mistake," he said flatly.

Now it was Joanna who stiffened. "A mistake?" she repeated. "Kissing me was a *mistake*?"

He grimaced. "That's not what I...that's not what I meant."

"By all means, please enlighten me, then." Kneeling, she began to collect the papers that had been knocked to the floor. Her fingers brushed against the ear loop of his spectacles. Wordlessly, she picked them up and extended her arm above her head.

"Thank you." Kincaid took the spectacles. He was quiet for a few seconds before he said, "I'm afraid this isn't the first time I've had…feelings for a client."

"You've feelings for me?" Jumping on his choice of words like a cat on a poor, unsuspecting mouse, Joanna gathered the stack of papers and leapt to her feet. "What sort of feelings?" she asked as her pulse fluttered.

This was what she'd been waiting for. Kincaid to actually *express* his emotions instead of concealing them behind that damned stone wall. Who knew all it would take was a bit of heavy fondling? Heavens, had she known *that* she might have been tempted to kiss him the first day she walked into his office! It certainly would have saved them both some time, and she quivered when she thought of all the climaxes—was that the right word for it? She thought that was the right word for it—she could have had between then and now.

Unfortunately, her newfound hope quickly withered like a flower denied rain when she saw the expression upon Kincaid's countenance.

"You're a truly lovely woman, Miss Thorncroft," he began.

"Oh, dear," she mumbled. Nothing, in the history of all humankind, had ever gone well after a sentence began with "you're a truly lovely woman".

"But—"

"Here it comes," she sighed.

"I would kindly ask you to forget this ever happened."

Joanna stared blankly at him. "You want me to *forget* you had your hand on my—"

"Yes," he said hastily. "Yes, that's precisely what I want you to do."

"I was going to say shoulder."

His eyebrow raised. "Of course. Because Americans are known for their *propriety*."

A valid point.

Biting on the inside of her cheek, she placed the papers on his desk, then pivoted to face him, her gaze (and her heart) troubled. "I must be honest. I don't know if I *can* forget."

"You must try, or else..."

"Or else?" she said softly.

"Or else I would advise you to find another private investigator, Miss Thorncroft."

He wouldn't dare.

Except he would, and they both knew it.

"You can still call me Joanna," she offered. "If you'd like."

His jaw clenched. "I don't believe that would be wise, Miss Thorncroft."

Oh, for heaven's sake. It was just a name. Except it wasn't.

And they both knew it.

Her name was a barrier. One of the last that stood between them and...well, more of what had happened on the desk.

Joanna would have liked more.

She would have liked more very much.

But it was clear that while Kincaid had enjoyed himself (he *had* enjoyed himself, hadn't he?), there was no interest in a repeat performance.

"All right," she conceded. "I shall endeavor to do as you've requested and forget this ever happened. Except...why can't we enjoy each other's company? We are both adults."

Heat flared in his gaze. "Are you asking for an affair, Miss Thorncroft?"

"No." *Maybe.* Her hands gathered in the folds of her skirts. She tucked her thumbs in, nail digging ever-so-slightly into her the soft flesh of her palms. "Unless *you* wanted—"

"I do not," he said shortly.

Well, then.

That was blunt, wasn't it?

Except it was an answer, not a reason. And surely, surely there had to be a reason. Because they *did* enjoy each other's company. And they *were* both adults. And...why not? She wasn't married. Neither was Kincaid. He also didn't have a mistress, at least one that she knew about. From what she'd witnessed thus far, the detective was wedded to his work. Everything else came secondary, which was to be expected, she assumed, given the long hours his line of employment required. But surely his job did not exclude him from *all* pleasures.

Joanna knew it was wicked of her to want what she did.

But she also refused to believe it was wrong.

"I have a private meeting in half an hour." Kincaid gathered her hat and gloves. A not-terribly-subtle hint that it was time for her to leave. He ushered her to the door but she balked at the threshold, refusing to be dismissed so easily as that.

"Why?" Her lashes swept across the tops of her cheeks as she glanced down, then back up, her brow creased in confusion. "Is it me? Have I done something?"

"You're my client," he said, as if that explained everything.

"And?" she persisted.

"And only a fool steps back into the fire after they've already been burned. Good day, Miss Thorncroft." Without further explanation, he shoved her into the foyer, closed the door…and locked it.

"GO AWAY," KINCAID growled when he felt a

nudge against his legs. "I'm not speaking to you."

Baring his tiny, white fangs, James gave a loud hiss before he leapt onto a chair and swatted at his master's hand.

"Bloody hell!" Kincaid swore when he felt a sharp stab of pain and saw four bright red claw marks across his knuckles. "What the devil was that for?"

The cat's tail swished through the air.

"Don't look at me like that."

James hissed again.

"It's not as if I *planned* for this to happen." Scowling, Kincaid began to pick up the books that were scattered across the floor. "I did the only thing I could do," he muttered, more to himself than to the cat, never mind that there didn't really need to be a distinction because it was a *cat*.

From the chair came the sound of a sniff that could only be described as disdainful.

Kincaid glared at James over his shoulder. "What? You think I should have an affair with her, don't you? An affair with an American. Bollocks on that." He slammed two books together. "It'd be like standing naked in the middle of a thunderstorm with an iron rod while I waited for lightning to strike me down."

But damned if the shock—and the resulting electrocution—wouldn't be worth it.

He meant what he'd said. He hadn't intended to kiss Joanna. In fact, it was the last thing he had wanted to do. But then *she* had kissed him. And once he tasted her lips…once he tasted her lips, he knew he'd never find anything else on earth so sweet no matter if he scoured the four corners.

Holding her in his arms had been like holding the sun. The sheer brightness of her passion had blinded him. Her lack of inhibitions had stunned him. The mewling noise she'd made when she came against his hand had undone him.

It was a wonder he'd stopped when he did.

It was a miracle he hadn't started where he'd left off when she suggested they have an affair.

A bloody *affair*.

The woman was out of her mind. And he was just as equally crazed, because for a fleeting moment…he'd actually considered it.

"Sleep," he muttered to himself as he returned the last book to the shelf. When was the last time his head had spent more than a few hours on his pillow? Not since the day a bold, brazen, red-haired hellion had darkened his door. He needed to sleep, and then he needed to eat, and then he needed to pretend this afternoon had never happened.

He only prayed Joanna would do the same.

Because if she tested his restraint…

James released a loud *meow*.

Kincaid looked at the cat. If he didn't know any better, he could have sworn his pet was smirking at him. "I can still throw you out, you damned bag of fleas," he threatened. "You think you're tough now. You wouldn't last a damned minute on the streets. A rat would eat you for dinner."

After a cool staring match, the cat lifted his hind leg and began to lick himself.

It was, to Kincaid's memory, the clearest "fuck you" he'd ever received.

"Sod off." Kicking off his boots, he headed upstairs.

CHAPTER ELEVEN

"WHAT DO YOU do when a man ignores you?" Joanna asked Evie. She sat on the edge of the sill in their shared room, a warm evening breeze tickling the curls at the nape of her neck. A heavy rain had fallen for most of the day. It had finally subsided after supper and she'd taken the opportunity to pry open a window. The wood had creaked in protest as if it hadn't been moved in a long while but, eventually, it had given way.

With enough effort, Joanna found most things usually did.

"I don't understand the question," Evie replied without bothering to look up from the game of solitaire she was playing by candlelight in the middle of the bed.

Joanna pursed her lips.

Three days had passed since the thing she'd

been ordered to forget had occurred in Kincaid's office. Three days of him barely talking to her, hardly looking at her, and definitely *not* kissing her.

It was as if their moment of passion—make that *moments* of passion—had never happened. And she knew that had been his intention. To pretend he'd never stroked her to orgasm atop his desk. But she'd had no way of knowing he would actually go *through* with it.

Gone was the man who licked her in places that still brought a blush to her cheeks whenever she thought of them. To her immense frustration, he was as cold and standoffish as he'd been the morning they'd first met.

Oh, he was unfailingly polite. Annoyingly dignified, even. But aside from a few questions about her mother, Kincaid refused to interact, leaving her to organize his shelves and sort his paperwork while he worked silently behind the desk he'd ravished her upon.

She was at her wit's end trying to make him notice her. Multiple times, she'd caught him staring, his hot gaze skittering across her skin like the lick of a flame. But as soon as she looked up, he scowled and looked away, a pulsing vein in his temple the only indication he wasn't as immune to her presence as he'd like her to believe.

"Men are complicated," she muttered, sliding off the sill to pace across the room. Her shadow painted a silhouette of a woman in a flowing nightdress, hair hanging in a thick braid down the middle of her back, narrow shoulders rigid with annoyance.

"Men are simple," said Evie, still studying her cards. "You've just never met one who didn't fall in love at first sight."

Joanna's mouth opened.

Closed.

"That's not true," she argued, but even to her own ears her protest lacked conviction.

"It is." Evie tapped a card against her chin. "For reasons that honestly escape me, you've been pursued since you turned sixteen. How many engagements have you turned down?"

"I…" Joanna trailed off as a guilty flush crept into her cheeks. It was shameful to admit, but she didn't have an answer. How could she *not* know how many wedding proposals she'd received? Maybe because they'd never seemed very meaningful.

A few carriage rides, a walk through the field, and then suddenly her suitor dropped down on bended knee and professed his undying love. Except they *didn't* love her. Not really. And not a single one had ever made her feel even a whisper of what Kincaid had.

"Six?" she guessed, nibbling her thumbnail.

"Eight, if you include Charles Gaines."

"It hasn't been *that* many."

"Eight," her sister repeated. "Eight perfectly acceptable suitors have asked you to marry them, and you refused every single one. Now, for the first time, you're taken with someone—I'll refrain from saying I told you so, but, well, I *did* tell you so—and he is not interested."

Joanna tucked her hands behind her back. "I don't know if I'd say he's not *interested*."

"Oh?" Evie queried. "Did something happen?"

Ordinarily, Joanna shared everything with her siblings, and they with her. But she hadn't shared her kiss with Kincaid. She didn't know why, exactly. Only that it seemed…private. A secret to be kept between the two of them. Which made her feel guilty, because the only reason she was in England to begin with was because a secret had been kept from *her*. But she simply wasn't ready to tell Evie the truth. Especially since she was still figuring out what the truth meant for herself.

"Not…exactly. I told you what he said to me the night we went searching for you at the pleasure gardens."

"That he wouldn't have to ask permission when he wanted to kiss you." A sly smile stole across Evie's lips. "Yes, I remember. The scoundrel."

Kincaid was, indeed, a scoundrel.

At least, part of him was.

A part Joanna had been desperately missing these past three days.

"I thought...after that....he might..." Her shoulder lifted in a shrug. "You know."

"Admit he cannot live another second of his life without you?" Evie suggested.

Joanna rolled her eyes. "Not exactly."

"It's called rejection." Finally ending her game of solitaire, Evie swung her legs over the edge of the bed and regarded her sister with an air of sympathy. "I've never experienced it myself, naturally. But I imagine it isn't very pleasant."

Rejection?

Was that what this heavy knot of emotion was in the pit of Joanna's throat? It tasted bittersweet, like the dandelion tea her grandmother forced her to drink whenever she was starting to come down with a cold.

"No," she said quietly. "It isn't very pleasant."

"Do you want to marry Kincaid?"

"What? *No*," said Joanna emphatically even as her flush deepened. Pressing her hands to her cheeks, she willed the warmth to subside. Marry Thomas Kincaid? She didn't want to marry him. The idea had never even crossed her mind. All right, maybe once. Or twice. Three times at the most. But she had never considered it *seriously*.

"Do not be ridiculous," she scoffed. "I just..."

"Want his tongue to hit the floor when he looks at you?"

"Maybe not the floor. But a chair would suffice." As her blush faded, she dropped her arms with a sigh. "At this rate, I'd even settle for a bookshelf."

"Thorncroft women do *not* settle," Evie declared. "If Kincaid is too foolish to see how wonderful you are then surely that is his problem, not yours. Chin up, sweeting. Soon, we'll find Mother's ring and be on our way back to Boston. Then this will all be nothing but a distant memory." Her nose wrinkled. "The number of eligible dukes in London has been *greatly* exaggerated. I've yet to meet a single one under the age of sixty."

"Have you tried looking in trees?" Joanna said innocently.

"Don't make me throw another pillow at you."

With another sigh, Joanna flung herself onto the bed with the sort of dramatic flair usually employed by Evie. "I just don't know what to do."

Carrying a candle to the mirror above the dressing table, Evie held the light up and inspected her reflection with a critical eye. "It rains far too much here. Does my skin appear sallow to you?"

"*Evie!*" Glaring, Joanna sat up on her elbows. "This is important."

"So is my complexion. All right, all right,"

Evie said when Joanna inhaled sharply. She set the candle aside and met her sister's gaze. "You want this detective's attention, and he isn't giving it to you. Is that the crux of the matter?"

"Well, when you put it like *that*, it doesn't sound very important."

"Matters of the heart always take precedence over practical feelings." Evie paused. "Did I make that up, or read it in a book? Regardless, do you even have a plan for what you are going to do with Kincaid's attention once you have it? You said you had no intention of marrying him."

"I don't know if I have *no* intention." She nibbled her bottom lip. "Anything is possible, I suppose."

"But you wouldn't *seriously* consider it," Evie said with a tittering laugh.

Joanna sat up. "Why not?"

"Because he isn't even titled."

"Neither is Charles Gaines."

"Yes, but titles don't matter in America."

"I am not going to be in England forever."

"You will if you marry an Englishman."

"What about an affair, then?" Joanna asked.

Evie stared at her. "Now I *know* you're jesting."

As a flicker of excitement stirred within her breast, Joanna stood up and began to pace the room. "What if I wasn't? Kincaid may not be acknowledging it at the moment, but there is an undeniable spark of attraction between us." *To put it mildly.* "Affairs are very common in this day and age." As the idea took root, her excitement grew. "We would be discreet."

"Absolutely not!" Evie cried.

Joanna stopped in front of the window. "Why?"

"Should I list the reasons? Fine." Extending her arm, Evie began tick off her fingers one by one. "You will ruin your reputation."

"Only if we're caught."

"You'll ruin yourself for marriage!"

"That is an antiquated notion based on the idea that virginity holds some sort of monetary value," Joanna said dismissively. "I should think a husband would prefer his wife to have a little experience."

Evie threw up her hands. "There's no reasoning with you."

"Because you do not have a valid counterargument."

"You need to learn to curb your impulsivity." A black curl slid across Evie's temple as she shook her head in exasperation. "It always leads to nothing but trouble."

Joanna leaned against the sill and set her jaw. "I'm not impulsive."

"Not impulsive?" said Evie incredulously. "*You* were the one who wanted to sell Mother's ring instead of marrying someone who was perfectly practical in every way. Then you dragged us halfway across the world on a moment's notice! You're constantly throwing yourself into situations without thinking of the consequences, and Kincaid is no different. How could you possibly even *think* of having an affair? Let alone an affair with a complete stranger!"

"Kincaid isn't a stranger." Joanna may not have known his secrets. But she *did* know the taste of his mouth. The feel of his hand skimming across her bare flesh. The weight of his body pressing against hers. "And Charles may have been suitable, but he wasn't suitable for *me*."

"And a detective is?"

"Maybe. Maybe not." She tapped a finger against her chin. "But I think I'd like to find out."

THE PICKLED PIG was dark, dingy, and reeked of cheap ale and piss. In short, it was the perfect meeting place for a man who didn't want to be noticed. Which the Duke of Hanover most decidedly did not.

Sterling entered the pub with his hat pulled low over his brow and a stern frown bracketing the edges of his mouth. Waving off a whore's lewd attempt at solicitation, he quickly located who he was meeting at a table in the corner blanketed by shadows.

"Bloody hell," he complained as he took off his coat and sank down into a wooden chair that was stained with beer and God only knew what else. "It stinks in here."

Kincaid looked up from the potato stew he'd been mindlessly shoveling into his mouth. "You said you needed somewhere discreet."

"The Ivy Bridge in Hyde Park is discreet. Cremorne Gardens after dark is discreet." Sterling watched dubiously as a barmaid carrying ale to a nearby table paused, tilted the pitcher to her lips, and took a long drink. "This is unsanitary."

Kincaid's lips stretched in the ghost of a smile. "Spoken like a true aristocrat."

"Regarding the pleasure gardens, you haven't been there lately by any chance, have you?"

"Why do you ask?" he said guardedly.

"It seems the Duke of Telford had an unfortunate run-in with an American chit and her protector. Ended up with a broken nose. Messy affair." Sterling cocked a brow. "Not that I blame whoever set Telford back on his heels. Bloke's a right twat. In fact, if I knew who it was, I'd buy him a drink. Your cup's looking a little empty there, Kincaid."

"I have no idea who punched Telford, if that's what you are asking." Lifting his tankard of ale, Kincaid finished it off then nudged it to the edge of the table. "But I'll take another."

"You sly bastard," Sterling grinned. "Things must be going well with your American if you're taking her to Cremorne."

Kincaid tensed. "She isn't *my* American."

"Whatever you have to tell yourself." Sterling gave an amiable shrug. Then his expression turned horrified. "Good God. That barmaid just dropped an entire pork leg on the floor and put it back on the plate."

"You wanted to meet somewhere you wouldn't be recognized," Kincaid reminded his friend.

"What I *want* is to not get typhoid." His gray eyes hardened. "And to clear my name. Have you any leads on who might have killed Eloise?"

When Sterling had first revealed he stood accused of murdering his mistress, Kincaid had been understandably shocked. Despite his tragic past—or perhaps because of it—Sterling could no more harm a woman than he could a fly.

Let alone bludgeon her to death in her own bedchamber.

But if the growing rumors in the *ton* were to be believed, that was precisely what he had done. Then he'd dismembered the body and dumped it in the Thames. Or buried it on the grounds of his estate in Sussex. Or left it out in the woods to be devoured by wild animals. The exact details varied depending on who was telling the story. But while no one could reach a general consensus on how Eloise's body had mysteriously disappeared, they all agreed on a single fact: the Duke of Hanover was a murderer.

And now it was Kincaid's job to prove he wasn't.

Since the House of Lords wasn't yet in session, no official charges had been brought, and that gave them some time. Had Sterling stood accused of anything besides murder, parliamentary privilege would have exonerated him. Unfortunately, it did not apply in this case. If Kincaid couldn't track down the *real* murderer, it was only a matter of weeks before Sterling would be arrested and put on trial before a jury of his peers.

"No, I haven't found anything yet. But that doesn't mean I won't," he said when Sterling muttered a curse and slumped back in his chair. "It's been less than a week."

A week that felt like a bloody year.

Ever since Miss Joanna Thorncroft had marched into his office and demanded Kincaid take her case, the hours had started to blur together. It wasn't long before he didn't know yesterday from tomorrow or the past from the present.

Her arrival had dredged up all sorts of things—emotions, feelings, memories—long believed forgotten. Things he didn't want to remember. Things he'd locked in a box before tossing the box into the deepest, darkest pit of his mind where it had remained...until Joanna showed up holding a key.

Joanna, with her eyes the color of the sky right before the last autumn leaf fell. Joanna, with her sharp wit and mischievous smile. Joanna, with her soft lips and skin that smelled of sunshine and violets.

Kincaid stirred his stew. Chunks of meat were beginning to congeal on the surface. He wasn't necessarily hungry, but he could not remember the last time he'd eaten. And while it was tempting, a man couldn't survive on passionate kisses alone. Particularly when he had banned himself from said kisses.

Being in the same room as Joanna these past three days had been pure, unadulterated torture. He was like a starving orphan with his face pressed to the window of a sweets shop. He could see the chocolate. He could almost taste it. But he couldn't have it. He couldn't have *her*. Even though all he wanted to do was drag her head back until those cornflower blue eyes saw him, only him, and then he wanted to kiss her again until the stars in the sky burned to ash.

"You seem distracted, old chap," Sterling commented.

Kincaid dropped his spoon and lifted his gaze. "Why do you say that?"

"Because I've asked you the same question

three times and you haven't responded." The duke leaned forward and rested his elbows on the table. "If you do not believe there is a way to prove my innocence, best tell me now. I'd rather hear it from you than the damned magistrate."

"No, it's not that. It's…bollocks." Kincaid gave a short, irritated shake of his head. He should have been focusing exclusively on Sterling's case. A case that was literally a matter of life and death.

Instead, he was dreaming about Joanna like some sort of lovesick fool. Had he learned *nothing* from Lavinia? The evil bitch who had gleefully torn his heart out of his chest, ripped it in half, and then shoved the bleeding organ back inside. He'd sworn he would never again blur the lines between his personal and professional life. Yet here he was, four years later, on the brink of doing precisely that.

Wasn't that the definition of madness? Doing the same thing over and over again while expecting a different result. Best lock himself up in bedlam now, for surely an insane asylum would be preferable to peeling the scars off his heart and exposing it to even more hurt. The kind of hurt he never wanted to feel again.

"It's nothing," he snapped. "She means nothing."

Sterling's brows lifted with interest. "*She?* You mean your American?"

"I told you that she isn't my American." He needed a drink. Throwing his hand in the air, he managed to snag the attention of a barmaid and held up two fingers. She sauntered over, a curvy brunette with an ample bosom. While Sterling openly admired the view—and gave the maid a light smack on her bottom as she walked away—Kincaid took a long, quenching drink.

"I take it back," said Sterling. "A dash of typhoid might be worth it."

"I'm sure she'd be willing to entertain any offer you made."

Instead of appearing pleased by the reminder that he could have whatever woman he desired, the duke looked oddly dejected. "They always are. But it's the title they want, not me. I know that's what Eloise wanted."

"Which is why you killed her," said Kincaid, carefully watching Sterling to gauge his reaction.

The duke was innocent, but that wouldn't matter if he displayed even a hint of guilt over his mistress' death. Thankfully, Sterling's expression did not waver, an indication he would do well under questioning…if it came to that.

"That's what they tell me." Sterling sipped his ale. "Does your American know that you fancy her?"

"For the last time," Kincaid said through gritted teeth, "she isn't mine. And I don't fancy anyone."

"Really? Because I haven't seen you this worked up since...never mind." Realizing his error a second too late, Sterling immediately stopped talking. But the damage had already been done, and they both knew what name he hadn't said.

"Lady Lavinia Townsend." A muscle ticked high in Kincaid's jaw.

"May her adulterous, lying soul rot in hell."

"She isn't dead."

"I know, I saw her just this past week at the Earl of Whitefield's garden party. I didn't want to mention it," Sterling said apologetically, "seeing as how you two...well, parted ways."

Parted ways.

How pleasant that made it sound.

Rather like calling the Black Death a mild cough, or Marie Antoinette's beheading a little nick.

He and Lavinia hadn't *parted ways*.

They'd scorched the damned earth.

And then she'd tried to bury him in it.

"When the witch finally does die," Sterling continued, "I can assure you there is only one direction she is traveling. And it's not up."

Kincaid's mouth twitched. He appreciated his friend's loyalty more than he could put into words. Society dictated the duke should have sided with Lavinia. She was, after all, the well-bred daughter of a marquess and the wife of one of Sterling's acquaintances. They'd run in the same circles since they were children. But Sterling had always made it clear where his allegiances lay, and Kincaid was grateful for it. Especially since he knew others did not look upon him so kindly.

Courtesy of Lavinia's lies and calculated deceit, his first year as a private investigator had almost been his last. Clients who had been with him since his first days as a peeler had suddenly acted as if he'd caught the plague, their minds poisoned against him by Lavinia's uncanny ability to spin fiction into fact. If not for sheer persistence and a little luck, he'd have gone belly up within six months. And he would have had no one to blame but himself for being gullible enough to fall for Lavinia's crocodile tears.

He was still deeply ashamed of how easily she'd been able to manipulate him. She hadn't only pulled the wool over his eyes. She'd changed him into a bloody sheep, and he hated her for it. He hated *himself* for it. Which was why he was determined that history was not going to repeat itself.

"If anyone has a pact with the devil, it's Lavinia." He drank his ale. "I never should have believed a word she told me."

"No," Sterling agreed. "You shouldn't have. But you're not the first man she deceived, and I'm certain you will not be the last. It's a bloody game to her. To all of them. The *ton*." Storm clouds gathered in his gaze. "There's nothing they delight in more than ruining reputations and spinning half-truths. It is their entertainment."

"You're a duke," Kincaid pointed out. "One could argue you are the very personification of that which you despise."

"One could also argue that you are deliberately trying to steer the topic of conversation away from your new client." Sterling leaned back in his chair, arms casually draped behind his neck. "Is she attractive, this American who isn't your American? A change of scenery could be a welcome distraction."

If Kincaid were a wolf, his hackles would have stood straight up. "She's not interested."

"Every woman is interested in a duke. It sort of comes with the territory."

"Not Joanna."

"On a first name basis, are we?" Gray eyes holding a glint of amusement, Sterling lowered his arms and took a casual sip of ale. "I thought you didn't fancy her."

"I don't," Kincaid said shortly. "But that doesn't mean you get to."

As far as he was concerned, no one did. Joanna wasn't his. He didn't claim her. He didn't want her. But neither could anyone else have her. If they tried, he'd kill them. Including Sterling. It was as simple—and bloody complicated—as that.

Scowling, he reached for his ale. Only to grunt in annoyance when he realized he'd already finished it off.

"Here," Sterling said, sliding his tankard across the table. "Have mine, although I don't know how you drink the stuff. Tastes like lukewarm piss."

"I've had worse."

"That's troubling. Speaking of piss, I'll be right back."

While Sterling went to relieve himself, Kincaid finished off the remainder of the ale and considered his soup, but the talk of Lavinia had soured his stomach.

She was a dark spot he couldn't scrub out. A stain he couldn't erase. A blemish he couldn't fix. If only he'd never met her. Never tried to help her. Never fallen in love.

In a way, however, he supposed it was good that he had. The consequences of his affair had taught him a valuable lesson. A difficult lesson, but a valuable one nevertheless. Because of Lavinia, he knew how easily a man could be destroyed from the inside. Because of Lavinia, he knew the sharp, slicing pain of betrayal. Because of Lavinia, he knew he could never give the broken shards of his heart away. Not even to Joanna. Which was why he had been trying his damned best to ignore her.

And failing miserably.

A man could no more ignore Joanna Thorn-croft than he could his next breath. A single kiss, and he craved her lips as much as he craved oxygen to breathe. He wanted her. He *needed* her. Which was exactly why he couldn't have her.

Need was an opportunity for exploitation.

Need was a vulnerability.

Need was a weakness.

And he'd made himself a promise. A promise that he would never be vulnerable or weak ever again. A promise that he intended to keep…no matter how strong the temptation was to break it.

He rubbed the sides of his temples where a dull ache had settled. The only solution, as he saw it, was to find Joanna's ring and get her the hell out of England. With an ocean between them, maybe he'd finally be able to stop thinking about her every bloody second of every bloody day. Because he couldn't go on like this.

Not unless he wanted to drive himself completely mad.

When Sterling returned, complaining of the ungodly stench radiating from the water closet, Kincaid's eyes narrowed thoughtfully.

Despite his best efforts, he hadn't yet made any headway on tracking down the ring or the man who had given it to Anne Thorncroft. The *Queen Mary's* manifest hadn't given him any clues, nor had his usual connections turned anything up. But his connections only extended so far, and given the ring's presumed origin, it may have simply been that it was in the hands of someone too far above his reach.

"I may need your help with something," he told Sterling. "A case."

"A case?" Visibly intrigued, the duke slid into his chair. "What sort of case?"

"The one that brought Joanna Thorncroft and her sister here."

"There's a sister?"

"No."

"But I haven't even—"

"*No*," Kincaid said firmly.

"All right," Sterling muttered. "What can I do?"

In short order, Kincaid explained the ring's history. How Joanna's mother had traveled to England when she was a young woman, and had an affair with a man who then gave her the priceless ruby before she'd returned to America and married Jacob Thorncroft.

"Wait," Sterling interrupted. "Then Joanna is really the illegitimate daughter of a British nobleman?"

Kincaid gave a clipped nod. "Yes. Given the ring's value, that is my working theory. I believe it is an heirloom that the family never had any plan of giving up or else they wouldn't have gone to such pains to retrieve it after more than two decades."

"Fascinating," said Sterling. "Absolutely fascinating. But you've had no leads?"

"None."

"Hmm."

"What is it?"

"I just find it interesting that you've hit such a wall when ordinarily you're quite good at all this detective business." Sterling drummed his fingers on the edge of the table. "Is it because you've genuinely exhausted all possibilities, or you secretly want your American to remain in London for as long as possible?"

"If you call her that again, I'm going to pick up this tankard and bash you over the head with it," Kincaid threatened.

Sterling clucked his tongue. "Striking one duke is an isolated incident, but striking two is the beginning of a pattern. Should I tell the Duke of Avalon to be on the lookout?"

"That depends."

"On?"

"If he's as big of an arse as you."

There weren't many people in London, or all of Great Britain, for that matter, who would dare deliver such an insult to a man of Sterling's station. But he didn't appear insulted. If anything, he looked amused.

"That's a crown I wear alone, I'm afraid."

"If I could find the ring and send Joanna

home on the next ship bound for Boston, I'd do it in a heartbeat." Maybe if he said it out loud, Kincaid thought, it would make it true. "But if the ring is being held by a family of great means, I haven't the resources to root it out."

"Which is where I come in, I suppose." A dark wave of hair slid across Sterling's brow as his head canted to the side. "A ruby in the shape of a heart, you said?"

"Surrounded by diamonds."

"It should be unusual enough to stand out. And the initials inscribed on the band?"

"JW."

"That narrows it down some."

"But not enough," said Kincaid.

"No," Sterling concurred. "Not enough. If only the name James wasn't so damned popular. And the W could refer to either a surname or a title."

Kincaid had come to the same deduction. "Short of stealing into every manor in Grosvenor Square under the cover of darkness, I've no way to ascertain the ring's whereabouts. But you rub elbows with the *ton* every day."

"Don't remind me," Sterling grimaced. "As it happens, there's a ball coming up at the end of the week. A prestigious affair to celebrate the Countess of Beresford's seventieth birthday. Her gout has rendered her unable to travel, which means the *ton* will be flocking in en masse from their country estates. I can get you in invitation, if you'd like."

Kincaid's gaze sharpened behind his spectacles. "It's expected to be well attended?"

"Everyone who is anyone will be there," the duke confirmed.

Which meant that Kincaid might not get a better opportunity to discover the identity of the elusive JW and the whereabouts of the ring before the London Season resumed in January. Five months from now. His teeth gnashed together. He couldn't have Joanna here for five more months. He didn't even want her here for five more *days*. His self-control was already hanging by a thread. Another encounter like the one in his office, and it would snap entirely.

Then all hell would break loose.

Sweet, sweet hell.

The kind a man wouldn't mind burning in.

"I'll take that invitation." Pushing his chair back, he rose to his feet and reached for his coat. "I need this finished."

Sterling stood as well. "What is it about this American that you dislike so much?"

Kincaid shoved his hands into his pockets where they curled into fists. "She's far too impetuous."

"And that's a bad thing?"

"It is when you lack the common sense to avoid danger."

"Ah." Sterling nodded in understanding. "The poor thing's a bit daft, is she? I find the pretty ones usually are."

Kincaid snorted. "Hardly. If anything, she's too intelligent for her own good. But she's also headstrong. Doesn't listen to a damned thing I say."

"Then why take her case?"

"A moment of temporary weakness that I've since regretted a thousand times over."

"Personally, I've always been fond of bold, headstrong women." A dimple that had made hearts flutter from London to Leeds flashed in Sterling's left cheek. "Especially in bed. It was what first drew me to Eloise. That, and her laugh. Like wind chimes in the breeze." His smile faded. "I need to find out who did this to her, Kincaid. For her sake as much as my own."

"We will. *I* will." His gaze skimmed across the crowded room, then returned to Sterling. "I'm going to question Eloise's household staff tomorrow."

"I'll go with you," the duke said at once, but Kincaid was already shaking his head.

"I won't get the answers I need with you hovering behind me. The servants won't talk if you're there." Because details were important, he removed his journal from an inside flap he'd had specially sewn into his coat and asked a passing barmaid for something to write with. She returned shortly with a pencil, worn down to a nub and chewed at the end, but it worked well enough. "Did the staff come with the house you rented for Eloise, or were they hired after?"

Sterling frowned. "How the devil am I supposed to know that? Eloise was in charge of all those matters."

Kincaid closed his journal. "It would help move the case along if you could provide *some* details."

The duke gave him a hearty slap on the back. "That's why I hired you." He sobered when he saw Kincaid's resulting expression. "They're not excellent, are they? My chances of getting out of this without being charged for her murder."

"No," Kincaid said bluntly. "They're not. Unless we can find the true culprit, you're going to be brought before the House of Lords. I'd find a good lawyer now."

"At least we have time on our side."

"That, and little else." Kincaid would have liked to reassure his friend. But having once been the unsuspecting recipient of false hope, he'd always rather give the truth. No matter how hard it was to hear. "I'll let you know if I learn anything of note tomorrow. Try to get a good night's sleep."

"Aye," Sterling said dryly. "After all this joviality, I'm sure I'll sleep like a baby. By the by, I'd be remiss if I didn't remind you that not every woman is like Lavinia."

"Duly noted," Kincaid said, his tone unmistakably curt.

"She was awful," Sterling went on. "There's no denying it. And what she did—"

"I don't care to have this conversation."

"—there's no excuse for it. Hell, there's not even a good reason other than her being a scheming whore. But she's a single fish in a large pond. Maybe it's time you have a go at another. Who knows? You may even prefer the American variety." The duke's eyebrows wiggled suggestively. "Headstrong or not, I've heard they've quite a good mouth on them."

The picture *that* brought to mind was not one Kincaid cared to contemplate.

Not unless he wanted to spring a cockstand in the middle of the bloody pub.

"Sod off." He slapped a handful of coins onto the table to pay for their drinks and then walked out, Sterling's rich laughter ringing in his ears.

MIDNIGHT FOUND KINCAID laid out flat on the bed in his office, scotch in one hand and regret in the other. Lifting his head, he tilted the bottle back and took a generous swallow before dropping it onto the ground where it rolled, empty, across the floorboards and under his desk.

He wasn't a man who drank to excess. His set of skills required a sharp mind and quick wit, neither of which were conducive to drinking himself into oblivion. But once he'd finished his first glass of scotch, it seemed only right to have another, and after that was done, James, the rascal, had knocked the glass onto the floor and broken it, so what else could he have done but drink directly from the bottle?

A poor decision, that. One he'd regret more come morning, he imagined, as right now he found the heaviness of his limbs and the numbness in his skull rather pleasant. It was certainly a welcome distraction from his memories of Lavinia...and his thoughts of Joanna.

The first he understood.

The second he...didn't.

Kincaid had always enjoyed women. Their gentle voices. Their soft curves. Their silky curls nestled between plump thighs. That enjoyment had led to the loss of his virginity at sixteen when he'd fumbled his way through tupping Betsy Graham in the hayloft above her father's forge. Not his best performance, but he had always been a quick learner. His past mistresses certainly never had reason to complain. Suffice it to say, Kincaid considered himself to be well versed in passion.

He knew what it felt like.

He knew what to expect.

Yet his attraction to Joanna was unlike anything he'd ever experienced before.

Even with Lavinia.

When he and Joanna had kissed, it had been almost *carnal* in nature; raw and pulsing, like a carnivore demanding to be fed. A fitting analogy, seeing as he'd snarled like a wolf when her velvety core had clenched, hot and wet, around his fingers.

On a groan, his head fell back and hit the pillow. What the bollocks was he going to do?

Not think about her, he ordered himself fiercely.

If he didn't think about her, then he wouldn't want her. If he didn't want her, then this war between his head and his heart could finally cease.

It was a sound plan. The best his drunken arse could come up with, at any rate. It even worked...until he fell asleep.

And dreamed only of Joanna.

CHAPTER TWELVE

J OANNA SMELLED THE scotch before she entered
  Kincaid's office. Woodsy with an underlying
hint of peat moss, the scent of it filled her nostrils
as soon as she stepped into the foyer. Her brow
furrowing, she left her cloak and hat on as she
made her way to the door. It was partially ajar,
and her brisk knock pushed it all the way open to
reveal the usual cluttered disorder. As well as
Kincaid, only partially clothed, sprawled on the
bed in the corner.

With a gasp, she slammed the door shut. The
sound struck the silence like a gunshot, and she
cringed when she heard the unmistakable *thump*
of a body striking the floor, followed by a
strangled curse.

"Fuck," Kincaid groaned, his voice muffled by
the wood between them. "Sterling, is that you?"

"I'm—I'm afraid not. I am terribly sorry,"

Joanna apologized as she hesitantly opened the door. "I didn't mean to wake you. I didn't realize you were,"—*passed out drunk in your office without a shirt on*—"indisposed. I can return later, if you'd like."

"No," he said, to her immense surprise. "Come in." Grimacing, he managed to push himself up into a sitting position before he leaned back against the bedrail and covered his face with his hands. "You don't happen to see a shirt anywhere, do you? And coffee." Amber eyes shot through with red peeked hopefully at her from between his fingers. "I'd pay a king's ransom for a cup of coffee."

Joanna did not see any clothing strewn about, but there was half a cup of coffee on the corner of his desk. "Will this do?" she asked, holding it out to him. "It's cold. I could make a—"

"It's fine," he said, snatching the ceramic mug out of her hand.

She watched, bemused, as Kincaid guzzled the coffee down before staggering to his feet. When he squinted, she immediately guessed what the problem was and began to look for his spectacles. After a brief search, she found the wire-rimmed glasses underneath his pillow.

"Here," she said. "These should help."

He accepted the spectacles and slipped them on, then blinked and frowned at her as his gaze refocused. "I...thank you, Miss Thorncroft." As a ruddy flush began to spread up his neck and into his face, he averted his stare to a spot on the wall several inches above her head. "I apologize that you have to see me like this. It's inappropriate, and inexcusable. If you'd be so kind as to leave—"

"I am not going anywhere," she interrupted. This may not have been how she'd planned to begin their day together, but she wasn't about to let him shoo her away like a pesky fly. For nearly half the night, she'd stayed awake. While Evie slept, her soft snores resonating through the bedroom like the rising and falling of the tide, Joanna's thoughts had been centered on Kincaid. And what she would do when she saw him in the morning.

Her *plan* had been to boldly enter his office, command his attention, and inform him, in no uncertain terms, that they were no longer going to ignore each other or what had happened between them.

No more hiding.

No more pretending.

They needed to put their emotions out in the open, and let what would happen…well, happen.

But she couldn't make any demands of him *now*. It'd be the equivalent of kicking a sad puppy. A sad, miserable puppy that smelled like scotch and looked as if it wanted to crawl under a rock and die. Which meant that if she wanted him to acknowledge the feelings that she *knew* existed between them, she would have to be subtle about it.

Unfortunately, subtlety wasn't exactly her strong point.

"What was that?" she asked when he mumbled something unintelligible.

"*Stubborn*," he enunciated clearly. "I said you're stubborn, Miss Thorncroft."

She smiled. "Thank you."

Kincaid glowered. "That wasn't a compliment."

"No, oddly enough it never seems to be. Oh, there's your shirt." Spying the garment crumpled underneath the bed, she knelt down and picked it up. The shirt smelled of him. Were he not staring at her with daggers in his eyes, she might have been tempted to bury her face in the folds of the soft fabric and inhale his scent.

"I'll take that," he said stiffly. With great reluctance, she handed it over and watched, nails digging into her hips, as he quickly dressed himself, his fingers working nimbly to push the buttons into place. But try as he might, he couldn't secure his right sleeve cuff. After observing him struggle for nearly a minute, she rolled her eyes and stepped forward.

"Let me." Bending her head in concentration, Joanna easily slid the pewter button through the tiny hole. "There you are, all done." But she didn't move away, and neither did Kincaid. Her attention drawn to a long, narrow scar on his wrist that had silvered with age, she gently ran her thumb across the mark.

"What happened?" she asked, glancing up at him from beneath her lashes. He stood impossibly still, the shallow rise and fall of his chest the only indication he was still breathing.

"I needed to break a window," he said.

"With your *hand*?"

"There wasn't a hammer available."

"It must have been very painful." Acting on impulse, she lowered her head and ever-so-gently pressed her lips to the small scar. "There," she murmured. "All better."

Above her Kincaid let out a hiss. *"Miss Thorncroft."*

"Yes?" she said softly, tilting her chin up. The piercing intensity she saw in the depths of his eyes sent her pulse skittering. Sitting behind his desk with his spectacles and his journal, Kincaid could have easily passed for a mild-mannered professor. But when they were face to face, chest to chest, thigh to thigh, there wasn't anything the least bit *mild* about him.

"We swore we wouldn't do this again," he said roughly, even as he reached out and tucked a loose curl behind her ear, the back of his fingers brushing along the curved edge.

His gaze dropped to her mouth.

Her belly quivered in anticipation.

"Maybe *you* swore," she said. "But I never make promises I have no intention of keeping."

He squeezed his eyes shut. "Joanna…"

It was the first time he'd spoken her first name, and it felt exhilarating to hear it spill from his lips. It felt good. It felt…it felt *natural*. She wanted to hear him say her name again. And again. She wanted to hear him say it in a shout. She wanted to hear him say it in a whisper. She wanted to hear him say it as his mouth glided along her skin and she came alive beneath his touch.

His eyes still closed, he rested his temple against hers in a gesture that was achingly vulnerable. "We cannot."

She was filled with the urge to wrap her arms around him and draw him to her breast. To soothe him as one might a child. Because while his reasons for always yanking away at the last possible moment were still unknown to her, something was clear: Kincaid was in pain. The deep, wrenching pain that only came after a great loss.

Joanna had learned what that pain felt like after her father died. And again, when she'd learned the secrets her parents had kept hidden from her. It was not a burden she wished on anyone. Least of all Kincaid, who may have been gruff and surly on the outside, but whose heart was pure and true. If she could have carried some of the weight, she would have. But to do that, she needed to know what demons haunted him.

"Why?" she asked gently, splaying her hands across his chest. "Why can't we?"

On ragged breath, he lifted his head. "Because it wouldn't be right."

"With everything that's happened, it is the only thing that *does* seem right." She went to cup the side of his face, but he caught her wrist.

"No," he said hoarsely, dragging her arm away. "I won't repeat past mistakes."

"What kind of mistakes?"

His eyes met hers, and the bleakness she saw in his gaze tugged straight at her heart. "The kind I cannot afford to make again." He released her arm, stepped away, and raked his hands through his hair, fingers disappearing in the tangled locks of brown. "Miss Thorncroft, I'd like you to leave. We can reconvene on the morrow."

And they were back to Miss Thorncroft again.

How utterly disappointing.

"I am not going anywhere." Marching briskly across the room, she poured a glass of water from a pitcher on the edge of his desk. "You are going to drink this, I am going to make fresh coffee, and then we are going to go about our day as usual. You may not want me here. But I've a job to do, and so do you."

If Kincaid refused to kiss her (and he called

her the stubborn one), then the least he could do was honor their agreement. Which meant until their trial period expired or the ring was found, she was to stay on as his secretary. A position she could hardly fulfill if she wasn't in his office.

Subtlety, she reminded herself as she thrust the glass at him. Subtlety...and patience. Just because Kincaid wasn't ready to admit his feelings for her didn't mean he did not have them. They were there. She was sure of it. As sure of anything she'd ever been in her life.

And maybe she *was* impulsive, to want an affair. Maybe she was even foolish.

But she was also determined.

Because of Kincaid, she knew what it felt like to be aroused. To be wanted. To be *desired*. And she wasn't going to just give all that up and return to her humdrum courtships with suitors like Charles Gaines.

No matter how perfectly practical they were.

"You're an exceedingly difficult woman, Miss Thorncroft," said Kincaid darkly as he accepted the water.

"Thank you."

"That wasn't a compliment." The corners of his eyes crinkling, he brought the glass to his lips.

If Joanna didn't know any better, she'd think he was actually *grinning*.

"I'll start the coffee." As she left the room, she could feel his eyes burning a hole in her backside with every step she took. A small, catlike smile teasing her mouth, she gave an extra tilt of her hips as she went through the doorway and all but heard him groan.

Her smile widened.

Poor handsome, emotionally aloof detective.

He really didn't stand a chance.

JOANNA WORKED THROUGH the morning, sorting through piles of old missives and bills, while Kincaid tallied numbers and wrote letters. They were quiet, but it was a comfortable sort of silence, and more than once she glanced up to discover Kincaid staring at her, his gaze oddly contemplative.

Shortly after lunch—buttered bread, thin slices of leftover roasted mutton, and cold pudding—which they ate together in the sparsely decorated dining room, Kincaid put on his long jacket and hat and reached for his journal.

"I have a call to make," he said brusquely. "You can finish what you're doing and see yourself out. I don't have anything else for you to do today."

"Where are you going?" she asked.

He gave the curved brim of his bowler an absent tug. "To question the staff in a case I've agreed to take on for a personal friend. I should not be long, but I wouldn't want you to wait for me to return. I'm sure you have better things to do."

She really didn't, which was why she hastily grabbed her burgundy frock coat and followed after him. Wherever Kincaid was going, that was where she wanted to be. Mostly because she found herself perpetually drawn to him, and a little bit because she wanted to see what Kincaid's job consisted of when he wasn't behind his desk. Compared to alphabetizing paperwork, questioning servants sounded downright thrilling.

Not shockingly, Kincaid was less than pleased.

"What are you doing, Miss Thorncroft?" he asked when she caught up to him on the front path after giving James a farewell scratch behind his ears and a tiny piece of leftover mutton.

"Accompanying you," she replied cheerfully before she preceded him through the gate and onto the sidewalk. A light breeze stirred the air, teasing the tiny wisps of hair at the nape of her neck. She had "forgotten" her bonnet in the office, and no inclination to retrieve it. Evie was adamant that too much sun stained the skin with freckles, but Joanna rather liked the tiny collection of dots across her nose and cheeks.

"I do not recall extending you an invitation," Kincaid said, casting her an irate glare over his shoulder as he secured the gate.

"Which is why I invited myself. I *am* your secretary." She knew it was naughty of her, but Joanna did so enjoy annoying him. She loved the way his eyes flashed when he was angry, revealing tiny fragments of gold in the irises that only appeared when his temper ran high. She loved the way he ran his hands through his hair, leaving the ends disheveled. And she especially loved the heated way he stared at her, as if he didn't know whether he wanted to strangle her...or kiss her.

"No," he said flatly. "Out of the question."

"I won't get in the way," she said, batting her lashes. Flirting may have been a foreign concept but, in this battle of wiles and wits, there was no weapon she wasn't willing to try. "I won't even say a word."

Kincaid snorted. "I find that hard to believe."

"All right, maybe a *few* words," she allowed. "But I truly believe I'd be very useful."

"And how is that?" he asked, not bothering to disguise his skepticism.

She lifted her chin. "For your information, I am an *excellent* judge of character."

"An excellent judge of character," he repeated.

"Indeed. For example, even though you act like a gruff, growly bear, I know that, deep down, you are a good, honest man. I also know that you always strive to do the right thing, even when that means taking on the case of an American who cannot afford to pay you a penny."

The gruff, growly bear frowned at her. "A decision which I am beginning to seriously reconsider."

"*And*," she continued, nonplussed by his surliness, "I know that you are far more enamored of that penniless American than you let on. In fact, I think you might even *like* her. Very much. You're simply afraid to admit it."

His jaw clenched. "I can assure you I am enamored of no one, Miss Thorncroft."

Joanna leaned in close. "It's all right," she said in a conspiratorial whisper. "I won't tell."

He glowered at her.

She grinned at him.

"Very well," he said at last. "You may accompany me—"

"Splendid!"

"—*if* you can remain quiet and keep your thoughts to yourself."

"That should not be a problem." Her head tilted. "Although, what if—"

"No."

"But I might have a—"

"No."

"What if *they* talk to—"

"No."

She huffed out a breath. "Fine. I'll hold my

tongue and stand in the corner, just like a well-behaved lady should."

"You're many things, Miss Thorncroft," he said wryly. "Well-behaved isn't one of them."

"Thank you."

He stared at her for a moment, his amber gaze impossible to read. Then he held out his arm. "You're welcome."

Side by side, the penniless American and the growly bear set off down the sidewalk.

CHAPTER THIRTEEN

THEIR DESTINATION WAS Mayfair, a district in West London that bordered Hyde Park. Predominately comprised of tree-lined streets and brick townhouses, it was an affluent area for those who could not afford Grosvenor Square, but were far wealthier than the poor souls condemned to the rookeries in the East End.

Kincaid led the way to a home with a blue door. Tall and narrow, its walkway was in need of a good sweeping and the mortar between the bricks was beginning to crumble but, otherwise, it was in fair condition, discernable from the other houses only by the color of its entrance.

He knocked, then glanced at Joanna out of the corners of his eyes. "Remember, you are—"

"Not even here," she said sweetly.

"Why are you being so agreeable?" Suspicion flickered in his gaze. "What are you planning?"

"Why do I have to be planning something?" Their walk, while not long, had been brisk, and she was beginning to perspire beneath the weight of her coat. Shrugging out of the garment, she laid it over her arms and regarded Kincaid with an innocent smile. "You needn't worry. I shall endeavor to be on my best behavior."

His expression darkened. "That's *exactly* what worries me."

Joanna made a scoffing noise. "You hate me when I don't listen, and you hate me when I do. You've placed me at a severe disadvantage, Kincaid."

"I don't hate you, Miss Thorncroft, I—"

Unfortunately, whatever Kincaid felt for her would have to wait for, at that very inconvenient moment, the blue door opened to reveal a butler. At least, Joanna assumed he was a butler. She'd never met one personally. But she had read about them in her beloved gothic romances.

They were always dressed in black (which this man was) and looked disapproving (which he certainly did). Invariably, they were named Dobson or Gibbs, and were either a hindrance to the hero whenever he tried to visit his lady love or gave sage pieces of wisdom which no one ever seemed to heed.

"Can I be of assistance?" the butler asked coolly.

"Yes." Kincaid stepped forward, filling the

doorway with his long, lanky frame and forcing the servant to take a step back. "My name is Thomas Kincaid. I believe you were told to expect me. I have a few questions for the staff in regards to Miss Eloise Bancroft."

A mottled red crept up the sides of the butler's neck. "I am afraid that will not be possible. We were not given a time, and the servants are busy. Not to mention they, and I, have already been interviewed extensively by Scotland Yard." He spared a dismissive glance at Joanna before refocusing his ire on Kincaid. "Should you have any further questions, I would direct you there."

"If I wanted to go to Scotland Yard, I would be at Scotland Yard. Mind your step, Miss Thorncroft." Grasping Joanna's elbow, Kincaid steered her past the blustering butler and into a high-ceilinged foyer that had been stripped of all its furnishings.

While Kincaid conversed with the butler in low, furious tones, Joanna wandered over to the wall and absently ran her fingertip along the wainscoting. She frowned when her glove came away covered in a black layer of dust. If the servants were otherwise engaged, as the butler had indicated, they certainly were doing something other than cleaning. The marble tile was scuffed, the windows were dull, and the chandelier hanging above her head was filled with cobwebs. The house appeared as though it had not received a proper cleaning in weeks, if not months.

"Who is Miss Eloise Bancroft?" she asked Kincaid after the butler had stormed off, muttering about "inconveniences" and "we will see about this". What a truly unpleasant man. "Does she live here?"

"She *lived* here," the detective corrected. "She was murdered the same day you arrived in London. I've been hired to find the culprit."

Joanna's eyes widened. "This is a *murder* investigation?"

"Indeed. Well, suspected murder, I suppose, as Eloise's body has not yet been found." Removing his spectacles, he polished the lenses with his handkerchief before slipping them back on. "Dumped in the Thames, most likely."

She suppressed a shudder. "But...then how do you know she was murdered, and not kidnapped? Or maybe she ran away."

"Given the amount of blood that was found splattered on the walls of her bedchamber, I doubt very much she is still alive," he said, speaking with the casual bluntness of someone who had witnessed enough violence and death to be unfazed by it.

Unaccustomed to the darker side of Kincaid's profession, Joanna pressed a hand to her mouth as bile burned the back of her tongue at the vivid picture his words invoked. "How awful," she whispered. "That poor woman."

He let out an oath. "I apologize, Miss Thorn-croft. I should have curbed my tongue. I am used to keeping company with other peelers." In two powerful strides, he was across the room and had his hands resting protectively on either side of her waist. "You shouldn't be here. I shouldn't have brought you here. Let me take you to the office, or to your boarding house. Whichever you prefer."

As her initial unease subsided, Joanna slowly exhaled. She may have been startled by Kincaid's carelessly graphic description of the crime, but she was no shrinking violet.

"I *prefer* you not think of me as a helpless damsel who is in danger of swooning at the first mention of blood. We Americans are made of sterner stuff than that." *And hotter fire*, she added silently as she felt Kincaid's thumbs pressing into her hipbones through the combined layers of her dress and petticoat.

A few inches higher, and he'd be touching her ribcage. Then her breasts. Her nipples tingled, swelling to hard buds that strained against her bodice as heat pulsed between her thighs. Her slender throat convulsed in a forced swallow. There was a time and place for passion; the middle of a stranger's foyer wasn't it. Unless Kincaid indicated otherwise, of course.

At this rate, she was willing to kiss him in the

broom closet.

Or the pantry.

Even the library would suffice.

Books and desire...would could be better?

She peeked up at him to find he was staring intently at her, his gaze fixated on her mouth. She wet her lips, and he made a hoarse sound as his grip tightened, dragging her even closer until the only two things separating them were their clothing and his unwillingness to succumb to his potent desire.

"Miss Thorncroft." His hand left her hip to glide along her cheek. "*Joanna*."

"Yes?" she said breathlessly.

"I—"

But once again, they were interrupted. This time by a young maid.

"Mr. Brown said you wanted to speak with me?" the servant asked timidly.

"You've *got* to be jesting," Joanna muttered as she discreetly adjusted her bodice.

Kincaid's reaction was a bit more...extreme.

Like a fox who'd been sighted in the hen house, he all but bolted away from her. One second he was there and the next he was at least seven feet across the room, his spectacles askew, his countenance suffused with color, and a noticeable bulge between his thighs.

As she turned away to hide her snicker, she could feel Kincaid glaring at her. A moment of awkward silence, and then he addressed the maid as if there weren't a raging arousal in his trousers. A testament, Joanna supposed, to his professionalism.

"Yes, I'd like to have a word," he said. "Miss…?"

"Abigail, sir. Abigail Groshen." The maid clutched her apron with knotted fists. Her knuckles were as white as the cap on her head, and her face was of a similar pallor, causing her blonde eyebrows to stand out in stark contrast against her milky skin.

"Were you employed for the entirety of Miss Bancroft's tenure here, Miss Groshen?"

Her gaze darting nervously, Abigail gave the tiniest of nods.

"Good," Kincaid said sharply. "Then I've questions for you."

With a frightened squeak, the maid took a step in retreat. "F—for me? But I just work in the kitchens, sir."

"That is a sufficient position for the information I require. Where were you on the night Miss Bancroft was murdered?"

"Oh for heaven's sake," Joanna cut in when Abigail's eyes grew huge. "Can you not see you're scaring the poor girl out of her wits?"

Kincaid frowned. "What the devil do you mean?"

Joanna didn't know whether to laugh or

shake her head, so she did both. Kincaid excelled at a wide variety of things, but putting the opposite sex at ease with his charm was certainly not one of them. It was obvious to see why he had been a good policeman and was now a successful private investigator. He was intelligent, level-headed, and intensely focused on whatever task lay in front of him. But that focus often lent itself to a decided lack of emotion and empathy. Whether it was accidental or on purpose, the effect remained the same. Kincaid often came across as hard and cold, but he was more than that. So much more.

Abigail Groshen may not have seen it. How could she, when he was barking demands at her left and right? But Joanna did. More than that, she *felt* it. Kincaid might have portrayed himself as a gruff, grumbly bear, but there wasn't a doubt in her mind that if the maid required it, he'd be the first to give her the shirt off his back.

Why he refused to show that side of himself more often, Joanna hadn't the faintest idea. Maybe he saw it as a weakness. Or maybe he was just exhaustingly stubborn. Whatever the reason, she had no issue in taking it upon herself to soften his rough edges.

"There is no need to fret," she told the maid kindly. "What my esteemed partner *meant* to say is that we just have a few questions, and we'd be very appreciative if you could help us find the answers. We recognize the ability of the household staff to notice and hear things that others might miss. It's a valuable skill, Miss Groshen, which most do not appreciate. Why don't we continue this in the parlor? I'm sure it would be much more comfortable."

"Partner?" Kincaid growled in her ear as Abigail preceded them into the parlor. "What happened to pretending you're not even here?"

Joanna smirked. "We can discuss my fee later."

Unlike the foyer, this parlor had furniture, but the walls had been stripped of their paintings, leaving behind large squares of gold and ivory paper that were noticeably lighter than the space surrounding them. It was rather strange that such a fine house in such a fine neighborhood would be all but barren on the inside. Joanna wondered if it was a sign of financial strain. If so, did it have anything to do with Miss Bancroft's tragic death?

"You should let me question her," she told Kincaid out of the corner of her mouth. "She'll open up more to another woman. And I'm not terrifying."

"Neither am I," he said, appearing vaguely insulted. "I wear spectacles."

"You're not terrifying to *me*." She patted his hand. "But you've terrified our witness, and she is not going to say anything useful to you. If she even says anything at all without requiring smelling salts."

"She isn't *our* witness because this isn't *our* case. It's mine." A muscle leapt in his cheek. "Has anyone ever told you what a bloody pain in the arse you are, Miss Thorncroft?"

"You're the first one today," she said. Then she waited patiently.

It did not take long.

"Fine," Kincaid bit out. "Have at it. But I doubt you'll obtain any helpful information. She's just a scullery maid."

Accepting the challenge with a toss of her head, Joanna marched past Kincaid and sat down in a leather wing chair opposite Abigail. Kincaid, his countenance inscrutable, took up a position beside the window, pushing the curtain aside to peer out at the street beyond. His lean body was casually postured, but she knew by the tension in his shoulders that he was listening keenly to every word.

"Well then," she began, giving the maid an encouraging smile. "I suppose I should start by introducing myself. I am Joanna Thorncroft. You can call me Jo, if you'd like. My sisters do. Jo when they're happy with me, and Joanna when they're not. Do you have any sisters, Miss Groshen?"

Abigail twisted her fingers together on her lap. "Three. I—I'm the youngest."

"That would be my sister Claire." As she

spoke Claire's name aloud, Joanna felt a pang in her chest. She hadn't allowed herself the chance to miss her sister, as every time she thought of sweet, gentle Claire, it filled her with sadness. She wished they could have all made the journey to London together, but Claire was where she was supposed to be, and it was a relief to know someone was watching over their grandmother. Even if Ruth remained adamant that she didn't need any special care. "I'm the eldest, and Evie is in the middle. I don't know what I'd do if there was another one."

"It made for a busy household growing up." Abigail managed a trembling smile. "My sisters are all maids as well."

"It's a fine profession." She leaned forward. "How long have you worked for Miss Bancroft?"

The maid flicked a frightened glance at Kincaid. "Umm…"

"Don't mind him," said Joanna with a dismissive wave. "I know he comes across all gruff and brooding, but I can assure you he's as harmless as a potato."

A warning snarl emanated from the window.

"See?" she said brightly. "All growl and no bite. You're perfectly safe, Abigail."

"If you say so," Abigail said doubtfully. Still, she managed to wrench her gaze away from Kincaid and, after a moment's pause, answered Joanna's question. "I worked for Miss Bancroft for two years. Mostly in the kitchen, as I said. Hannah—that's Hannah Adamson—was Miss Bancroft's personal maid, but I...I did fill in on occasion when Hannah wasn't feeling well. Miss Bancroft liked the way I curled her hair." The maid's voice thickened. "She said—she said I was good enough to work for a real lady, one day. She was even going to give me a recommendation, but..."

"She disappeared," Joanna filled in gently when Abigail fell silent.

The maid began to cry. "I knew something was w—wrong that night. Miss Bancroft wasn't herself."

"How do you mean?" Joanna reached inside her reticule and procured a linen handkerchief. Handing it to Abigail, she glanced discreetly at Kincaid over her shoulder. He was fixated on the maid, his brows drawn sharply together over the bridge of his spectacles. Every muscle in his body was coiled tight, like a lion about to spring.

So much for the scullery maid not having any helpful information, Joanna thought smugly.

Accepting the handkerchief, Abigail blew loudly into it, then dabbed at her wet cheeks. "Miss Bancroft was agitated. Pacing back and forth. She kept asking if he was here yet."

"Who?" Kincaid demanded. "Who was she waiting for?"

Clutching the handkerchief, Abigail recoiled.

"I...I..."

"It's all right," Joanna said soothingly even as she shot Kincaid a warning glare. "You're safe here with me. We're just trying to get to the truth and find out who might have harmed Miss Bancroft. Do you remember who she was expecting that night?"

"She was waiting for her—her benefactor. The Duke of Hanover. He arrived two hours late, and they went upstairs to...to Miss Bancroft's bedchamber."

"That's odd, isn't it? Why would she bring her benefactor up to her...*oh*," Joanna squeaked when Abigail flushed and Kincaid cleared his throat. "He was *that* type of benefactor. I understand. Erm...what happened then?"

"Nothing out of the usual, until the next morning when I brought Miss Bancroft her breakfast tray and...and I saw all the blood. It was *everywhere*," Abigail wailed as big fat tears began to roll down her cheeks.

"Take a deep breath," Joanna advised. Crossing over to the maid, she sat beside her and rested a hand on her knee.

As an older sibling, Joanna was accustomed to wiping tears and cleaning up scrapes. When Evie and Claire were children, they'd come to her countless times to heal their injuries, both the ones in their hearts and the ones on their persons. The night Father died, they'd climbed into

Joanna's bed to sleep beside her, and hadn't left for the next month. Her sisters didn't need her now as much as they had then. They'd all grown past the point of mending their bumps and bruises with a kiss. But she still knew how to give comfort when it was needed.

"That's it," she told Abigail as the maid's sobs began to abate. "You're doing a splendid job. I cannot imagine how difficult this must be for you. Especially since you were so well acquainted with Miss Bancroft."

"She was a l—lovely woman," Abigail sniffled. "But sometimes…"

"Sometimes?" Joanna prodded delicately.

"Have you ever felt as if someone is h—hiding something?"

"What do you mean?"

"Not a treasure. But a—a secret." The maid's fingers moved fretfully over the handkerchief, smoothing the damp fabric out before bunching it into a ball and then smoothing it out again in a rhythm that seemed to bring her a sense of calm. "A secret they didn't want anyone else to know."

Of its own accord, Joanna's gaze was pulled towards Kincaid. "All the time," she murmured.

"That's how Miss Bancroft was acting. At least, the past month or so. Ever since *he* came to call."

"The Duke of Hanover?"

"No." Abigail gave a jerky shake of her head.

"I—I don't know his name. She never said."

Kincaid cleared his throat. He met Joanna's gaze, drew a circle around his face, then looked pointedly at Abigail. His intent was clear, and she gave a small nod to indicate she understood.

"Miss Groshen, do you remember what this man looked like?"

"I...I don't know." The maid bit her lip. "He was tall."

"Taller than Kincaid?"

"The—the same height, I believe. Except his hair was lighter. And his e-eyes." Abigail faltered, then gave a shudder. "I know a person can't have black eyes. But he did. Black as pitch, they were. I was—I was glad when he never returned."

"Did he threaten Miss Bancroft in any way?"

"No. Not that I heard, at least. He was only here for a minute. But after he left...she was never the same." The handkerchief fluttered to the floor as the maid abruptly stood. "If that's everything, I should return to my duties. Mr. Brown does not like us to dally."

"We're grateful for all of your help, Miss Groshen. I've only two more questions, and then you can be on your way." Standing as well, Joanna subtly positioned herself between the maid and the door. "You mentioned you were the first to enter Miss Bancroft's bedchamber that horrible morning. Where was Hannah, her personal maid? Shouldn't she have been serving

Miss Bancroft her breakfast?"

"Hannah left over a fortnight ago," said Abigail. "To care for her sick grandfather in Bedford. She hasn't come back. I sent her a letter, but I've yet to hear anything."

"That's unusual, isn't it?" Before Joanna and her siblings were forced to sell their childhood home, they'd employed a staff of five. Not enough for each sister to have their own maid, but they had shared one, as well as a governess. Which meant Joanna knew firsthand the unique relationship that could be formed between servants and those that employed them. She'd certainly considered Lucy, their maid, to be a close confidant as well as a friend. It broke all their hearts, Lucy's included, when they were forced to let her go; the loss softened only by the knowledge that she'd gone on to a splendid family.

Because of her own experience, Joanna couldn't think of a single reason why Hannah wouldn't have immediately returned when she learned of what had happened to Miss Bancroft. If something ill had ever befallen Joanna, or either of her sisters, Lucy would have been there without a moment's delay.

Surely it was worthy to note that the person who had known the victim best hadn't bothered to return after Miss Bancroft's walls were found stained with blood.

"Can I leave now?" Abigail asked with a desperate glance at the door.

"A final question, Miss Groshen," said Kincaid, his voice notably softer than it was when the interrogation first began. "The night before Miss Bancroft was presumably killed, you mentioned the Duke of Hanover paid her a visit. Did you see him leave?"

"N—not that I recall."

"Are you absolutely certain?"

The maid gave a hesitant nod. "I believe so."

"Did you *hear* him leave?" Kincaid persisted. "Footsteps on the stairs, carriage wheels on the gravel? Anything that might indicate he was not in the house between the hours of two in the morning and when you entered the bedchamber? When *did* you enter the bedchamber, Miss Groshen? The exact time, if you please."

"The e—exact time?" Abigail paled. "Um, I'm not sure. After seven, as Miss Bancroft hates to be woken early. But before nine, as she was expecting guests for morning tea. Is that helpful?"

"Exceedingly." Joanna gave the maid's shoulder a squeeze. "Thank you, Miss Groshen. We will be in touch if we need anything further."

"I wasn't done," Kincaid said after Abigail had fled the room.

"Perhaps, but she was."

Kincaid came to stand beside her. Arms crossed, he stared at the door as he said, "You did a fair job, Miss Thorncroft."

"I did, didn't I?" she said, pleased with the reluctant praise. Investigative work wasn't nearly as difficult as Kincaid had tried to make it appear. It required the ability to piece things together that might not seem, at least on the surface, as if they were connected. In that way, it wasn't unlike a jigsaw puzzle.

And she'd always enjoyed trying to solve things.

Family secrets. Murders. Stubborn detectives.

What was the difference, really?

After questioning three more servants, none of whom had any information to give, they saw themselves out.

"I believe that went well," Joanna remarked as they headed back towards the office. "At least we've several suspects. Are we going to call upon the Duke of Hanover next? From what Miss Groshen said, he was the last person to see Miss Bancroft alive. *And* he had reason to see her dead."

"What reason?" Kincaid said curtly. "Eloise was his mistress. By all accounts, they were happy together."

"Yes, but Miss Groshen indicated there was another man in the picture. Perhaps Hanover suspected something illicit was going on, and he became jealous." Joanna's eyes lit up. "A crime of passion. After it was done, he panicked and disposed of the body. Just like in *The Mysterious Murder of Madame Madelynn*."

"The Mysterious Murder of *who*? Never mind," Kincaid said before she could answer. "You've an active imagination, Miss Thorncroft, but your theory is misguided. The Duke of Hanover is innocent."

"How do you know that?"

"Because the duke hired me to find Eloise's killer."

Joanna stopped short. "You're working for a *murderer*?"

"Sterling—the Duke of Hanover—did not murder anyone."

"You sound absolutely positive."

"I am."

"Why?" she asked, confused. "Do you have any evidence that clears him of wrongdoing?"

"Not exactly," he hedged.

"Then how can you be so sure?" This may have been Joanna's first attempt at crime solving, but even she knew that evidence—or lack thereof—was a strong indicator of guilt. The Duke of Hanover had an intimate relationship with the victim. There was no indication he'd left the residence until *after* she was killed. Client or not, he had to be their number one suspect. And yet, Kincaid did not seem to be of the same opinion.

"I've known Sterling for a long time." Kincaid's mouth settled into a grim line. "He is more than a client, he is a close personal friend. Which is how I know, beyond a shadow of a doubt and despite all the clues to the contrary, that he no more harmed Eloise than you or I did."

Joanna studied Kincaid closely. The indent between his brows. The lines of tension in the corners of his eyes. The steady throb of his pulse underneath his jaw. "All right," she said simply. "I believe you."

He blinked at her, visibly startled. "You do?"

"Are you surprised?"

"It takes an innate sense of trust to believe someone when all of the facts point in a different direction." There was an endearing note of bewilderment in Kincaid's tone. As if he couldn't understand why anyone would have such faith in him.

Sweet, stubborn man, Joanna thought with affection.

Why could he not see what she did?

That he was worthy of her trust...and so much more.

"If you say the Duke of Hanover is innocent, then he is innocent." Seeing the top of his shirt had come undone, she reached out to fix it, and their hands collided as he did the same. Wordlessly, his fingers slid over the top of hers as she bent her head in concentration and slipped the small wood button back into its hole, then pressed her palm to the middle of his chest where she could feel the *thump thump, thump thump* of his heartbeat. "There. Now all we have left to do is prove who *really* killed his mistress."

Kincaid stiffened beneath her touch. "There is no 'we', Miss Thorncroft."

She gave a light laugh. "But of course there is. Without me, you wouldn't have learned about the man with the black eyes or Hannah's coincidental disappearance. We may not be partners, but we make an excellent team." Lips curving, she peered up at him from beneath her lashes…and her smile froze in place. "You're being serious."

"This is a *murder* investigation. With the murderer still at large." Taking her hand, he deliberately moved it away from his chest. For an instant, his fingers remained locked with hers. Then his countenance hardened, and he released his grip. "I gave you the courtesy of accompanying me today, but—"

"The *courtesy*?"

"—this is not to become a regular occurrence. You are a secretary, not a detective."

And Kincaid was an ass.

Not the donkey kind.

"If it wasn't for me, Miss Groshen never would have given us any information. I believe the words you are looking for are, 'Thank you, Miss Thorncroft, for your invaluable assistance.

Couldn't have done it without you. Bang up job.'" Eyes flashing, she spun on her heel, her only intent to get as far away from him as fast as possible.

If she'd been paying attention to her surroundings, she would have seen the team of Belgian drafts pulling a heavy cart piled high with crates of milk. But her focus wasn't on the street she needed to cross, it was on Kincaid. And with anger clouding her vision, she stepped carelessly off the edge of the curb and directly into the path of the oncoming horses.

"JOANNA!" Kincaid's shout cut through the air like the slash of a whip...

A second too late.

CHAPTER FOURTEEN

JOANNA STOPPED AT the sound of her name.
Brimming with righteous indignation, she
whirled around, ready to give Kincaid a piece of
her mind.

"Who do you think you—*heavens,*" she
gasped when she saw the wagon barreling down
on her.

The driver pulled frantically on the reins, but
the draft horses were too large, their bodies too
cumbersome. She willed her legs to move, but
they were stuck to the ground. She threw her
hands up in front of her face, preparing for the
impact...

Out of nowhere, a hard force slammed into
her from behind, and she was flung out of the
path of the horses with nary a second to spare.
Kincaid, her stunned mind barely had time to
register before he tucked her against him and

they rolled across the cobblestone.

The wagon clattered by, the driver shouting at them as he passed, but Joanna couldn't hear above the roaring in her ears.

Her entire body was tingling with adrenaline. Blood dripped from a scrape on her elbow and her shoulder ached from where it had struck the ground. But it was Kincaid who had taken the brunt of the impact.

He was stretched out beneath her, his long frame cushioning hers. There was a cut above his right brow. Another on his chin. His spectacles had been knocked askew. She could feel the wild pounding of his heart through his clothes, its erratic rhythm keeping time with her own as she managed to push herself up into a half-sitting position, her splayed fingers filling the narrow gaps in his ribcage.

"You—you *saved* me," she said in amazement. "How did you move so *quickly*?"

His gaze fell to her arm, and his eyebrows shot together. "You're bleeding."

"It's nothing. A scratch." But if not for Kincaid's swift actions, she knew it would have been far, far worse. With a tender smile, she straightened his glasses. "There. That's better," she said quietly. "You need to be able to see."

And she needed to have patience.

Rome wasn't built in a day, and stubborn detectives didn't open their hearts in a week. But they *did* risk their lives to save others, and what more could she ask than that? Maybe Kincaid couldn't say what he felt for her in words. But his actions had said all that she needed to hear.

"I see *you*, Miss Thorncroft," he said huskily.

As the world continued on all around them, with no one giving any mind to the couple crouched on the side of the street, he gathered her in his arms.

She tucked her head beneath his chin.

They were two fragments of a whole, clicking into place. Just like a puzzle not yet solved, it seemed they had nothing that connected them together. She was an American bluestocking. He was a British detective. Their paths never should have intersected, let alone become entwined. But then the unsolved part of the puzzle became smaller. And suddenly, it became obvious where the last pieces needed to go.

This was all Joanna wanted. To want, and be wanted in return. To protect, and be protected in return. To love, and to be loved in return.

Her breath caught.

Did she *love* Kincaid?

As frustrating as it could be, she loved arguing with him. She loved coaxing these precious moments of vulnerability out of him. She loved the way he made her burn.

If she wasn't *in* love with him, then she was falling.

No, not falling.

This tingling inside of her wasn't a simple descent of gravity.

It was a spinning. A twirling. A *dancing*.

She was waltzing with Kincaid. And for once, they were moving in unison.

Until he exhaled, and abruptly hauled her to her feet.

"You little fool," he growled as any traces of softness vanished in a *poof* of proverbial smoke. "You could have been killed. You almost *were* killed. What the devil were you thinking, stepping off the pavement like that without looking first? You are *never* to put your life at risk like that again." He gave her a small, painless shake. "Do you understand me?"

Taken aback by the dark fury burning in his eyes, Joanna was slow to respond. She felt as if she'd been languishing in a hot bath, only to have a bucket of cold water suddenly dumped on her head. Where had it come from? Better yet, what was its purpose?

"Would...would that have bothered you?" she asked. "If I were hurt?"

"Would it have bothered me?" he repeated incredulously. "Would it have *bothered* me? Yes, it bloody well would have! What sort of stupid question is that?"

Why, he's scared, she realized.

Frightened out of his wits, really.

Because of *her*.

She could all but feel Kincaid's anger vibrating in the air. But beneath all that bristling, tumultuous rage was panic and fear. Fear that he wouldn't have felt...unless he felt what she did. Daring to risk his wrath, she stretched up and gently brushed a lock of hair off his forehead.

"Why?" she whispered.

"Because you're my client, and I'm responsible for you."

She shook her head. "Why?"

"Because you're my secretary, and I don't have time to find another."

"*Why?*" she persisted.

She wanted—she needed—to hear him say it. Actions were all well and good, but sometimes words were the only thing that could fill a heart. If he was going to drain her emotions like this, he couldn't leave her empty. He had to give her *something*. Something to fill her until the next kiss. Something to sustain her until the next soft moment. Something to give her hope that when she was done spinning, and twirling, and falling, he would catch her.

He would always catch her.

Because he was right. She *could* have been killed. And maybe it was selfish of her but, before she died, she wanted what kings went to war for. She wanted what sonnets were made of. She wanted what poets wrote about.

Lust, and longing, and love.

She wanted it *all,* damnit.

And she wanted it with Kincaid.

"I understand your reservations," she began when he remained wrapped in icy silence. "I would have them, too, if I were in your place and a stranger arrived unannounced on my doorstep, demanding things. Making me feel things I didn't want to feel. But I know that I'm more than *just* your client. I'm more than *just* your secretary." Wide eyes framed with thick lashes implored him to open up to her. To lower his guard. To come out from behind his wall of stone. To trust her as she trusted him. With her secrets, with her life…and with her heart. "I do not want to keep going in circles."

"What *do* you want?" he demanded, all raw tension and simmering angst.

"You, Thomas Kincaid," she said with quiet conviction. "I want you. And I know—"

"You don't *know* anything," he snarled. "Not about me. Not about what you're asking. *Nothing.*"

"Kincaid—"

But he was already walking away.

And this time, there was no one to catch her when she fell.

KINCAID *HAD* TO walk away. If he didn't, he would have touched her again. If he'd touched her, he would have kissed her. And if he'd kissed her...if he'd kissed her, this time, he wouldn't have stopped until he'd devoured her whole. So he forced himself to let her go, and he resisted the urge to look over his shoulder.

He knew he was being a bloody sod, leaving a bleeding woman in the middle of the pavement to venture home by herself. But given the alternative, this was surely the safest option for them both.

Joanna was young and naïve. She was full of hope and stars and everything bright and magical. She didn't understand what she was asking of him. She didn't understand what she was risking. She didn't understand what she stood to lose.

But he did.

He understood that when you played with your heart, you didn't always win.

And the pain wasn't worth the reward.

Kincaid considered himself to be a practical man. Which was why, in his *head*, he knew Joanna was different from Lavinia. As different as the warm sun from the cool, cold moon. But it was his *heart* that needed convincing, and it was his heart he refused to risk. Not again. Not even for a titian-haired goddess with eyes of blue fire and an unbridled spirit that rivaled the four winds.

He shoved his hands into the pockets of his coat as he walked, his stormy expression hastening pedestrians out of his path. He passed by his office without stopping and proceeded on to Grafton Street, a fashionable address on the outskirts of Mayfair.

If there was a surefire way to distract his mind and stop himself from turning around and marching right back to Joanna like a poor, besotted dunce, it was to bury himself in his work.

He'd gone as far as he could with Sterling's case. For now, at least. And Joanna was right, which only served to heighten his temper. Although this anger was self-directed. Because she'd held her own as well as any seasoned peeler, and he never should have doubted her. Not for an instant. But couldn't she see the danger she'd be in if she continued? He couldn't let her be part of the hunt for a bloody *murderer*.

If something happened to her, it would be the end of him.

He did not know when or how that had come to be.

He just knew it was.

What he felt for Joanna…what he felt for Joanna was stronger than anything he'd ever known. And that terrified him, as it should have. As it would any normal, sane person. When you were burned once, you didn't stick your damned hand back into the fire. If Lavinia had left his heart filled with gnarled, puckered scars, then Joanna was going to turn it to ash.

It was only a matter of time.

Which was why he needed to get her the hell out of London.

The sooner, the better.

The sheer terror he'd experienced when he saw her step in front of those horses...he didn't want to feel that ever again. He didn't want to feel this yearning inside of him. He didn't want to feel *anything*.

Not if it meant giving up everything.

Unfortunately, stubborn minx that she was, he knew Joanna wasn't going to return to America until she had answers. Answers he was determined to provide. As much for her sake as his.

He was hoping the Countess of Beresford's ball would lead him to the ring, and Joanna's birth father. In his gut, he knew that if he found one, he'd find the other. In the meantime, he'd been using her grandmother's maiden name of Ellinwood to track down any remaining relatives that might still be residing in the city. He'd withheld his search only because he hadn't wanted to disappoint her if he came up empty. And thus far, that was precisely what had happened.

Over the past few days, after Joanna had left

his office, he'd walked all over London, knocking on door after door. Ellinwood wasn't an exceedingly common surname, but there were enough families who shared it to make the task an arduous one.

He had one last residence to check. A manor on Green Street, not too far from the house they'd just left. In this section of Mayfair, however, the homes did not share walls and the gardens were considerably larger, a subtle indication of wealth and privilege.

He knocked on the door. A maid answered. After accepting his card, she ushered him into the front parlor.

"I was not told Lady Ellinwood was expecting anyone, but I will tell her you are here," she said before discreetly sliding the pocket doors closed.

Hands clasped behind his back, Kincaid circled the room, the restless energy still moving through his veins from when he'd snatched Joanna from certain death making it impossible to sit or to settle.

Thankfully, he was not kept waiting for long.

Within a few minutes, the pocket doors opened to reveal an elderly woman with a hawkish nose, gray hair pinned beneath a lace cap, and a thin mouth. She wore a mauve-colored gown that rustled as she walked, its skirt decorated with too many pleats and bows to count. In her right hand, she held a cane, its whalebone handle worn smooth.

"I was told you requested to see me?" she asked, her voice scratchy with age.

"Indeed, Lady Ellinwood." On instinct, Kincaid bowed lower and longer than he should have, and was rewarded for the gratuitous act when he caught a glint of approval in Lady Ellinwood's eyes as he straightened. "I am a private investigator, hired by a young woman to find any family ties she might have in England. Your name brought me here. It should not take more than a moment of your time to discover whether you are, in fact, the family she has been seeking."

Instead of looking annoyed by his intrusion (as nearly every other person whose door he'd knocked upon had, their lives far too busy to be bothered by a random stranger, and a detective at that), Lady Ellinwood appeared resigned.

"She's an American? This young woman who has hired you."

"Yes, she is," Kincaid said earnestly as anticipation gripped him. "How did you know that?"

With a sigh, Lady Ellinwood leaned heavily onto her cane. "Because I suspected she would come here eventually. Her mother did."

"Anne Thorncroft," he supplied.

Lady Ellinwood's gaze sharpened. "My niece's name was Pratt when I met her. The only daughter of my dear sister and her ne'er-do-well American husband. Joseph's blood must have been strong, because Anne received most of it. A more rebellious, disobedient child I've never met. I won't say I wasn't glad when she left. In the dead of the night, like a thief. Fitting, I suppose, given what she had stolen."

"What did she steal?"

Lady Ellinwood blinked. "Why, the Duke of Caldwell's granddaughter, of course."

CHAPTER FIFTEEN

JOANNA THORNCROFT WAS the illegitimate granddaughter of a duke.

The knowledge resonated within Kincaid's head like a gun being shot, its bullet tearing through any number of bodies before it reached its intended target.

Over tea and cucumber sandwiches, Lady Ellinwood explained to him in brisk, no-nonsense terms of what had transpired when Anne Thorncroft came to London for her Season debut…and the fallout that occurred after she had left.

It was, Joanna's great-aunt told him, the worst kept secret in all of the *ton*. People had since forgotten, naturally. There'd been far too many scandals over the past two decades to keep track of this one in particular. But she remembered. And she had no compunctions in revealing everything she knew.

"I was glad when Mabel returned to London with Anne. My sister and I were always close, and I was devastated when she ran off with that American scoundrel. Mabel's daughter deserved a proper come out. She *was* half-British, after all. Unfortunately, I learned too late that that side didn't take."

"You did mention she was rebellious." Although he'd placed a sandwich on his plate, Kincaid did not eat. Instead, he dined on Lady Ellinwood's every word, using them to form a picture of Joanna's mother. A woman who, for better or worse, had obviously passed her traits on to her eldest daughter.

"Oh, worse than *that*," said Lady Ellinwood, rolling her eyes. "The girl was too independent for her own good. Everyone agreed. Mabel needed to take a firm hand with her, but she never did. Never dared to, if I am being honest. When Anne found herself caught up in an affair with the Duke of Caldwell's eldest son, I was *not* surprised."

"What was his name?" Kincaid asked. "The son."

"Jason Weston, Marquess of Dorchester."

JW.

"He'd buried his wife a month before the Season began," Lady Ellinwood continued. "She died in childbirth. Twins, you understand. A boy and a girl. They both survived, but Lady Dorchester, may her soul rest in peace, did not. A tragedy, really. The *ton* agreed as a collective to give the marquess his year of mourning before he remarried. Even though there were *plenty* of eligible young ladies who could have benefited immensely from such a match. But what are we, as a Society, if we do not uphold our word?"

A bunch of greedy lemmings, Kincaid thought silently.

"Quite right, Lady Ellinwood."

"Well, as you can probably guess, Anne did not adhere to our unspoken agreement. Within a week of her arrival, she was seen everywhere with the marquess. In the park. At the theater. They attended a private musicale at Kensington Palace! In the presence of a chaperone, naturally, but *still.*" Lady Ellinwood paused to take a sip of her tea. "It was the very height of scandal. Especially after it became clear that the little chit was expecting."

"Why didn't the marquess offer to marry her?" Kincaid frowned. He knew that in Lady Ellinwood's retelling, the Marquess of Dorchester was the victim and Anne was the perpetrator, but he saw it in a very different light.

Kincaid saw a young woman in a new country. Who missed her home, and the sweetheart she'd left behind. Whose headstrong nature did not permit her to fit in with the *ton's* simpering elite. Who was lost, and lonely, and so far out of her depth she was all but drowning. He saw an older man. Titled, experienced, a new father who should have been home with his infant children. Perhaps the marquess' interest in Anne began innocently enough. A harmless flirtation to take his mind off the death of his wife. But as soon as he put his hands on an innocent, it had devolved into something else.

"The pregnancy was not common knowledge," said Lady Ellinwood before she stuffed a cucumber sandwich into her mouth and use a linen napkin to neatly brush the crumbs from her chin. "I only suspected it because I accidentally walked in on Anne after she was sick in a chamber pot. Still, I'm certain the marquess would have done right by her had she not run off. Do you know Mabel didn't even tell me they were leaving? I was humiliated. *Humiliated.*"

"I can only imagine how difficult this all was for you," Kincaid said blandly. "What happened then?"

"You mean after my sister and deflowered niece returned to America?"

He gave a clipped nod. It was becoming increasingly difficult to maintain a passive expression while Lady Ellinwood besmirched Joanna's mother, but he was doing his best. With the exception of the Marquess of Dorchester, he was unlikely to find another source of such credible information. Because of Lady Ellinwood, he already knew infinitely more than he had, and he intended to present what he'd learned to Joanna as soon as he figured out a way to soften the shock that was certain to come when she discovered who her real father was.

A lord would have been remarkable enough.

But to be the offspring of a marquess...granddaughter of a duke...

Some—most—would have been elated by the news. But he wasn't sure how Joanna, who seemed to put no value in the peerage or titles, was going to take it.

Would she be happy or sad? Calm or overwhelmed? Excited or nervous?

Whatever her reaction, he knew one thing.

He wanted to be there.

Because he never should have left.

"I received a letter when Anne married that doctor," Lady Ellinwood said. "And when she had her bastard. A girl, so I was told. Judith or June or something or rather. I really cannot recall, it was so long ago."

Kincaid dropped his plate. It hit the table with a loud clatter, spilling his uneaten sandwich onto the floor. "Careful," he said icily. "That is my client you are speaking about, and her name is Joanna."

"I assure you I do not care *what* her name is. She is meaningless to me."

"Well she isn't meaningless to me!" Kincaid shouted. The admission caught both of them off guard, but he did not regret his impassioned words. Not when they rang with truth. "Joanna may not be a member of the peerage," he continued through gritted teeth, "but as far as I am concerned, that is a quality, not a flaw. You may not have liked your niece, Lady Ellinwood, but you would do well to learn a thing or two from her daughter. Joanna has more courage and integrity in her little finger than the *ton* has within its collective body. You should be grateful to have such a remarkable young woman in your family."

Lady Ellinwood's lips all but disappeared as she pressed them together. "I believe it may be time for you to see yourself out, Detective."

"I believe you're right." There was nothing more he could learn here, and he feared what else he might say if he remained. Retrieving the sandwich, Kincaid slapped it onto the plate and then stood up.

With the use of her cane, Lady Ellinwood did the same. As if he were a criminal she needed to keep an eye on lest he make off with the silver, she followed him all the way to the door. "When you see my grandniece, you might mention that I have no interest in meeting her. It's clear the chit has woven a spell over you, the same as her mother did to the poor Marquess of Dorchester, and I want no part of it. I have been charged with raising my grandchild, and I will not have my grandniece exposing my darling Rosemary to her wicked ways."

"You've actually three grandnieces," Kincaid informed her, biting down hard on the inside of his cheek to refrain from saying what he *really* wanted to. He'd never felt such an overwhelming wave of protectiveness before. Not for anyone. It was a primal urge that tinged the edges of his vision red and made him want to beat his chest like a bloody madman. Instead, he settled for a flinty stare. "Joanna has two sisters, Evelyn and Claire."

Lady Ellinwood sniffed. "Not all from different fathers, I hope."

With that, she closed the door in his face.

"What *happened* to you?" Evie asked, her eyes widening with alarm when Joanna swept past her and marched into their shared room with all of the righteous anger exclusively reserved for a woman spurned.

"Thomas Kincaid," Joanna fumed as she tossed her frock coat onto the bed. "And a milk wagon."

"A *milk* wagon? You're bleeding!" Wetting a towel in one of the buckets they'd been using to collect rainwater, Evie motioned for Joanna to sit in a chair and began to tend to her wound.

"It's nothing more than a scratch," Joanna said, holding out her arm. "I don't even feel it."

It was true, she didn't. She *couldn't*. Not over the anger pulsing through her veins. She didn't know if she'd ever been this enraged in her entire life. Her whole body was vibrating with fury. Or maybe those were tiny aftershocks of all the adrenaline still making its way through her bloodstream. She had, after all, nearly died.

And Kincaid had walked away.

The bastard had *walked away*, leaving her humiliated...and hurt.

Joanna had never been *hurt* by a man before. Exasperated; more times than she cared to count. Bored; it went without saying. But she'd never felt her heart wrench inside of her chest. Never felt her throat swell with emotion, or the pit of her stomach fill with despair.

If this was what rejection felt like, she wanted no part of it.

"What happened?" Evie repeated. Having finished cleaning the scrape, she wrapped it with a linen handkerchief, secured the makeshift bandage with a ribbon, and then picked up a brush. "Your hair looks as though it's been through a windstorm. Hold still."

Joanna set her jaw and glared forcefully at the wall as Evie pulled the pins from her hair and carefully began to work the comb through the tangled curls "I wasn't paying attention to where I was going, and was nearly run over by a milk wagon. Kincaid saved me. Then, in an act of complete and utter idiocy, I poured my heart out to him."

Evie's hands stilled. "Why on earth would you do that?"

"Because that is what you do when you're falling in love. All the books say so."

"Oh, Jo," her sister said in quiet dismay. "You're not, are you? Falling in love with him, that is."

"Well not *anymore*." Even as she spoke the denial out loud, Joanna knew it wasn't true. Love wasn't a faucet to be turned off and on. Even when you shoved the handle down as hard as you could (and she was really putting all her weight into it), water continued to drip.

Kincaid may have walked away, but her heart hadn't gone with him.

It was still inside her chest.

A little cracked. A little bloody. But still beating.

For *him*.

A man with the emotional range of a turnip.

Why couldn't she have felt this way for Charles? Or any of her other suitors who, in Evie's words, would have been "perfectly practical in every single way"? At the very least, they had never made her tremble with fury. But they'd never made her tremble with desire, either.

"*Ouch*," she exclaimed when her sister tugged on a snarl a little too hard.

"Sorry." Putting the brush down, Evie began to attack the knot with her fingers. "I can see that you're upset. Which you have every reason to be. But…"

"But?" Joanna asked.

"Maybe this is for the best. You know it never would have worked. You and the detective. A bit of flirtation is all well and good. I could have done with a harmless dalliance myself during our time here. But it wasn't ever going to go any further. There." Holding up the lock of hair she'd been untangling for inspection, Evie gave a satisfied nod and let it fall before moving on to the next. "Mrs. Benedict has invited us to join her for dinner at the Claridge Hotel. Apparently it is *the* place to meet—"

"Wait," Joanna interrupted. "What do you mean Kincaid and I weren't ever going to go any further?"

"Exactly what I said. Tilt you head forward. No, too far. There. Perfect." She began brushing again. Long, slow strokes of the comb that would have felt wonderful if Joanna' stomach wasn't twisted in knots. "From what you've described, Kincaid appears like a nice enough fellow. His boorish behavior notwithstanding, he *did* save your life. He also agreed to find the ring without requiring so much as a pittance. A good thing, as we're nearly out of money as it is. How is that going, by the by?"

"Finding the ring?"

"Yes."

"I...I don't know." Joanna touched her bandage, her fingers absently tracing across the smooth satin ribbon. "Kincaid has not brought it up lately, and I have not asked."

"You haven't *asked*? That ring is the entire reason we're here!"

"I understand that," she said defensively. "I'm sure he is working on it."

"He had better work fast. We haven't an infinite amount of time and resources to spend here, Jo. We *will* have to return home eventually. Which is another reason why you and Kincaid would never suit. You live an ocean away from each other. Would you stay in London, or would he return with us to Boston?"

"I *am* half-British." It was the first time she had acknowledged her heritage out loud. Surprisingly, it did not feel nearly as strange as she had been expecting. "We could remain here, at least for a while. It is where Kincaid has made a name for himself, and I've always wanted to travel. To see new sights. To get out of Somerville. This could be the chance I've been waiting for."

If only Kincaid had the ability to see what was right in front of him, she added silently.

How could a *detective* miss something so obvious?

If her heart didn't still hurt, it would have been comical.

Instead, it was just wrenchingly ironic.

Evie tapped the comb against her palm. "You'd never see Grandmother, or Claire, again."

"There *are* these things called ships. Surely you've heard of them."

"Don't be difficult. And move your head back."

Joanna complied, then felt a gentle tugging on her scalp as Evie twisted her unruly mane into a long braid. "Regardless, it is a moot point," she said, staring at the ceiling. "Kincaid has made it clear he wants nothing to do with me outside of a professional capacity, and I can hardly force him."

"His loss and your gain," Evie said dismissively as she twisted the braid into a bun and secured it with pins. "It is not as if he is titled, or even exceedingly wealthy. You can do far better. There. All finished."

"Thank you." Wincing, Joanna stood up. Now that her anger was beginning to subside, her aches and pains from being thrown to the ground were starting to catch up to her.

In like a lion, out like a lamb, was how their

father used to describe his eldest daughter's temper. While Evie could brood for hours (sometimes even days) when riled, Joanna rarely stayed mad for more than five minutes. It was both a blessing and a curse, for anger allowed her to ignore her emotions. Releasing it forced her to confront them. And she wasn't ready to accept Kincaid was capable of treating her with such callousness. Because it meant she was wrong. It meant she'd been wrong all along.

There wasn't anything between them.

There'd never been anything between them.

And she *was* just his secretary.

"Are you all right?" Evie asked when Joanna limped to the old wooden dresser they were both forced to share. Evie had claimed the vast majority of space, but Joanna had managed to retain the top drawer. In it, she kept an extra pair of gloves, stockings with the heels rubbed bare, a handkerchief painstakingly embroidered with her initials (the patience and attention to detail sewing required had always proven to be a challenge), a vial of perfume, two spare buttons, and a bar of chocolate wrapped in wax paper that she'd brought with her all the way across the Atlantic.

"Yes," she replied as she snapped off a tiny piece of chocolate and popped it in her mouth. It was deliciously sweet, with undertones of black cherry. Precisely the treat she needed to help restore her spirits. "Only a tad sore."

If she were home, she would have drawn a hot bath. But as they were only allotted a certain amount of water per day courtesy of Mrs. Privet's draconian rules (and none of it was particularly hot), she would have to make do with some mild stretching and rainwater.

She was leaning down to touch the scuffed toes of her leather ankle boots when there was a loud, staccato knock at the door.

"Is rent due again already?" she asked Evie, who shook her head.

"Not for another three days. It's probably Mrs. Benedict." But when Evie opened the door, it wasn't their kindly neighbor standing on the other side of it.

"Hello," came Kincaid's deep, somber voice. "You must be Miss Thorncroft's sister."

Her heart in her throat, Joanna jerked upright.

"And you must be Kincaid," Evie said with all the warmth of a snowstorm in the middle of February. "Come to check on Joanna after you abandoned her in the street, have we?"

Kincaid's piercing stare shot past Evie and landed squarely on Joanna. Behind the clear lenses of his spectacles, his eyes were as dark as coffee and, above them, his brows were drawn together in a taut line. "Are you all right?"

Why did everyone keep asking her that?

She'd taken a tumble, not fallen off a bridge.

And the pain she felt in her body was nothing compared to the aching in her heart.

"I am fine." She pursed her lips. "Not that *you* care."

"I do care, Miss Thorncroft," he said roughly. "I care too damned much."

Evie's gaze darted between them. "If you need me, I'll be, ah, down the hall."

Off she dashed, leaving Joanna and Kincaid to stare at each other across the room.

"What do you really want?" she asked. "What are you doing here?"

"I wanted to make sure you made it back."

She wrapped her arms around herself. "You mean after you stormed off and left me."

"Yes, I…" His Adam's apple bobbed in a hard swallow. "I have no excuse, Miss Thorncroft. No reason to do what I did. It was wrong, and I apologize. If I could go back and change my behavior, I would have escorted you to the boarding house as any gentleman should."

Her eyebrow lifted. "You're no gentleman, Thomas Kincaid."

The hint of a smile broke the severe line of his mouth. "Not around you, at any rate."

"Is that a compliment or a complaint?" she said coyly.

"I honestly don't know."

"You can come in, if you'd like." Grabbing

the chair she'd sat in while Evie repaired her hair, she turned it to face the bed and then retrieved what remained of her slab of chocolate. "It's not as fancy as your office, but there's someplace to sit, and sweets."

"I'd hardly describe my office as fancy," Kincaid said with a snort.

"It's better than it was. Come on," she coaxed, waving the chocolate at him. "I'd like to clear the air between us, and there are things we need to discuss."

His expression wary, he took one step into the room, then another, before he stopped short.

"All the way. You can sit here," she said, gesturing at the chair. "And close the door. Mrs. Holden, three doors down, is notorious for eavesdropping."

"I really don't think—" he began tersely.

"Oh for heaven's sake. I won't *bite*."

The mattress creaked as she rested on the corner. After a moment's hesitation, Kincaid reluctantly nudged the door shut, but did not sit.

"Chocolate?" she offered, cracking off a piece.

"No, thank you. Miss Thorncroft—"

"I was very angry with you, Kincaid." She met his gaze without blinking. "For what you said, and what you did."

His shoulders tensed. "I understand, and as I said, I am—"

"Fortunately for you, it's not in my nature to

stay angry for long."

Goodness, but he was handsome. Standing there, all flustered and flushed. He hadn't bothered to change his clothes since the last time she'd seen him, and there was a hole torn in his trousers as well as a dirt stain on his shirt. At least he'd cleaned the cut above his brow and on his chin. They weren't deep, and they wouldn't scar. But they did give him an air of reckless danger that she found *very* becoming.

"Why did you leave?" she asked. "You said you had no excuse or reason, but I know that isn't true. You were upset by what I shared with you. About my personal feelings."

"Yes," he said without further explanation.

"Why? And this time, I deserve an answer. It's the least you can do for what you did." She bit off a piece of chocolate and waited while it melted on her tongue.

Kincaid ran a hand over his mouth. "I…"

"It is all right," she said softly. "You can tell me."

He sat in the chair. Heavily, she noted, as if he carried an enormous, invisible weight. Removing his spectacles, he slid them into the front pocket of his vest and massaged the bridge of his nose. "I was still working for Scotland Yard when I met her. I'd just been made an inspector, and given my own division. I had two dozen men under my command, which meant I could delegate the smaller cases and pursue the larger ones myself. Lord Townsend was such a case. Someone was stealing from him. A servant, he suspected. Though he had no proof. Over the course of my investigation, I stayed at his country estate. That was where his wife and I first struck up a...rapport, I suppose you could call it."

Joanna's eyes widened ever-so-slightly, but she didn't interject. This was Kincaid's story to tell, and having waited this long, she wasn't going to risk giving him a reason to stop telling it.

"Lady Townsend told me things about her marriage. At the time, I believed they were true." Kincaid's hand dropped from his face. He spread his knees apart and rested his elbows upon them, his eyes on the floor between his feet as he continued to speak in the low, impersonal tone of someone recalling the weather. "She implied that her husband was cruel. That he shouted unnecessarily, and drank too much, and struck her where he was certain no one would see the bruises. All lies," Kincaid sat flatly as he straightened in his chair. "But I did not realize that at the time, and I...I developed feelings for her. I wanted to protect her."

Of course he had, Joanna thought. Because that was what Kincaid did. He protected people. And shame on this Lady Townsend for taking advantage of his giving nature. For using what came naturally to him and twisting it into something perverse.

"We began an affair." He met Joanna's gaze and then looked quickly away as a cord of muscle stood out in his neck. "I am not proud of it. I knew she was married. That she was not mine to have. But we made plans to run away together. I was going to leave Scotland Yard. She was going to leave her husband. We were to meet at dawn. I already had a private coach arranged to take us to Edinburgh."

"But she didn't meet you," Joanna said, unable to keep her silence any longer.

"No, she did not." He closed his eyes, and her heart ached at the raw pain she saw flash across his countenance. "I waited in the rain for hours. When I finally came to terms with the fact that she was not coming, I returned to Scotland Yard. Where I promptly found myself arrested and thrown in a cell."

"For what?" she said indignantly.

"Lady Townsend told her husband about the affair, and implied that I had…forced it on her."

"But that's not what happened!" she cried, aghast that a woman would lie about something so serious.

"Can you be that certain?" he asked hollowly. "Others weren't. Good men I'd served beside for years suddenly could not look me in the eyes."

"Then they did not know you as I do, Kincaid." She sprang off the bed and was beside him in an instant, her hand on his thigh, her gaze imploring him to believe and trust in what she was saying. Even though now she finally understood why trusting was difficult for him. "What Lady Townsend did was wicked and cruel. Not only to you, but to *all* women who have the courage to bring their abuse to light only to find themselves doubted and disbelieved."

He clenched his jaw. "I never should have become romantically involved with a client's wife. That blame is mine, and mine alone."

"No, you probably shouldn't have," Joanna agreed, ignoring the twinge of jealousy she felt at the idea of Kincaid with someone else. Of him caring for someone else. Of him *loving* someone else, when he refused to love her. "But if there is blame to be had, this Lady Townsend owns her fair share of it."

"Lord Townsend agreed to withdraw the charges if I left Scotland Yard. My captain requested my resignation that day, and I gave it."

Joanna's lips parted in protest. "But if you were innocent—"

"A trial would have resulted in a scandal, no matter the outcome. A scandal which would have eroded the public's faith in the peelers. It was the right decision."

"So that's why you became a private investigator."

He gave a brusque nod.

"Did you...did you ever see Lady Townsend again?"

Beneath her hand, his leg stiffened. "Shortly after I opened my new business, she arrived unannounced. Even after everything had happened...I still asked if she was all right. If she needed anything. If her husband was treating her well." He dragged his fingers through his hair. "What a bloody fool I was."

"What did she say?"

His mouth twisted in a humorless smile. "She said that Lord Townsend never raised his hand to her. She said he was busy with his mistress, and she was bored, and she'd always wondered what it would be like to have an affair with a commoner."

Joanna's breath expelled in a shocked gasp that rocked her back onto her heels. The *nerve* of that woman! To nearly ruin a life because she was tired of her dull, perfect life and seeking entertainment. Had she any comprehension of what she had done to Kincaid? Of the hurt she'd caused? The hurt she *continued* to cause? For it was clear that even though years had passed, Kincaid was still affected by what had happened. And why wouldn't he be?

He had loved Lady Townsend. Joanna heard it in his voice. Saw in his eyes. Felt it in the unconscious clench of his muscles whenever he spoke her name. He had loved her, and she had betrayed him. In one of the worst ways a woman *could* betray a man. Not out of desperation. Not out of necessity. But because she was *bored*.

It was almost beyond belief.

"I am sorry, Kincaid. I am terribly, terribly sorry. I had no idea." Sliding her hand to his knee, Joanna shifted her weight until she was crouched directly in front of him. His head was down. His arms were limp at his sides. He appeared defeated. And she hated, she *hated* to see him this way.

Which was why she did something *she* probably shouldn't have.

She stood up and stepped between Kincaid's thighs. He lifted his head, his eyes dark and wary. But he did not say anything, and neither did Joanna. The only sound in the room was their ragged breathing as she slid her arms around his neck. She wet her lips. Swallowed once, twice, and her heart pitched inside of her chest.

And then she kissed him.

CHAPTER SIXTEEN

During his first year at Scotland Yard, Kincaid had been ordered to investigate an abandoned factory in the middle of the night. Although the factory, once home to the largest manufacturing company in London, had been shut down for nearly half a decade, the owner continued to store large pieces of expensive equipment inside the crumbling brick building, and he was worried about trespassers after he'd passed by and seen a flicker of candlelight from within.

Kincaid was on the third floor when a storm rolled in over the Thames, bringing with it a wall of thick, eerie, gray fog that spilled through the broken windows and pooled on the floor like dragon's breath.

He'd begun to make his way back down the rickety staircase when he heard it. The unmistakable creak of a board, followed by the scrape of something heavy being dragged across the floor directly below him.

Withdrawing his pistol from the folds of his greatcoat, he had descended the stairs as silently as a cat, every muscle in his body poised to strike. Except it was as black as pitch inside the factory, and with the bloody fog on top of it he did not see the man behind him until it was too late.

The pistol went flying when he was tackled to the ground. Grunting, cursing, he grappled with his attacker, managing to land as many blows as he received despite his unfamiliarity with his surroundings and the damned faceless bastard outweighing him by at least two stone.

A blow to his jaw sent him reeling. As blood filled his mouth, he reached for the knife he always kept tucked in his boot. As he grasped the hilt, lightning exploded across the sky.

The massive bolt lit up the factory, allowing Kincaid to see the second assailant charging towards him with a metal pipe clenched between his meaty fists. Kincaid ducked, then spun around and slid his knife between the man's ribs. The pipe fell with a clatter, and both of the brutes scurried off into the darkness like rats into the sewer.

Breathing heavily, Kincaid bent forward, his hands on his knees and his head hanging limply as his heartbeat gradually slowed. He spat out a mouthful of blood, then staggered to the nearest wall and leaned against it as a boom of thunder shook the factory.

If not for the lightning, he would have been dead with his head bashed open. That violent surge of electricity had saved him. More than that, it had changed him. In those few precious moments between the blinding white flash and driving his blade into flesh, he had been faced with his own mortality. His triumphs and his failures. All he had accomplished...and everything he had yet to do.

When Joanna leaned down and kissed him, another bolt of lightning, straight from the hand of Zeus, shot across the sky.

This one came from inside of his soul, but its point of origin made it no less potent or powerful. And as he wrapped his arms around the tempestuous, fiery American who had been driving him wild since she first sauntered into his office, Kincaid's life was changed as it had been then in that dark factory all those years ago.

Why, he asked himself as their lips parted and he sampled the delicious nectar of her mouth. Why had he denied himself this? Why had he damned himself to hell when he could have been living in heaven?

Yanking up her skirt and all the blasted petti-coats that were underneath it, he grasped her hips and lifted her effortlessly onto his lap. Her knees hugged his ribs, her boots falling to the floor with a soft *thud* as she hooked her ankles around the back of his chair.

His cock surged between them, hard as a railroad pike, and her neck muffled his groan when she wiggled closer, inadvertently stroking herself on his arousal.

Had her kiss happened ten minutes ago, he would have stopped their desires here. Before it went too far for either of them to control. They were already teetering on the brink. A ship about to plunge into deep, untested waters. But having stripped his soul bare, he had no inhibitions left. No compulsions to do what was right. What was honorable.

And thus, he chose what was wicked.

But how could this be wicked when it felt so bloody *good*?

His fingers dove into Joanna's coiffure, scattering pins in every direction as his mouth forged a blazing trail down her neck to her shoulder, which he nipped before burying his face between her breasts.

She leaned away from him, shamelessly offering her taut nipples to his tongue. He licked them through her gown, but the fabric mocked him. With a growl, he grabbed the back of her dress and quite simply tore it away, along with the cotton shift underneath. This time, she wore no corset, for which he was exceedingly grateful, and a whistle of appreciation formed between his lips as the sinking sun bathed her naked skin in an orange glow.

"Better," he murmured as he devoured the sight of her breasts. Perfectly formed, they were neither too large nor too small, rounded beneath and slightly concave on top, with nipples painted a dusky rose. "Much better."

He suckled one sweet tip and then the other, lavishing attention upon the sensitive buds until Joanna was all but writhing and her slender arms trembled from the exertion of holding herself upright. Lifting his head, he gazed at her from eyes heavy lidded with lust. Her cheeks were flush with color. Her hair cascaded over her body in a luxurious wave of crimson. Her lips were parted, her breaths coming in small, little pants.

She was a vision. A masterpiece. A goddess.

He'd never seen anyone so beautiful. He was almost afraid to touch her, for fear that some of his darkness might tarnish such raw, ravishing magnificence. But how could he deny himself such delicious pleasure?

As need warred with logic, as past mistakes mingled with new, he picked her up and changed their positions so that she was sitting in the chair and he was kneeling in the middle of her long legs. A few tugs, and her drawers and stockings were gone until the only thing she wore was her perfume. It wrapped around him in a haze of violet that reminded him of the first day they'd met. She'd smelled of rain, then. Rain and flowers and a hint of desperation.

With the exception of the rain, nothing had changed.

His knees dug into the floorboards as he braced his hands on the armrests of the chair, his hungry gaze drawn to the auburn curls nestled at the apex of Joanna's thighs. She was already damp with passion, and a growl rumbled deep in his throat as he imagined sinking his hard, pulsing length into all of that wet, clenching velvet.

"Let me taste you," he said hoarsely, lifting his head. "Just a taste."

Her brows drew together. "I don't under— *oh*," she gasped when he sank between her legs. A gasp that turned into a moan when he pressed his mouth to the inside of her knee and began to kiss his way up, up, up until he reached the center of all her breathless passion.

Using his thumbs, he delicately parted her folds to reveal the glistening pearl within. His hands sliding around to cup her plump bottom, he lifted her to his lips, a king dining on a banquet of riches.

"Kincaid? Kincaid. *Kincaid!*" She spoke his name as a question, an answer, and a plea as he began to lick with slow, lazy sweeps of his tongue. Her fingers tangled in his hair, nails digging into his scalp.

When the flames threatened to consume them both, he slid a finger into her. Just up to the first knuckle and then back out as he used his mouth to tease and torment her small nub. Gradually, he worked his way to the second knuckle, and then the third.

Her head thrashed. Her legs wrapped convulsively around his hips. He sensed that she was teetering on the brink, and even the gentlest of nudges would send her spiraling into oblivion. But this time, he wanted to go with her. This time, he wanted to jump off that peak together.

Drawing out her ecstasy, he loosened his trousers and sought his own. Using the moisture gathered at the head of his cock to stroke himself as he stroked her, he brought them swiftly to the brink where they teetered, their breaths and souls entwined, before he tightened his fist while simultaneously plunging his tongue into all that slick, satin heat.

Side by side, they fell.

"MY OTHER STOCKING is under the bed, I believe. Thank you," Joanna said when Kincaid retrieved it for her.

Pointing her toes, she guided the crumpled linen up and over her calf before securing it with a plain ribbon tied in a knot. "I think that should do it," she said breathlessly. "Except for my shoes."

"And your hair," he said quietly as he lifted a curl off her shoulder, a rare half-smile tugging at the corner of his mouth.

The same mouth that had just brought her unimaginable pleasure.

It looked the same, she thought. It was the same shape. The same color. But, of course, it wasn't the same at all. Not now, not when she knew what that mouth was capable of.

Pure, unadulterated sin.

And she'd loved every decadent second of it.

In all of her wildest imaginings, she never dreamed of a man doing to her what Kincaid had just done. When he first kissed her down *there* she'd been stunned speechless. Even a tad embarrassed. Now, she wondered if anything of a carnal nature would ever shock her again.

She very much hoped it would.

"Evie's going to be furious with me," she said ruefully as she gathered her disheveled hair at the nape of her neck.

"Your sister." Kincaid's countenance went blank. "I forgot about her. Had she walked in…"

"But she didn't," Joanna said when he trailed away.

And thank goodness for that, or Evie would have seen *much* more than she wanted.

"Still, I should have known better." Retrieving his spectacles from his waistcoat, he gave them a brief cleaning before placing them on his face. "I could have behaved better. Miss Thorncroft—"

"If you apologize, I am going to take this shoe,"—reaching blindly under the chair, she managed to retrieve an ankle boot—"and hit you over the head with it. We were both willing participants in what happened, Kincaid. If anything, *I* should be the one to apologize for taking advantage of your weakened emotional state."

His eyes narrowed. "My weakened what?"

"Nothing," she said cheerfully. Dropping the shoe, she bounded to her feet.

She felt...weightless. Energized. As if she could conquer anything in her path. Which was a good thing, as the object currently in her path was a six foot, three inch, scowling detective who appeared as if he didn't know whether he wanted to kiss her again or bolt out the door.

Kiss, she decided, making the choice for him.

Lightly pursing her lips, she pressed them to his rough cheek where he'd allowed a day's worth of bristle to grow, then tucked a lock of hair behind his ear. "Thank you entrusting such a personal piece of your past with me. It helps me to understand why you've put up such a guard."

His gaze endearingly tender, he trailed a

fingertip along her jawline, then flicked the middle of her chin. "I do not have my guard up."

Joanna gave a tiny snort. "Any higher and the Chinese would accuse you of stealing a section of their Great Wall."

"You're not nearly as amusing as you think you are, Miss Thorncroft."

"And you're not nearly as cold as you think you are, *Mr.* Kincaid." Canting her head, she poked the middle of his chest. "Given where your mouth has been, I believe it would be socially acceptable if you began calling me Joanna."

To her great delight, he actually *blushed*.

How utterly adorable.

As she went to the dressing mirror and attempted to repair her coiffure, all traces of lingering anger faded away as stars brightened her eyes and love swept into her heart, carried on a wind of hope and possibility.

Now that she knew *why* Kincaid was the way he was, his infuriating behavior made perfect sense. Why he would start to get close to her, only to abruptly withdraw. Why he always seemed to be fighting *himself* as much as he fought her. Why he was so fixated on her role as his client, as if it were an insurmountable hurdle that couldn't possibly be overcome.

She did not blame him for the way he'd acted. Not after learning how Lady Townsend had used him, manipulated him, and then discarded him as if he were a shawl that had fallen out of favor.

What a wretched, vile thing to do.

Collecting a handful of pins, she began to place them indiscriminately amidst her curls. Without Evie's skill or patience for elaborate hairstyles, the best she could manage was a loose bun coiled on top of her head that was more or less centered, but it would have to do.

When Kincaid came up behind her and rested his hands on her shoulders, she met his gaze in the mirror. "What do you think?" she asked, batting her lashes.

"I think you look perfect. Miss Thorncroft—"

"Joanna," she reminded him.

A shadow flickered across his face. "Joanna, there is much we need to—"

The door burst open.

"Are you coming with us to the hotel or not?" Evie demanded, her expression vexed. "Mrs. Benedict and I have been waiting downstairs for *hours*."

"Oh, it hasn't been hours." Joanna frowned when she saw that Kincaid was now all the way on the other side of the room by the window. Given his quickness, and his abhorrence for being caught in any sort of intimate position with her, she supposed she was lucky he wasn't on the roof. But how nice it would have been if he'd stayed right where he was.

"Well it's been a long time and—what on earth happened to your hair?" Evie gasped.

Joanna touched the bun. "It...fell out."

"It fell *out*?" She looked at Kincaid in suspicion. "I do not want to speculate what you two were doing up here, but I am nearly positive it wasn't proper. Jo, let us go. I can fix that nest on your head in the carriage. We've reservations, and Mrs. Benedict said the host is very strict with them. If we miss our table, it will be given to someone else!"

"The horror," Joanna said dryly. Gathering her coat, hat, and gloves, she slipped back into her ankle boots, then slanted Kincaid a glance. "Would you be kind enough to accompany us to the door?"

Together, they reached the receiving parlor where Mrs. Benedict was fretfully pacing.

"*There* you are," she said, visibly relieved. "Our hansom cab is waiting."

"Our apologies, my sister and the detective were discussing the case," Evie said smoothly.

"Oh! Have you managed to locate the ring yet?" Mrs. Benedict asked Kincaid. "So tragic, what happened."

"Not yet," said Kincaid. "Although I have a solid lead."

"You *do*?" Joanna and Evie said in unison.

"What didn't you tell me?" Joanna demanded.

"I was going to," he said meaningfully, "but we discussed the *other* case instead."

"Ah, yes. The...the other case," she said as her cheeks warmed.

Evie's gaze swept back and forth between them before she grabbed Joanna's arm. "Whatever it is will have to wait until tomorrow, because our table will not. Goodbye, Mr. Kincaid. It was nice to meet you at last."

"You as well, Miss Thorncroft." He tipped his head at Joanna. "Miss Thorncroft."

"Joanna" she mouthed over her shoulder as Evie dragged her away.

She thought—but couldn't be sure—that Kincaid smiled.

CHAPTER SEVENTEEN

THE SUN SANK low over the Thames, painting the sky a vivid red as Kincaid made his way home. There was a spring in his step. A lightness in his heart. And his mouth...his mouth hurt, actually.

Bemused, Kincaid stopped in front of a store shop window and glanced at his reflection. Why, he was *grinning*, he realized. And doing so was deploying muscles that he hadn't used in years.

How...strange.

Or maybe it wasn't strange at all. Maybe this was how people were *supposed* to feel. When they were happy. Which he was. For the first time in a long time, mayhap in forever, he was *happy*.

As a child, abandoned and unloved, he hadn't known happiness. He thought he'd found it with Scotland Yard, but now that he looked back, he wasn't so sure.

He had been driven, certainly. Driven to succeed. Driven to make a difference. Driven to bloody well *survive*. But all of that meaningless death and disregard for human life had already started to take its toll well before he tendered his resignation.

He thought he was happy with Lavinia. And he was. In the beginning. Yet, if he was being completely honest with himself, a part of him had always known, or at the very least suspected, that something wasn't right. Because love, true love, did not come with attachments or ultimatums. Which was all Lavinia had ever given him. That, and a lasting distrust for all members of the opposite sex.

Then he'd started his own business. Where he was, if not happy, at least content. And that contentment had sufficed.

Until Joanna.

Absently touching the side of his neck where her lips had left a faint purple bruise, he resumed walking, his ridiculous grin larger than ever.

Joanna had turned his entire world upside down.

She'd forced him to take a good, hard look at himself and ask if *this* was what he wanted. A plain life. A tranquil life. A life with purpose but no passion. A life with direction but no desire.

The answer...the answer was obvious.

He wanted Joanna.

He'd *always* wanted Joanna.

And all the chaotic, impulsive joy that she carried with her wherever she went.

When he had rescued her from the horses, his want for her, his desperate *need*, had terrified him. And it still did. But overriding that sense of fear was the knowledge that he didn't have to be afraid. His past need not direct his future. He had made mistakes with Lavinia. Horrific mistakes. But how much longer was he going to punish himself? How much longer was he going to make himself suffer? How much longer was he going to keep himself from being happy?

Joanna made him happy.

Being with her, hell, just being in the same *room* as her was like feeling the first rays of sun on his face after a long, cold night. She'd brought him out of the darkness, and he had never seen her equal. Not even in Lavinia. For Joanna's beauty flowed from the inside, while Lavinia's only existed on the surface, like an apple that was shiny on the surface but black and rotten at the core.

He'd allowed that rot to infect him.

To *change* him.

But not anymore.

Kincaid had just begun to whistle—whistle!— when he rounded a corner...and slammed into a lady walking her small, furry rat.

No, not a rat, he registered as he grasped the

woman by her shoulders to keep her from falling and the tiny rodent began to yap at his ankles. A dog. A fluffy white dog with a pink ribbon collar.

He recognized the collar first.

Lavinia had always been partial to pink, and she dressed all of her animals—three Persian cats and four Pomeranians, the last he knew—in the color.

Then he smelled her perfume. That, too, was unchanged.

Too sweet, like an orange left to wither on the branch, it invaded his nostrils as he automatically bent to retrieve the parcel that had gone flying when he had collided...with Lady Lavinia Townsend.

Slow to stand, he considered throwing the wrapped box at her and running in the opposite direction. But that wasn't how you defeated your demons.

"Lady Townsend." His tone a step below frigid, he held out the box. It contained shoes, if he had to guess. Shopping seemed to be the only thing that brought Lavinia genuine happiness. And wasn't it sad, if that were true?

For so long, he had been so *angry* with her. Eventually, that anger had turned to bitterness, and that bitterness to solemn resolve never to open his heart again. But maybe...maybe Lavinia had never deserved his anger. Maybe what he should have given her all this time was his pity.

She had everything anyone could have ever wanted. A title, immeasurable wealth, good health, popularity. Despite all that, she was still wasn't happy. She'd never *been* happy. Because happy people did not hurt those they loved.

"Why, as I live and breathe, it's Thomas Kincaid," Lavinia purred, her voice—a little breathy with a touch of smoke—precisely as he remembered it.

As his gaze swept across her in a brusque, passionless examination, he wasn't surprised to discover the rest of her was just the same as he remembered. Whatever pact Lavinia had made with the devil, it was working.

Fair haired and green-eyed, she had the soft, pastel allure of a porcelain doll. Her eyebrows, a shade darker than the pale blonde hair styled in a twist beneath a blue felt hat with feathers, were delicately arched. Her cheekbones were sharp and distinguished. There was nary a freckle or blemish to be found on her roses and cream complexion, and her lips were soft and carried a light sheen. The dress she wore had been tailored to fit snugly over her petite frame, with a taffeta bustle to draw focus to curves that Kincaid knew firsthand were greatly exaggerated.

Still, she was undeniably attractive.

Stunning even.

But having touched Joanna's tangled hair, and kissed the freckles on her nose, and marveled at all of her perfect imperfections, he had a new appreciation for the flower growing wild in an open field over the cultured rose in a glasshouse garden.

Lavinia may have been beautiful. But her beauty was frail and cold, like moonlight. Whereas Joanna was as vibrant as the sun.

And he knew which he preferred.

"What are you doing here, Lavinia?" he asked shortly. "You're a long way from Grosvenor Square."

"I came to do some shopping." She patted the box she'd tucked into the crook of her arm. "And to see how an old friend is doing. How *are* you doing, darling? I hope you don't mind me saying so, but you look a little tired. Work keeping you up late?"

He gritted his teeth. "We are not friends. And my work is none of your concern."

She gave a cluck of her tongue. "I suppose you're right...except a tiny bird told me that you've been hired by an American to find a family heirloom that was stolen, and I thought I might be able to offer some assistance."

Kincaid shuttered his surprise behind a bland stare. As far as he'd been aware, no one had known about Joanna except for Sterling. And his friend certainly wouldn't have repeated the details of the case to *Lavinia*, of all people. So how the hell had she learned about the ring?

"I don't know what you're talking about." He went to move past her, but she stepped directly into his path. The rat bared its teeth.

"Now, now, no need to pretend, darling. You can trust me."

"No," he said, glaring down at her. "I really can't."

She sighed loudly. "Are we back to this? I told you it was all a terrible misunderstanding. I feel awful about what happened. Simply *awful*. Which is why I've come to make amends. I do not expect you to forgive me. But my dearest hope is that one day we really *can* be friends again." Reaching out, she trailed a gloved fingertip down the middle of his chest, then gazed up at her him beneath her lashes. "Don't you miss what we had, darling? I do."

Repulsed where he once would have felt aroused, Kincaid grabbed her wrist right before she reached the waistband of his trousers. "I don't miss a single thing about you, Lavinia."

Her plump lips pursed in a pout. "Regardless, I'd still like to help you. Which is why I am going to help you."

"I do not want, or need, your help," he said, dropping her hand as if it were a hot coal.

"But of course you do. Or rather, that delightful American that you've placed under your wing does. She must be beside herself with excitement to have learned that she is the Duke of Caldwell's granddaughter. Even given her illegitimacy, it is *quite* the coup."

"How the hell do you know that?" he snapped.

Lavinia gave a tittering laugh. "If you wanted to keep the girl a secret, then you should have been more careful before you went digging for answers into her past. Lady Ellinwood's closest acquaintance, Mrs. Goshen, is a *notorious* gossip. Cannot keep her mouth closed, the poor thing."

Kincaid had never intended to keep Joanna a secret. But he sure as hell had wanted to tell her the truth about her birth father before Lavinia Townsend found out, or the rest of the *ton*, for that matter. Because if this many people knew already, it was only a matter of days—if not hours—before the news spread like wildfire.

Damn Lady Ellinwood.

Damn her.

She may not have had any interest in meeting her great-nieces, but she certainly had no issues with talking about them. Did she not understand what a tenuous position Joanna was in? And what might befall her if word of her mother's affair with the Marquess of Dorchester became public fodder?

"What do you think will happen when everyone finds out?" Lavinia asked, echoing Kincaid's exact thoughts. "A scandal of this magnitude will shake the *ton* to its core. And just in time for the

Countess of Beresford's birthday celebration. How delightful!"

His gaze slid to Lavinia's mouth and the sly smile that resided there. Lady Ellinwood might not have recognized the potential harm she was causing by recklessly sharing information that was not hers to share.

But Lady Townsend certainly did.

"What do you want?" he asked bluntly.

Lavinia splayed her fingers across the top of her breasts. "Why, only to help you, as I said. And your American. Joanna Thorncroft, isn't it? Lady Ellinwood implied you were *quite* protective of her when you two met. Then there was that little scuffle at the pleasure gardens with the Duke of Telford. If I didn't know any better, I'd start to believe you were sweet on your client, darling." Her smile grew razor sharp. "You've certainly a type, haven't you?"

His hands curled into fists. "You and Joanna are *nothing* alike."

Lavinia's nose wrinkled. "Goodness, I should hope not. She's an American, for heaven's sake. They're practically heathens. Still, I wish her no ill-will. Which is why I am going to tell you that the ring you are looking for is in the possession of her brother, Lord Weston, the Earl of Hawkridge." Lavinia's head tipped. "Or rather, should I say *half*-brother. Words has it he intends to use the ring to propose to the lady he has been courting. Some mouse of a girl, I cannot even remember her name. But they will both be attending the ball."

It was valuable information.

But Kincaid was not so naïve to believe that it came without a cost.

"What is in it for you, Lavinia?" he growled.

Her green eyes widened, all innocence and feigned compassion. "Can I not offer my assistance without expecting anything in return?

"No," he said without hesitation.

"Fine." For an instant, her façade slipped, revealing the ugliness lurking beneath the glossy veneer of polish and perfection. "If I can't have you, then neither can some ill-bred American upstart."

He stared incredulously at her. "You cannot be *jealous*. Our affair ended over four years ago."

"But I still think about you, darling. Don't you think about me and all the fun we used to have?" Her gaze took on a sensual gleam. "Do you remember that inn at Haymarket Square where we—"

"*Enough*," he said loudly. "I remember everything, Lavinia. Including all of the lies you told."

"A little exaggeration here and there," she scoffed. "Hardly anything worthy of note."

"You told me your husband beat you."

"He did threaten to cut off my allowance."

"You told me you were going to leave him."

"Oh, darling." Her voice dripping with sympathy, she leaned forward and patted his cheek. "We all say things under duress. But I could never leave Lord Townsend for a *commoner*. What sort of life could you possibly provide? Please, darling. We must be realistic about these things. That's not to say we cannot enjoy ourselves." Her hand slid lower, her thumb skimming along his jawbone. "In any manner of ways."

"I don't want anything to do with you," he said tersely as he jerked out of her reach. Four years ago, her touch would have ignited a twisted feeling of desire inside of him. Twisted because he'd known it was wrong, but he had still wanted her. Or rather, he'd wanted the woman she'd been pretending to be. But now that he saw her for what she really was, he felt nothing but revulsion.

Lavinia's mouth thinned. "Because of your red-haired American tart?"

"Do not speak of Joanna again," he warned in a soft, silky voice that was far more dangerous than any yell or bluster.

Unfortunately, Lavinia did not heed his warning.

Scooping up her yapping rat, she held the fur ball pinned against her waist as she said, "When everyone learns who Joanna Thorncroft is, it won't matter that she is illegitimate. It won't even matter if the Duke of Caldwell acknowledges her or gives her the cut direct. She'll still be beyond you, darling. You're an unwanted orphan who left Scotland Yard in disgrace while she is the daughter of a marquess. The *ton* is going to adore her." Lavinia ran her tongue across her fangs. "Before they chew her up and spit her back out, that is. She doesn't belong here. And she certainly doesn't belong with *you*. Find the girl's ring, and let her return home. It is the least she deserves after what the poor thing has been through."

Something inside of Kincaid tightened, like a clock spring drawn a tick too hard to the left. Sweat, cold and clammy, broke out along his temple. He swept it away with the back of his hand, but he couldn't wipe away the knowledge that Lavinia was right.

He had spent all of this time trying to convince himself that he *couldn't* love Joanna that he never stopped to consider if he *should*.

What future could they possibly have together? If she remained here, with him, she'd be leaving her family and the only home she'd ever known behind. Not to mention the fact that she was practically royalty and he...he was exactly what Lavinia had said he was. An unwanted orphan who had left Scotland Yard in disgrace.

He could go with Joanna to America. But his work, his *livelihood*, was here, in London. Dare he give it up and begin anew? What if he failed? What if he promised her the moon and was unable to give her even a star?

He couldn't do that to her.

He wouldn't.

Because happy people didn't hurt those they loved.

CHAPTER EIGHTEEN

THE NEXT MORNING, Joanna was positively elated when Kincaid took her to Hyde Park, a 350-acre marvel of bridle paths, wooded trails, and memorial fountains. With Kensington Palace on one end and the Serpentine Lake in the middle, it was the largest green space in all of London. On the narrow footpath upon which she and Kincaid walked step in step, there wasn't room for curricles or carriages. But on the main thoroughfare, they breezed past at a brisk pace, along with riders and pedestrians, all enjoying the crisp, cool morning air that only late August could bring.

The sky was a clear, flawless blue with nary a cloud in sight. From the branches of towering oaks, birds chirped a cheerful tune, their sweet melody echoing the joy that sang in Joanna's heart.

As elated as she felt, it was a wonder she wasn't skipping.

Or spontaneously bursting into song, even though she was completely and utterly tone-deaf. But that didn't matter, because she was in love.

Not maybe in love.

Not falling in love.

In love.

With the man walking beside her.

Thomas Kincaid, detective and wicked kisser extraordinaire.

The best part was she knew he loved her, too.

Oh, he hadn't said it yet. At least not in so many words. But how could he have shared his deepest secret if he didn't love her? How could he have kissed her with such passion, if he didn't love her? It was only a matter of time before he told her. And she was fairly confident he was going to do it soon, for else why would he have brought her to this beautiful place? Surely not *just* to share news of the case. Although she was looking forward to that as well.

How dark and dismal things had seemed yesterday afternoon! Yet if there was a single lesson she'd learned over the past three months, it was that everything could change in the blink of an eye.

Three months ago, she had been in the process of turning down yet another mundane proposal from a well-meaning suitor. Now, she was holding the arm of a British detective she was madly in love with who was trying to recover a stolen ring that had been given to her mother by a father she'd never known existed.

In all her wildest dreams, she could not have imagined that this was where she would end up. All of those twists and turns, all the heartache and the tears, had led her *here*. To Hyde Park. With Kincaid. And surely that was worth all the doubt and uncertainty.

For if not, what was the point?

Kincaid led her to the middle of a bridge with wide, wooden planks and a railing that had once been painted white but was now beginning to peel. He'd spoken little since he'd met her at his front door and turned her towards the park before she could even step foot in the foyer. All of the glances she'd stolen at him out of the corners of her eyes had revealed a pensive expression, his thoughts concealed behind a wall of calm stoicism.

He seemed…resolute.

As if he'd come to a decision.

And she all but beamed, because she knew what that decision was.

Practically, they'd have a few things to work out. Where they were going to live, for instance. She missed Claire and Grandmother. She missed them so much that sometimes her yearning to see their faces and hear their voices felt like a physical illness. But she did not miss Somerville, or her small place inside of it.

The village had stifled her spirit. For some, like Claire, who had no ambitions to leave, knowing every person who walked down the street was a comfort. For others, like Evie, it was an opportunity to be the biggest fish in a tiny pond. But for Joanna, it was, and always had been, a reminder of all the places she'd yet to see and all the life she'd yet to live.

She had done more in the past ten weeks than she had in the past ten years. All of it because she had finally left Somerville. Aside from her family, did she really have any reason to go back? She *liked* London. The chaotic business of it. The pleasure gardens. Mayfair. The theater district. This park. The seemingly endless sprawl of businesses, and homes, and museums. If she lived to be a hundred, she wouldn't be able to see them all. But she'd very much like to accept the challenge.

If—when—they found Mother's ring and sold it, the money could buy an endless amount of trips across the pond. She and Kincaid could see her grandmother and sisters as often as they liked, or even invite them to visit. It certainly wouldn't be convenient. An eight-week voyage was hardly the definition of expediency. But it *would* be possible. And sometimes, possibility was all a person could ask for.

"Look!" she gasped suddenly, her attention captured by a flash of silver in the clear water beneath the bridge. "There's fish. At least a dozen of them."

Kincaid joined her at the rail, his thigh pressing intimately against her hip as he followed the direction of her gaze. "Trout, if I had to guess. When Queen Caroline ordered the Serpentine built by damming up the River Westbourne, she had all manner of trout brought in from surrounding streams. Most perished. Trout are notoriously fickle creatures, and do not adapt to change easily." Sunlight reflected off the fish's scales as they swam lazily upstream. "But some managed to survive. These are most likely their great-great-great-descendants. Speaking of which...I've found your family, Miss Thorncroft."

"You *did*?" she asked, too overwhelmed with excitement to notice he'd reverted to using her surname. "When? Where? Who? Tell me all about them!"

Amber eyes tender behind his spectacles, Kincaid gently brushed a curl off her cheek. "Perhaps we should sit, and I'll tell you all that I have learned."

They went to a bench underneath a weeping willow. There, cocooned in a sweeping cloak of green, he told her about finding Lady Ellinwood and the conversation they'd had over tea and cucumber sandwiches.

"I have a great-aunt," Joanna whispered, not knowing whether she was thrilled or apprehensive by the news. A bit of both, she decided. Along with a slew of countless other emotions she couldn't possibly begin to name.

"And a cousin," said Kincaid, resting his hand on top of hers. "Rosemary. From the way Lady Ellinwood spoke about her, I should think she is similar in age to you and your sisters."

"I want to meet them." Joanna's fingers curled inward, nails digging into her palms through the thin fabric of her kid gloves. "My aunt and my cousin. I want to meet them, Kincaid. As soon as possible."

He hesitated. "It seems there was some...strain that developed between Lady Ellinwood and her late sister, Mabel. Your grandmother. They did not reconcile their differences before Mabel passed and Lady Ellinwood still harbors resentment which she has transferred to you and your sisters."

"To *us*? But we've never met her!"

He squeezed her hand. "I am certain, in time, she will come around."

"I should hope so." Joanna gave an irritated shake of her head. "It's quite presumptuous of her, isn't it, to form an opinion before we have even been introduced? Granted, I am not everyone's cup of tea, but she should at least *meet* me before she decides I'm too loud and opinionated."

The corners of Kincaid's mouth twitched. "Apparently, your mother, whom Lady Ellinwood described as 'rebellious' and 'disobedient', left an indelible impression."

"Good." Squaring her shoulders, Joanna sat up a little straighter. "I am glad that she did. Does...does my great-aunt know who my father—my birth father—is?"

Kincaid stiffened and withdrew his hand. Crossing his arms, he stared out through the long boughs of the willow tree as Joanna held her breath. "I am not sure how to tell you this, Miss Thorncroft. Only to warn you that it may come as a bit of a...surprise."

A hundred different thoughts raced through Joanna's mind. Was her father dead? Was he a criminal? Did he not want to be found?

"Go—go ahead," she managed. "Out with it."

Surely the anticipation was worse than whatever Kincaid was about to say.

"Your birth father is Lord Jason Weston, Marquess of Dorchester. His father is the Duke of Caldwell." Kincaid turned his head and met her stunned gaze without blinking. "Miss Thorncroft...you're the illegitimate daughter of one of the wealthiest and most powerful men in all of England."

⇶⇷

WHEN JOANNA'S FACE drained of all color, Kincaid could have kicked himself.

Bloody hell, but he should have handled that better.

Could have handled it better, if not for the lump inside of his throat. A lump that had grown so large at the sight of Joanna, pretty as a picture standing on his doorstep in a blue dress that matched her eyes, it had all but suffocated him.

Maybe he deserved to be suffocated, for what he was about to do.

What he *had* to do.

He knew she wasn't going to understand. He knew she was going to be furious with him. But he'd rather have her anger than her disappointment. Rather give her a temporary bruise than a lifetime of hurt. Because every word that Lavinia had said to him last evening still rang true in the light of day.

You're an unwanted orphan who left Scotland Yard in disgrace while she is the daughter of a marquess.

She doesn't belong here.

And she certainly doesn't belong with you.

He wasn't good enough for Joanna. He never had been. He never would be. And the only solace to be found in letting her go was knowing that he was doing what was best for both of them.

Or at least, what was best for her. Surely this *wrenching* in his chest wasn't good for him. A person wasn't designed to be torn apart from the inside out. Yet, that was precisely what he was doing. For Joanna, and the life she deserved to live far away from him, and the *ton*, and all the danger she'd inadvertently placed herself in since she got here.

Because ultimately, that was what he wanted. That was *all* he wanted. For her to be safe. For her to be loved. For her to be treasured.

He'd do it himself if he could.

After he'd left the boarding house yesterday, he believed that he *would*.

Until Lavinia had reminded him of what he'd forgotten. That love wasn't only comprised of happiness and merriment and golden sunsets. There was pain as well. Pain, and suffering, and betrayal. He didn't want to feel that again. More than that, he didn't want Joanna to feel it. Which was why he was determined to shield her tender heart from such misery.

Even if it killed him.

"Miss Thorncroft?" Resisting the urge to gather her in his arms and tuck her head beneath his chin, he awkwardly stretched his arm along the bench, his hand hovering over her right shoulder. Her slender body was radiating with tension, her fingers latched together so tightly in her lap that her knuckles gleamed white in the dappled sunlight shimmering down through the willow tree. "Do you understand what I said?"

He did not like her silence.

Quiet did not become Joanna.

She was loud, and bright, and fiery.

A burning comet hurtling across the sky.

But sitting beside him now, with her cheeks as white as snow and her eyes bright with shock, she looked as defenseless as a newborn fawn.

"I...I think I do." She blinked slowly. "I'm not sure. Is...is my great-aunt positive? About the Marquess of...Dom...Din..."

"Dorchester," he provided.

"That's it." Her breasts lifted as she drew a deep breath. "The Marquess of Dorchester. Is Lady Ellinwood certain that *he* is really my birth father?"

"Yes, she seems to be."

"But that does not make any sense." A line furrowed Joanna's brow as she met his gaze. "My mother wasn't even a lady. She was an *American*. Not to say she wasn't beautiful. There is a painting of her above our mantel, she was...well, she was breathtaking. I wish you could have seen her."

I am looking right at her, he thought silently.

Kincaid may never have met Anne Thorncroft but, from what had been described of her, she'd been just as vivacious, and independent, and strong-willed as her eldest daughter. Were Anne still alive, he could only imagine the amount of pride she would have had for Joanna.

"Americans carry their own sort of unique appeal," he said gruffly. Unable to stop himself, he skimmed his fingertips along the delicate vertebrae running up the back of Joanna's neck. An auburn curl wound around his finger as she closed her eyes and leaned into his touch, resting her head on his shoulder.

"Does he know about me?" she asked. "The marquess."

"I like to believe that if he did, he would have reached out to you." Kincaid stroked her arm. "From everything I've heard, Dorchester is a hard, but fair man. Which leads me to suspect your mother never told him she was expecting before she left London."

Joanna sat up. "Then why go to the trouble of stealing the ring after all these years?"

Kincaid had asked himself the same question, and he thought he finally had an answer.

"You also have a half-brother, Miss Thorncroft. Three years older. The Earl of Hawkridge."

"I am related to a duke, a marquess, *and* an earl?" She gave a quick, disbelieving shake of her head. "Evie is going to be *so* jealous."

"Apparently, the earl is about to propose. As I said initially, heirlooms are quite important to the aristocracy."

"You're saying my half-brother stole my mother's ring to use for his *engagement*?"

"Indeed."

"But that's ludicrous!" she exclaimed, jumping off the bench in a swirl of indignation and blue skirts. "Why couldn't he just buy another ring? Why did he have to take *this* one? Does he have any idea the trouble he has caused?"

"I don't know," Kincaid admitted. "But I intend to find out. There is a ball in two days at the private estate of the Countess of Beresford, and the Earl of Hawkridge will be there. I'll speak to him, explain the situation, and see if he is willing to return the ring. Hopefully, he'll have no issue parting with it once he realizes how much it means to you and your sisters."

"Hopefully," Joanna repeated darkly, her brows drawing together. Then her expression abruptly lightened. "I have a brother, and a father, and a *grandfather*. And a great-aunt, and a cousin! Will they all be at the ball? What should I wear? Oh, Evie is going to beside herself when she finds out where we're going. I'd best tell her as soon as possible. It's going to take her a week to prepare, and we've only two days."

This was the part Kincaid had been dreading.

He cleared his throat, where the lump had nearly doubled in size, and rose to his feet. "Miss Thorncroft—"

"You keep calling me that," she interrupted with a smile. A smile that gradually faded as she studied his face. "Kincaid, why do you keep calling me that?"

Because I need the wall to go back up between us.

Because I cannot allow myself to love you.

Because you are better off without me.

"We have reached the end of our week-long trial, Miss Thorncroft."

"Yes, but—"

"Seven days. That was our agreement."

Her mouth opened. Closed. "What—what are you saying?

"That for all intents and purposes, our time together is done." He spoke in calm, precise, level tones. He had to, or else he'd yell. And if he yelled, he was very much afraid he might humiliate himself and cry. "I've located the ring and, barring any unforeseen circumstances, should be able to deliver it to you promptly. There is no need for you to attend the ball. In fact, I think it would be wise if you began preparing for your journey back."

"My journey back?" She swatted at a leaf tickling her cheek. "Back to where?"

"Home, Miss Thorncroft. Where you belong."

She stared blankly at him for a moment. "But...but I *love* you," she said in the small, confused voice of a child who had just been told that Father Christmas was not real. "I thought...that's why...don't you love me, too?"

A knife plunged between his shoulder blades would have hurt less. Love her? He loved her more than the sun loved the moon. More than the ocean loved the sky. It was *because* he loved her...that he was letting her go. "Our personal feelings are irrelevant, Miss Thorncroft. This is what's best. For both of us."

Heat rose to her cheeks. Hurt filled her eyes. Raising her arm, she jabbed a finger at his chest with enough force that he stumbled back a step.

"You," she cried, "are the most idiotic man I have *ever* met!"

Then she turned on her heel and marched away, leaving Kincaid to wonder what the devil he'd done...and why, after years spent trying not repeat past mistakes, it felt as if he'd just committed the gravest one of all.

CHAPTER NINETEEN

JOANNA COULD NOT remember how she had returned to the boarding house. The walk was a blur, obscured by the glassy sheen in her eyes and the rage in her heart.

Evie wasn't there when she stormed into their room. All the better, for Joanna preferred to fall apart in private.

And fall apart, she did.

Little pieces fractured off first. The first time she'd met Kincaid. The first small pulse of heat. The first kiss. Remembering them was like ripping a bandage off a fresh wound and watching blood spill out with no way to stop it.

The shape of his mouth when he smiled.

The sound of his laughter, so husky and rare.

The way his eyes crinkled when he was annoyed with her.

And the warmth that flooded them when he

was pleased.

The sight, the sound, the scent of him wrapped around her like a cloak as she paced the room, then stood by the window, then collapsed onto the bed in a ball of torment and tears.

How could he do this to her? How could he be *this* insensitive?

The bastard had made her fall in love with him! No one else had ever done that before. No one else had ever taken a piece of her heart.

And no one else had ever given it back to her broken and bloody.

Did she mean so little to him after everything they'd shared? Did he hate her this much? For surely, hate was the only emotion that could drive a person to treat someone with such callousness and cruelty.

She'd always known he was cold...and after he told her about Lavinia, she finally knew why.

But this...

There was no explanation for this.

No reason.

Nothing Kincaid could possibly say to make it better.

Because the only thing worse than giving someone hope was snatching it away.

And he had done both.

A pillow muffled her sobs as she buried her face in the scratchy feathers. Joanna did not know how long she had purged herself of all the hurt and the heartache, but when her tears finally subsided and she could draw a breath without knives slicing at her throat, she felt...empty. And empty was a good thing, as it meant she *didn't* feel wounded, or sad, or angry.

Well, maybe a *little* angry.

"Thomas Kincaid is a pigeon-livered ratbag and I despise the very air he breathes," she announced when Evie entered the room.

Cautiously closing the door behind her, Evie set down a collection of parcels on the floor and then regarded her sibling with an arched brow. "The same Thomas Kincaid who you were alone with in here yesterday when your hair mysteriously came undone and I found your petticoat behind the dressing table?"

"You couldn't have found my petticoat. I made sure to put it back on after...oh," Joanna muttered when Evie pursed her lips. "That was quite clever."

"Jo, you didn't—"

"No. *No*," Joanna repeated firmly when her sister appeared unconvinced. "We did kiss. But we didn't...that is to say, I am not a ruined woman."

"Just a devastated one, then. Jo..." Crossing to the bed, Evie sat down and draped her arm around Joanna's back. "What *happened*?"

Like a ribbon unraveling, Joanna came undone at the sympathy in her sister's tone. Laying her head on Evie's lap, something she hadn't done since they were children, she recited what Kincaid had told her when he'd ended their agreement, pausing here and there to use Evie's skirt as a handkerchief to blot at her eyes and nose.

Her sister listened in silence, and when Joanna had finally purged herself of every horrible detail, she stroked her hair and said, "You're right. He *is* a pigeon-livered ratbag. The nerve!"

Evie's indignation felt good. Like cold water trickled over a fresh burn. It didn't take the pain away—nothing could do that—but it did serve to lessen the sting, and Joanna was grateful for whatever reprieve she could get.

"I don't w—want him to be pigeon-livered," she sniffled.

"I know, sweeting. I know."

"Pigeons are h—horrid creatures. Do you remember when that white one pecked my sandwich out of my hand?"

"Horrid," Evie agreed. "Absolutely horrid."

"I thought he was going to tell me that he *loved* me." Grabbing a fistful of Evie's dress, she blew loudly into the fabric. "Instead, he told me to go *home!*"

"Jo, I am heartbroken for you. Truly." As she spoke, Evie gently but firmly tugged her skirt out of Joanna's hand. "But this *is* silk, and stains are impossible to get out. Particularly of the nasal discharge variety."

Joanna wiped her nose with the back of her hand and sat up. "I'm sorry."

"It's quite all right." Going to the wash basin, Evie wet the edge of a towel and began to dab at the damp circle of tears in the middle of her dress. When she was finished, she rinsed the towel clean, sprayed it with one of her many perfume bottles, and then brought it over to Joanna. "Here. Let me wipe your face. I made this chamomile tonic myself, and it should help with your blotchiness."

Joanna rubbed her swollen eyes. "My face is blotchy?"

"Do you recall what Claire looked like after she climbed the apple tree and was stung by hornets?"

Just the memory made Joanna wince. "Yes. She was nearly unrecognizable."

"This is much worse." With all the tender care of a mother bathing her child, Evie ran the damp towel across Joanna's forehead, cheeks, and chin. "There." She tapped the end of Joanna's nose. "That's much better, sweeting."

"You're being so kind to me."

"We're sisters," Evie said, as if that was an answer.

And in many ways, Joanna supposed, it was.

She and Evie may have fought, but they were always there for each other when it mattered.

Without hesitation. Without reservation. They were sisters first, and their bond was unbreakable.

Foolishly, she thought she had found that same bond with Kincaid.

She should have known better.

There *was* something between them.

But it wasn't enough.

She wasn't enough.

Or perhaps, his demons were simply too great.

Either way, maybe it was time to finally admit they were not meant to be together...and love wasn't meant to be this hard.

"There's something else I need to tell you." Letting herself fall back onto the mattress, Joanna stared at the ceiling where a leak in the roof had turned the plaster a dull yellow. Mold was beginning to grow along the edges. But then, that was what happened with problems when they were not addressed. They didn't disappear. They didn't vanish. Instead, they grew larger and larger, until they couldn't be ignored.

Like a family secret left to fester.

Or a detective who refused to acknowledge what was right in front of him.

"What is it?" Evie asked, sitting on the corner of the bed.

Joanna pushed herself up onto her elbows. "I don't know how you're going to react."

"Let me decide that," said Evie. Then she

gave a small gasp. "Is it the ring? Kincaid mentioned he had a lead. Has he found it?"

Joanna bit her lip. "Not exactly...but he knows who has it."

"Who?" Evie demanded.

"Perhaps I should start at the beginning."

"You'd best start *somewhere*, or else I'm likely to die of anticipation."

"I don't think people can die of anticipation."

"*Jo.*"

"All right, all right. Give me a moment," she grumbled. "I'm still figuring it out myself. It seems Mother's affair wasn't just with anyone. According to our great-aunt—"

"We have an aunt?" Evie interrupted. "When did we get one of those?"

"A great-aunt," Joanna clarified. "Lady Ellinwood. She is our grandmother's sister on Mother's side. We've never met her because she has never left England. She married a viscount, who has since passed, and is the guardian of Miss Rosemary Stanhope, our cousin. Or second cousin. Third, maybe? I am not sure how that works, to be honest. At some point, we're going to need to write this all down."

"What happened to Rosemary's parents?"

"They died, I assume."

Evie frowned. "People tend to expire quite frequently in our family, don't they?"

"So it would appear."

"At least we had a viscount for a while," Evie said optimistically. "That's exciting!"

Just wait, Joanna thought silently.

"During Mother's stay in London, it seems Lady Ellinwood was privy to many of the intimate details about her life, including her affair with my birth father." Joanna paused. She was not trying to be deliberately climactic. She merely needed a chance to gather her thoughts. To center herself around the enormity of what she was about to reveal. Because once she spoke the truth out loud, there would be no taking it back. No undoing what was about to be done. And even though answers were what she'd sought when she'd come to London, these were not the *ones* she'd been expecting.

How could she?

How could she possibly have anticipated that this *was* where her searching would lead? To a great-aunt and a cousin, to a father and a grandfather, to a *half-brother*. She had a half-brother! A half-brother who was as much a part of her blood as Evie or Claire.

A half-brother who had set this all in motion when he took what wasn't his to take.

It was ironic, really.

If he hadn't stolen the ring, none of this would have happened. Coming to England. Falling in love with Kincaid. Discovering the identity of her birth father. In an obscure way, the

Earl of Hawkridge had found *her*.

She was simply following the trail he'd left behind.

"Jo?" Evie scooted across the bed until they were side by side. Reaching for Joanna's hand, she linked their fingers together. "If you don't want to reveal his name, I will not ask you for it. We can get the ring and go home. Pretend all of this was a bad dream."

There was a part of Joanna that wanted to do precisely that. To take what they'd come for and return to where they'd come from. To forget the last nine weeks had ever existed.

If she did that, she'd be leaving behind all of the bad.

The hurt.

The misery.

The heartache.

But she'd also be leaving behind all of the *good*.

The butterflies in her belly.

The thrill of Kincaid's touch.

The feel of his mouth on hers.

Was it better to have been in love and had your heart shattered, or to have never known love at all? A question for the ages, for she certainly didn't have the answer. Neither had Shakespeare, or Austen, or Alcott.

But she *did* know, deep in her soul, that having come this far, she couldn't go back. She couldn't pretend it had never happened. She couldn't ignore the love that still beat within her, even now. Even after all the pain. All the disappointment. All the anguish.

Because then, she'd be no better than Kincaid.

She took a long breath.

Counted to three.

Let it out slowly.

"My father is the Marquess of Dorchester. I am the illegitimate daughter of a marquess, the granddaughter of a duke, the sister of an earl." Without warning, tears flooded her eyes and thickened her voice. "I—I am in love with a detective. And I have never felt more unwanted in my entire life."

"Oh, Jo. I want you," Evie said fiercely. "Claire and Grandmother want you. Mother wanted you. And Father...I think Father wanted you most of all. Enough to raise another man's daughter as his own. Your family has always wanted you, Joanna. Always. You must know that."

It was exactly what Joanna needed to hear...and it gave her the strength to push aside her self-pity before it overwhelmed her. Squeezing Evie's hand, she forced herself to sit up. Then she dried her eyes (using her own dress this time), and squared her shoulders. "I do. I *do* know that. I just...I didn't realize a person could hurt like this, Evie. My heart." She laid a hand flat over her breasts. "My heart *hurts*."

"After all that you've endured, I would be surprised if it didn't. But you are strong. You are resilient. You are the most *stubborn* woman I have *ever* met. You'll get through this. The same as you've gotten through everything else. And in the end, you shall be the better for it." Evie was quiet for a moment. Then she nibbled her bottom lip and scratched her ear. "A *duke*, did you say?"

>>>><<<<

LORD WESTON, EARL of Hawkridge, was in a foul mood.

And he didn't care who knew it.

Stoic by nature, it took quite a bit to rile him up to the point of showing emotion in public.

When he was a boy of seven and fell off his pony, he hadn't shed a tear. Not even when it turned out his arm was broken in two places.

When he was a young lad of eighteen and the woman he fancied himself in love with married his best mate, he'd offered his congratulations and bought them a sterling silver tea set.

When he was a man of twenty-two and watched the thoroughbred he'd raised from a colt break down in the middle of The Ascot, he had calmly wielded the pistol that put the stallion out of its misery.

As a result, Weston was renowned throughout the *ton* for his control.

Cold, his friends called him.

Heartless, women said.

Yet when he stalked into his townhouse and slammed the door with enough force to rattle the windows, he wasn't cold or icy. In fact, steam was all but pouring out his ears. Yanking off his hat and coat, he tossed them at the poor, bewildered footman before going off in search of his sister, Lady Brynne. After a brief search of the first floor and its many rooms, he found her outside in the rose garden.

Painting.

"You're standing in my light," she said mildly when he stopped beside her, arms crossed and chest heaving from the exertion of his fast-paced walk from Hyde Park to the south end of Grosvenor Square.

"Put the brush down for a bloody second," he growled. "It's important."

A delicate blonde with hazel eyes that widened imperceptibly at her brother's tone, Brynne obediently stopped painting and swiveled in her chair to face him. "My goodness," she gasped. "Weston, you're...you're *sweating*."

He yanked his handkerchief out of his waistcoat pocket and mopped his temple. "Your point?"

"You never sweat. Are you...are you feeling ill?" she asked hesitantly.

No one ever questioned how Weston was feeling.

Especially his own family.

They all knew better.

"She's here," he bit out, flicking a glance at his sister's canvas. A shy woman, Brynne had always preferred painting to people, even as a small child. She never traveled anywhere without her extensive array of art supplies, and when the siblings had traveled to London together to attend the Countess of Beresford's ball, her brushes and paints and canvases had filled half the trunks.

"*Who* is here?" Brynne said, visibly confused. "Lady Martha? I was under the impression you invited her. Or have you changed your mind about proposing?"

"This isn't about Martha." At that moment, Weston couldn't have cared less about his bride-to-be. Not when there were more pressing matters to attend to. "This is about *her*."

"And by her, you mean..."

Birds hiding in the shrubbery took flight when he threw his hands towards the heavens. "Our sister!"

Brynne blinked. "We don't have a sister."

"The American."

"Oh, you mean *that* sister." Brynne turned

back to her painting and picked up her brush. "How nice. Do you think we should invite her over for tea?"

Weston raked both hands through his hair. As dark as Brynne's was light, it fell to his shoulders in a wave of black. "No, I don't think we should *invite her over for tea.*"

If he allowed it, Brynne would have had every injured animal and orphan in London living under their roof.

But Joanna Thorncroft wasn't injured.

And she damned sure wasn't an orphan.

He had spoken to her father—*their* father— just this morning. They'd discussed the weather. Weston's new string of thoroughbreds. The gambling hell opening on Third and Chesterfield. One topic noticeably absent from their conversation?

The Marquess of Dorchester's bastard daughter.

It was eighteen months to the day that Weston had discovered The Letter in his father's study. Cursed with insomnia and unable to sleep, he'd gone searching for a book to read to pass the hours until sunrise. A slim volume of poetry had caught his eye; *Leaves of Grass* by the American poet Walt Whitman.

The letter fell out as soon as he pulled the book off the shelf. Folded thrice over and yellowed with age, it had crackled when he picked it up and carefully laid it flat on his father's desk to read the delicate handwriting.

My Dear Jason it had begun, and Weston had almost stopped there. Some days, he wished that he had, as the letter had brought him nothing but trouble. But then, he had seen the date in the upper hand corner, and realized it had been written the year his mother passed, and he naively thought that it was from her. A voice from the past he still secretly yearned to hear, even all these years later. So he brought his candle closer, and as light from the orange flame licked across the old parchment, he started reading and didn't stop until he reached the end.

My Dear Jason,

First I should like to apologize for leaving as I did. I should have told you, but if I had done that I fear I never would have had the courage to return to Boston. And this is where I belong. Where I have always belonged. I shall treasure our time together, and hope you are able to do the same. I ask that you not follow me, or try to bring me back to you. I am happy and content where I am, and my greatest hope is that you can find the same happiness and contentment where you are. There may be an ocean between us, but you will forever be in my heart and a piece of you will always be with me.

I was not certain when I left, but I am

now. I am going to be a mother. Our love for each other has gifted us with a child. Again, I should have told you of my suspicions, but I know if I did, you'd have asked me to stay and I would have said yes. But in my heart, I've no wish to be a countess. That life is not for me, and I wouldn't have it for this child.

Jacob has agreed to marry me and raise the babe as our own. He is a good man. He will provide us with a good life. When the child comes of age, perhaps they can visit England as I did. And please know your invitation here is forever open. I wouldn't keep you from your own child, if that is your wish. But neither would I have them raised in an environment that I found so intolerable. I pray you can understand my decision and, some day, find it in yourself to forgive me.

All of my care,
Anne

Once, twice, a dozen times, Weston read the letter.

He kept waiting for it to change. For the words to magically rearrange themselves into something that made sense. But they never did.

What he'd hoped was a hidden letter from his mother had actually been a love note from his father's mistress. A mistress the Marquess of Dorchester had taken almost immediately after his wife died giving birth to Weston and Brynne. A mistress that had born him a child!

For five months, Weston kept what he'd learned to himself.

He hadn't even told Brynne the truth.

There was no reason to dig up old skeletons. No reason to burden his ailing grandfather, the Duke of Caldwell, with a decades-old scandal. No reason to drag the family name through the gossip pages.

But then he had met Lady Martha Smethwick and, finding her a suitable prospect for a wife (if a bit dull), had made the decision to propose. But when he went to ask his father for the family ring, a ring that had been passed down via the eldest son through five generations of carefully planned (if generally unhappy) Weston marriages, he was informed, in no uncertain terms, that it was…

"Gone," said Jason Weston, Marquess of Dorchester, without glancing up from his accounting ledger.

"What the hell do you mean, it's gone?" Weston had said in disbelief.

Jason tapped his pen on the edge of his desk. "I gave it away."

"To whom?" Weston had demanded, although the sinking pit in his stomach told him he already knew the answer. "You gave it to *her*, didn't you? Your mistress. Anne."

His father's head snapped up. "How do you

know that name?"

"Does it matter?"

Jason was quiet for a long while. Then he slumped in his chair, and shook his head. "I suppose not. Except Anne was never my mistress. She was...she was the love of my life."

Weston snorted. "You've never loved anyone."

"That's not true. I love you, and your sister."

"Then you've a damned interesting way of showing it," said Weston, thinking of all the years he'd spent at boarding school. All the times he'd reached out for affection, or acknowledgement, or anything, really, other than indifference. Only to be shoved aside, time and time again. Until, at long last, he stopped reaching out.

There was a reason Weston was cold. A reason he was described as heartless.

And that reason was sitting right in front of him.

The marquess stood up. "If I've been demanding of you over the years, it's because—"

"This isn't about me," Weston said curtly. "It's about the ring. And what you did with it."

A muscle tensed in Jason's jaw. A tall man, like his son, he still cut an intimidating figure at seven and fifty. "Purchase another. As I said, the ring is gone."

Weston met his father's gaze without flinching. "It wasn't yours to give away."

"Are you questioning my decision?"

"You mean your decision to give a two-hundred-year-old family heirloom away to your American mistress? Yes, I bloody well am." Unable to look his father in the eyes for all of the disgust bubbling up inside of him, Weston turned and strode to the window. Dorchester Park was a magnificent estate of over three thousand acres with the study overlooking a large, manmade pond. Focusing on a pair of swans swimming in lazy circles, he said tersely, "Did you ever bother to meet your bastard child?"

"Don't call her that," Jason said.

Her.

His father's mistress had born a girl.

"You've another daughter, then," he said dispassionately. "Congratulations."

"Her name is Joanna. And it was better that I never went to see her. She was raised to believe that another man was her father. I never wanted to dissuade her of that notion."

Of course not.

Why would the marquess care for a third child when he couldn't be bothered with his first two?

"Does Anne still have the ring?" Weston asked.

A long pause, and then…"I don't know."

Incredulous, he whirled to face his father. "You don't *know*?"

"Anne…Anne passed away when Joanna was still a young girl. Scarlet fever," Jason said heavily. "I don't know what became of the ring after that."

"And you never thought to find out?"

The marquess glared at his son. "Should I have arrived on their doorstep while they were still in mourning and order them to return it to me?"

"No, you never should have given it away to begin with." As a quiet rage took hold of him, the likes of which he was always exceedingly careful to control, Weston forced himself to take a step back. "Mama would have wanted my wife, the future mother of my children, to have the ring. Not some American harlot."

His father's face turned a deep, mottled red. "If you want it, then go find it."

And that was what Weston did. With no leads to go on other than a name and a location, he hired the best personal investigator that his vast wealth could buy to find the ring. In a twist of incredible fate, Weston's search coincided with the ring appearing at a jeweler's shop in Boston. The investigator, Harrison, had already paid off every jeweler within thirty miles of the city to immediately notify him should a priceless heart-shaped ruby be brought to them, and when it did, he had one of his so-called "pocket boys" nab the ring and steal onto the first ship bound for

London.

As soon as the ring was in Weston's possession, he had paid the investigator twice his asking fee, then another hundred pounds for his discretion. He still hadn't bothered to tell his father. As far as he was concerned, the marquess didn't deserve to know. But he had shared all that he knew with Brynne, if only because the weight of it all was better shared between two people, and if she were to ever discover he'd kept a secret of this magnitude from her, she'd never speak another word to him again.

And that was it.

The matter was resolved.

Or at least it *had* been until this morning when he rode through Hyde Park...and saw his damned half-sister.

Weston wouldn't have known who she was if not for the picture the investigator had his pocket boy draw at Weston's request. Sheer curiosity had driven him to want to know what Joanna looked like, even though he had absolutely no intention of ever meeting his father's bastard.

The sketch had been childish and lacking in detail, but it was accurate enough that when Weston saw the tall, red-haired, blue-eyed woman marching through the park, he knew at once who she was.

What he didn't know was what the hell she

was doing here.

"Do you think she's come for the ring?" he asked Brynne.

His sister tapped her paintbrush against her chin. "One would assume. You *did* steal it from her."

"You cannot steal what is rightfully yours," he growled.

"But if it was left to her by her mother—"

"That doesn't matter."

"It matters a great deal to her, I believe, if she's traveled all the way to London." Brynne crossed her legs at the knee. "What are you going to do, West? If our sister asks for the ring back."

"I'll tell her that I'll give it to her." He smiled grimly. "Over my cold, dead body."

CHAPTER TWENTY

WHEN A KNOCK sounded at the door early in the morning, Joanna buried her nose in her book. "If that's Kincaid," she said scathingly, "tell him I am not in."

After pouring out her innermost feelings to Evie and crying a few more tears, Joanna had picked herself up, dusted herself off, and decided that a man wasn't going to ruin what little time in London she had left.

Even a man who had stolen her heart.

She would need it back at some point. As the daughter of a doctor, she was fairly certain a person couldn't go parading about with an empty hole in their chest where a vital organ ought to be.

But not today.

Today, she refused to think about Kincaid at all.

JILLIAN EATON

Except he was knocking on the door at half-past seven.

Which made him rather hard to ignore.

Pigeon-livered ratbag, indeed.

"Our room is the size of a henhouse," Evie pointed out as she abandoned her garden of powders and creams, cinched her dressing robe, and went to the door. "I'm fairly certain he is going to see you."

"Not. In," Joanna repeated.

"Fine," Evie sighed. The door creaked on its hinges as she opened the door a crack. "I am terribly sorry, but—oh. *You're* not who I was expecting."

"Is that a good thing or a bad thing?" asked a woman whose voice Joanna had never heard before. It was light, and melodious, and she could tell their visitor was smiling even though Evie was blocking the doorway.

"Who is it?" she asked, closing her book and swinging her legs over the side of the bed.

"Not Kincaid," Evie replied. "Are you still out?"

"No, I'm in."

"You're *not* in, or you're—"

"For heaven's sake," Joanna grumbled. In two steps, she was across the room—it really was the size of a henhouse—and peering over Evie's shoulder at a curvy brunette with a heart-shaped face, twinkling eyes that couldn't decide whether they wanted to be blue or gray, and a beaming smile that stretched ear to ear.

"Oh," she gasped in delight, "I am *so* happy to finally meet you!"

Joanna grunted when the young woman flung her arms around both sisters and gave them a hug that was astonishingly strong for her petite size.

"Help me," Evie mouthed.

"Er, it's nice to meet you as well," Joanna said as she carefully extracted herself from the enthusiastic embrace. "Who are you, exactly?"

"Of *course.*" Using her palm, the brunette gave herself a light smack in the middle of her forehead. "I always forget that part. Or rather, I never get to do it as not many people are interested in meeting me." Her grin unwavering, she stuck out the hand she'd just used to hit herself. "Miss Rosemary Stanhope. I am your—"

"Cousin," Joanna said, stunned. "You're our cousin."

Evie turned to her. *"This* is our cousin?"

Rosemary's nose wrinkled. "Are you disappointed? It is all right. I am accustomed to it."

"Disappointed?" Joanna repeated. "We're *thrilled*! Aren't we Evie?"

"I could have done without the hug."

Joanna pressed her lips together.

"Yes, yes." Immediately putting on her most charming smile, Evie shook Rosemary's hand.

"Absolutely thrilled."

"Come inside, come inside. I apologize for the mess," Joanna said with a pointed glance at the dressing table which was all but hidden beneath Evie's various creams and pots and potions, "but we were not expecting company."

"I'd hoped to surprise you," Rosemary confessed. "Or else I would have sent word."

"This is a wonderful surprise, and please do not take this unkindly, but...what are you doing here?" Sitting on the bed and leaving the chairs for her cousin and sister, Joanna's head tilted in confusion. "I was under the impression our great-aunt was not exactly...eager to make our acquaintance."

"She's not," Rosemary said. "I mean, she is. Well, she *will* be. Eventually. But my grandmother can be quite...set in her ways."

"We know the feeling," Evie said dryly.

"How did you find us?" Joanna asked.

Color bloomed in Rosemary's cheeks as she sat down. "I, er...that is to say, I followed the detective yesterday after he left our house," she confessed, smoothing a wrinkle on her skirt. "He led me straight here. I would have come in, except I lost my nerve. But I found it again this morning. Try and try again, as my grandmother always says! Usually, she's referring to my failed attempts at landing a suitor, but I thought it could apply to this, as well."

"We're glad that you are here." Refusing to acknowledge the tightening in her throat at the mention of Kincaid, Joanna forced a smile onto her face. It wasn't exceedingly difficult. She *was* happy to meet her cousin. Elated, really. But over all that elation was a dark, heavy raincloud.

A raincloud made all by the heavier by the knowledge that she *should* have been ecstatic.

After weeks of uncertainty, she had everything she could have ever possibly asked for. The location of her mother's ring. The identity of her birth father. And other family, besides! That was everything she'd come to England to find. But in seeking those answers, she'd found something else. Something even more valuable.

Love.

True love.

Or so she'd allowed herself to believe.

Now when she returned to Somerville, she'd have the ring, and the knowledge of where she came from. But she'd be leaving her heart behind in London. More than that, she'd be leaving behind the possibility of what could have been. What *would* have been, if not for Kincaid's inability to give what they both desperately needed.

Did he really think she would hurt him, as that other woman had? That she would take his love and twist it into something unrecognizable? Or was he just so badly wounded from what had happened to him that he was unable to see the light of what could be through the shadows of what had been?

That was an answer Joanna did *not* have.

Because Kincaid had refused to give it.

Once again, he had just closed himself off and pushed her away.

As if she meant nothing.

As if *they* meant nothing.

And maybe that was what hurt worst of all. Not that he'd all but shoved her out the door, but that he hadn't even been willing to *try*.

"You seem upset," Rosemary observed, her smile wavering as she looked at Joanna. "I shouldn't have come. I'm sorry." She started to stand. "I will go, and—"

"It's not you," Joanna said hurriedly. "Honest. It's…it's something else. *Someone* else. Please stay. There is so much I'd like to ask you."

Sinking back down into her seat, Rosemary clucked her tongue in sympathy. "It's the Marquess of Dorchester, isn't it? Silly me. If I found out my father wasn't who I thought he was, I'd be upset as well."

Joanna exchanged a quick, startled glance with Evie. "How do *you* know about the marquess?" she asked, puzzled. "I was under the impression it was…well, that it was a bit of a secret."

Rosemary giggled. Then her eyes widened.

"Oh. Oh, you're *serious*. Nothing in the *ton* is a secret. Not really. Plus, I may have...erm...eavesdropped on my grandmother and Mr. Kincaid. I didn't mean to." Her round cheeks flushed, reminding Joanna of the doll that Claire used to carry around with her everywhere she went. "It's just that we do not get many visitors, and I thought the detective may have been a suitor come to call, and so...I pressed my ear to the door and listened to the entire conversation."

"Have you met him?" Joanna slid to the edge of the mattress. "My...that is to say, the Marquess of Dorchester."

"We have been introduced," Rosemary nodded. "I even danced with the Earl of Hawkridge once." Her blush intensified. "I trounced on his instep so hard that he walked with a limp for the rest of the night. He never asked to sign his name to my card again."

"What are they like?" Joanna asked earnestly. Try as she might, she'd been unable to form a picture of her birth father and her half-brother in her head. Perhaps because every time that she'd tried, her thoughts just kept veering back to Kincaid, like a moth that couldn't leave an open flame alone even though it knew that if it got too close it would singe its wings.

"The marquess and the earl?" Rosemary asked.

Joanna nodded.

"We don't really...that is to say, our social circles don't intersect with any sort of regularity. Probably due to the fact that mine is shaped more like a square." She smiled apologetically. "Rest assured that you are going to be far more popular than I. People don't tend to notice plain."

"You're not plain," Joanna protested. "Is she, Evie?"

"I've seen worse," said Evie. For her, it was a very high compliment indeed.

"It's all right," Rosemary said with a shrug. "I don't mind. Truth be told, there are many good things about being a wallflower. No one ever notices when I go back for thirds at the sweets table. And I'd much rather read a book than remember the steps to a waltz."

"Reading is *much* more important than dancing," Joanna agreed. She hesitated, and then asked, "What does he look like, my half-brother? I have been trying to conjure an image of him in my mind, and...." Her hands lifted in the air. "I cannot."

"He's *very* handsome," Rosemary said at once. Then she gasped, and covered her mouth as another pink blush stole across her cheeks. "I shouldn't have said that. You're his sister. I mean, his half-sister. I mean, his—"

"It is all right," Joanna said gently. "Please do not feel flustered on my account."

Evie perked up. "Handsome, did you say?"

"Oh, for heaven's sake." Joanna muffled a snort as she noted the calculating gleam in Evie's eyes. "He's my *brother*. Surely you can set your sights on someone else. Anyone else, really."

"He is your *half*-brother. With absolutely no relation to me. *And* he is an earl."

"I was under the impression you wanted a duke."

"If I could find one, I'd happily marry him. Until then...tell us more about the Earl of Hawkridge," Evie ordered Rosemary, who bit her lip.

"Well..." their cousin began. "He is quite tall. And he has black hair, unlike his sister—"

"He has a sister?" Joanna interrupted. "*I* have a sister?"

Kincaid had failed to mention that part.

Then again, he'd failed at a lot of things.

"Yes. Lady Brynne. They're twins."

Weston and Brynne.

Evie and Claire.

As Joanna shook her head in disbelief, she struggled to wrap her mind around the idea that her number of siblings had just doubled.

"How long are you planning to be in London?" asked Rosemary. "There's so much I'd like to show you. Are you staying through Christmas?"

Evie glanced at Joanna, whose gaze fell to her

lap as a sharp pang resounded within her chest.

"We're leaving soon," she said, drawing a circle around her knee. "Most likely within the next day or two."

"But you cannot," said Rosemary, positively aghast. "You'll miss the Countess of Beresford's birthday celebration. She's throwing an enormous ball. *Everyone* will be in attendance."

Joanna's pulse leapt. She knew that name; Kincaid had spoken it in the park before he'd stomped on her heart. Her half-brother was going to be at the ball. As well as Kincaid, and maybe even the ring. "Did you say the Countess of Beresford?"

Evie gripped her chair. "Did you say *ball*?"

"It's going to be an absolute crush," said Rosemary. Then she frowned. "I am not looking forward to it, if I were being honest. As I said, I am not exceedingly popular." Her nose wrinkled. "People find me odd. I think it is the squirrel."

"I don't think you're odd at all," Joanna declared, and she meant it. Rosemary may have been a tad shy and awkward, but that's what made her so endearing. They'd only just met, and already Joanna had the feeling they were going to be good friends.

Unfortunately, it seemed Evie had a different opinion in regards to Rosemary's unique charm.

"I'm terribly sorry," she said politely. "You have a squirrel?"

"Sir Reginald." Rosemary patted her shoulder. "He usually sits here, but I left him at home this morning. I did not want to make a poor first impression."

Evie edged her chair back a few inches. "I see."

"Sir Reginald sounds delightful," said Joanna with a reproachful glare at her sister, whose eyebrows rose as if to say, "What would you have me do? She has a pet *squirrel*". "When is the ball, again?"

"Tomorrow night. Which is why you cannot leave yet!" Rosemary gazed anxiously between them. "I always sit in the corner by myself. And Grandmother said this time I have to leave my book at home. But if you were there with me, it would be entirely different! I've always wanted a sister. But surely cousins are the next best thing! Oh, *please* say you'll come. Please?"

Joanna looked at Evie.

Evie looked at Joanna.

"Yes," they said in unison. "We'd love to."

UNFORTUNATELY, IT SEEMED attending a ball wasn't as easy as saying "yes".

According to Evie, none of the dresses they'd brought with them were suitable. Which meant

Joanna spent the rest of her day traipsing about London in search of a gown that was not only within their meager budget, but ready to wear.

Finding the Holy Grail would have been a far easier task, but at least it provided a welcome distraction from her constant thoughts of Kincaid. Never mind that they were soon to be at the same ball. She wasn't going there to see him. Definitely not. She was going there to spend time with her cousin, and to possibly catch a glimpse—or mayhap even meet—her brother, the Earl of Hawkridge.

Truth be told, Joanna didn't know *how* she felt about her newfound family.

It was, in a word, overwhelming.

And difficult to fully comprehend.

Joanna did not care that her father was titled or "one of the most wealthiest and powerful men in England". She would have been pleased if he were a baker or a blacksmith or a candle maker. Such an occupation certainly would have lent itself to fewer complications.

Showing up on the doorstep of a baker and announcing herself as his long-lost daughter was one thing.

But arriving at the private estate of a marquess…well, that was something else entirely.

Add to that an earl, and a duke!

It was almost too much.

It *was* too much.

What did she know about British aristocracy? Their rules and rigid propriety. Their customs and traditions. When—if—they were introduced, she wasn't going to fit in.

She, an American who hated bonnets and didn't have the foggiest idea of which fork to use for dessert, would stick out like the proverbial sore thumb. Having already been rejected once, she didn't know if she had it in her to face rejection again.

But there *was* always the chance, however slight, that she would be welcomed with open arms. Which was why she was attending the ball. To catch a glimpse of her half-brother from afar and see if he was someone whom she might get on with, as she had with Rosemary. Well, that, and if she didn't go, Evie would murder her in her sleep.

Joanna hadn't seen her sister this happy since they'd left Somerville. All she'd wanted this entire time was to go to a ball. And Joanna wasn't going to be the one to deny her that small pleasure. Especially given how well Evie was handling everything.

To Joanna's surprise—and relief—her sister hadn't been jealous, or put out by the revelation that her sister had noble blood running through her veins. Quite the opposite. She was absolutely *thrilled* by the news, and saw this ball as the first of many.

But first, they needed gowns.

After walking for what felt like hours, they found a small, inconspicuous shop tucked away off the main thoroughfare. It didn't look like much from the outside, but the windows were clean and someone had taken care to plant flowers along the edge of the short walkway. Joanna hoped it was a promising sign of what awaited them inside, for her legs were beginning to tire and her head felt heavy on her shoulders.

She wanted a bath, and a nap, and a glass of wine. Not necessarily in that order. But Evie was determined to find the perfect gown, and when she got that certain glint in her eyes, no one could dissuade her.

Especially not Joanna.

A cheerful bell announced their entrance. Almost at once, they were greeted by a short, plump woman with black hair streaked with gray and a kind smile.

"*Bonjour,*" she said, her voice warm and welcoming and undeniably French. "How can I be of assistance?"

"We have been invited to the Countess of Beresford's ball," Evie said with thinly veiled excitement. "And we are in need of the appropriate attire."

The dressmaker blinked in confusion. "But is zee ball not tomorrow?"

"Exactly," Evie said solemnly.

"We've hardly any money and little to trade." As this was their seventh stop, Joanna saw no reason to beat around the bush. "But we would be appreciative of anything you might have that we could use. A dress that was returned, or didn't fit, perhaps. We're not picky."

The dressmaker placed her hands on her rounded hips and sniffed. "Clients do not *return* dresses to Mademoiselle Claudette."

Evie elbowed Joanna sharply in the ribs. "You've insulted her!" she hissed. "Clients do not return dresses to Mademoiselle Claudette."

Joanna resisted the urge to roll her eyes. "I heard her. I *am* standing right next to you."

"Well, go stand over there," she said, pointing across the tiny shop. "Let me handle this."

With no desire to argue, Joanna did as she was told. Absently running her fingers along the edge of a wooden mannequin, she waited while Evie and Mademoiselle Claudette spoke in low, quick tones. There was an audible gasp, a torrent of French, and Joanna turned just in time to see the dressmaker clap both hands to her cheeks.

"I have zee perfect gowns for you and your sister!" she announced. "Zey were commissioned by the Earl of Tremont for his wife, but zey were meant for greater things."

"I'm sorry," Joanna began with a reproachful look at Evie, "but we don't have that sort of money. I wish we did—"

"Tra la la," Mademoiselle Claudette scoffed. "I should be zee one paying you! Do not move a muscle. I'll be right back to take your measurements. If I work through zee night, the gowns shall be ready in time. You will be zee talk of zee *ton!*"

"What did you do?" Joanna demanded as soon as the dressmaker had disappeared behind a heavy velvet curtain. "We couldn't buy a potato sack if we wanted, let alone dresses that are intended for a countess!"

Evie shrugged. "I simply told her who you are and promised to tell anyone who asks that our gowns were designed by Mademoiselle Claudette."

"What do you mean, you told her who I am?" Joanna asked suspiciously. "Why would she care about a penniless American?"

"But you're not a penniless American, are you?" Evie wandered over to a shelf stuffed with bolts of fabric and removed a small swatch of violet silk. "You're the daughter of the Marquess of Dorchester."

Joanna paled. "You didn't tell that to the dressmaker, did you?"

"Why wouldn't I? It's the truth." Evie held the silk to her face. "Does this pair with my complexion, or wash me out?"

"*Evelyn.*"

"Oh, don't be upset with me. We needed the

gowns, and we weren't about to be given them by asking nicely. We've lost so much, Jo. Our parents. Our home. Mother's ring." Lowering the fabric, Evie gave it a fond pat before she returned it to the shelf. "Maybe this is the world's way of repaying us. Of giving us something back after all that we've gone through. That *you've* gone through."

Her sister did have a point.

They *had* been through a lot. More than Joanna would ever wish upon anyone else. Surely two dresses and a ball weren't too much to ask for in return. Still, she felt a flicker of discomfort at using her father—a father she'd never met—as currency.

"Just…do not do it again, all right?" she said.

"*Fine*," Evie sighed.

Mademoiselle Claudette returned, armed with a cloth measuring tape draped around her neck and a dozen pins held between her lips. One at a time, she ordered the sisters onto a wooden dais where she measured, poked, and prodded until Joanna was on the verge of leaping into the first rowboat she could find and paddling back to America. At long last, the dressmaker nodded in satisfaction and tucked her measuring tape between her breasts.

"Zee gowns will be ready tomorrow. Come in zee morning for a final fitting."

"Another one?" Joanna groaned.

"We cannot wait," Evie beamed as she put on her hat and knotted the strings beneath her chin. "Thank you, Mademoiselle. What an honor to be dressed by the finest *modiste* in all of London."

"Thank *you*," Claudette replied as she led them to the door and waved farewell.

CHAPTER TWENTY-ONE

"**Y**OU LOOK LIKE shite," Sterling commented as Kincaid climbed into the duke's carriage. With a crack of the whip and a slap of the reins, the glossy black town coach lurched forward, headed for Beresford Manor in the middle of Grosvenor Square.

"This is *your* tailcoat," Kincaid reminded his so-called friend as he tugged at his sleeve.

"Aye, and you look like shite in it."

"Sod off." While he was not lacking for clothing, Kincaid did not have the formal attire required of such a prestigious event as the Countess of Beresford's ball. Sterling had sent his tailor over in the later afternoon to dress him accordingly. The sizes of the two men were similar enough that only a few lines had needed to be adjusted. When the tailor was finished, Kincaid had glanced at himself in the mirror and was startled to see a nabob staring back.

He hated that his first thought had been of Joanna. Of what she would think of his appearance, and if she would prefer his regular attire to being trussed up like a damned penguin. He hated it not because he didn't *want* to think about her.

But because he did not deserve to.

After the way he'd ended things between them…after the hurt he'd seen in those beautiful, blue eyes…he didn't deserve to breathe the same air as she did.

Joanna had given him her heart to care for.

And he'd returned it to her in pieces.

Just as Lavinia had done to him.

In the carriage's inky interior, Sterling's teeth flashed white. "Had a row with your American, did you? Either that, or one of those flea-infested felines you insist on keeping in your house died."

The duke's abhorrence for any animal smaller than a horse was well known. Normally, Kincaid found his friend's aversion amusing if only because he knew the *real* reason Sterling despised cute, fluffy creatures. When he was a child, Sterling had been bitten by his mother's terrier in a very…*sensitive* area. Since then, he had developed an innate distrust for any tiny creature with teeth.

But this time, Kincaid didn't chuckle.

He didn't even crack a smile.

"My cats are well, and Miss Thorncroft and I did not have a *row*." He stared out the window. "I chose to end our...partnership."

"Why the devil would you do that?" Sterling asked.

"If tonight goes according to plan, Miss Thorncroft's ring will be in my possession by the end of the evening and both she and her sister can depart on the next ship bound for Boston."

Little more than a week ago, those very words had brought him a sense of relief.

Find the ring, give it to Joanna, and send her back to where she'd come from.

But tonight, he felt nothing but despair...and doubt.

"That's the bloodiest stupid idea I've ever heard," Sterling said with a snort. "Should I tell you why?"

"No," Kincaid said unequivocally.

"First, because it's obvious you're in love with the chit. And second, because the Earl of Hawkridge is the meanest, most frigid bastard I've ever met in my life. You've a better chance of winning a derby race with a damned donkey than getting him to give you that ring."

Kincaid's gaze flew away from the window. "How the hell do you know about the Earl of Hawkridge and his connection to Joanna?"

"Who *doesn't* know?" Removing a silver flask from his pocket, Sterling took a sip and offered it to Kincaid, who declined with a curt shake of his head. "You're aware of how fast gossip travels once it's let out of the bottle. I'm a bit annoyed I didn't figure it out myself. JW. Jason Weston. 'Tis obvious now, isn't it? All of it happened before my time, naturally, but I've heard whispers over the years about the Marquess of Dorchester and his American mistress. No idea they ever had a child, though. Or that that child was your client." Grinning, Sterling nudged Kincaid in the side. "You sly dog. Going after the granddaughter of a duke. Smart on you."

"I didn't *go after* the granddaughter of a duke," Kincaid scowled. "I didn't know who she was when I—"

"Fell in love with her?" Sterling finished when Kincaid stopped himself short. "It's all right, old chap. Happens to the best of us. I must say, all this chatter about your American has done me a great service. Haven't had a single person look at me as if I were a crazed murderer in at least a day."

"Congratulations," Kincaid said bitterly.

The duke lifted a cool brow. "Thank you. Given that the detective I hired has done bugger all to clear my name, I need whatever reprieve I can get."

Guilt filled Kincaid. "I am sorry. I..." Removing his spectacles, he buried his head in his hands and groaned. "I'm a bloody mess."

"That much is obvious. Care for a nip of that scotch, now?"

Blindly, he reached for the flask and raised it to his mouth. "I fucked it up," he said before he took a long swallow and handed the liquor back.

"Fucked what up?"

"Everything." The carriage rolled to a halt. They'd reached their destination, but neither man made an attempt to disembark. "From the start, I told myself not to get involved with Joanna. I *knew* how it was going to end. Along the way, something changed, and I...I saw a future between us. How, when, it didn't matter. I saw it. It was there. Then I spoke with Lavinia—"

"*Lavinia* Lavinia?" Sterling interjected. "The blonde bitch who enjoys yanking the wings off of flies just to watch them squirm? You're the fly in that analogy, by the by."

Kincaid pinched the bridge of his nose and then sat back, letting his head fall against the seat with a soft *thud*. "I know."

"Tell me you didn't listen to a word that scheming harlot said."

He closed his eyes.

Sterling cursed under his breath.

"God*damnit*, man. You let her get inside your head *again*?"

"She raised some valid points," Kincaid defended.

"Did she? Or did she merely say what you

wanted to hear?"

"I didn't…I don't…Bloody hell."

Sterling was right. He'd listened to Lavinia because she *had* told him what he wanted to hear. Not on the surface, but down deep. Where the keystone to the wall he'd built around his heart was buried. He'd listened to her because it had been easier than embracing the alternative. He'd listened to her because he was still afraid.

Afraid of losing his heart.

Afraid of losing *himself*.

But was that not what he'd done when he watched the brightness dim in Joanna's eyes?

He had put that hurt inside of her.

He had taken away her smile.

He had…he had done to Joanna what Lavinia had done to him.

The realization hit Kincaid like a brick to the face.

Mentally reeling, he grabbed Sterling's flask again and gulped it down.

Joanna wasn't better off without him.

And he sure as hell wasn't better off without *her*.

She challenged him in ways that no one else ever had. Because no one else knew him like she did. Joanna *saw* him. The good and the bad. The light and the dark. She loved him despite his flaws and his imperfections. She loved him even though he'd done everything in his power to keep her at arm's length.

She *loved* him.

Without reservation.

Without ulterior motives.

Without demanding anything of him in return.

Having never felt that type of love before, was it any wonder he'd been suspicious of it? Was it any wonder that he'd squandered it? If Lavinia had taught him anything, it was that commitment did not come without painful consequences. But whatever sickness they'd had between them, it was never love. Which meant he hadn't ever known what love really was.

Until he'd met Joanna.

Kincaid's grip tightened around the flask.

What a *fool* he was!

All this time, he'd been running from something he'd never even had. And then when he *did* have it, when it was in his grasp and he had only to close his hand around it, he'd allowed Lavinia to yank it away.

Which he was certain had been her intention all along.

"Oi, save some for me," the duke complained, yanking the flask out of Kincaid's grip. "Do you've any idea how many debutantes are going to be in there tonight? I need all the liquid fortitude I can get."

And Kincaid needed another chance with

Joanna.

A chance he damned well didn't deserve.

But one he was going to take anyways.

"I have to speak with her," he muttered, raking a hand through his hair.

"Your American?" Sterling asked.

For once, Kincaid didn't try to correct him. Because Joanna *was* his.

That is, if she'd take him back.

"Yes," he said, already calculating the time it would take to hail a hansom cab and get across London to the boarding house.

"Then you're in luck," said Sterling cheerfully, pointing out the window towards the marble pillars guarding the front entrance of the manor where guests were lined up in a long queue waiting to be admitted. "Because there she is."

"THIS IS IT." Her face tinged pink with excitement and a dusting of rouge, Evie's gloved fingernails dug into Joanna's arm as a butler dressed in formal black accepted their invitations (courtesy of Rosemary) and waved them onward. "Our official debut into London High Society!"

"Is it an official debut when no one knows who we are?" Joanna wondered aloud as they followed the crowd through an enormous foyer with hand-painted tile on the floor and gold chandeliers hanging from the ceiling. By her count, there had to be at least two hundred people in attendance. Most likely even double that, as she hadn't actually *seen* the ballroom yet. It loomed before them, guarded by towering doors painted a vivid blue with naked cherubs at the top and clouds at the bottom.

She and Evie shuffled ahead at a snail's pace, giving her plenty of opportunity to take in her surroundings…and the other guests.

Before their father died, Joanna and her sisters had hosted a ball at their stately manor in town. There had been dancing, and singing, and vases filled with white roses. At the time, she'd thought it was the very height of elegance. But when compared to the Countess of Beresford's birthday celebration, it might as well have been a picnic on a grassy knoll.

The sheer size of the estate was intimidating enough. Why, the foyer alone was the entire size of their cottage! Pair that with footmen milling about carrying sparkling glasses of champagne, real-life swans roaming the front gardens, the most exquisite gowns Joanna had ever laid eyes upon, and the entire affair was absolutely mind-boggling.

A subtle sweep of the room (her third, as it so happened) revealed a sea of unfamiliar faces. She was looking for her cousin. Definitely *not* Kincaid.

But if she happened to see him, well, wasn't it better to know where he was? Better to prepare herself ahead of time for the inevitable pain she was going to feel when she saw him. Better to get control of her recalcitrant emotions now rather than later. Because if she started crying again, not only was she going to be disappointed in herself, Evie would be furious. Her sister had already warned her that tears did not come out of silk, and Joanna's dress was made out of yards of it.

A mossy green that complemented her titian mane, it had a wide-necked bodice that sat just off her shoulders, sleeves adorned with ivory rosettes, and a large skirt decorated with embossed tulle. The gown was simplistic in design, allowing Joanna's natural beauty to shine through. Evie had twisted her hair into a pile of curls on the top of her head, accentuating the length of her neck and the height of her cheekbones. Candlelight reflected off the alabaster pearls at her ears and throat, the only jewelry she wore. Elbow-length satin gloves, borrowed from Mademoiselle Claudette's vast collection of accessories, completed her attire.

When Joanna had gazed at her reflection before they left the boarding house, she'd been hard-pressed to recognize herself. In some ways, she felt like a butterfly, set free from its cocoon. In other ways, it was as if she were staring at a stranger.

And a stranger was staring back.

Was *this* what her life would have been like if she were raised in London? Fancy gowns and elegant balls and so much tulle beneath her dress she was all but swimming in it.

There would have been no racing through the fields in her bare feet, or skinning her knees climbing trees, or "forgetting" her bonnet when she went to run errands.

For all its hardship, her upbringing had been free of societal constructs. For which she would always be grateful, as she didn't even need to enter the ballroom to know that this world, with its glitter and pomp, wasn't for her. Which was why, perhaps, she'd found herself instinctively drawn to Kincaid. Who, unlike her previous suitors, had never cared what she wore or how loudly she spoke or if she didn't wear a hat.

There wasn't a minute during their time together that she'd ever felt as if she were pretending to be someone else. Someone less intelligent. Someone more proper. Someone other than precisely who she was.

And he'd loved her for it!

She knew he had.

Which made his betrayal all the more cutting.

When sharp needles pricked the corners of her eyes, she blinked them furiously away. She hadn't come here to bemoan her broken heart or dissolve in a puddle of self-pity. She was here to support Rosemary, who didn't fit in with the *ton* any more than Joanna did. She was here to give Evie her shining moment in the spotlight, for if ever that was a person designed to flourish in such a setting, it was her sister. And she was here to see her half-brother. Who, if he was a man of decency, would agree to return the ring so that she and Evie might at long last return home. Wearier and, hopefully, wiser from their voyage across the pond.

The sky blue doors opened, admitting the next rush of bodies, of which Joanna and Evie were a part. They formed another line at the top of a wide staircase which led down into the middle of the sunken ballroom, a vast space lit with dozens of crystal chandeliers, polished wood floors, and windows framed with red velvet drapes. Chairs lined the one side, a buffet of food and drink occupied the other, and the back doors, all glass, were propped open to reveal a stone terrace and the torchlit rose garden beyond. An orchestra comprised of violinists, harpists, and even a pianist played from a second-floor balcony overlooking the room, their music guiding the dancers through the steps of a complicated waltz.

When it was over, everyone clapped, and the butler at the head of the stairs began to announce the arrival of new guests before another dance began.

What a slow, unwieldy process Joanna thought as she and Evie gradually moved closer to the stairs. If it were up to her, she'd let everyone in at once. No need for such revelry. Why, a person was as likely to spend as much time in a line as they were dancing. But then, it wasn't her decision to make. She was simply a spectator. A spectator who very much wished the buffet table had chocolate-covered marzipan.

When it was finally her and Evie's turn to be recognized, Evie told their names to the butler. Joanna started to walk down the steps before he could bellow them out (for a man short in stature, he was really quite loud), but Evie grabbed her arm.

"*Wait*," she hissed. "This is the best part."

Sucking in a mouthful of air, the butler puffed out his chest and shouted, *"Miss Joanna Thorncroft and Miss Evelyn Thorncroft of Somerville, Massachusetts."*

The entire room went absolutely silent.

Had a pin dropped, everyone would have dove for cover.

In unison, every pair of eyes turned to the top of the staircase.

Evie gave Joanna a small nudge. "Still think no one knows who we are?"

CHAPTER TWENTY-TWO

EVERYONE WAS STARING at them. The worst part was, they weren't even trying to hide it. As Joanna descended the stairs with her heart in her throat and her hand wrapped so tightly around Evie's arm she wouldn't have been surprised if she left a permanent mark, she cursed herself for ever agreeing to attend the ball in the first place.

There wasn't very much she was afraid of.

Not heights, or spiders, or the dark.

Not even snakes.

But a room filled with three hundred strangers watching her with all the intensity of a pack of bloodthirsty wolves ready to spring on their unsuspecting American prey?

That was terrifying.

She dared a glance out of the corners of her eyes to see if Evie was equally intimidated. She really should have known better. While Joanna was resisting the urge to run for the nearest exit, Evie was basking in the glow of the limelight.

Radiant in a violet gown that brought out the deep blue in her eyes, Evie floated down the steps with all the inherent grace of a young queen. As they neared the bottom and the crowd surged towards them, her poise did not waver.

"Good evening," she said sweetly. "Lovely weather. So nice to meet you, Lady Dillinger. A pleasure, Lord Concord. What a beautiful dress, Miss Hathwick…"

Struggling to find courage in her sister's composure, Joanna forced a smile and a few mumbled words. But as the circle grew smaller, and the amount of people waiting to be introduced to the long-lost granddaughter of the Duke of Caldwell grew larger, panic began to set in.

Then, out of nowhere, a dark angel came to her rescue.

"Joanna." A hand closed around her elbow. "Come with me."

Kincaid.

She didn't hesitate.

She didn't question.

Grabbing the back of his coat, she let him lead her out of the throng to a door beneath the balcony where the orchestra was picking up their instruments in preparation for the next dance.

But before Kincaid could open the door, a woman stepped in front of it.

"Hello," she purred, fluttering her lashes. "Fancy meeting you here."

Joanna stepped out from behind Kincaid. "Who is this?"

A muscle quivered in his jaw. "Lady Lavinia Townsend."

This was Lavinia Townsend? This blonde, petite woman with sharp green eyes and a shark's smile?

She didn't hesitate.

She didn't question.

Drawing her arm back as far as it would go, Joanna brought it forward and punched Lady Lavinia Townsend right in the middle of her smirking face.

With a guttural wail, Lavinia collapsed to the ground in a pool of peach satin.

Shaking out her fist, Joanna gave her first genuine grin of the night. "That felt good."

Kincaid stared at her in astonishment. "That was…"

"Long overdue?" she suggested.

"Yes," he said. "Exceedingly."

Together, they walked around Lavinia and through the door which led to a hallway filled with family portraits in gold filigreed frames. Another door led to a library, dimly lit by a crackling fire. Books of all types lined the walls and were stacked on tables and chairs. There was a desk in the far corner, and a set of matching sofas upholstered in pink velvet with rosewood trim in the middle.

Joanna sat on one sofa. After pouring her a glass of water from a pitcher by the desk, Kincaid sat on the other.

Her gaze on the logs burning in the hearth, she sipped slowly from her glass. "This is better. I don't know what I expected from my first British ball, but it wasn't that."

"The *ton* is not known for its subtlety. Once word began circulating about who you were, a spark was ignited. And your appearance on that stairwell fanned the flames." His eyes swept across her, the touch of them on her body hotter than any fire. "How could they *not* have noticed you? Especially tonight. You are gorgeous, Joanna."

So they were back to Joanna again, were they?

With a compliment, besides.

Her lips pressed together. She didn't want his flattery. She didn't want *anything* from him. Except...except to fill this void inside of her. To make her forget, just for a little while, all the weight pressing against her chest. To ease the ache in her heart.

And there was only one way she knew to do that.

"I am glad you came," he went on, amber eyes somber behind the clear lenses of his spectacles. "I have something to say to you. Something I should have said two days ago in the park. Joanna—"

"I don't want your words." Setting her glass aside with a deliberate click, she rose to her feet and walked closer to him until his legs were covered by her voluminous skirt and she could see the leap of his pulse at the base of his throat.

"Then what do you want?" he asked huskily. But she could tell by the rasp in his voice and the heat in his gaze that he already knew.

That he'd *always* known, just like she had, it would come to this.

Her mouth brushed against his, feather soft. She removed his spectacles and set them aside. Then she turned and bent her head forward, exposing the line of buttons keeping her dress closed. A long pause, a flash of orange as one of the logs in the hearth shifted, and then she felts his fingers at the nape of her neck.

One by one, he undid the buttons, knuckles tracing a tantalizing path down her spine to the small of her back. The gown fell to her waist, and she balanced herself on the edge of the sofa as she stepped out of it, then turned to face him.

Watching her, he loosened his cravat and then peeled off his tailcoat, letting it drop carelessly onto the thick rug. His waistcoat was next, and then his linen shirt.

Anticipation brought Joanna to the tips of her toes, her attention fixed to his torso as he bared his bronzed chest to the flickering firelight.

He was, in a word, magnificent.

All smooth skin and lean, taut muscles that clenched when she ran her hands along his body, exploring every nook and cranny, every flaw and scar, until there was no part of him that remained a mystery to her.

Above the waist, that is.

When his thumbs hooked into the waistband of his trousers, she held her breath, and released it on a slow, wondrous exhalation as he exposed *all* of himself. Every long, thick inch revealed for her viewing pleasure. She was reminded of the Greek statues at Cremorne Gardens. Except Kincaid was carved from flesh and blood instead of stone. At least on the outside. And for now, for *this*, that was all that concerned her.

It was her turn to undress next. No tiny task, given her number of undergarments. But she managed it well enough, and with only the tiniest bit of shyness. When she finally stood naked before Kincaid, she struggled not to give in to her natural instinct and cover her breasts. A good thing, as that seemed to be where his main focus was.

Heavy lidded, his gaze rose slowly to her face.

Their eyes met.

"Are you sure?" he asked.

"With every fiber of my being," she replied.

As the strains of Chopin's *Spring Waltz* sounded faintly from the hallway, Joanna and Kincaid came together. It was not the feverish rush to climax that they'd sought in the boarding house, or the bold lust she'd instigated in his office, but rather a purposeful unraveling of all the ties and restraints that had kept their ultimate desire bound.

He kissed her gently, his tongue sweeping between her lips. Her fingers glided along the sculpted valley of his chest, her soft belly pressing against the hard, pulsing root of his passion.

The kiss deepened and then eased, like a tide washing up against the shore. She melted into his arms when he picked her up and carried her to one of the sofas, her auburn hair standing out in vivid contrast against all the pink velvet as he tenderly laid her upon the cushions.

Standing at the end of the sofa, he leaned over her and brushed a ringlet from her cheek. Her stomach drew inward when he pressed his lips to her jaw and then began to make his way down to her breasts, where he lingered for what felt like hours before he went lower, the short stubble on his chin scraping against her navel on his way to the curls between her thighs.

She gasped when he kissed her there, his

tongue seeking and finding the source of her ardor. Her toes curled. Her heartbeat sped up, then slowed as warmth seeped into her.

The rising temperature drove her spine off the sofa. She arched, her voice escaping on a breathy moan of wanton disbelief as Kincaid cupped her bottom and lifted her to his mouth. For days, months, *years* he brought her to the brink again and again, teasing her with his lips, his tongue, his fingers, until her temple was damp with perspiration and her entire body was trembling with need.

Only when her eyes were glazed and her arms were limp did he give her curls a final kiss and withdraw his fingers from her wet, clenching heat.

The sofa was wide enough for his knees to fit on either side of her waist. He pinned her lightly in place as he lowered himself with exquisite control, and her nails dug into his back when she felt the press of his manhood, already slick, at her entrance.

He slid inside of her. There was a token resistance, a slight sensation of tugging, but he'd taken such care to prepare her that there wasn't so much as a flicker of pain. Just ecstasy. Sweet, sweet ecstasy that expanded with every subtle rock of his hips.

When he sheathed himself completely inside of her, they both gasped. The sensation was such that she burrowed her face in the crook of his neck to keep herself from crying out. Beneath her hands, his muscles bunched and coiled from the force of his restraint.

Slowly, so slowly she could have wept, he began to move again and, this time, she moved with him. Their glistening bodies bathed in firelight and their hearts racing in tandem, they rode towards the elusive crest of sweet surrender.

And plummeted together.

WESTON WAS LATE to the ball.

One of his mares had showed signs of being ready to foal, and he'd stayed by her side as she circled her stall and pawed restlessly at the straw. Ultimately, it had been a false labor, and with Brynne snapping in his ear to hurry up, he'd changed his clothes and driven them to Beresford Manor in his curricle.

The slight, two-wheeled carriage was a decade out of fashion, but he still preferred it to the cumbersome town coach whenever he needed to get somewhere with haste. Not wanting all the fuss that accompanied the main entrance, he went in through the terrace at the back while Brynne skipped off to meet her friends.

His guarded expression warding off any who

might have been tempted to engage in a simple conversation, he was afforded a wide swath of space as he made his way across the ballroom. He was searching for a tall redhead. If his half-sister was here, as she was rumored to be, he'd like to promptly dissuade her of any notions she might have of taking the ring back.

If she wanted to meet their father, he wasn't going to stop her. In fact, he'd wish her good luck: the marquess was notably difficult to get an audience with, even for his own children. To the best of Weston's knowledge, the old man was currently on holiday in France. There was no telling when he'd return. Or if he would even be bothered to meet with his illegitimate daughter when he did.

Mostly likely, the marquess would simply throw money at the problem and wash his hands of it. That was, after all, what'd he done with Weston and Brynne for their entire lives.

In many ways, Joanna was fortunate she'd been raised across the pond.

She certainly hadn't missed any warm family gatherings on this side of it.

His attention drawn by a large gathering at the base of the master staircase, he approached warily, a lion circling its hunting ground. To his annoyance, there were no redheads to be found in the crowd. But there *was* a slight brunette trapped in the midst of the melee, her diminutive frame nearly lost in the sea of people.

The urge to protect her caught Weston off guard.

Quite frankly, he was not the rescuing type.

Which was why he surprised himself when he surged forward, fighting his way through the dukes and the debutantes to where the young lady stood, holding her own but losing noticeable ground.

"Do you care to dance?" He hadn't signed her card. He didn't even know her name. But that didn't matter. When she turned her head and he caught his first glimpse of her cornflower blue eyes, nothing did.

Noise faded. Color receded. The crowd melted away.

There was only Weston...and the most stunningly beautiful woman he'd ever seen.

A fairy, was his first irrational thought. Plucked from the woods and waters wild.

She studied him for a moment beneath high, arching brows a shade darker than her hair. Her skin was ivory tinged with the slightest hint of rose on the apples of her cheeks. Her mouth was full, the top lip just a tad heavier than the bottom and shaped like Cupid's bow. As Weston gazed at her, utterly transfixed, she smiled, slow and sure. Then she held out her gloved hand.

"I would love to."

They walked out of the crush and into each

other's arms. The Viennese waltz required its participants to be intimately close and their steps to be perfectly in tune lest they fall out of rhythm. As with all other things, Weston was a good dancer. It wasn't that gracefulness required of such a dance came naturally to him, but rather that his governesses and tutors had never allowed him to be subpar at anything.

A boy of eight should have been hunting for frogs in the stream or racing his pony through the fields. He had been walking circles around the drawing room, a vase filled with freezing cold water balanced on his head and his arms trembling from the weight of the books his dance instructor had forced him to hold.

The lessons, however barbaric they might have been, had paid off.

Weston rarely—if ever—made a misstep, and if he did, he was his own harshest critic.

He did not expect perfection.

He *demanded* it.

Which was why it was a pleasure to discover that his blue-eyed fairy was just as good, if not better, than he was at the waltz.

She moved with a natural grace that could not be taught, her hands fluttering from his shoulder to his waist and her small feet moving with impeccable timing. He spun her away from him and then brought her back, his retraction a bit more forceful than necessary so that she bumped against his chest.

"I am sorry, my lord." Her voice was as soft and light as the rest of her; a rainbow dancing on a sunbeam.

"The error was mine," he said without apology, as the act had been intentional and he did not regret her breasts pressing against his jacket. Countless layers of clothing between them, and he'd still felt a shock.

When was the last time he had been shocked by anything, let alone *anyone*?

The edge of her mouth curled upward. "I suspected as much, but am always loath to point out other's errors unless they are deserving of it."

"And I am not deserving of critique?" he asked, arching a brow.

"That remains to be seen," she said coyly.

They stepped seamlessly around a slower, clumsily moving couple.

Weston adjusted his grip on her waist, his hand enveloping a large portion of her back and the slightest curve of her bottom. "What is your name?" he asked. "You are not from around here."

"Was it the accent that gave it away?"

"That, and I never forget a face."

"Do you find it memorable?" She tilted her chin. "My face, that is."

"You're beautiful." It wasn't praise so much as a statement of fact. "Only a blind man could forget you."

"And you're not blind."

"I am not," he confirmed.

"Just rude, then, for asking me to introduce myself to you when it is a gentleman's duty to introduce himself to the lady."

Unbidden, a roguish grin claimed his lips. "I never said I was a gentleman."

"That's fine, as I never claimed to be a lady."

They gazed at each other.

The music swelled, a final crescendo, and then stopped.

Sliding his hand to the end of her fingertips and taking a step backwards, he lowered himself into a deep bow. "Lord Weston Weston, Earl of Hawkridge."

"You've the same name twice," she said as he straightened.

"So I have been told."

"Why would your parents—*my goodness*," she gasped, her blue eyes widening. "You're the Earl of Hawkridge!"

"Does my reputation precede me?" he said dryly. "Unfortunately, it's most likely worse than what you have heard."

She tugged her hand free of his grip. "No, it's not that."

"Then what is it?" he asked.

"You—you have my mother's ring."

Weston stiffened. "You're not Joanna Thorncroft."

"Of course not." Her chin lifted a notch. "I am her sister, Evelyn."

All at once, he remembered what it felt like when he'd lost his balance and that pitcher of icy water had rained down on him. "That is why you are here, then." His voice dropped several degrees. "For the ring."

She lifted her slender shoulder in a shrug. "And for the dukes, but it seems they're in alarmingly short supply. This is rather fortuitous that our paths have crossed. Do you have the ring on you? May I have it? It means a great deal to me and my sisters, and I—"

"No," he said flatly.

She blinked at him. "No, you don't have the ring on you, or no I cannot have it?"

"Both." His countenance hardened. "I don't know what you possibly hoped to accomplish by coming to London, but you and your sister can sod off all the way back to Boston because you're not getting your greedy hands on my family's ring ever again."

With that, he stalked away.

KINCAID HELPED JOANNA back into her gown.

It was surprisingly heavy, and he marveled at

her ability to wear it all night. But then, everything she did was a marvel to him.

Including what they'd just done on a pink sofa in the Countess of Beresford's library.

He knew he should have felt guilty, but he didn't. He could he?

A sunset did not feel guilt for painting the sky in reds and oranges so bright and beautiful it sometimes hurt to look at. A flower did not feel guilt for growing where it shouldn't and spreading its beauty far and wide. A poet did not feel guilt for writing a sonnet so wrenchingly poignant that it made the reader cry.

And thus neither would Kincaid feel guilt for loving the woman he was in love with.

Loving the woman he was *destined* to be with.

He was not a man who looked to the heavens for answers, or believed in cosmic powers beyond his understanding. Logic and reason were his driving forces. But surely, there was some type of fate at play. Some kind of destiny, decades in the making, which had brought him and Joanna to this spot in the world at this precise moment in time.

And who was he to argue with the stars?

"There." Sliding the last button of her dress into place, he kissed her bare shoulder. "You're ready."

"For what?" she asked, turning towards him

in a rustle of silk and taffeta. Her eyes were luminous in the dim light, her cheeks flushed, her lips slightly swollen. She was a goddess brought to life, an earthly Athena of courage, and wit, and daring.

"To be married." It wasn't until Kincaid glanced around for his jacket that he realized he still hadn't found his spectacles. The room blurred, then abruptly came into vivid focus when Joanna jumped in front of him.

"*Married?*" she repeated.

"Indeed." Ah, there was his jacket. Draped over the arm of a chair. But he didn't dare reach for it. Not when Joanna was glaring at him as if he'd just eaten all the marzipan. "Is that a problem?"

"Perhaps my memory is the problem, as I do not remember even being engaged." Those luminous eyes narrowed. "When did you ask me to marry you, Kincaid? The last I recall, you had ended our agreement and told me I should prepare to return to America."

The icy shard of glass in her tone was his first inkling that whatever he was attempting to do, it wasn't going very well. The finger drilling into his chest was the second. "I, ah—"

"I told you that I loved you, and you told me—what was it? Oh, yes—that our personal feelings are *irrelevant*. What has changed between then and now?"

Of its accord, his gaze slipped to the pink sofa.

Joanna bristled.

"You want to marry me out of some outdated philosophy that a woman is ruined once she has lost her virginity, is that it?" she asked.

"Yes. No," he corrected hastily when her eyes flashed a deep, dark blue. "No, that's not it at all. That is to say, I would do right by you, Joanna."

He needed better words.

The *right* words.

He wanted to tell her how much he loved her. How much he cared. How much she meant to him. But when he opened his mouth, those words did not come. They were trapped inside of him. Stuck beneath the keystone that, although cracked and battered, still stood. The final barrier between keeping his heart safely guarded...and entrusting Joanna with it.

"You would do right by me," she said dubiously. "What does that mean?"

"I..." Frustrated, he plunged his hands into his hair. Why couldn't he take that last step? Why couldn't he commit himself in the way she wanted him to? What was so bloody wrong with him that he was unable to tell the woman he loved what she needed to hear? What she *deserved* to hear? "Joanna, I..."

Her gaze softened. "Yes, Kincaid?"

He drew a breath. Maybe...maybe he didn't

have to give his heart away all at once. Surely, that would be safer. A piece now, and a piece when they married. A piece when he finally found the words to tell her that he loved her. A piece when they had their first child.

That was better, he decided as the knot of tension in the middle of his temple uncoiled ever-so-slightly. That was best.

For both of them.

"I have always honored my obligations," he began. "I know a priest who can marry us tomorrow, if that is what you would like."

"What I would like is to not be thought of as an *obligation*."

Kincaid frowned. "That isn't what I meant."

"But it's what you said." Wrapping her arms around herself, she began to back slowly towards the door. "More than that, it is what you *haven't* said that tells me everything I need to hear. I am not a pretty vase to be put on a shelf. And I am not a duty to be fulfilled. I am a woman with hopes and dreams and aspirations that go far beyond being some man's *obligation*. I believed you, of all people, saw that." Her voice thickened. "Goodbye, Kincaid."

It wasn't until after Joanna had left, closing the door quietly behind her, that Kincaid understood a heart torn into pieces was still broken.

"THERE YOU ARE," said Evie, coming up to Joanna just as she was poised to flee onto the stone terrace. "I've been looking everywhere."

Joanna brushed her fingers across her lips. They felt hot to the touch, and she feared there was a sign hanging above her head in bold lettering that read *"Recently Ravished"*. But if there was, it seemed her sister was unable to see it, for Evie hardly spared her a glance.

"I met your half-brother," she continued. "The Earl of Hawkridge. Do you know his name is Weston *Weston*? How peculiar."

Stunned, Joanna lowered her arm as hope fluttered feebly in her chest. She felt drained. Physically. Emotionally. Like a rag that had been wrung out too many times. But if she couldn't have Kincaid, then maybe at least she could have this instead. It wasn't everything she wanted. But it was something. And when a person was clinging by their fingernails, they'd be foolish not to reach for whatever was thrown at them. "You met my half-brother? What was he like? Did you by chance bring up Mother's ring? Is he agreeable to returning it to us?"

Evie gave a snort. "Weston is the most *selfish*, domineering, *arrogant* lout I've ever had the misfortune of encountering. He absolutely, positively, is *never* giving Mother's ring back."

Joanna's hope sank like a rock where it sat, along with her heart, at the bottom of her stomach in a pool of bitterness and regret. "Then all of this was for naught," she said softly.

Their journey to London.

Falling in love with Kincaid.

Finding her birth father.

It had all amounted to *nothing*.

"But not to worry," Evie went on brightly. "Because I have a foolproof plan."

"We cannot steal the ring."

Evie blinked. "Steal it? Don't be absurd. I'm not going to *steal* anything." Her eyes gleamed. "I'm going to marry Weston Weston, the Earl of Hawkridge."

CHAPTER TWENTY-THREE

"**I**S THAT EVERYTHING?" Joanna asked, bending down to peer under the bed. It was three days after the disastrous ball at Beresford Manor, and she and Evie were preparing to leave the boarding house once and for all...with two separate destinations in mind.

Joanna was headed for the docks, where she would board a ship and sail home.

Evie was waiting on a carriage to take her to Hawkridge Manor where she was to be Lady Brynne's surprise guest at a month-long house party. The key word being surprise, for if Weston knew that Evelyn Thorncroft was on her way to his country estate, he would have undoubtedly barred the gates and dispatched the hounds.

Joanna still did not know precisely how it had come to be. She had quit the ball early while Evie had stayed on. Sometime during the night, *her* sister had struck up a conversation with *Weston's* sister (she really did need to get started on that family tree) and the two women had hit it off famously. The best of friends, Evie had gushed to Joanna when she'd finally made it back to their room at half-past two in the morning.

"She'd love to meet you," Evie had gone on. "Cousin Rosemary sends her best wishes as well. Apparently Sir Reginald the squirrel scurried out the door just as she was getting ready to depart for the ball and it took her over two hours to find him again. I say she should have let him have his freedom, but she really is attached to the little thing."

Now Evie took a final glance around the room, and nodded. "That is everything except for the letters you'd like me to deliver."

"Thank you. I wouldn't want to forget those." Reaching inside her bag, Joanna procured four letters. One for Rosemary, one for Brynne, one for Weston, and one for her father, the Marquess of Dorchester. She'd composed a fifth in her head for Kincaid, but she hadn't been able to put her thoughts to paper. Not when her wounds were still so fresh. Her hurt too deep.

It was why she was returning to Somerville, even though Brynne had extended the same invitation to her as she had Evie. But Joanna couldn't stand to stay another minute in a place that had brought her such heartache.

So she was leaving.

This very afternoon.

In the spring, she had every plan to return. By then, she was confident her pain would have subsided. And if she saw Kincaid, or even if she didn't, it would not matter. Because she wouldn't love him anymore. She wouldn't feel this...this terrible *ache* in her chest anymore.

In some ways, she was like an injured animal seeking a cave to shelter in until its cuts healed. Not that she preferred to think of it that way. She wasn't retreating, or running. For once, she was simply making herself accept the full, unvarnished truth.

Kincaid did not love her.

He never had.

And she would rather be alone than married to someone who thought of her as an obligation.

There were *some* things about London she would miss. The sheer size of the city, for one. Every time she'd turned a corner, she had seen a new sight or heard a new sound. The food, while different, had been delicious (particularly the sweets). And then there was the work she had done for Kincaid. The work she had done *with* Kincaid.

While sorting paperwork hadn't suited her restless nature, she had immensely enjoyed questioning the maid, Abigail, and trying to fit all the pieces together to form a picture of what had happened to the Duke of Hanover's mistress. Not only that, but she'd been good at it.

Even if Kincaid had been reluctant with his praise.

She wondered if she might not give detective work a go when she returned to Somerville. Not that the sleepy village was inundated with crimes, but things occasionally went missing and needed to be found, the same as any other place. She needed *something* to keep herself busy. Something to keep her mind off the detective she was leaving behind.

"Drats," Evie exclaimed when they had wrestled their luggage down the stairs and dropped it beside the front door. "It's raining."

So it was. Somewhere between a mist and a downpour, water fell steadily from a gray, gloomy sky with even darker clouds on the horizon.

"But your coach is here," said Joanna, pointing out the window at a shiny black landau carriage, its top closed to guard against the foul weather.

The sisters smiled sadly at each other.

"Are you sure this is what you want to do?" Evie asked. "I can go with you."

"And give up marrying an earl?" Joanna said with a wry smile. "I think not."

"I am only doing it to get Mother's ring. The second Weston proposes and slips the ring on my finger, I'll be on my way home."

"That's quite devious, even for you."

Evie pursed her lips. "Fair is fair. He took it from us, I am merely taking it back."

"While enjoying the life of a proper lady in the meantime."

"If *you're* not going to, I might as well."

Joanna suppressed a shudder. "That ball was all I needed to know that the *ton* and I are a poor match."

"Well, I adored every bit of it."

"I am aware, as that's all you've talked about for the past two days." Smiling fondly, Joanna reached out and straightened Evie's hat. "Enjoy your house party. You'll have everyone eating out of the palm of your hand before the first week is done."

Evie blushed with pleasure. "Do you really think so?"

"How could anyone *not* love you? I do." With that, Joanna wrapped her arms around her sister. They rocked back and forth before breaking apart.

Evie lifted her bag. "I can stay until your cab arrives, if you'd like."

"No, go on," said Joanna, gesturing at the door. "Your driver is waiting."

She watched until the landau had turned the corner, and then tucked her old carpet bag under her arm and set off in the rain. The docks weren't far, and she would rather not waste what little amount of money she had left on fare for a hansom cab.

But after ten minutes of walking in the cold, damp wet, Joanna realized she wasn't heading to the shipyard at all.

Instead, she was a street away from Kincaid's office.

Faltering, she ducked beneath a canvas awning.

Where was she going?

Better yet, what was she *doing?*

Her fingers curled, nails digging into her palms as her pulse began to race.

She wasn't giving up.

That's what she was doing.

Because Thorncroft women *did not settle.*

Dropping her luggage where she stood, she set off with a determined stride.

By the time she reached Kincaid's doorstep, her newfound resolve had waned, but it was still there, fighting its way through all the hurt and the heartache. Above her, thunder boomed and lightning slashed across a sky that had gone as dark as pitch. But the storm paled in comparison to the tempest within her.

She knocked on the door. And when Kincaid did not answer, she began to pound.

Without warning, the door was yanked inward. "It's pouring. What the hell do you—

Joanna."

She caught a glimpse of his amber eyes wide with shock before he grabbed her by the waist and pulled her inside. He brought her straight into his office, then whipped off her spencer jacket before all but shoving her into a chair.

"You're soaked to the bone," he muttered. "Here, drink this."

She accepted the coffee. It must have been freshly brewed, for steam rose from the top of the cup in a plume of wispy smoke. She took a sip. Wrinkled her nose. "Before you hire another secretary, make sure she knows how to make proper coffee."

He leaned against his desk. Crossed his arms. Uncrossed them. "I am not going to hire another secretary. Joanna, what are you doing here? I thought you were leaving London."

"I was. I *am*." She tried another drink of the bitter brew, then shook her head and put it on the floor. "What do you mean, you're not going to hire someone else? If you let all of that sorting I did be for naught, I swear that I'll—"

"I could never replace you, Joanna." His husky admission caught her off guard. "You're irreplaceable."

A tremble worked its way down her spine. From the rain, she told herself. Just from the rain. "That's not what you said in the library."

"Because I...what are you doing here?" he

repeated.

She looked at her lap, then boldly lifted her chin. "If someone is going to walk away, it is not going to be me. I love you, Kincaid. I hate it. I wish I didn't. But I do. And I cannot leave until I hear you tell me that you don't. That you *don't* love me. That you don't see a future between us. That you don't want to be with me."

"*Joanna.*" In an instant, he was on his knees before her with his hand on her thigh. "Do you honestly think I was ever going to let you go?" He glanced meaningfully to the corner of his room, and she followed his gaze to a large, battered-looking, leather suitcase.

Her eyes cut back to his in confusion. "You were...you were going to follow me?"

"To the ends of the earth, if that is what it takes. I am sorry." His grip tightened on her leg. "I am sorry I didn't have the words then, but I've been practicing with James—"

"You've been practicing with your *cat*?" she interrupted.

"That damned feline is your most ardent admirer. Second only to me." A crooked smile lifted the side of his mouth and melted her heart. "I love you, Joanna Thorncroft. I loved you the first time you stood on my doorstep in the rain, I love you now, and I will love you forever. Every strong, intelligent, beautiful, obstinate inch of you."

Her eyebrows pinched. "I don't know if I would describe me as *obstinate*—"

He silenced her with a kiss. A kiss that went on for a very, very, *very* long time. When it was done, she found herself sitting on his lap, her head tucked against his chest and her fingers entwined with his.

"After what happened with Lavinia, I was afraid to fall in love again," he admitted without reservation. "I saw giving yourself and your heart to someone as a weakness. A vulnerability. But what Lavinia and I had...it was never love. I wish I had understood that sooner. It might have saved both of us quite a lot of aggravation."

She rolled her eyes. "Do you think?"

He nipped her earlobe, then drew it between his teeth to suckle as she sighed. "Behave," he murmured, "or I'll do what I should have done the first day you marched into my office and toss you onto my bed."

"Oh, yes, *please*."

His chuckle warmed her neck. Then he sobered. "You are the daughter of a marquess. The granddaughter of a duke. Even illegitimate, you could have almost any lord you desired. I come from humble beginnings, Joanna. And while you will never want for anything, I cannot give you the life that could be yours with a nobleman."

"The only noble man that I desire is holding me right now." She tilted her head and kissed him again. Long, slow, and sweet. "I don't care for the *ton*. I understand why my mother left it all behind to seek a life of quiet normalcy in America."

"Speaking of which…" He slipped his hand free of hers to sweep a strand of damp hair out of her face. "Our luggage is already packed. The ship departs in an hour. We could go to Boston. I could meet your grandmother and Claire. I could ask their permission in person, rather than a letter."

Her temple creased. "Their permission for what?"

"To marry you. Not out of obligation," he said hurriedly when her lips parted. "But because I have absolutely no intention of ever letting you off my lap."

She smiled at that. "But your life is here, in London."

He brushed his knuckles along her cheek. "My life is wherever *you* are."

"I would like my grandmother to meet you," she agreed. "But Evie is staying here, at least for the time being. It probably makes sense for us all to sail together. At the very least, she is going to need someone to hold her bucket when she gets sick. Not to mention, you and I have a case to solve for the Duke of Hanover."

Kincaid's brows arched above the thin rims of his spectacles. "Do we?"

"Yes." She blinked innocently at him. "I *am*

your partner, aren't I?"

"I believe I've just had a position for secretary open up."

Joanna grimaced. "I refuse to do any more organizing."

"That's all right." He skimmed his mouth along her jaw. "I'm fairly certain you'll be busy doing *other* things."

Gasping when his hands slipped to her breasts and his thumbs glided across her nipples, she squirmed against him. "I should like equal pay for equal work."

"Keep wiggling like that, and you can have whatever you like."

"*Kincaid!*" Squealing, she clung to his shoulders when he scooped her up and carried her upstairs...to a life filled with exciting possibility and a love destined to last forever.

THE END

About the Author

Jillian Eaton grew up in Maine and now lives in Pennsylvania on a farmette with her husband and their three boys. They share the farm with a cattle dog, an old draft mule, a thoroughbred, and a mini-donkey—all rescues. When she isn't writing, Jillian enjoys spending time with her animals, gardening, reading, and going on long walks with her family.

CPSIA information can be obtained
at www.ICGtesting.com
Printed in the USA
BVHW041728030521
606361BV00006B/81

9 781953 455574